J M BRISCOE

THE

GIRL

WITH

THE

GREEN

EYES

# The Girl with the Green Eyes

by

## J M Briscoe

Cover photo by Dmytro Tolokonov-unsplash

Cover design by Jason Anscomb

Interior design by BAD PRESS iNK

ISBN: 978-1-8384577-2-3

published by www.badpress.ink

To Gary, Lara, Annabelle and Ben –
all of my everything

I was nine years and two months old when I realised that there was something wrong with me. I had suspected for some time that I was a bit different to some of my friends. That some of the things I said and did – not to mention some of the things that just seemed to happen around me – were a bit... off. Like the time everyone in my class was laughing at Jason Miller doing impressions in the playground and I just stood there, not laughing, until, one by one they all turned to me and fell silent. Or that day in the park when my sister, Maya, turned from her perch on the climbing frame and gave me the oddest look until I glanced behind me to see a great crowd of toddlers all clustered about, just watching me. And then there was Katie Jennings, that little moron from next door. Well, I warned her what would happen if she kept lying to me.

I didn't know why I was different. I didn't do it on purpose. I never demanded that my friends stop laughing at Jason. I didn't *make* those little kids follow me out of the playground and halfway home. It wasn't my fault their parents all freaked out. And with Katie... well, *someone* needed to punish her. Every time one of these things happened, I'd see the way other people were looking at me – my friends, my sister, my mother – and that feeling would tickle over the surface of my skin like a mosquito looking for a juicy spot to pierce. *Oh. That wasn't normal. That*

1

*wasn't 'right'. That was the off thing, again.* But I didn't know for sure that it was *wrong*. Not until the day in September when my mother bundled me into the car, drove me hundreds of miles to the house of a stranger and told him: *Bella is defective. You need to take her back.*

## Autumn, 1995

It was strange that she'd come to pick me up from school. I sat there in the back seat, frowning at the back of her head, biting my lip against all the questions bundling to get out. *What's going on? Why am I here? Where are you taking me?* It would be no good to voice any of them. I had seen the tightness of her jaw, the ragged ends of two of her fingernails, the wild fray to the back of her normally-pristine bob of hair. This was not a day to ask questions.

My mother was a tricky species. One day she'd be full of smiles, twisting my dark curls gently in her fingers and talking about a beautiful new lace dress she had ordered specially for me. The next her eyes would turn callous and hungry, reminding me of the seagulls we saw whenever we visited the coast; beady, cold, empty. *Don't stand like that, who do you think you are – Princess Di? Take that skirt off immediately, it's Maya's. I don't care if she said you could have it, it's not yours. You are not entitled just because you look the way you do! Get away from me, stop looking at me like that with those eyes. I will tear them out, then we will see how well you can bat them! Get out of my sight before...*

My dad was always there, though, with his soft arms and his gentle voice telling me not to take any notice. My older brother and sister would roll their eyes at me too, and whisper: *The python's awake, run!* And even though I knew as well as they that it only ever seemed to be *me* who awoke this hissing, maleficent-eyed monster within our mother, I tried to do as they said. After all, I still came top in all the tests at school, I was still lead ballerina at the local dance studio, people still said I was beautiful and, when I looked in the mirror, I knew they were right. I held my chin solidly and bundled the small, stony hurt of my mother's flinches and hisses into a knot which I tried hard not to feel at the back of my throat when I swallowed. And, after a day or two, the monster would recede, my mother would revert to sweetness and smiles and I'd come into my room to find something pretty and new on my bed. It was a strange, uneasy sort of life, but it was our normal. And, apart from the worst times, I never really gave it much thought. I certainly never anticipated that one day the serpent would strike.

I don't remember how long we drove. At some point I fell asleep and woke to find the roads darkened and shrivelled into single lanes. I sat in a hunch, waiting. Waiting for the tinny whine of the radio to give in to the massing waves of static. Waiting for the feeling to come back to my stiff limbs. Waiting to see if we were actually heading somewhere… Or if my mother was simply driving until the world outside had become wild enough to pull over, open my door, shove me out and drive away.

'Where *are* we?' I asked when I could no longer hold it in, staring at a flock of sheep staggered impossibly on a grey-green hillside. My mother, radiating tension from every inch of her body, forced the car into a lower gear and bent further over the steering wheel as we growled up a steep lane.

'Cumbria,' she replied, meaninglessly. 'Don't talk to me, I need to concentrate.'

Shutting my eyes, I let the trickling stream of fear tumble into the knot in my throat and clenched my fists until they ticked and juddered with my heartbeat. I wished, so hard my mouth trembled with the words, that I could be grown up, that I could look at her with the same shuddery glare she used on me, that I could push her away when her hands closed around my upper arms with their skin-pinching grip, that I could just... stop her. I sat and wished until all that existed was the wishing, the focus of hatred, the pounding ache of it, and slowly I felt a tiny bit of control return.

**October, 2018**

*Friday*

Flintworth University is as large, grey, and soulless as the average airport. Purpose-built sometime in the mid-nineties, everything inside it has supposedly been designed to encourage great thinking, from the little reflection nooks nestled into the corridors to the large-but-not-intimidating lecture theatres. The professors sneer, calling it *inspirationally uninspired*, but I like it here. I like the anonymity, the blandness, the total, undeniable genericness. It's academic enough, sure. I believe it reached the top 40 universities in the UK this year; and it certainly doesn't damage a person's CV to work here. Nestled in the heart of Flintworth town a few miles into the more affordable side of the M25, it is just close enough to hang off the academic coattails of the fancier London establishments... but no one with any truly lofty ambitions chooses Flintworth, whether they be student or faculty. Which makes it ideal for someone whose primary ambition is to keep firmly beneath the radar of all such people.

Even so, I don't often give lectures. My colleagues think it's due to a charmingly unfortunate fear of public speaking. They've grown comfortable with the sweetly shy, pretty-faced Dr Elodie Guerre who chooses the blocky, practical white coats over the expensive tailored ones, wears sensible shoes, keeps her blonde hair pinned back and her nails clipped short for her work in the lab. They're smug for a week if they persuade me to join them for a drink at one of the too-expensive-for-students wine bars in the city after work on a Friday night. I smile, blush when I need to, flirt with the gentle hint of French vowels when required, let them patronise, pity, lust... It works. It has worked, for more than ten years. Until today. Today Ted Costings is home with the flu. Today my line manager Thomas Willbury has cajoled me into stepping into Ted's place and lecturing a small group of third year undergrads on the ethics of genetic engineering. Professor Willbury is 47, on his third unhappy marriage and has three or perhaps four children, some of whom he doesn't see, none of whose birthdays he can remember. He wears cheap shoes but drinks good wine, and has a taste for shy, throaty blondes. I let him think he's in with a chance.

The Russell Building has seven lecture theatres, all around half the size of a leisure centre swimming pool. We're in the inspirationally named Theatre Six today, where the gently tiered seating curves around the lectern like a cupped hand. I glance up from the front of the room at the students as they jostle and joke their way into their seats and I feel the blush waiting, ready, beneath the surface of my cheeks. Dr Willbury kneels beside me as I snap the charging cable into the back of my laptop. I know he can sense the nervousness wafting from me like heat from a steaming mug.

'Alright, Els?'

I smile tightly and adjust the glasses I don't need. It's a mark of how enmeshed with Elodie's identity I've become that I barely register my own spasm of irritation at his repulsive choice of nickname. I certainly don't let it echo across my careful face.

'I'm OK... I mean, I think I'll be fine once I get going...' I bite my lip, injecting just a slight hint of the accent which I know shoots straight to his groin. He nods reassuringly and rubs my shoulder. His hand blazes with heat through my Zara blazer and I gulp bravely, allowing a little of the blush to trickle prettily across Elodie's powdered cheeks. He grins back.

'Maybe we could go for a drink afterwards... celebrate your successful influence over the minds of tomorrow!'

'Well. Maybe...'

A mechanical clock chimes somewhere within the depths of the building. I get to my feet, placing my laptop carefully on the lectern as Willbury switches on the smart board behind me. The screen immediately animates with my first slide: *Genetic Modification: Key Scientific Development or Monstrosity of Nature?*

Silence settles around the room and this time it's much more difficult to keep up the pretence. Self-consciousness, embarrassment, bashful unease... I've been Elodie for years, but she has never been an easy mask to harness, no matter how much I trust her.

I gaze around at the faces, some still with the pockmarks of adolescence, others older than my own, a few with the aloof, challenging eyebrows of anticipation, others vaguely attempting to grasp the meaning of the words through fogs of exhaustion or hangovers, and one or two just blank. Theatre Six does not allow for shadowy corners, every inch of the audience is spot lit. The woman at the end of the back row is bending forward, though, the first time I look up. The second time, once I've begun speaking with only the slightest, prettiest little tremor to

Elodie's sultry voice, I spot her. I don't pause. I don't stumble blindly from my position. I don't even think I blink. We lock eyes for a second and I know she knows. I know that just as I see past the crow's feet nestled in the corners of her eyes, the thickened arms under her cheap shirt and the swoosh of cropped hair covering most of her forehead to the bright eyed twenty-two-year-old lurking derisively in her past, she sees *me.* Through the fake glasses, the brown contact lenses beneath them, the blonde wig swept into its neat chignon. The overwhelming irony of my lecture's subject matter. She smirks and gets to her feet, slinging a large purple rucksack over her shoulder and it takes everything... everything I have built and clung onto by the tips of Elodie's neat little fingernails over the past ten years not to spring away from my laptop and leap after her. Instead, I keep my eyes forward and don't even pause as Felix Bryden walks quickly out of the hall, taking all of my everything with her.

After I round up the lecture to surprisingly loud applause, I manage to shake Willbury off with an excuse about feeling a migraine coming on. He doesn't pout too irritatingly; Elodie is, after all, sadly prone to migraines. I pack up my laptop and gather a few essentials from my lab on my way out of the building. It's late October and the air is stiff with the promise of winter. Apple-cheeked students kick up leaves and talk loudly and importantly about the lofty concepts with which they think we should all be concerned. I keep my eyes down as I scurry past them and into the car park. It is only once I've slid onto the soft leather driver's seat of my BMW that I let out a long, shuddery breath and glance carefully around. To my left runs the path towards the student halls of residence, dappled in russet leaves and bark chippings. To my right there are more cars, the braying students, and a few stragglers clutching bags and binders and walking with self-conscious purpose. And, straight ahead, the squatting, grey Russell Building. No sign of *her.* No sign either of the old, red Fiesta in which I learned to smoke, drive and a few other things besides. *Well of course not.* It's been thirteen years. The Fiesta would be long gone by now.

I lean my head back against the headrest, letting the cool fabric seep fingers of calm around my skull and across my forehead. This is it. I knew this day would happen. I knew one of them would track me down eventually. Sighing, I slot my key into the ignition and spring the engine into life. I'm surprised by the swell of regret I feel when I realise I won't see the Russell Building, or my quiet little lab within it, again. That my small department of almost-friends will not benefit, now, from the increased funding directed by Willbury's favour. John could have had that new microscope he'd been sighing over. Glenda might have been able to retire.

*Come on, Bella, what is this? Almost weeping over John and Glenda and some old lech you didn't get a chance to home-wreck? This isn't you. You don't feel. Not like this.*

The voice cuts across my sadness like a whip. She always did know exactly what to say to tear me into action, even if it drew blood. My ears ring with the echo of her words and I swallow hard as I pull the car into gear and begin to crawl out of the car park.

*That's better. No time for useless reminiscence. They've found you. You know what that means. He won't be far behind.*

I do know that. I bite my lip hard as I take a left out of campus and indicate to join the traffic winding its way across town, towards the High School. As I speed away from Flintworth University and Professor Thomas Willbury and Dr Elodie Guerre, I make sure I don't look back.

**Autumn, 1995**

It was almost dark by the time the car pulled to a slow, crunching stop. Peering out of the window as my mother opened her car door with a whoosh of cool air, I stared. The building before me was unlike anything I'd ever seen. Castle was my first thought – but were castles meant to be so... muddled up? The structure appeared to be made out of random grey stones, some of them no bigger than beach pebbles, others larger than I was. Windows – some narrow slits, some stained glass, and others plain modern slabs – were strewn at random across the front, occasionally interrupted by great climbing fingers of ivy. In the centre of the building a pair of heavy iron-bolted double doors glared as if ready for invasion but then along the nearside there were other doors – plain, wooden ones like the doors at school. Everywhere I looked there seemed to be one thing which immediately contradicted another. It was a bit like watching an old stooped granny hobbling along only for her to turn around and reveal bright pink highlights and a tutu.

'Out, now.' My mother's voice made me jump and I tore my eyes from the strange building to look at her. She stood with my car door in her hand, her eyes snapping irritably from me to the building as if worried it might disappear if we didn't approach it fast enough. I bit my lip, unbuckled my seat belt, and followed her as she marched sharply up to one of the heavy, grand front doors and knocked. She did not look at me again.

'Hola?' The door was opened by a short woman with very little neck and a body stacked in round tiers like a wedding cake. She wore a plain black dress, dark hair pulled into a bun at the back of her head and a wary, narrow-eyed expression.

'I'm here to see Dr Frederick Blake,' my mother barked at the woman. 'I'm Julia D'accourt, this is Bella. He's expecting us.'

'OK,' the woman said and, somewhat reluctantly, stepped backwards to let us in. 'I tell him you here,' she added, her accent thick.

I stepped into a dark, tall-ceilinged entranceway behind my mother and the woman's gaze fell upon me. I smiled sweetly, expecting her face to crease into the same beam adults usually wore when I looked at them like that. Instead, she glowered even more than she had done at my mother and muttered something under her breath in a language I didn't know. Then she turned and hurried into a room leading off to the right of the hallway, her footsteps plodding but quick on the large flagstones. I swallowed, my dismay at her reaction settling into the fear already churning violently around my stomach. It was difficult to keep my face expressionless.

'Mrs D'accourt?'

The voice echoed around the dingy entranceway and my mother jumped, which made me smile. I turned around to see a tall, thin man standing in a doorway a few feet down from the one through which the foreign woman had disappeared. He looked at the two of us through round glasses perched on the end of a knobbly nose, his silhouette glowing slightly by a soft warm-looking light coming from the room behind him. His black hair was streaked liberally with white and swooshed almost completely straight up from his head like he was a cartoon character who had put his finger in an electric socket.

'Hello there,' he rumbled, holding his hand out to me, who was closest. 'I'm Dr Frederick Blake.'

His hand was warm and dryly calloused like my father's. Just the feel of it in my own was enough to chase away a few swallows of the fear in my stomach. I gave the man my sweetest, shyest smile and was, to my relief, rewarded with an echoing grin. I decided, however, to hold off the lisp as I shook his hand firmly and replied, 'I'm Bella D'accourt. Pleased to meet you, sir.'

'Dr Blake,' my mother stepped forward, her hands tangling together anxiously. 'Please, I need... What we discussed on the telephone... have you—?'

'Please, Mrs D'accourt, shall we step into my office?'

He gestured to the glowing doorway. My mother nodded smartly and trod with quick, clicking steps across the stones and past him. I followed.

The fire was the first thing I noticed. It crackled merrily under a brick archway, which crested like a tunnel under shelves upon shelves of books. They lined the far wall like knobbly, dusty wallpaper and several of the shelves bowed and sagged in places. A ladder leant haphazardly on one side of the fire, old and rickety looking. In front of the fireplace lay a rug with swirly patterns, a sofa with curling arms and a cracked leather armchair. It was more like a sitting room than an office, I thought, even as I noticed the writing desk nestled under a large many-paned window looking out over the wild tumbling hills of the country just barely visible outside.

'Please, sit,' Dr Blake gestured to the sofa. My mother crossed stiffly over to it; her face as whitely pinched as it had been since she'd picked me up from school. She sat on the edge nearest to the leather armchair, staring at the fire with an odd, glazed look. Realising that Dr Blake wasn't going to move until I did, I reluctantly followed her and perched on the sofa's opposite side.

'So,' Dr Blake settled himself into the armchair and crossed his legs, revealing bright purple socks. 'How can I help?'

'My family... my children... you may not remember all the details. It was a long time ago and I don't know how many others there were... But anyway, we were among the last to participate in your... genetic selection programme. Project A, you called it...?'

I didn't need to see my mother to know she was holding her chin up defiantly the way she always did on the rare occasions she spoke about Project A. It was the same way my brother Silas held his head when explaining that his D in maths was surely the teacher's fault for not teaching him properly.

'Yes?' Dr Blake blinked and smiled politely in a way that didn't give away whether he remembered us or not. I could tell my mother didn't know either, because she stammered as she continued:

'Well... er, my children were the ones in the project, obviously. My eldest, Silas, he's fifteen now,' and here her voice allowed a bit of warmth, as if it had finally absorbed a little of the glow from the fire which sprang hungrily at our bodies.

'We wanted him to be ambitiously athletic. He's the national champion in long-distance running, tennis, squash, swimming... He could compete in the 2000

14

Olympics, if it were allowed. Our daughter Maya is just thirteen, but she's getting ready to sit A-Levels in maths, biology and computing. She's published three novels and can speak five languages. They're... well they're everything we wanted. They're everything you said they would be...'

'*Could* be. We just provided the potential,' Dr Blake interjected, his eyes warm as they flickered to mine. My mother merely twitched his words away with an irritated little gesture I knew well as her face hardened.

'My husband was the one who wanted a third. A dainty little girl to pamper and princess. Maya – she's never really liked girly things. My husband built her a doll's house when she was about four and she spent the afternoon dismantling it, working out where everything went, before putting it all back together again, better than he had. Anyway... We argued but in the end I gave in. What harm, I thought, in having a pretty little girl to dress up and take shopping? Maybe she'd be a stage prodigy or a famous model...'

'Mrs D'accourt—'

'And look at her! We asked for beauty and grace... Even as a newborn, she was the most breathtaking baby anyone could even *imagine.* Never a blemish on her skin, her hair silky smooth, her eyes huge with the longest lashes... She wore her babygros like high couture and as she's grown older, she's only become more beautiful. She's Snow-bloody-White.'

Her words spat against my skin like little bullets of ice. I kept my head lowered, suddenly exhausted in an overwhelming fall-asleep-on-the-floor way I hadn't felt in years. I didn't want to look at Dr Blake. I didn't want to have to think about how I should look at Dr Blake. In any case, I could feel his discomfort hovering in the room like an awkward smell.

'Perhaps, Mrs D'accourt, it would be best to—'

'It's not the beauty that's the problem. If she were an ordinary little girl in other ways... But she's *not*. She uses her looks, sure, but there's something else, something about the way she... manipulates everyone. She has this weird cold influence... The kids at school... her siblings... teachers, strangers, even my husband... they don't see it. But there's something that's just *not right*. She's like a robot... She doesn't seem to *feel* the way normal children do... but the worst thing is the way everyone else is around her. You should've seen her on her first day at nursery school. She was three years old. Most of the kids were crying, clinging to their parents or tearing about, exploring all the toys... In we walk with Bella. She stood there, looking around like a living doll, not a hair out of place, dress pristine, socks pulled up just so... She didn't want to hold my hand, she just stood there... and it was like there was some sort of weird *pull*. The other kids, they all stopped and then they just kind of *flocked* to her. Like the Pied Piper. It was... *creepy*. And there are other things. She has a way of getting what she wants... making people *do* things... even bad things. This little girl who came to our house the other day, Katie... Poor little Katie, I can't even...

'Look, what I'm trying to say is I think we made a mistake... *You* made a mistake. There's something very, very wrong here. Bella is defective. You have to take her back.'

'Mrs D'accourt!' Dr Blake stood up. His height, the firmness of his voice, the way his hands trembled a little at his sides... it was enough, finally, to stop my mother's venomous tirade. She looked up in surprise.

'Perhaps it might be best to continue this

conversation in private?'

My mother snorted and waved a hand dismissively as if he'd offered her a distasteful beverage.

'Bella? If you go through those doors over there, you'll find a schoolroom with lots of children's books and a few toys and games. They belong to my son but I'm sure he won't mind you having a look. Then when your mother and I have finished here we'll give you a call, OK?'

Wordlessly, I slipped off the sofa and made for the double doors he indicated. I wouldn't look at either of them. It was like she'd stripped me naked right there on the rug and the shame stung all the worse for knowing they could see it like a hideous, blistering rash upon my face. *Cold. Creepy. Defective.* I stumbled blindly into the brightly lit adjoining room without looking up, so I didn't notice the boy staring at me from the leather armchair until he spoke.

'Huh,' he chirped, his voice girlishly young, though when I turned to him in surprise the first thing I noticed were how long his legs were as they dangled endlessly over the chair leg. He looked me up and down and smirked, 'You're not *that* pretty.'

**October, 2018**

*Friday*

The car door is open and I'm halfway out before I stop myself. It's only 2.30pm. Ariana's school does not dismiss its pupils for another hour. *So what?* Something deep and visceral screams at me to pull myself out of the car, march into 8R's English class and haul my daughter out, appearances be damned. The larger, calmer part of myself coolly lowers my body back into the car and shuts the door again with a click. It's 2.30. Ariana is no fool; I have drummed enough awareness into her by now for alarm bells to ring should any strange person try to remove her from school an hour before home time. She'll be fine. I inhale slowly and let my gaze flicker to my reflection in the rear-view mirror. *Shit!* I let my breath out with a furious whoosh. I'm still dressed as Elodie bloody Guerre. Of course I am. Elodie leaves her lab at 3.15pm every day and arrives at her neat, two-bedroom apartment at 3.25pm, give or take a minute or five. She steps into the bathroom and, within a few minutes, ceases to exist. Ariana, whose bus drops her off at 3.55pm, comes home to her green-eyed, brunette mum called Bella; younger than most of her friends' parents, strict and reclusive to the point of being really quite annoying but still, just mum.

There had been a time when Ariana was as familiar with my alter-ego as I was. The days when we hadn't long lived here and my life revolved around establishing Elodie's neat little life in her lab, the spectre of discovery looming over my shoulder every time we left the flat. It was all much simpler then. At home, I was Mama with the eyes that matched hers and the hair which betrayed its dark roots every few weeks. Outside the flat, on the way to school, in the supermarket and parks I was Elodie – French, discernibly blonde beneath hats and head-bands, brown-eyed, nervous. But then, in time, the questions had begun. What was I doing to my hair in the bathroom? Why did I dye it yellow? Why did I have to put different eyes in when we went out? Why should I have to disguise myself, when I was already using a pretend name? Why shouldn't she be allowed to dye her hair blonde too, wouldn't we look more blendy-inny if we matched? And, eventually: why did I have to use a stupid, embarrassing accent around her teachers and her friends' dads? Why did I wear so many hats? Why did I always have to be so *different* to everyone else's mum? So, as time passed and no one found us, we'd lulled into a compromise. I cut my hair out of the bleach and let the coffee curls flow more and more into the long spirals I recognised. At home I was Bella. At work, I donned the brown contacts and a pretty, blonde wig and became Elodie. When Ariana moved up to secondary school, I let her take the bus and on the rare times I joined her for parents' evenings, talks or plays, I wore my hair pinned neatly, my contacts remained brown and no one got close to a first name basis. As long as my work in the genetics lab was conducted by Elodie, the fear could be kept at bay. This was where the danger lay, after all. In the exploration of what made people the way they were... This, the field where Bella D'accourt was most at home, was also the place where she was the most discoverable. Well. I had been right about that, at least.

Glancing around at the cul-de-sac, deathly quiet in the before-school-run lull, I reach up and quickly remove my wig and my glasses. I place them neatly in separate resealable plastic bags within my large handbag and release my hair from its scraped-back bun. My forehead instantly relaxes and my hands are steady as I click on the car's interior light and neatly remove my contact lenses. I'm only here for pick up, after all, and I need my eyes free for the journey ahead. I blink at myself in the mirror, my eyes flashing more severely emerald than ever now they have been unsheathed from Elodie's muddy gaze. I glance around again, calm but unable to shake off the sudden feeling of nakedness, as if Ralph might suddenly pop up from beneath my car window and shout, *Ah ha! Fee wasn't so sure, but I knew it was you, Beast!*

See. I know what needs to be done. And I can do it without being a robot, I think, as I steady my pulse and tuck a loose curl behind my ear. It's strange... There was a time when I prided myself on my own careful premeditation. My life was all sharp perfect edges and neat corners. Nothing out of place, never a word spoken without being measured and judged carefully first. Then Ariana came along and wrenched everything out of kilter with one sweep of her tiny, starfish hands. Nowadays the only times I truly feel like my old self is, ironically, when I'm in Elodie's lab, measuring, calculating, perfecting.

I spend the next hour playing word games on my phone, allowing my brain to whirr its way past the tension and the worry and into safe, meaningless territory. At five minutes to the bell, I put on a pair of sunglasses and text

Ariana to let her know I'm here. She doesn't reply and so as the bell goes, I feel my neck tighten like a lizard's as I peer among the bottle-green blazers and drooping school jumpers for her. The sun glares out from behind a cloud and swarms into my face as I lean over the dashboard. I sigh and pull the sun visor down. It's as I'm straightening back up that I see her. She's meandering along among a group of four girls, all of them with identical leather shoulder bags and long hair in various shades of brown. They all wear their socks pulled high and their skirts short, and as they turn to wave at one of them peeling away to walk down the hill, they almost look like clones from the back, save for a few inches difference in height. I frown, irritation itching along my arms and into my fingers, which tap along the steering wheel. So this is why Ariana insists upon spending half an hour every morning straightening the long, spiral curls she inherited from me into the generic sheet of blandness flowing down her back. I watch as the tallest girl – Lucy, if I remember rightly, though Ri rarely talks about her friends with me and hasn't mentioned bringing them home in over six months – whispers in my daughter's ear and points over her shoulder at a group of boys. They're kicking something suspiciously square and book-like between them and seem completely oblivious to the fresh wave of giggles bursting from the pre-teen girls in their direction. They also look about three years younger than their female counterparts, their faces still rounded with baby-fat, knees scruffy with grass and voices high-pitched as they call to one another.

Eventually Ariana throws a cursory glance towards my car in a way which instantly tells me she's not only been aware of it all this time but has deliberately taken her time, knowing full well I only ever come to pick her up when there's an urgent reason behind it. I swallow another lump of frustration and resist the urge to pummel the horn as she tosses her golden chestnut hair over her shoulder and waggles her fingers at her friends. Finally, deliberately slowly, she makes her way towards me with light, delicate steps only slightly jarred with the self-conscious awkwardness of adolescence.

'What are *you* doing here?' she grunts without looking at me as she throws her school bag into the foot-well and flumps ungracefully into the passenger seat. I roll my freshly rouged lips together as I flip the indicator on and pull out in front of a slow-moving Peugeot. Ariana sighs dramatically, rolling her eyes, glancing out of the window and, eventually, looks across at me.

'We're leaving,' I say, shortly, as the traffic lights at the top of the hill turn red and I brake sharply.

'Leaving? What d'you mean, leaving?'

'Exactly what I said. We're leaving.'

'Leaving… leaving school? Leaving Flintworth? Going on holiday? Leaving our senses? Taking ourselves off to the funny farm… I'm going to need a bit more to go on, Mum…'

I sigh and perch my sunglasses on the top of my head before I turn and look at her. Her eyes, as bright and green and clear as my own, widen back at me.

'You mean…?'

'I mean it's time to leave. That thing I warned you might happen has happened. They've found us. The bad people have found us. So we've got to go. Turn your phone off, please.'

The traffic light changes and I flick my sunglasses back into place as I pull the BMW forward and join the A-road leading towards the motorway, the opposite direction of home. Thank goodness I never bought Ariana the kitten she's been begging for since she was six.

'But... can't we just go to the police? Get them to protect us or something?'

'The police won't help. You know that. I've *explained* this, Ri...'

'Well, can't we at least go home first?' The panic in her voice cuts right into me like a thousand shards of invisible glass. I push it down and smooth over it with forced calm. *Now* is the time to be a robot.

'You know we can't...'

'But all my stuff! My clothes, my books... My *Doggy*...' And suddenly all the hair flicking at boys, the rolled-up skirt and the careful borrowing of my make-up over the last few months has gone, leaving a scared little girl who just wants the toy she's slept with since she was a baby. She hunkers down in her seat, bringing her knees up and burying her face in them.

'I'm sorry, Ri...'

'No, you're not. You don't even *care*. I don't want to leave – I'm supposed to be going to Lucy's party next week!'

'I know, I don't want to go either–'

'Yeah, *right*.'

I sigh again. There's no point arguing with her when she's like this. Instead, I turn on the radio and we lapse into silence as the car fills with shallow voices and hollow, repetitive melody.

'We can buy you new clothes,' I say, eventually. She sniffs and wipes her nose on her school skirt. I can't help but wince, though I don't say anything.

'We can't buy another Doggy though, can we? You didn't think of that when you were all caught up in the drama, did you?'

23

'Look, Ri,' I pause as the lights leading onto the motorway turn red and we draw to a halt. I turn to her and she immediately buries her head into her bony knees again. It can't be comfortable, but apparently it's preferable to looking at me. 'We've been through this. You're not like the other kids. We're not like other families. We look the same, but—'

'Yeah, yeah, yeah. Bad people are looking for us. So I have to be good and not invite my friends home or have an Instagram account or even Twitter and Snapchat like everyone else in the *entire universe*...'

'Not just bad people... You remember what I told you? About the man I used to work with? About what he did? And what *they* can do, tracking us using our phones?'

This time she does look up and within the childish petulance on her face there passes a shadow of pure fear. I know she is remembering the nightmares which would call me to her in the middle of the night, her pyjamas wet and clinging, white face streaming as her small body trembled with the echoes of terror, just from the stories I'd told her. I couldn't be sorry, though. I'd known, even as I held her to me and soothed it only temporarily back down, that we both needed her terror to keep us safe. To keep her careful. Even now, at twelve and a half, she feels the reverberations of that fear; I can see it like a hood dropping blackly in front of her eyes. She grasps her phone and presses a finger to a button until the screen flashes, once, and turns black.

'*Go*,' she whispers, as the light turns green. I pull the car into gear and we speed onto the motorway. There is no more arguing.

## Autumn, 1995

'…you're not *that* pretty.'

I was too surprised to reply to him immediately, so I just stood there with my mouth open, proving him irritatingly right. He chuckled, pushed his glasses up his long nose and dipped it back into the book lying open across his knees. A few years older than me, he had the same long limbs and nose as his father, though his eyes behind the thin lenses were a rich brown and his face was a little more angular, a little less soft – but that might have just been the way he was staring at me.

'You're his son, right? Dr Blake's, I mean?'

'And she said your sister was the genius…'

He didn't look up from his book, but I sniffed anyway and put my nose in the air.

'It's rude to eavesdrop, you know.'

He shrugged. I swallowed the urge to run over, pluck his paperback out of his hands and hit him smartly over the head with it.

'What kind of a name is Bella D'accourt, anyway?'

'*My* name,' I replied, deciding to ignore him as I trotted back over to the double doors, listening intently at the join in the middle as the rumble of voices started up again in the room beyond.

'It helps if you lie on the floor and put your ear against

the gap under the door.'

I narrowed my eyes at him, but still he didn't look up. Nobody ever spent this long in the same room as me without looking *at* me except my mother. The boiling urge to physically strike him kept creeping higher, but there was something fascinating about his determined indifference too.

'What's *your* name then?' I asked, mainly as a way of keeping him talking as I got down on my hands and knees.

'Ralph. It's French, isn't it?'

'Is it?'

'D'accourt, I mean. Doesn't it mean *OK*?'

'That's a different spelling.'

'Still, pronunciation's the same. Bella's easy. Beautiful. *Apparently.* Guessing your dad chose that one...'

'I don't know,' I mumbled, blowing dust from the carpet before placing my cheek against its scratchy surface. It smelled of old footsteps – of memories and mysteries and strange things I didn't understand. For a moment we were both silent as my mother's voice slithered into the room like a viper, its hiss an undertow you could only hear if you listened for it.

'...not what we agreed to. Obviously something went wrong – one of *your people* made a mistake. Mixed something sinister in the gene pool. Maybe they even did it on purpose as some sort of sicko experiment...'

'Mrs D'accourt, I can assure you that the genetic modification of our clients was done under the *strictest* control settings. And besides, no individual was ever given more than one predominant set of enhanced traits. That was a control *rule.* Your son, for example, would have been given the cocktail for physical elitism – strong muscles, fast metabolism, athletic build, et cetera. Bella's cocktail would have been for the enhancement of her natural beauty and grace. Nothing more.'

'So where's it come from then, this ability for manipulation?'

'Not from any intervention *we* made, Mrs D'accourt, I can assure you. Any other traits the child possesses can only be natural.'

'There's nothing *natural* about it. Do you know what I caught her doing the other day? I mentioned Katie from next door, didn't I? We had her over to play. The two of them had a board game out in the living room. I went upstairs to talk to the cleaner and next thing I heard were screams — awful, bone-chilling screams coming from the kitchen…'

I sat up so abruptly it felt as if the floor had lurched under me. Ralph was staring at me now, his eyes bright with curiosity under his slightly furrowed brow.

'What did you *do*?'

'I thought you couldn't hear unless you put your head down there?' I said accusingly. He merely shrugged, his fingers loose around his book now as he contemplated me with at least as much interest as I'd shown him.

'Seriously, what'd you do to your friend?'

'Why did you make me get down there in the dirty carpet if I didn't need to? That's just… that's stupid.'

'Not as stupid as you looked with your bum sticking in the air. Are you seriously not going to tell me what all the screaming was about with your friend?'

'None of your business.'

I lowered myself back onto the carpet, only remembering once I was down there that I didn't need to be. Still, I'd look more stupid getting back up again and at least this way I didn't have to look at him. The conversation

27

in the room beyond had moved on slightly.

'...disturbing, but I don't know what I can do to help you. Have you considered taking Bella to a childhood therapist? Perhaps having family counselling?'

'Pah! Of course I have. They spent twenty minutes with her and came out saying she was one of the sweetest, most well-adjusted little girls they'd ever met and that any issues between us were caused by *my* own insecurities and psychological disturbances or some such nonsense.'

I smiled into the carpet, remembering how fast my mother's face had drained of all colour and then filled up again like the sudden swoosh of flames in a newly-lit boiler.

'So what would you like me to do, Mrs D'accourt?'

'*Fix* her! Take her in for testing, scan her brain – open her up if you have to! Get a bloody pastor in here for an exorcism...'

'Mrs D'accourt, this is your *child*.'

'That is no normal child!' I could tell from the pitch of her voice that my mother had leapt to her feet. 'That is some... some sort of *beast* you and your dodgy little cronies have cooked up using mine and my husband's DNA... And I won't have it, I tell you! I won't have it under my roof any longer! Not until you've fixed it!'

'Mrs D'accourt, I can't just take custody of your child. What does your husband say about this?'

He doesn't even know, I wanted to shout. Daddy would never let her bring me here. Daddy doesn't think there's anything wrong with me. Daddy says I'm perfect, his little lovely.

'He... he isn't best pleased. But this is something we've been arguing over for months now. Perhaps even years. He... well, after that incident with little Katie, he stopped arguing. He's agreed that perhaps there's something in you taking a look... seeing what you can discover.'

I couldn't listen anymore. I felt sick with her words, like they'd crept into my stomach and churned it into a badness which sent whiffs of noxious poison up into my throat. Not trusting my hands or arms to push myself up, I simply rolled away from the door onto my back. My eyes instinctively went to the chair, but with a start I realised that Ralph had left it.

'Hah, that's funny!' His voice floated across from the other side of the room. Frowning, I raised myself onto shaky elbows to see him standing in front of yet another full-to-bursting set of bookshelves. He was peering into a large red volume and smirking so widely I could almost hear the glee of it like a crowing, triumphant magpie.

'What?'

'What she called you. *Beast.* I knew I'd read something about the term the other day... *The gift of reason differentiates humanity from the beasts.* Figures, really.'

I lay there a moment longer as he met my burning gaze with cheerful smugness.

'Differentiates means to differ, by the way. In case you're too *beautiful* to know...'

I kept staring. He needed to shut up. I needed to make him.

'I wanted to know what it smelled like,' I said, keeping my voice low and cool. 'Burning flesh. But I didn't want to hurt myself. So I got her to do it. Katie. She was irritating me, she kept cheating at the game we were playing and then lying about it. I don't like it when people lie to me. So I talked to her. Said things. The right things. To make her wonder what it smelled like too. And to make her think that wondering it was all *her* idea in the first place. Then I showed her how to turn on the hob.'

He wasn't laughing at me anymore. He was staring at me much like my mother had, when she'd come downstairs and found us, me shrieking because that's what any concerned child would do when they found their friend holding their hand over an open gas flame, Katie hysterical. No one blamed me. Katie told them all that it had been her idea and that she had waited until I was in the bathroom so I wouldn't stop her. Her mum had even given me a hug at the hospital when we waited for her hand to be bandaged, saying that I must have had an awful fright. Only my own mother looked at me with that awful, empty blackness. That *knowing*.

Two days later, here I was in this odd, half-castle, half-home. Me, my mother, a strange doctor who may or may not have been wearing the same half-disgusted, half-grudgingly fascinated look his son was currently throwing my way, and him – Ralph. The boy with the book who'd said I wasn't that pretty. At least none of them were laughing at me anymore.

**October, 2018**

*Friday*

'You're sure it was her?'

'Dom. Please. Who are you talking to here?'

'I mean… it just… this *place*…'

The young man gestures around him at the sparsely furnished flat. He and the woman are standing in the middle of the living room, where a striped rag rug covering the hardwood floor provides the only splash of colour. The walls are a blemish-free magnolia, the sofas are brown leather and match the walnut dining table and two dining chairs. The pictures on the walls are generic mass-order prints of the type usually found in hospital wards or cheap hotel rooms, there's an archway on the far side of the room leading to a stainless-steel kitchen where, the woman can tell even from here, there isn't so much as a coffee cup left out of place.

'What's your point? It's like a showroom in here.' She gestures to the TV, where a single speck of dust clings to the edge of the screen. 'This is *exactly* the sort of place she'd live…'

She trails a finger along the dining room table and wrinkles her nose, though there is nothing to smell.

'Is it?' Dominic picks something up from the matching

coffee table and shows it to the woman. It's a photograph of a grinning child, a girl aged around ten with long, curly hair of a shade somewhere between honey and tree-bark. She peers up from a swing her legs are too long and gangly for, laughing with her entire face, including the large, startlingly green eyes. The woman sucks her teeth but can't suppress the shudder which sweeps her entire upper body.

'She has a little girl,' Dominic says, softly.

'We don't know that for sure,' the woman replies quickly, unconvincingly. 'It could be a relative we don't know about... or a friend's daughter...'

'Look at those eyes, Fee. They're *hers*. I wonder why Ralph never said anything...'

'Maybe he didn't know...' They exchange a glance and both look away, quickly.

'C'mon,' Dominic puts the photo down quickly, 'Let's check the other rooms.'

He's already halfway across the room before the woman moves, so he doesn't see her swiftly reach for the photo and place it, carefully, in the purple rucksack which she then slings over her shoulder.

It's later, when the evening has moved into a thick black night and Dominic can barely hide the enormous yawns shuddering through his long skinny form, that the two of them finally accept the occupants of the flat are not going to return that night. As they leave, switching off lights and pulling the door closed until it locks behind them, they both know they are delaying the inevitable. The call. Admitting defeat. Dominic knows it will probably have to be him who makes it, as Felix drove. All she needs to do is start the engine and turn to him. His stomach fizzles uncomfortably as he folds himself into the Fiesta's passenger seat, his knees nudging uncomfortably against the glove compartment. He eases the seat backwards. They'd been expecting at least one extra passenger tonight and despite Felix's scorn, he hadn't wanted to make Bella any more uncomfortable than necessary. Felix's phone cuts through the silence just as she slots the key into the ignition and turns on the heating. Both of them can see their breath in front of their faces.

'Shit.' She reaches for her phone and sighs when she sees the caller's name. She fiddles with the heating dial and a waft of stale, cold air hits Dominic square in the face. She smirks briefly as she presses the green answer button, but Dom can sense the tightness in her jaw, the apprehension knotting her brows as she barks, 'Ralph, hi... No, not exactly...'

Dominic sighs, listening but unable to hear more than a gentle, murmuring echo of Ralph's voice. His mind wanders back to the flat in the building next to them. There was no longer any question that Bella D'accourt – or Elodie Guerre as the records on the flat's rental agreement showed – had a young girl living with her and that, judging by the few but tell-tale photos tacked to a mirror in the girl's violet, haphazardly tidy room, she could be no one but Bella's child. He hadn't been able to stop the lump of worry seizing his throat as he'd studied a photo of the girl, around twelve now, smiling from a group selfie with a gaggle of other, similar aged kids.

Felix's voice brings him back to the present like a swipe over the head. 'No, I'm sure... There was the photo I mentioned and a couple more in the kid's bedroom... The girl's hair is lighter but she has her exact eyes... You know as well as I do there's no mistaking Bella's eyes... Yeah...

Judging by the stuff in the bedroom, I'd say about eleven or twelve… Definitely no older than young teen… Yep… No, afraid not. There was another photo in Bella's bedroom…'

She reaches forward and digs a small frame out of the backpack nestled between her boots. Spotting other photos in the bag's depths, some framed, some loose, Dominic bites his lip uneasily, but says nothing. Felix holds the picture between finger and thumb and describes it into the phone.

'It's a few years old, but it's the same kid alright. Aged about four or five. And Bella – looking pretty much the same as she ever did – she's there with her arms around her… I know, weird, right? I wouldn't believe it either if I didn't have the damn evidence sitting here in my lap… Right… Yep… OK, we're on our way.'

She hangs up and chucks the phone into her backpack, tugging the old car into gear and indicating to pull into the empty street without looking at Dominic. He can see the spots of heat on her pale cheeks though, even in the dull wash of the street lights.

'You took her photos…' he says quietly, as she urges the car forward to join the dual carriageway.

'We need evidence to show Ralph, Dom. You know what he's like – he has to see something for himself to really believe in it. Specially something like this. Besides, it's not like she's going to come back. You saw that place.'

'Yeah, nothing was missing… There were clothes in the cupboards and shoes lined up in the shoe rack. Plenty of fresh food still in the fridge…'

'Come on, Dom, I know you're young but you weren't *that* young when Bella lived at the ARC. You remember what she was like. How *careful* she was about everything. She probably had an escape bag packed and in the back of her car… God knows where she is now.'

'So why did we spend the evening in her flat, then?'

Felix shrugs as if his question is a persistent, irritating fly.

'Why do we do anything… Blake thought it was a good idea. Anyway, you know as well as I do that we're not the only ones on Bella's tail. I did her a favour, taking these,' she gestures at her bag.

'It's not like it wasn't noticeable there was a child living there…'

'No, but at least now it won't be glaringly obvious what she looks like.'

'Mm. I'm still not sure about taking them.'

Felix sighs and flexes her arms as the Fiesta eases to a stop at a red light. 'You know your problem, don't you, Dom? You're too soft. Too soft by a mile…'

Dominic glares out of the window and doesn't answer, knowing she's right and hating her for it.

**October, 2018**

*Friday*

The drive is long and exhausting. I take several detours on winding country lanes that make me shudder with the memory of that silent journey up into the Lake District with my mother all those years ago. We stop only when we need to, and I pay in cash for the things we buy. Ariana's questions subside into grunts and eye-rolls, and exhaustion eventually overcomes her as we wind our way out of the Blackdown Hills and into Devon. I glance over as she dips her head onto her wadded-up school coat and her eyes disappear bit by bit until finally they're nothing but lids and long black lashes. I don't know what I'm going to do about her school. An illness might buy us some time, but it won't be long before questions are asked, reports are made... Everything is all so much more complicated when a child is involved. I'd known this might happen. Had planned for it, puzzled over it, even – in the darker, most boring moments of Elodie's day – daydreamed about it... But now, with the reality rushing bleakly past the window and swarming round my chest... I can't help but go over all the mistakes I might have made, the open doors, the breadcrumbs of decisions that could have brought us here.

*What good does thinking like that do, Bella? You're here now. You need to move forward. Best not to call her school at all, leave the screen completely blank. Harder to trace someone who simply disappears.*

Right. Then they get the authorities involved, we become missing persons and a whole lot of questions are raised about who the hell Elodie Guerre is. Not to mention our faces plastered all over the internet...

*Come on. Do you really think he doesn't know? That Felix and Ralph found you on their own after 13 years? This has Lychen written all over it. He's the one with all the resources. All the power. He always was.*

But how? How did he find me?

*Not just how. Why. Why now?*

I sigh and grit my teeth, blinking hard against the exhaustion prickling at my eyes. I've been driving for over five hours and we're still at least two from our destination. I glance at the battered A-Z map leaning on Ariana's knees. It's fallen slightly as she's curled herself into a comfier position and I ease it back gently. I can just about make out the route from the A38 into the depths of Cornwall. I don't dare put the postcode into my phone's map. In fact, I haven't switched my phone back on since leaving Flintworth. I know Felix. Even back in 2005 she could hack into what were the very cutting edge of satellite navigation systems. It's one of the reasons Lychen was so interested in her joining his new team.

Lychen.

I try not to, but in the depths of the dark, silent car, with just the dwindling tail and headlights of strangers around me, my mind swarms back to the last time I saw him. His eyes, those shards of nothingness, piercing me from across the stage. Seeing into me, exposing my hidden parts, the secrets he'd wrenched so forcefully upon the two of us. His fist in my hair, the jack-knife of pain... *Sooner or later you're going to have to choose a side, Bella... Before the choice is taken from you...* His grip like an icy metal clamp around my arms, my neck... I shudder, gritting my teeth harder and this time I stop the nightmare before it deepens, before it takes me further into that crushing warm night in August. *I did choose,* I tell myself, firmly. *I chose my own side. And Ariana's.*

*Yes, but he never really left you, did he? He's still here, isn't he?*

The voice hardens, turns clipped around the edges of words, becomes cold... Becomes his.

*See. Here I am. In your head. And out of it. Always. And if I wanted more, I would take it. Like I did before. That was your choice, Bella. It could have been different... It would have been, if you'd just—*

*Shut up, shut up, get out, shut up!* I shake my head and switch the radio from static to one of Ariana's CDs, letting Harry Styles warble over him, masking his cruel taunts until they fade back into the darkest shadows of my head. I force myself to smile tightly, but it's not quite enough to stop the tingling in my throat, the quick feeling of tightness as if it had suddenly been grasped in the fist of a shadowy, icy hand.

It's past eleven by the time I finally pull the BMW to a halt outside the small, white brick cottage. I've only been here once before, long ago. Despite my many pit-stops to pour over the map, the country lanes it shows sprouting like noodles from the tiny village of Pethwick seem to have bred and multiplied in reality. Still, we're here now. Finally. I stare at the reassuringly dark windows, the deserted driveway, the sloping, sand-strewn lane behind us illuminated only by the glare of my rear lights. It's too dark to see now, but I know that in the daylight we'll be surrounded by overgrown fields, tussocks of gorse, perhaps a distant sheep or two. The cottage lies at the bottom of a single-track lane sloping through a deserted valley. Over the hill there's a cliff and, far below, a spit of a beach almost too tiny to bother risking the treacherous route hidden behind boulders.

'Where *are* we?' Ariana groans. I glance over, not having realised she was awake.

'Cornwall. Near Pethwick. I'm not sure how near, exactly, it's not really a clear route.'

'Looks like we're at the crap end of the middle of nowhere,' she mutters as I switch off the engine and retrieve a pocket torch from the glove compartment.

'Yes, well… That's pretty much the idea,' I mumble back, pointing the torch into my handbag and locating the small set of rusting keys at the very bottom. We both climb out of the car and stand side by side at the gate at the end of the path winding towards the cottage's front door. The front garden is overgrown, but not derelict. I know someone will have been in to tend to it over the summer, during the busy season. The knowledge doesn't make the white building seem any more homely as it glares at us from the dark.

'Who does it belong to?' Ariana whispers, shivering and moving closer to my side.

'An old friend. She rents it out over the holidays but it's off-season at the moment so it's empty. Come on, let's go in. It's cold.'

I push on the gate and it swings open far easier than I expected, though the hinges give an angry squawk under my touch. I hitch my bag onto my shoulder and begin to walk. I'm five paces down, stepping carefully over the broken parts of the paving stones, when I realise Ariana isn't following. Turning, I shine the beam from my torch up towards her face and she winces. There's a wariness to her, a hesitation that blares like a little blinking worry light from her face. But she's not looking at the cottage, she's looking at me.

'What is it?' I can't help but let a little of my irritation show. It's late; I'm exhausted.

'This friend...' she says, slowly, pouting. 'She does *know* you've got the keys to her house, doesn't she? I mean... we're not like... trespassing or anything are we?'

We stare at one another coldly. I blink slowly. She looks down and her pout twists into a sulk as she shrugs and shuffles forwards behind me. How long, I wonder. How long do I have left before she refuses to follow? Before her burgeoning mistrust leads to her splitting away from me entirely?

**October, 2018**

*Friday*

The chain hotel they've been using as their base for the last week lies just under an hour's drive from Bella's flat in Flintworth. Felix and Dominic drive most of it in silence. As every mile passes, his mind becomes more consumed with the thoughts of the woman with the green eyes speeding far away from them, her heart flurrying ever faster with every glance she throws at the child sleeping next to her. The sweet-faced girl with the brownish-blonde hair, limbs folded delicately, face relaxed in innocent oblivion… He knows he's being soft. But as the journey rumbles north he can't stop the thoughts circling like vultures around his stomach. What is he doing?

Felix, meanwhile, is also occupied by images of the woman, only she sees the slipped opportunity, the wasted moment. Why hadn't she hung about at the university until the lecture had finished? She could have confronted Bella then and there before she'd had the chance to run. She could have ripped away the blonde wig in front of that fawning man who'd been staring like a lustful slave from the side of the lectern, asked loudly why Bella was pretending to be some French academic when they both knew she was about as French as Felix's stubby

41

fingernails... Maybe she'd have had the chance to give her a good shove. They'd been friends once, maybe, but even in the old days Felix had often fantasised about what it might feel like to give Bella D'accourt a good shove. She doesn't think about Ralph's instructions to confirm identity and report back as quickly as possible. She doesn't think about the danger Bella might have posed to *her* under threat. She doesn't think about the child. She very determinedly does not think about the child. And as they draw closer to the hotel, to Ralph, and Ethan, her husband, her thoughts turn to what sort of reception they might receive. She was the one in charge of tracking, after all. She was the one who gathered intelligence. She isn't scared of Ralph, but she knows he'll be disappointed in her and the thought sticks to the back of her throat like a large, stubborn crumb.

Ralph is the one to answer the door when Felix knocks, twenty minutes later. He barely nods, ushering them inside. Ethan is frowning over a laptop and a monitor screen, a box of noodles untouched next to him. He looks up as Felix approaches and his broad face splits into a relieved grin. Despite the nagging nibble of worry in her gullet, Felix finds some of her tension lifting away. *That's why I married you,* she thinks as she smiles, shortly, back at him. Dominic flops heavily onto one of the still pristinely made-up double beds behind them and sighs dramatically.

'Alright?' Ralph barks, glancing between the two of them.

'Fine... Just... annoyed we didn't get her,' Felix mutters.

'Never mind that now. We might still be able to work out where she's going. Fee, I want you to get onto the laptop and show me all the communications which lead us to Flintworth... I want to make sure we didn't overlook anything,' Ralph says, taking a gulp from a bottle of water.

'Right.' Felix nudges Ethan and he gratefully relinquishes the chair at the laptop, picking up the box of noodles.

'I had a go at getting started,' he says as he shovels a mouthful in with his fingers. 'But I couldn't get past the encryption.'

'Well, that's what I'm here for,' Felix says, her eyes already sweeping over the lines of code as her fingers flex across the familiar keys. 'And get a fork, animal.'

'What exactly did you find at the flat, Dom?' Ralph sinks into a chair opposite Dominic. Felix glances over at Dominic's bobbing Adam's apple and sighs in frustration.

'Show him the photos, Dom,' she snaps, before turning back to the screen. Within minutes she is caught within the snare of the code, her ears deaf to the rest of the room, her eyes only existing for the beautiful puzzle in front of her.

'Here.' Dominic reaches into Felix's backpack, throwing a furtive look her way as he does so, but she is fully immersed in the softly whirring machine before her. 'Fee took them from the flat. Two bedrooms, one of them clearly belonged to a young girl. *This* girl. All of it very tidy, nothing out of place. The whole flat, I mean, not just the kid's room – that was tidy too, but in a kind of forced way, if you see what I mean. Like when your parents make you clean up because your grandparents are coming round so you kind of shove things in boxes and under the bed even though they *never* go in your room so really there's no poi—'

His voice withers into a gulp as Ralph throws him a look over the top of the photo. He's got the one of the girl with her friends which had been fixed to the mirror in her room. Slowly he traces a finger over the green eyes of the smiling girl. He places the photo down and picks up the one from Bella's bedroom, the only one showing her along with the child. His breath floods slowly, hiss-like from his mouth as if it is his last and a stillness falls over him. The only sounds in the room come from the gentle tapping of Felix's fingers on the keyboard and Ethan's soft chewing over in the far corner by the window.

'So this is why she hid herself away for so long,' Ralph sighs, his dark brown eyes unfathomable as they feast upon the picture. 'How old, did you say?'

'There? About four or five, I'd say... I mean she's still got her baby teeth—'

'I mean now, Dom.'

'Oh. Right, of course. Sorry... About twelve, Fee reckoned?'

Ralph shuts his eyes for a moment and, when he opens them, he places the picture face down on the bed, turning away from it as if it couldn't be trusted.

'Bella left in August 2005,' he says softly into the shadows in front of him.

'Right, just after the big C-Project presentation when that kid, Rudy... Yeah. I was only a teenager myself at the time and I had a lot going on with my own part to play in the whole show... But I remember Bella there. She did that big talk... in that dress, with the... um...'

'Shut up, Dom,' Ethan growls. Dominic flushes. If Ralph notices, he doesn't spare him a glance.

'What?' Dominic turns around, 'The beauty is in the detail, right? Isn't that what Dr Blake always says? Remember everything, you never know what might be a crucial detail.'

'Getting a boner when you're thirteen is *never* a crucial detail, Dom,' Ethan slurps up a noodle and wipes his face with his large, meaty knuckle, grinning at Dom over the top.

'Fifteen,' Dom says, knowing he's blushing and wishing he could punch Ethan without risking the bones in his hand. And his arm, for that matter.

'Ralph.' Felix's voice brings them all to attention as if she has suddenly cast invisible lassos around their heads. *Is she going to ask?* Dominic wonders. Is she going to bring up the rumours surrounding Bella and Ralph that even he, at fifteen, hadn't been too self-obsessed to absorb? Is she going to mention the crashing coincidence of Bella's leaving following the strange way she and Ralph had been acting around one another in the weeks leading up to the presentation, not to mention the raging argument they were rumoured to have had the night she left? He can still picture Bella, chest fluttering delicately under the glistening emeralds on her dress, hair tumbling in loose curls around her face and teasing the bare skin of her back as she'd stepped onto that stage and ensnared every single watcher with the merest flickers of movement.

'Fee?'

'I've got it here. All the communications we were able to intercept between Lychen and... well...'

'Bella?' Ralph crosses the room in two strides of his long legs to hover over the back of Felix's chair like an anxious apostrophe. Dominic and Ethan exchange a glance before they both jump to their feet at the same time and scramble to get a look at the screen. Felix drags the open browser window over to the larger monitor so they can all read it easily.

'That's the thing... Knowing what we know now, I'm

45

not so sure it *was* Bella he was talking to... I mean, for one thing, why would she go to such lengths to conceal herself for so long only to open up a conversation on Twitter of all things?'

'Well, learning about the child certainly changes things...'

'Exactly.'

They all pause to read the few lines of the chat which Felix has managed to unencrypt.

> Conan68          ...like London or Manchester?
>
> LesYeuxVertes  Like I should be so lucky!!! Where do you live? I bet it's somewhere really fun.
>
> Conan68          Oh, I live all over. One week Paris, the next Dubai. I travel a lot. But London is my home. There's no place like it, really. Especially when you go away a lot, don't you think?
>
> LesYeuxVertes  I wouldn't know! I've never been! I've never really been anywhere fun!! Except Brighton beach once or twice in the summer!!!! I wish I...

'I always thought the language didn't seem quite right,' Felix murmurs. 'I assumed she was playing some sort of game, adopting some innocent, un-Bella-ish persona, but now... I mean the exclamation marks... What if it wasn't a persona at all? What if it actually was—'

'A twelve-year-old kid...'

'Well... yeah,' Felix looks up and shares a look with Ralph that Dominic can't work out. There's worry in it, but something more. Something deeper that takes him right back to being the skinny, awkward boy with too-big clothes, watching the grown-ups argue over things he *wouldn't understand.*

Ralph throws himself back from the chair so violently that Felix shoots forward several inches and has to catch the desk before it jabs into her stomach. He doesn't look at her, though, his eyes are wild, staring around at the room but not really seeing any of it. He pulls his hands through his hair until it stands straight up and for a moment he looks so uncannily like his father that Felix has to blink several times.

'Calm down,' she murmurs, trying not to sound alarmed. She's never seen quite so much of the whites of his eyes before. 'None of this is new information...'

'It *is* though, Felix! There's a kid involved!'

'And, from the looks of things, Lychen knew about her long before we did... and what's he done? Nothing. *We're* the ones who made the first move. We're the ones who went after Bella...'

'Yes, and look what's happened... For all we know this is exactly what he wanted. For all we know we could have driven them straight at him...'

'Look, why don't we just—'

'You don't get it, Felix! Thirteen years ago, right before the presentation... That summer... Bella and I... We...'

'I *do* get it, actually. I got it the moment you first looked at those bloody photographs. Give me some credit here, please.'

Ralph stares at her and, slowly, the fight whooshes out of him in a long breath. He sits, slowly, on the bed next to the small scatter of frames and prints. Felix realises, with some surprise, that she's on her feet. Ethan and Dom have retreated to the chairs nestled in the corner of the room. Ethan has picked up the half-empty noodle carton once again and Dominic is staring at the generic waves of the hotel room carpet as if wishing he could melt into it.

'I didn't think this could happen... I mean I know it *happens*. But I thought we were careful, you know?'

'It still happens, mate,' Ethan mumbles, though he's looking at Felix rather than Ralph. She smiles sadly and looks away. Ralph is entirely oblivious to the brief exchange. He drops his head forward onto his palms.

'Why didn't she tell me?' He looks like a long, limby grasshopper-type insect all folded over. Felix sighs and squeezes his shoulder.

'Who knows? I never understood that girl. Even when we were supposedly friends. She was – what, thirteen, fourteen – when I first began working at the ARC, and I wasn't all that much older... I practically grew up with her... We spent months together working on tasks and experiments for Project C and the presentation... and then she just upped and disappeared. Without a single word. She could have talked to me about the pregnancy, I could have helped her...'

Ralph shakes his head. 'I don't even know her name...' he mumbles to his knees.

'Look... there's nothing more we can do tonight. Tomorrow I'll give my contact at the police a shout, see if we can get a vehicle match using ANPR. We should be able to track her using the traffic cams. She can't hide. She knows that. Not forever. In the meantime... maybe it's time we gave your dad a call.'

'Oh *God*...'

'Yeah, but he's going to need an update, you know that.'

'Urgh. Right. Yeah, you're right.'

'Ralph... Lychen's not going to do anything to Bella.

You know that. She's probably the only person in the world who's safe from him. And I know what you're going to say – she's not the one you're worried about, except she *is,* of course, because who're you kidding? But anyway, the girl... she's Bella's daughter. She's done a pretty good job keeping her safe for the last twelve years... You're just going to have to trust her for a bit longer. Until we get to them...'

'Trust Bella. Right. *That* sounds like a sensible plan...'

'Come on, you know as well as I do that she doesn't let anyone take anything from her unless she's willing to let it go.'

'No... You're right,' Ralph looks up, rubbing his face. 'Right. I better get this over and done with. Where's my phone?'

'Here. Oh. And I took this from the girl's bedroom, too,' she pulls a hand out of her rucksack and throws something small and glittery onto the bed between them. It's a door sign, a personalised decal with flakes of white paint from the door still stuck to its underside. Ralph stares at it and, slowly, traces the letters with one long, skinny finger.

'Ariana...' he murmurs. 'That was my mother's name – everyone called her Ana.'

'Well, that confirms it, doesn't it? Congratulations,' Felix says, drily. 'You're a dad.'

**Autumn, 1995**

My mother didn't bother coming to say goodbye to me. In fact, I only realised she'd gone when I heard the sound of a car crawling across gravel. By the time I'd rolled over and climbed to my feet, Dr Blake had slid the double doors open and was standing there in the space between, looking at me with a strange, unreadable expression. I glanced past him to the far end of his office and saw the twin red lights of my mother's car tremble over the loose stones and turn slowly out of the driveway. By the time I looked back at Blake my face was smooth and impassive. Blake looked over my shoulder and his mouth twitched as he spotted his son.

'Ralph... I didn't know you were down here...'

I glanced behind me and Ralph, who was back in his chair with his book folded over his lap as if he hadn't moved at all the whole time I'd been in the room, shrugged.

'I came down to read.'

'Hmm,' Blake stared at him a bit longer as if he were trying to decide whether to accuse him of eavesdropping. If he were my mother and Ralph were me, he'd have started yelling by now, I thought. If he were my father, he would smile indulgently and call me a little pickle. Blake did neither. He looked at Ralph in a way I'd never seen any adult look at a child, let alone their own. It was like they worked together or something, like they had some sort of understanding that was far too grown up for silly pet names or childish reprimands. I decided, then and there, that that was how I wanted to be looked at, too. If the cutesy cuddles with Daddy came hand in hand with my mother's cold eyes and wrinkled nose, I'd rather be treated like a colleague. I didn't know then, of course, that the subject of my parenting was already a moot point.

'Anyhow, I'm sure you two will have introduced yourselves, but for the sake of formalities, this here is Ralph Blake. He's my son. And how old are you now, Ralph? Eleven?'

'Turned twelve in May, father dear.'

Blake chuckled and his eyes twinkled behind their spectacles. 'Of course. May the twelfth. I get his birthday right but I get muddled with the years. Ralph, this is Bella D'accourt. She's going to be staying with us for a bit...'

'I am?' I wasn't at all surprised by the news, but thought I should probably act as if I were.

'Yes... I'm not sure how long for, but your mother and I have decided it's for the best for now...' Some unspoken understanding passed between him and Ralph again. Ralph slowly placed his book down and got to his feet. They both watched me as if worried I might burst into tears or rush out of the door after my mother. When I did neither they both seemed to sag a little in relief. I had to bite my cheek not to laugh. Men were so simple.

'Are you hungry, Bella?' Dr Blake turned towards me. 'We've eaten already but I can ask Ramona to make you a sandwich or something if you'd like one?'

'No thank you,' I replied, my stomach empty but too knotted to contemplate food.

'Well, then... I'll show you to the guest room...

Normally my wife would be around but I'm afraid she's a bit under the weather at the moment.'

'Oh,' I said, unable to contain my surprise. For some reason I hadn't factored in Ralph having a mother, which was silly, I realised. Everyone had a mother. This house – the parts I'd seen so far, at least – just seemed so... male... I couldn't imagine a mother figure flittering about, dropping kisses on Ralph's head or smoothing Dr Blake's sticky-uppy hair.

'She has cancer,' Ralph said, shortly, his eyes locked onto mine as if in challenge. Blake was leading the way out of the room so I couldn't see his reaction, but I thought I saw his shoulders twitch just a little. I glanced from one to the other and said nothing.

In the hallway there were two suitcases, one of which was the bright pink Minnie Mouse pull-along my dad had bought me for our holiday to Florida last year. The other was black and plain. Both seemed out of place on the old, shiny-worn flagstones. I glimpsed myself in a tall, dusty-edged mirror as Blake took a suitcase in each hand. My face seemed paler than usual, but otherwise I looked the same as I always did. I wondered, bitterly, how long my mother had had those suitcases ready. Whether the contents would be jumbled, panic-strewn like the time Maya forgot about a school trip and had had to pack everything the morning she was due to leave. I'd laughed when she'd told me afterwards that she'd had to borrow underwear from a friend when she realised she'd packed about seven vests but only one pair of pants. I blinked slowly, and forced myself to stop thinking about my sister and home. The walls around me loomed tall and full of shadows. Ralph brushed past us and disappeared up a winding staircase with a threadbare carpet. Blake gestured for me to follow and together we began to climb.

'Here we are… I'm afraid it's not very… Well… It might not be much like what you're used to…'

We stood in the doorway of a large room roughly twice the size of my pink, frilly bedroom at home. The bed was a huge expanse of dark purple velvet with at least six pillows and cushions. The wooden ends curved over like the downstairs sofa arms – I'd later be told it was a sleigh bed, which always made me think of Christmas. Opposite the bed stood a tall, double-doored wardrobe with swirling patterns set into the dark wood. An old rocking chair, dusty but comfy-looking with an old, velvet pillow which matched the bed's eiderdown, stood in the corner of the room and the rest… The rest was mostly empty, apart from a full-length mirror propped against the wall and a friendly-looking striped rug over the bare floorboards. It was like the room had been furnished by someone who hadn't decided what might need to go in it and had run out of furniture before they'd made up their mind. A huge, many-paned window set into the far wall overlooked the driveway. I stared at it, remembering the mismatch of window styles I'd spotted from the driveway and wondering where this one fitted. As Blake gently set my cases down on the rug, I felt very small.

'I'm afraid there's no en-suite, but there's a bathroom out here on the left… There should be plenty of towels and things… And there's only my wife's private studio along with a couple of other guest rooms on this floor, but they're all empty so it's all nice and quiet…' He glanced around, his hands suddenly looking too large at the ends of his arms.

'I'm sorry my wife's not around… Hopefully she'll be feeling a little stronger in the morning and will be able to meet you...'

'OK,' I said, swallowing an involuntary tremble which threatened to wobble into my voice. I couldn't remember ever feeling so... lost. My brain told me it was normal, even felt a sprig of wry amusement that, for once, I was reacting the way any other nine-year-old might at finding themselves in a strange place with strange people.

'I... er...' Blake cleared his throat and pushed a hand through his hair, making it stick up even more. 'We used to read to Ralph at bedtime... When he was younger... Even when he was about your age and could read as well as I'm sure you can... which reminds me, I'll ask him to dig out some books for you tomorrow, and we'll see about moving a bookshelf in here. It's not a proper bedroom without books, after all...'

I smiled, thinking about his study downstairs and wondering if *any* room was a proper room without books in this house. Blake grinned back, barely hiding his relief. He'd clearly still been a little worried I was about to get hysterical or something. After all, he didn't really know me – he only had my mother's word for what I was like, so far. I could hardly blame him for looking nervous.

'But, er, if you'd like me to read to you, I'd be more than happy.'

'Thank you, Dr Blake,' I replied, sweetly. 'But I'm just really tired. I think if it's OK with you I'll just go to bed.'

'Of course, of course... Well, like I said – bathroom's on the left. Ana and I – that's my wife, Ralph's mum – we're just upstairs, first door on the right. If you need anything. Or if you're, you know, scared or worried. But really, don't mind any creaks or anything. It's an old house. I like to think it sings a little in the dark... Sleep well.'

'Thank you. You too.'

I waited until he pulled the door closed with a click, then I crossed the room to the suitcases. Barely taking a breath, I pushed the pink one onto its side and unzipped it. Every item was folded and ironed. There were clothes I hadn't seen for weeks. My mother must have been putting them away, readying them long before the day I hurt Katie. I dug through the jumpers and skirts, tights, socks and jeans until my hands closed over something soft and familiar. I drew out the small, cuddly dog my father had brought home from a business trip three years ago. I'd never really liked teddies or cuddly things. I'd posed with them, rubbed my face into them and smiled sweetly from their fur if someone was watching, especially if they had a camera out; but I'd never bothered having them in my bed. That night, though, I kept the dog near me as I pulled my favourite nightie from the case. I took the dog when I tiptoed to the bathroom, clutching the new toothbrush I'd found in the second suitcase alongside shampoo, my hairbrush, and several books, some of which she must have taken from my school bag that very week. And, when I finally hoisted myself onto the cavernous double bed, fanning the pillows around me and pulling several layers of velvet, blanket, and sheets back until I could wriggle into its cool depths, the dog came with me.

I lay in the darkness, curled around myself – a small, kidney-shaped nugget of warmth in the cold horizon of sheets – stroking the dog's fur. I didn't cry. I thought about my parents, my brother, my sister, and my home. I thought about my school, teachers, and friends. I thought about my dance lessons. Weekends spent playing with my friends; visiting grandparents; holidays; ballet shows; Christmases; birthdays. *That's over now,* I thought, and the voice thinking it rang with sternness. *That part is finished. There's no point thinking about them. They erased me. They were too weak.* But it was hard to stop, now I'd started, now that the images swarmed past the wall my brain scrambled to lay before them and my imagination reached over the top. My father's eyes closing in defeat in the darkness of my parents' bedroom as my mother mimed a hand burning over a stove top. My brother and sister glancing at one another in alarm over the dinner table as they realised I wasn't coming home. What was it my mother had said about me? *She doesn't seem to feel the way normal children do.* I rolled onto my back, clenching and unclenching my toes as my feet stretched into the middle of the bed. *She's like a robot.* My mother, ironing and folding the clothes she had chosen for me and placing them, one by one, into a small, pink suitcase. *Robots don't feel. Robots don't cry.* I didn't cry. I held the dog next to my face and, as my mind sank towards the close, welcome blankness of sleep, it occurred to me that its fur smelled, ever so slightly, of burning flesh.

**October, 2018**

*Saturday*

At first it's a bit like being on holiday. Ariana wakes up and, before she even opens her eyes, she can smell the ocean. Seagulls shriek and she can't help but smile as she rolls into the soft duvet which smells only a little bit musty. Then she opens her eyes. The room is small, just big enough for the single bed she lies in, a white wooden chair where she dumped her school bag and uniform the night before and a small night-stand. White linen curtains barely filter the stream of morning light from the small window above the foot of the bed. She sits up, tugs the curtains open and stares. Greenness stretches as far as she can see. The small window is completely full of fields, swarming upwards in hilly waves. There are a few dark, greyish spots which might be sheep in the very distance, and a wind turbine spikes into the sky on top of a hill to the far left. On the right she can just make out a blueish grey line which *might* be the sea at the very edges of the green tussocks. She knows there's a closer bit of beach somewhere, though. Mum said so last night. She said they could go and find it today or tomorrow.

Ariana sighs and looks down at the faded, baggy T-shirt she slept in. Like everything here, it's unfamiliar. Mum said they'd shop for new clothes today, but she doesn't know what she'll wear until then. There were a few outfits in the large wardrobe in Mum's room last night, which is where they found this shirt, but they all looked suspiciously mannish to Ariana. Mum, of course, has her own clothes packed neatly into a holdall Ariana had never seen before last night when it appeared, as if by magic, in the boot of the car. Ariana doesn't know how to feel about that. She wants to shove it to the back of her head like she's been doing with all the weird, unexplained things she's been noticing more and more about her mother over the last few years. But now… Now here she is, sitting in a tiny bedroom with too much white in it for it to feel like *anyone's* bedroom, let alone hers, probably two thousand miles or more away from her friends, her room, her Doggy…

Ariana sniffs and, with a wallop, all the lightness she felt just minutes ago is gone, leaving heavy stones in its place. Her mind swarms with the darkness of the night before. The look on her mother's face when she told her they'd been found… The man from her nightmares. He looms too tall, his face a featureless smear, his hands claw through the air towards her, looking to pull her apart and put her back together as something monstrous… *Stop*, Ariana tells herself. *Just stop.*

Swallowing hard, she shakes her head and listens carefully. She can hear her mother moving around downstairs, the sound of clinking and a kettle coming to the boil. Aware every moment of every noise, she edges to the other end of the bed and reaches for her school bag. At least that's one good thing about a box room, she thinks, everything is reachable from the bed. Listening so hard her ears almost ring with effort, she reaches into her bag, past the books, past the spiky sequins of her pencil case and into the very bottom where her fingers close around her phone. Her mother had warned her not to use it, but surely just a few minutes, just to check her messages, wouldn't hurt… She's seen the police dramas on TV, the ones when they triangulate signals and stuff. It always takes them ages, that's why the kidnappers never spend too long on the phone… surely this is the same thing.

She swipes the WhatsApp notifications from her friends away and taps on the internet. It takes ages to load, at least ten seconds. The little icon at the top isn't even 3G let alone 4, it's some symbol she doesn't recognise and it flickers on and off. Ariana can feel her unease growing and is two seconds from throwing the phone back into her bag before, finally, the page loads. Instagram. No notifications. She scrolls for a bit through the newsfeed until the pictures of her friends grinning, the #FridayFeels and the Saturday lie-in selfies begin to make her throat ache again. She closes the tab and brings up Twitter. Her heart flutters so loudly in her ears she can barely hear the soft steps crossing into the living room downstairs. No messages. No new followers. She only has a handful, after all, and only one of them isn't some randomer. Only one of them has even sent her a direct message. She thinks about typing something out now. Telling him about the journey down here, how weird everything is, how scary it feels. How she doesn't know if she really is safe now, despite what Mum says. And the deepest, most shadowy worry of all, that she doesn't know if she can even trust her own mother, anyway… He would understand. He'd say something clever and cool. He'd make it OK.

'Ariana, are you awake? I've made you a cup of tea!' Her mother's voice, light and musical like she's about to burst into song, comes from the hallway outside the room and Ariana jumps. Quickly she holds down the off button and chucks the phone back into her bag just as the door opens.

'Oh good, you're up,' her mother smiles, looking as unruffled and serene as if this really were some sort of lovely, impromptu holiday. Ariana frowns at her.

'I didn't hear you coming,' she mutters. 'You made me jump.'

Bella shrugs and places a steaming mug down on the bedside table.

'Good news,' she says, not bothering to respond to Ariana's grumble. 'I've found you some clothes.'

'I am *not* wearing anything else out of that musty old wardrobe in your room,' Ariana sniffs, glancing down at the T-shirt again. 'There's probably moths in there.'

Bella frowns briefly, but quickly smooths her face back into its neutral, smiling expression. She's obviously decided that determinedly cheerful will be her tack for the day. She herself is already fully dressed in a pair of dark designer jeans and a pressed, acid-green blouse which makes the colour of her eyes sharper than ever.

'No, I mean I've found some of *your* clothes. I *knew* I'd packed a bag for you as well, you know, just in case... I just didn't spot it in the dark last night. Some of the stuff might be a bit small now... I think the last time I put new things in there was in the spring...'

'Great.'

'But we should be able to find you something suitable for today. Then we'll go into town and buy you some new things, alright?'

'OK...' Ariana reaches for her mug and bends her head over it.

'Right… Well, I'll let you drink your tea. Good job we picked up a few bits from that petrol station last night, there's barely anything in the cupboards except a few tins of beans and some rice… Anyway, I'll go make us some toast. Careful with that tea on the white duvet. See you in a bit.'

Ariana sips so she doesn't have to reply. As her mother leaves the room she listens carefully, but despite the old floorboards of the house and the general moans and creaks which seemed to wake her every few minutes during the night, her mother's footfalls don't seem to make so much as a squeak on her way back downstairs. *Like a ghost*, Ariana thinks, and before she has the chance to suppress the urge, she shudders and two drops of tea splotch heavily onto the sea of whiteness beneath.

**October, 2018**

*Saturday*

For all my determined positivity, the first morning doesn't go well. The cottage is comfortable enough, with its mismatched furniture and odd assortment of amenities – fifteen knives but only three forks, a broom, dustpan and brush but no vacuum cleaner – but it's cold even for the mild October day and I can't work out the heating system. Last time I was here – seven, no, eight years ago – was during the summer. There's a fireplace set into the stones of the small living room wall, but the guard has a lock on it and a small sign says that guests are not permitted to use it unless they're staying over Christmas. By 10am I've had to dig my old cashmere cardigan out of the holdall and by eleven I'm wondering whether I'll need to resort to wearing one of the old throws from the sofa around my shoulders. The temperature is the least of Ariana's complaints, however.

'When can I use my phone again?' she demands sullenly, as she trudges into the kitchen a good 45 minutes after I took her her tea. She hasn't, I notice, brought her empty mug downstairs but I decide against making her go and retrieve it. Who knows how long we're going to be marooned here together, after all. There's no point making the atmosphere even more fractious.

'Safer not to,' I say, carefully keeping my voice as casual as possible as I slide the toaster into action.

'What, *ever?*' Ariana is a vision of shock. With her hair all dishevelled like a golden cloud around her shoulders, the too-big shirt she slept in hanging off one skinny shoulder and her hands curling into fists, she looks like some sort of fierce, neglected waif.

'It probably wouldn't work here anyway. Sandra – that's my friend who owns this place – she markets it as a sort of retreat for artists and such like. That's why it's so remote. It's great for getting work done, last time I came I practically wrote a whole dissertation in one day and still had time to discover the little beach down the cliff path before dark. But you'd be lucky to get reception here let alone internet...'

'So what's the harm in trying, then?'

I take a deep breath, trying to soothe the frustration as it jags around my skull before it has the chance to muscle into a full-blown headache.

'Look, you don't *need* the internet, do you? There're plenty of books,' I gesture to the neat bookshelf standing next to the sofa.

'What*ever*,' Ariana mumbles, stomping over to the armchair and throwing herself into it, reaching for the TV remote. The room instantly fills with the voices of the latest reality show she's into and her body visibly relaxes into the cushions. I roll my eyes and turn back to the sink, trying to remember how much cash is in the leather holdall now upstairs and whether it will stretch to two new phones. My fingers itch for my own phone nestled in my handbag, longing to switch it on, check for messages and send an email to Sandra to let her know we're here and ask how to work the heating.

Despite what Ariana might think, Sandra gave me her spare key long ago – back in the days when Elodie was a wide-eyed young thing just starting out as a PhD student in London. I'd let her glimpse a baby photo of Ariana and she'd 'pulled' the story of her troublesome father out of me. This, of course, was only after I'd overheard her mentioning her small remote holiday home down in Cornwall to one of the other professors after class one day. A few days later I'd gone to her for advice on my thesis and left with a spare key and permission to use the cottage whenever I might need, providing it wasn't during the school holidays. I doubt Ariana remembers me leaving her for a few nights back in the days when juggling a demanding pre-schooler and a full-time undergraduate degree had seemed almost impossible. The days when I'd still had a person I could trust to look after her.

Ariana's next tantrum occurs approximately half an hour later when we're upstairs in her bedroom. As promised, I show her the clothes I've found tucked into an old canvas tote in the back of the BMW. Unfortunately, as I warned, they are all a little on the snug side. The T-shirts are fine if a little unseasonal, and she cheers up no end once I tell her she can borrow my second-favourite cashmere jumper to go over the top. Then she tries on the jeans and bursts into tears when she can't do up the zipper.

I try my best. I put on my patient face, the one I use when Willbury won't take no for an answer and keeps finding excuses to touch me. I make my voice calm and gentle. I swallow the rage. I bury the burning urge to shake her, to yell at her to pull herself to-fucking-gether already. But when she refuses to listen, says she can't possibly go out like this because she is a disgusting, fat mess bursting out of her jeans and continues to wallow in the passionate glory of her own self-pity, I feel myself snap.

'Why? *Why* can't I just leave you here while I go to buy new clothes? Because, Ariana, I can't. Because there are people *looking* for us. Dangerous people. And it's not a case of *if* they find us, it's *when*. And I'm damned if I'm risking that happening during the hours I happen to have left my twelve-year-old daughter home on her own just because she's had a pathetic hissy fit over something so trivial as *what she's going to wear.*'

'Like you would ever step out of the house wearing jeans that were a size too small!'

'I did it all the time when I was bloody pregnant!'

'I can just imagine how much you must have *loved* that! I don't know why you even *had* me! It's not like I've ever had a life *worth living!*'

I clench my fists until my nails cut into my palms, then I slowly force myself to relax them. My head is pounding; it always does when we argue. I take a breath and count to five silently, trying not to think about who might be coming closer with every passing moment. It's not like us going into town for supplies is going to delay them.

'Look,' I say, and then stop until my jaw is fully unclenched. 'Look. This is just an hour or so of your whole, entire life. I'll show you a trick with a hairband I know that will keep your jeans up without doing the zip. You can hide it with my sweater. Just please, *please* get ready so we can go. I... I don't just want to pick up clothes, OK? There are other things we need.'

'Like what?'

'Nothing... Just... things that will help me sleep better at night.'

'Really,' Ariana snorts, though she grudgingly picks up

her hairbrush from the bedside table and begins dragging it through her unruly mane. 'Like an extra blanket? Don't think I haven't noticed this place is practically a *crypt* it's so cold.'

'Yes, well, I'm sure once I get hold of Sandra she'll let me know the code for the central heating. I'll transfer her some money for the bill. We should be fine using it sparingly until it gets really cold, then perhaps we'll have to see if one of her housekeepers has a key for the fireplace... Providing the cottage isn't let for Christmas...'

'We might be staying here as long as *Christmas?*' Ariana pauses, one arm in my sweater and one arm out.

'I don't know.'

'I thought you said those people that were after us – that man. I thought you said he'd find us if we stayed in one place too long...'

'I didn't say that, but it's certainly a possibility. Which is why we need to find, among other things, somewhere that sells cheap, pay-as-you-go phones.'

Finally, fully-dressed, Ariana follows me silently down the wooden steps to the landing. I reach for our coats, wishing I'd brought my thicker, winter parka with the fur lining instead of the lightweight autumn mac I'd shrugged on without a care for yesterday's mild morning in Flintworth. When I turn, Ariana is ready and waiting with her school shoes and coat on, but her face is still troubled.

'What is it?' I sigh, more impatiently that I intended.

'These bad people... is it just you they're after or both of us? You always said they were cross because you took work stuff they thought was theirs... And that if they – *he* – ever found you he'd hunt you down to try and take the things back...'

'Yes...'

'So why couldn't I have just stayed behind if it was just you he was after? I could've stayed with Lucy or Yasmin... *Their* mums wouldn't have minded... Why did I have to be dragged all the way out here too?' She looks at her feet as she says it, knowing it's wrong, knowing how it sounds to me but saying it anyway.

'Because it's not as simple as that. Yes, it's me they're looking for, not you. But they'll have gone to the flat. They'll know about you too, now. If I'd left you behind... God knows where you'd be by now.'

She looks up and we stare at each other for a few moments.

'If you're getting a new phone... can I have one, too?'

I pick up my car keys without breaking eye contact.

'We'll see.'

Ariana sighs and, for the tenth time that minute, tugs my sweater lower over her waistband before stomping begrudgingly towards me and finally – *finally* – we leave the house.

**Autumn, 1995**

Ralph's mum was a hugger. I'd had a plan of how to act. I'd woken up, in fact, in that deep, soft prairie of a bed with my plan fully formed in my head. I'd be polite. I'd be nice. I wouldn't baby myself, I wouldn't lisp and I wouldn't use my *unnaturalness,* as my mother had put it, to manipulate anyone into behaving how I wanted them to. If they didn't like me – and the strange notion made my insides twist, I have to admit – then I'd just have to get on with it the same way other people did.

I got out of bed and dressed in a plain white T-shirt and a new pinafore dress my mother had ordered for me a few weeks earlier. I chose it because it was pretty, I told myself, not because *she'd* said it looked sweet. I didn't care what *she* thought anymore. I combed my hair and slid an Alice band over it to keep it off my face. I made the bed as best I could, left the stuffed dog on one of the pillows, crossed the room and slowly made my way downstairs, following the murmur of voices coming from somewhere nearby. Polite, nice, plain, I thought to myself, as I turned right instead of towards the rooms I'd been in the night before. I paused in front of two heavy-set doors and waited until Ralph's voice rang out from the closest one.

'...school though, Dad, she's going to be way behind...'

'Not necessarily, kiddo... You should see what her

sister's capable of… In line for a Nobel prize at the age of fifteen, that one.'

I took a breath before Dr Blake's words could filter through and make me think about my family again, and, using both hands, pushed the heavy door open. The first thing I noticed was the table, because it was massive and round, like the ones I'd seen illustrated in books about King Arthur and his knights. The second thing I noticed were the people. Blake, closest to me, his knife poised mid-buttering of his toast, his eyes bright and smiling beneath his spectacles as he beamed at me.

'Ah, here she is! Morning, Bella, hope you slept well?'

'Yes, thank you,' I said, as I glanced from him to Ralph, who seemed caught between surprise and embarrassment as he swallowed a mouthful of cereal and frowned into his bowl. I had barely had a chance to look from Ralph to the woman next to him before she got to her feet. All I noticed was a headscarf with bright, rainbow colours that seemed to strike an odd chord in the midst of the room's glossy formality, a pale face with large, dark eyes and then she was coming at me and before I could even think, let alone step backwards, her arms were around me.

'Oh my poor darling, you must be so scared and tired and confused… I'm sorry I wasn't able to take care of you last night, I wasn't feeling my best and had to go to bed early… If I'd only *known*… but then I don't suppose any of us did, did we?'

She paused for breath, I breathed in her scent – a mixture of musky, expensive perfume like the ones my mother would squirt onto her wrists in the shops but never buy, and something else I couldn't identify. Something slightly off, like bread on the cusp of growing mould. Just as I was wondering whether I should perhaps put my arms around her and hug her back she peeled me away and knelt to take a proper a look at me. I looked straight back at her and did the same. She had no eyebrows, but her brown eyes were bright and her lashes thick. Her cheeks sagged a little more than my mother's and her skin had a soft, almost powdery look to it, though nothing about her, from the quickness of her movements to the sweet, singsong lilt of her voice, seemed old. I blinked and waited for her to tell us all how beautiful I was, but again she surprised me.

'Bella… Such a lovely, strong Italian name. My name is Italian also – Ariana – although everyone here calls me Ana. You can call me that too for now if you like. Now, Miss Bella, are you hungry? We have toast and cereals…'

She steered me round the edge of the table and into the empty chair next to hers, and all the while her eyes never left my face. I frowned a little and tried to think about food.

'Um…'

I was aware of Ralph exchanging significant looks with his father and knew I must seem like a total idiot, but it was like Ana had waved a magic wand and scrambled everything in my brain. I couldn't work out what was going on. I was used to adults fawning over me but, apart from close family, there was always a degree of detachment about it… Ana acted as if she'd known me all my life, like she'd already decided I was going to stay there forever. Had she not heard the story about Katie's hand?

'I know everything probably feels a bit topsy turvy at the moment,' Ana said as she pulled a plate of white toast towards us and put a slice on my place. 'But it's important to eat so we stay strong. It's what the doctors are always telling me, isn't it my love?'

'It is,' Blake agreed, still with that sparkly look in his

eye as if he were in the middle of a wonderful joke. I frowned and wordlessly accepted the butter dish as he offered it to me.

Once I'd swallowed enough toast to satisfy Ana, she took me by the hand and said she was going to show me around.

'Don't wear yourself out, darling,' Dr Blake murmured as she bent to kiss him on our way past his chair.

'And don't *you* forget Ralphie's chemistry test this morning,' Ana replied, ruffling Ralph's hair as he scowled at the pair of us. I smiled back at him serenely, remembering the way he'd embarrassed me the previous night.

Ana led me out into the hallway. Instead of taking a left into one of the book-filled rooms I'd been in last night, however, she marched me straight ahead and opened another heavy door on our right. In contrast to the bulky furnishings and book-scented mustiness of the other rooms, this one was light and airy. A large mirror threw our faces back at us as we entered. The walls seemed higher in here, with large, swooping arches set into them. The floor was different too, instead of the flagstones and heavy carpets of the hallway and dining room, this room had the smooth, shiny, wood-looking floor I recognised from my ballet studio. With surprise I spotted a barre along the end of the room facing the mirror. Two large windows beamed great rectangles of sun onto the centre of the floor. For the first time since my mother bundled me into the car, I took a long, deep breath.

'Yes,' Ana said, softly, and I turned to see her watching me closely. 'I thought you'd like this room. You dance, yes?'

I nodded.

'Ballet?'

'I started tap and modern a few years ago as well, but I've been doing ballet since I was three.'

'I thought so. I don't dance as much anymore, but I will continue your teaching here.' The way she said it didn't sound like a question. In fact, she didn't even look at me to see my nod. I wondered what she would do if I refused... And, with a strange, novel feeling I'd never felt before, I realised that in all likelihood she would simply disregard it and teach me anyway. I shifted from one foot to another, unsure of how to feel about this strange woman who seemed to be an entirely different kind of adult to all those I'd met so far. I wondered if I should say something, test her, find the thing that made her tired eyes sparkle and use that to get what I wanted, but then I wondered what exactly it was I wanted, after all... And as I was wondering about that, my eyes caught the large, gilded-framed portrait hanging in a slightly shadowed corner of the room next to the window.

'Oh!' I said, unable not to. The portrait showed a woman, her arms outstretched as her leg extended endlessly behind her in arabesque, her face upturned but unmistakable.

'Yes,' Ana murmured, coming to stand beside me as I moved towards the picture. 'That was painted just five years ago.'

I glanced from her back to the picture. There was no denying the staggering difference I saw. The real Ana was still delicate and graceful, and even I could tell she moved the same way my ballet teacher did, as if every mundane step were poised to launch her into a jeté or pirouette. But the Ana in the picture... her hair was thick, long and shiningly dark as it tumbled rebelliously below her shoulders. Her face smiled delicately from the frame, the eyes bright beneath dark curves of eyebrows; it wasn't just that she was beautiful, she was beyond beautiful. As if the joy of the movement, the dance, were shining from every part of her, lighting her up from within and catching all around it within its glow.

'I know,' Ana said on my right, 'I look *very* different with eyebrows, don't I?'

I looked at her in surprise and she looked back and suddenly I knew that it wasn't that she hadn't noticed my beauty or didn't agree with it. She *understood* it.

'It's easier now, though. Eyebrows are a good filter. I never realised that until I became ill. I wouldn't change it, in some ways. Now people… They look at me less, but they listen to me more. I'm different too, I *make* them listen.

'But come on, now is not the time to lurk in dusty dance studios when there are whole grounds to explore and a beautiful day outside… Come, this dingy old Manor is best viewed from the *outside,* I've always thought.'

And with that, she took up my hand again in her papery-soft one and steered me, with all the graceful wire of a professionally trained dancer, away from the studio and out into the blazingly fresh air.

**October, 2018**

*Saturday*

'There! See, there it is.'

'Where? I can only see that Warburtons lorry...'

'Right there to the right of it, in the middle lane.'

'What, that shadowy little smudge?'

'That would be the back bumper of a BMW X5 in metallic blue...'

'How the hell can you be so *sure?*'

'Because, dear boy, this is what I *do.*' Felix sits back in the hotel chair and rubs her eyes, smirking.

'D'you think we should wake them?' Dominic glances over towards the beds and Felix follows his gaze. It's barely lunchtime but they've been tracking the X5 all morning and most of the previous night. Ethan lies sprawled like an overgrown teddy bear on one bed, Ralph is curled into a long-legged comma with his back to them in the other. It took Ralph a particularly long time to drop off and Felix feels a heavy clench of pity as she regards him now.

'No. Let's see if we can get a bit more first.'

'Really? We know they're in Cornwall...'

'Yeah, and have you seen the size of Cornwall lately? Not to mention how very much of it *isn't* plastered with traffic and CCTV cams. Wonder why she chose it...'

'Right... So you think we're going to lose the trail?'

'I'd be surprised if this wasn't the last camera sighting we get, but let's carry on down the A38 a bit more, see if we can spot which junction she took at least... Actually, you can do that, can't you? You remember the code I showed you? It's in this window here if you want to copy and paste...'

'Oh... er, OK...'

'Come on, Dom, don't tell me you weren't paying attention... This is why you're here after all. If I get stabbed in the gut, we need someone in possession of at least two neurones to keep tabs on everyone electronically...'

'Yeah, yeah, I know. I just didn't realise I'd be taking over... right now... is all... but it's cool, of course it is...' Dom withers under Felix's heavy eyebrows and sinks quickly into the chair she vacates.

'Good,' she says as, tentatively, his fingers find their places on the keys. 'I'm going to dig into the telecoms side of it, see if I can get a trace on the phone...'

'Really? You think Bella would have left herself exposed that way?'

'No. Of course not. But I *do* think I know a bit more about how to trace a phone than she does. And I'm guessing young Ariana isn't half as careful about covering her tracks as her dear old mumsie...'

'Oh...' Dom mutters, swallowing hard as Felix draws up a second chair and pulls another laptop out of the purple backpack next to her. He watches her just long enough for her to twitch irritably, and then turns swiftly back to his own screen. *On your head*, he thinks, unable to stop the image of Bella's face as he last remembers seeing it all those years ago, so full of life her entire body seemed to take on a shimmery, other-worldly quality as she'd moved onstage, her voice as rich and far-reaching as a full orchestra. The audience staring at her with uniform, unsettling blankness upon their faces. He shudders, wondering if Felix remembers Bella the same way, and whether she's thought of what the other woman might do when she realises how they've traced her. How they're going to find her.

By noon the chill of the morning has lifted and by the time Ariana and I take our supermarket sandwiches and make our way to the deserted sea front, I can tell I'm not the only one feeling lighter. Still, I almost tense up in surprise when Ariana takes my arm and leans her head on my shoulder as we step carefully down a narrow, wooden boardwalk and onto the sand. The tide is out, leaving an eye-widening expanse of golden-grey beach, seaweed-strewn outcrops of rock and dozens of pools. I glance sideways at Ariana, thinking that not so very long ago she'd have immediately deserted her shoes – autumn or not – and sprinted towards the nearest rock pool to see what she might find. Even now I see her eyeing them, though she then glances down at her brand-new trainers and stops to inspect them delicately.

'Let's not go too far onto the wet bit,' she says, still examining her feet. 'I don't want to mess these up.'

'You could take them off,' I suggest, mildly. 'It's not that cold now.'

She shrugs.

'Maybe later.'

We make our way towards a dry-looking scatter of large rocks and settle there, folding our coats for padding. Still, the hardness of the rock seems to seep through and I find a slow ache beginning to spread upwards in my back like a sprouting tree. Ariana, on the other hand, nestles back into her rock as if it were the plushest of armchairs and reaches for her sandwich and the new phone I've just bought her. She's wearing one of three new pairs of jeans, and though she hasn't given up my cashmere sweater yet, there's an identical one in a smaller size nestled in one of the shopping bags along with enough other items to ensure her good mood lasts at least until tomorrow morning, if I'm lucky.

If I'm honest, though, it's not just Ariana's improved spirits which has lifted the heavy, stone-like lump I've carried in my chest ever since I first glimpsed Felix in my lecture theatre just twenty-four hours ago. It's not even my own new phone, a basic model with a reassuringly anonymous pay-as-you-go SIM, slotted next to my old, switched off model in my handbag. It's the other thing. The thing I bought during the ten minutes I left Ariana to try on the over-priced hoodies and T-shirts in the surf shop and ducked next door into the fishing supply store. The blade is at the very edge of being legal at three inches long. It has a smooth, leather sheath. It's unlikely I'll ever need to use it, but just the feel of it, the handle reassuringly cool and solid under my fingertips, is enough because I know that I *can* if I have to. It would be as easy as it was to transform the shop owner's gaze from high-eyebrowed suspicion into the bemused, slightly dazed smile he wore as I left. My mother's voice growls, caught somewhere between disdain and a deep smugness, that she'd known all along what I was, what I could be. *It's no surprise, Mamma. Just because we never talked about it, doesn't mean I didn't know too.*

'Mum... Mum! I want to go and see that puppy, that's

OK, isn't it?'

I glance over and spot a boy around Ariana's age walking a small retriever a few dozen feet away.

'Sure, go on then. Remember to ask first before petting it, OK?'

'Yeah, yeah…' And she's off, trainers and socks discarded – though carefully, on top of her rock alongside her sandwich wrapper – new jeans rolled up, long legs wheeling across the sand with the strange, gangly rhythm I still haven't quite gotten used to. She was such a petite child like I had been; the new height that's slowly stretched her over the last year has caught me off guard.

I switch on my new phone as Ariana's giggle drifts across the sand towards me. The screen is blank, blue. Anonymous. No photos. No defining features. I slide it into my bag and draw out my old iPhone. The screen is blank at the moment, of course, but if I were to switch it on, I'd see Ariana turning a cartwheel. The lock screen is her grinning up at me from her twelfth birthday cake back in April. I hold the phone gently for a moment as the urge to switch it on battles, briefly, with the dominant instinct to throw it as far as I can towards the distant sea. Instead, I make sure Ariana isn't watching, then I turn, find a sharp outcrop of rock and bring the phone down on it, hard, until the screen is shattered beyond repair. Then I gather the shards, wrap them and the phone up in my sandwich wrapper and pop it into a rubbish bag. There's a bin for dog mess on the way up from the beach. That'll do.

**Autumn, 1995**

Ana kept hold of my hand the entire time we walked down the driveway and then turned left; through a twisted metal side gate I hadn't spotted the night before. She talked about the roses which bloomed in the spring, how every year since she fell ill, 'Freddie' had had the gardeners plant different breeds in different colours to surprise her. That this year's crop had been a particularly startling shade of pink which had clashed with everything in every room they were placed in once cut and that actually, she wished they would just plant plain white ones. She tugged me over to see a small tangle of apple trees where Ralph, she told me, sometimes still climbed with a book and a can of something fizzy when it was warm out. Across a neatly trimmed lawn and through another gate we walked and all the while I watched her and waited, patiently, for her to say what I could sense bubbling so close to the surface. Finally, as she pulled the gate closed behind us, she stopped, took me by the shoulders and steered me around until I was facing the opposite direction of the great house.

'There. See it?'

Of course I saw it, I wanted to say. Before us a path tumbled through long, wild grasses dotted with gorse and bracken, leading into a small copse of tall trees and out, in flashes of pale brown between more tussocks. I tracked its progress over a small hill and there it disappeared, but it wasn't difficult to work out where it went. The gleaming tower in the distance was about as different to the Blake house as a building could be. While the Manor rose half-heartedly with its uneven stones and strange, mismatched windows, this building shot straight up, an oily-black tooth alone in the mouth of the rolling hills and distant mountains.

'Do you know what that place is?' Ana breathed; her face close to mine as she bent forward to see it from my level. I shook my head.

'That, my dear, is where you came from. Where you *really* came from. You, your brother, your sister and about fifty other children around the same ages as you three. It is called the Aspira Research Centre and it is everything, *everything* that is important and cutting edge in the field of genetic engineering and manipulation.'

At the word *manipulation* I felt my shoulders tense beneath her grip, but she didn't let go. If anything, she held me tighter as if worried I might suddenly fly away from her.

'Do you have any idea how special you are, Miss Bella? You are one of only a handful... They don't make genetically selected children anymore the way they did when you were conceived, you know... I believe you are among the youngest, as it was around the time you were born, perhaps even before, that the ethics committee of the government got wind of Freddie's project and cut all funding. Just a blip, though, as it turns out.'

She still had me by the shoulders, with one arm encircling my chest now. It was almost like a hug, though I could feel every bone in her long, sinewy arm cutting into my breast a little more with every breath I took. And every one of those breaths seemed to be shrinking a little smaller. She was very slowly crushing me, I realised, but when I tried to move, her other hand gripped easily around my arm and pinned it to my side. Her voice when she spoke was as light as it had been when we were discussing ballet back in the dance studio.

'We got more funding. A lot more. Private investors this time. No more vain, rich idiots after their designer babies. Everything is changing now. That building there... The ARC... That's where real magic is happening. Genetic manipulation which goes beyond making a child run fast or solve quadratic equations when they're four... We're pushing the very foundations, Bella, of what it is that makes us human.'

'Please,' I gasped, as my breath juddered and my lungs began to scream. 'I can't... please...'

'Don't you realise how lucky you are to be here with us? You get to be part of this... Part of the future, part of *evolution*... You understand that, right?'

'Yes.' It came out as a slip of a word, a hiss, as the last of my oxygen escaped my lips. And then, all at once, she let me go. I staggered forwards and took several gulps of air, my eyes never leaving the big, black building in front of me. Ana didn't say anything as my frantic gasps slowly subsided to normality. I turned, slowly, eyes narrowed, to face her. She wasn't even looking at me, she was still gazing at that big black building with a faraway look in her bright eyes. I wondered if she realised she'd almost suffocated me with her bare hands, but then her gaze snapped downwards to mine and to her own hands, which she brought up in front of her as if they were covered in paint and she'd only just noticed.

'People always underestimate the beautiful,' she said, quietly. I found myself leaning towards her so I could hear, not daring to actually step closer, but not quite able to turn away.

'They think that we are ruled by our beauty. That when it leaves us, part of us leaves too... Reducing us to less than what we were before. Some half-thing who is pleased by pretty roses and gentle voices and sweet faces. That just because we are weak in body some of the time, the rest of it can be forgotten...' She stared at her hands a moment longer and then dropped them, turning back to me. Her voice became hard again, purposeful.

'I lied, earlier. I knew you were coming back here. You were born here, you know. In Cumbria. I was there at the hospital. I saw your brother born, your sister too – it was part of the package, our presence there after the birth to check for any anomalies. Physical anomalies, that is. I remember watching them take you home, your father was already besotted, your mother was dazed... I knew they couldn't hope to keep you, though nine years is longer than I would have guessed. I have my husband to thank for that, of course. He's been keeping tabs on you for some time, keeping an eye on the situation with your mother. He didn't tell me – didn't want to *worry* me, cause any undue stress, that's what he said, of course – but I found out. He didn't want to bring you here yet... Didn't think you should be separated from your family so young. But he didn't *see* you... None of them did... Do... Not like I do.' She was looking at me like I was holding the cure for cancer in my hands. Like she wasn't sure if she wanted to reach out and hug me or crush me to death properly this time.

'Your parents certainly didn't. You may have their genetic base layers and DNA, but you were never really theirs. To them you are nothing more than a pretty girl with green eyes. They didn't *make* you. I did. Do you understand what I'm telling you?'

I nodded because in that moment, nothing else existed. I forgot how to execute a triple pirouette. I forgot how old I was. I forgot I was beautiful Bella D'accourt with the pink bedroom in the large house in Weston-on-the-Hill. All that mattered was her and what she was saying and her hands, reaching, and I tried to think about genes and DNA and science but all I could think about was her... Strong and beautiful as she had been in the ballet portrait, but this time dressed in a snowy white lab coat and holding a syringe with a tiny baby squeezed into it. A tiny me baby, ready to live and grow in my mother's belly, but always belonging to someone else.

Then, suddenly, Ana laughed. It came out like a bird's call, high and joyful but eerie too. I frowned and she laughed more. Then she held out her hand.

'Come on, Miss Bella. Let me show you the climbing frame and the swing set. Ralphie likes to let us think he doesn't go on it anymore, but once again it is autumn and yet somehow the leaves never settle on it for long...'

I didn't move, but she stepped forward and took my hand anyway. Her grip was as tight as the arm around my chest had been and for a second I felt almost paralysed once again by the crushing sensation, but the next I took in a cool lungful of the crisp autumn air and was fine again. The hand squeezed, though, as if telling me something underneath her light, airy words about the lovely apple crumble Ramona made.

I can crush you, it was saying. I made you but I can still crush you.

**October, 2018**

*Saturday*

The boy's name is Jacob. He and Ariana wander up and down the soft sand, talking about his friends and his school and the party he's going to next weekend which, according to some unknown person called Lolo with whom Jacob seems to assume Ariana is intimately familiar, will have real alcohol and no parents. You can come, if you're still about, he says, casually. Ariana knows he's trying to impress her. Knows that he's probably only year seven, judging by his lack of inches and his voice which occasionally pitches from unexpected squeaks to low growls that make her turn her head to avoid laughing. Still, he has nice eyes. And the way he looks at her makes her feel all glowy. Added to the new clothes and the fact that Mum clearly hasn't noticed that this sweater is now pretty much hers, Ariana feels better than she would have thought possible a few hours earlier.

'I'd better go,' she says, when they've exhausted a mostly one-sided discussion about survival versus creative mode on Minecraft and she's worked out where he lives, what school he goes to and where this party is going to be next weekend without actually asking any of the questions outright.

'Alright,' he shrugs, gazing past her as she kneels to

pet the puppy once again. 'Is that your mum?' She glances up and watches him gaze.

'Yeah,' she mutters.

'Nice,' he replies, grinning obliviously as she rolls her eyes.

'Whatever,' she scowls, getting to her feet and brushing the sand from her knees.

'Hey, Anna…?'

'Ariana. Ri.'

'Ariana. Cool name. Like Ariana Grande. Can I have your number? You know, so I can text you about the party?'

'Sure.'

The sun blinks and bursts suddenly from behind a cloud as Ariana watches Jacob and the dog meander slowly up the boardwalk and back towards the town. Then she turns towards her mother, who is sitting straight-backed on her rock as if it were a throne, thumbs tapping away on the new phone, identical to the one Ariana can just make out on the rock next to her where she left it to do its loading up thing. *Can I have your number?* Ah. She'd given him her old number. Of course she had. Well, never mind. Switching it back on again this morning clearly hadn't brought fire and brimstone down on them, surely checking it just once more wouldn't be a problem… Just to get Jacob's number, of course…

The weak sunshine seeps into Ariana's body and nestles deliciously with the small, bubbling secret within her and she begins to run. Sea air fills her lungs in great, whooshing blasts of freshness. Her feet pummel the smooth sand and dig into it, making her stagger a little, and her arms wheel but there's no one to see her look stupid. Her hair billows behind her and she knows it will take ages to detangle, but she doesn't care, the world is in front of her and everything is fresh and a boy has her number, her mother doesn't need to know, and even the scary darkness lurking beneath the surface of her thoughts isn't enough to stop her.

Bella looks up just in time to slip her phone into her coat pocket and get to her feet as Ariana launches herself at her.

'Argh! You're freezing!' Bella exclaims as Ariana's hands find exposed skin, but there's a smile in her voice and when Ariana peels away, her mother's green eyes sparkle with warmth.

'Nice puppy?' she asks innocently.

'Yes. She was a sweet little dog. Only three months old. So cute!' Ariana sinks onto one of the flat rocks and begins trying to dust the sand from her feet using her sock.

'Yeah, the *dog* was cute. *That's* why you're blushing!'

'Shuddup...'

They lapse into a comfortable silence as Ariana finishes with one foot and eases it into her new trainer before starting on the other. She looks up and glances to her left, along the wide expanse of shining sand which the sea has unpeeled several metres further in the time since they arrived.

'Can we walk back that way? To the cottage I mean?'

'Along the beach? I'm not sure... I suppose it might be possible with the tide out... You'd have to time it right, though, otherwise you could get stuck in one of the coves...'

'We should try it...'

'Maybe tomorrow. There's that tiny beach I told you about, though it's quite tricky to find. Hidden by a big outcrop if I remember rightly. If we find that we'll be able to see.'

'It'll be nice to have our own private beach,' Ariana sighs as she pulls her second trainer on and stuffs her dirty socks into her back pocket.

'What's that? Is that your phone? What happened?'

'I broke it,' her mother replies, simply. Ariana looks at her as the sun suddenly slips beneath a cloud and throws the entire beach into shadow. Rather than fade, Bella's eyes seem to burn all the brighter in the sudden gloom, like two rings of something poisonous that should belong in a laboratory behind a screen.

'But I thought you said just keeping them off would be OK...'

Bella shrugs and glances away quickly, her gaze sweeping across the huge plain of sand in front of them. Ariana shivers a little as the chill seeps under the soft wool of her sweater.

'They found us once,' Bella murmurs, hooking her handbag over her shoulder and picking up one of the shopping bags. Ariana tucks her new phone into her jeans pocket and reaches for the other bags. Wordlessly they make their way back along the sand and the boardwalk, and though Bella does not glance around again, Ariana can't help but throw the beach a quick, worried glance behind her shoulder as if expecting the sea itself to peel back further still and reveal a band of marching, dark figures heading for them.

### Sunday

'Got it,' Felix murmurs softly to herself. She blinks several times and then glances around her at the soft darkness of the hotel room. She feels as if she's just woken up from a long, fidgety sleep. Next to her, Dominic lies back in his desk chair, his head lolling to one side as his mouth slacks open, and the occasional snore grunts deeper than Felix thinks she's ever heard his voice. Past him, Ethan is still sprawled in the middle of the closest bed. He won't move until he wakes, she knows. But Ralph has shifted so he's facing her, still curled in a foetal position with one arm thrown over most of his face like a sulking child.

The smell in the room has reached new levels of hideousness and Felix gets to her feet, her limbs clacking as she flexes her muscles and reaches for the small window across the desk. She opens it and waits for the cool night air to trickle pleasantly over her face before she sits back down and draws her feet up under her. Exhaustion lurks somewhere close by, but for now the pounding excitement is still too great as she turns back to the screen where a small, red dot blinks insistently next to a large, blue expanse. Zooming in until the small town and its yellow stretch of beach bear labels, Felix draws a pen and pad next to her and begins to scribble, bringing up a second tab to check timings.

> *07.32 Sat. Co-ords: 50.272843, 5276786.*
> *Near Penglathen beach & Pethwick town,*
> *village? Instagram and Twitter check.*
> *Phone switched off at 07.37.*
>
> *13.24 Co-ords as above. Switched on.*
> *Missed call from unsaved number reg. to*
> *Jacob Woollcott, aged 11.7, res. Pethwick,*
> *Cornwall. Switched off at 13.28.*

'New boyfriend, Ariana?' Felix murmurs softly as she

notes down three new texts from the same number, none of them read.

'What's that?' Ralph's voice, unexpectedly alert, sweeps through the room and makes her jump so hard the chair squeaks several inches back from the desk. Dominic grunts as Felix turns around, but he doesn't wake. Ralph slides with serpentine movements from the bed and quickly comes over to the desk. He glances at Dominic once before slowly easing his chair out of his way.

'Have you found them? Why didn't you wake me?'

'Because I literally found them about five seconds ago,' Felix replies, realising her voice has turned hoarse with lack of sleep. She clears her throat and shows him her notes.

'Penglathen Beach? Where's that, Wales?'

'Cornwall. Dom and I tracked them using the traffic cams but we lost them when they turned off the A30... But I still know a few tricks on the telecoms side...'

'You tracked Bella's phone?'

'Ha! No. I tried. I eventually managed to track the device using her address, but that phone's been switched off since Friday afternoon, big surprise. But then I thought about those Twitter messages and wondered if I could get a trace on the device used to send them... Et voila...'

'Ah... Beast... Letting Ana have a mobile phone at her age...'

'Ariana.'

'Right... Still getting used to the idea.'

'Might help if you got her name right. You know, if you're going to meet her and all...'

Ralph looks momentarily terrified at the suggestion. He recovers quickly, though, swallows and glances from the screen to Felix's notes.

'So this is her phone, then? Where are they now?'

'It doesn't really work like that. The software I have only alerts me when activity is present... So I can see where she was when she switched it on yesterday morning and then again in the afternoon.'

'Which is...'

'Somewhere just on the coast here. There's no label on Google Maps so it's likely to be a private address, remote...'

'What about a tent?'

They look at each other, both of them trying to imagine Bella D'accourt camping in a field.

'Never mind,' Ralph smiles wryly and straightens up. He's so tall Felix has to crane her neck to see the parts of his face which aren't hidden in the room's long shadows.

'So they're skulking in Cornwall... Shouldn't take us too long to get there if we leave shortly...'

'Nope. I might have to have a kip in the car, though... I'm done in...' Felix stifles a second shoulder-shuddering yawn. Ralph doesn't seem to notice; he's gazing at a spot on the wall behind the desk and frowning.

'I don't get it... Bella's so careful with her own stuff – she switches off her phone, makes sure the traffic cams don't track her too far... But then she just lets her kid have free reign over social media? Messaging God-knows-who...? And now, letting her use her phone when she's been careful enough to turn her own off? Surely she'd realise we could track her that way?'

Felix shrugs. 'Like I've said before, I've long given up trying to understand Bella. But if I had to guess, I'd say it's one of two options. One, this is an almost-teenager we're dealing with here. Probably a bloody clever one too.

There's every chance Bella doesn't even know she's got a phone; let alone how she's using it...'

She looks up and catches the brief grin which flits over Ralph's face. She looks away, fighting a sudden, painful lump in her throat. She waits until she's sure her voice won't shiver before she continues.

'Number two... Well, that's a lot more worrying...'

'What is it?'

'Well, number two is that Bella knows exactly what's happening and that this is all playing into some bigger plan. Which means...'

'We're playing into her hands and doing exactly what she wants us to do...'

'Yep...'

They lapse into silence. Felix's eyes find the newly vacated bed, its sheets rumpled but soft-looking, the warmth left by Ralph's body beckoning to her across the room...

'It doesn't change anything, though. Maybe if it was just her. But Fee, this is a kid. *My* kid. We can't just wait around for Lychen to get there first. Even if it is some kind of trap...'

'I know...' Felix sighs and wrenches her gaze from the bed back to the screen. 'Better wake the others then, hadn't you?'

**October, 2018**

*Sunday*

'Shall we go for a walk in a bit? See if we can find that private beach?'

'Mmm,' Ariana doesn't look up from her new phone. She's been curled around it in the armchair for almost the entirety of our second morning at the cottage.

'It'll be good to get some fresh air...'

'Yeah,' she grunts scathingly, 'because fresh air is something in real short supply living here...'

'Staying,' I correct quietly, placing my empty coffee mug in the sink.

'I thought you said we'd be safe now we've changed our phones and everything.'

'I said we were safe*r*. Besides, I finally got hold of Sandra last night – she said it's fine for us to be here at the moment but the week after next is half-term and the cottage is booked out then, so we'll have to make a move anyway.'

*Not that you were ever still going to be here by then...*

'So where'll we go?' Ariana is fully focused on me now, her eyes wide under her wild bush of hair which seems to have expanded even more overnight. I turn away from her and begin placing more of the breakfast things in the sink.

'Well, I have to confirm a few things, but I was thinking we could perhaps go and stay with my sister...'

'Your sister?'

'Yes, she's up in North Devon which isn't too far from here.'

'I didn't know I had an aunt.'

'Why would you? I've never mentioned her. We don't stay in touch much, just the odd email here and there. I don't think I've even told her about you...'

*Of course you haven't.*

'What about my grandparents? Are they still alive? They probably are, right? You're what, fortyish? That wouldn't make them *that* old...'

I turn to stare at her coldly. 'I'm thirty-two. As you well know.'

'Whatever... So do I have a long-lost granny somewhere just dying to shower me with twelve years' worth of birthday and Christmas presents?'

'I have no idea,' I say, shortly, turning back to the sink and pulling the tap on until the sound of water drowns out any more questions. By the time I've washed my plate and mug, she's lost once again in her phone. A trickle of suspicion winds its way down my insides like a cold finger tracing my spine.

'What're you so absorbed in, anyway? You don't have any of your friends' numbers on there and the internet can't be strong enough for most games...'

'There's a few I've downloaded,' Ariana replies vaguely, though she doesn't meet my eye when she glances up, briefly. 'My signal's not so bad over here, anyway...'

'You do remember the conditions for you having that phone... Everything I told you about being careful...'

'*Yes,* Mum. God. I'm not an idiot. I haven't contacted anyone from home. Like you said, I don't have anyone's number on here anyway. I look at their Instas sometimes, just to see them. That's allowed, right?'

I ignore her heavy sarcasm and sigh, 'As long as you don't write anyth–'

'I *know*!' Her tone slices through my head like an icy blade and we both frown.

'I'll call the school tomorrow,' I say slowly, looking away. 'I'll tell them you've got glandular fever. That should buy us the couple of weeks until half-term, at least...' I let my voice drift vaguely as Ariana goes back to her phone. I'm just about to suggest the walk again when she puts the phone on the arm of the chair and stands up.

'I'm going to go and have a shower, see if I can sort out my stupid hair. The sea air's turned me into Hermione bloody Granger. I don't know how *yours* stays so sleek,' she mutters, reaching for her phone as she makes for the stairs.

'Hold on a sec, could you just pass me that mug and plate there? While the water's still warm?'

'*Fine,*' Ariana sighs, retracting her outstretched arm and redirecting it to where she's balanced a mug and plate precariously on the other arm of the chair. I smile tightly as she hands them over and wait until her stomps have retreated all the way upstairs, across the hallway and into the bathroom before I glance back at the phone left abandoned on the arm of the chair.

Ariana pulls her mother's cashmere sweater back over her head before fanning her wet hair out over her shoulders. She rubs an area clear on the clouded mirror and stares at herself. A spot is brewing under the skin on her chin. It's only a red smudge at the moment, but she can feel the skin tightening with soreness. She pulls a face and glances unnecessarily over her shoulder before opening the cabinet and rooting about in her mother's wash bag. Extracting a small, expensive-looking bottle of hair serum, she slowly begins unscrewing the top.

'Ari*ana!*'

Ariana drops the bottle on the bathmat with a muffled thump. Serum begins to leak over her bare toes and she swears under her breath, kneeling to gather up the bottle.

'*Ariana!* Come down here, *now!*'

Uh-oh. Ariana quickly replaces the bottle and automatically checks her jeans pocket for her phone. It's not there. Crap. She remembers going to pick it up on the way upstairs… Then nothing. Heart pummelling her chest as if trying to break out of it, she makes her way out of the bathroom and plods down the stairs.

Bella is standing in the centre of the living room, staring at Ariana's phone. To anyone else her mother's posture would seem unremarkable, just another person checking the weather or scrolling through messages. But when she looks up, her eyes glare like two jets of green fire shooting straight for Ariana's head.

'Look,' Ariana starts, and has to clear her throat because it's gone completely dry. 'Look. It's just that boy I met yesterday at the beach. Jacob. We've just been talking… about school stuff and Minecraft and some party he's going to and I was going to ask you—'

'Not that, *this.*' Bella holds up the phone and, reluctantly, Ariana moves forward into the room to see the screen. When she recognises the Twitter page her heart seems to gallop right into her throat and wait there like a large, quivering mass. Her profile pic – a close-up shot of her left eye – is a green speck in the corner of the page, which is mostly taken up by direct messages.

'Conan68?' Bella spits the name, her voice like venom, 'I assume this is a close and personal friend? Someone you've known for years from school perhaps?'

'Um...'

'Because I can't imagine why else you would be so *idiotic* as to disclose such personal information. I mean, I've only scrolled so far but already I've been able to work out your age, your school, what town you *live in...*'

'I never said—'

'You didn't need to, the clues are there, Ariana. Have I really taught you so little? Are you really this *stupid?*'

'Look, it's not like that. He's not *bad* like those people you're trying to hide from... It's not like that – *I* found *him...*'

'What?'

'Look, it's not what you think. He's not some dodgy old creeper trying to groom me into something gross. I mean he *is* old, like forty-one I think he said, but... Mum? What is it?'

Ariana has never seen a person's face drain of colour. She's read about how when someone has a terrible shock, they go pale and sometimes faint, but it's never happened in front of her eyes before. Now, though, even her mother's lips have gone the colour of cream and when she sinks downwards onto the coffee table, the movement is jerky and instinctive, as if her legs simply can't hold her anymore. Ariana has never seen her mother move like that.

'Mum?'

'Forty-one?' Bella is still holding the phone in one hand, but the other is gripping the table beneath her as if she's scared it will jolt away if she doesn't keep hold of it.

'Yeah... but listen, it's not sketchy I swear. It was Lucy...

We had a big argument a few weeks ago. It was stupid – she was taking selfies with Yas and I happened to be in the background of one, only she didn't notice before she posted it on Instagram. Don't look like that, I got her to delete it – it was only on Insta for like an hour or something. Anyway, she didn't want to delete it because it was a really good shot of her, and it'd got loads of comments, including one from Oliver Mason. She really likes him and even though she could crop me out and post like the exact same shot it would mean his comment wouldn't be there and... well, anyway she didn't talk to me for about a week afterwards. And when she did start talking to me again, she was all weird and wanted to know why everything was such a big deal with me being on social media and stuff... So I told her what *you* told me to say, that we were in witness protection from my dad who was violent and abusive and stuff. And she said that surely things might have changed in twelve years... and maybe if we could work out who he was and see if he was even still alive or in prison or something, that you could have peace of mind and I could have an Instagram account...

'Lucy's really good with tech stuff – she once showed me how she disabled a tracker device thing her dad put on her phone – so she did most of the work. I made her promise not to use our names or give anything away, and she didn't, I swear. She used a reverse photo search like they do on Catfish on MTV and it came up with a lot of false hits but eventually she found a *really* old photo of the side of your face in some random person's Facebook album from like 2005... And there was a guy near you who she reckoned looked a bit like me. He wasn't on Facebook either, but she did the photo search thing again and found him on Twitter...'

There's a long pause. Bella's still a delicate shade of bone-white. She blinks a few times and finally focuses on Ariana's face. And, this time, it's Ariana's turn to feel the icy trickle of fear as she realises that her mother isn't just furious anymore, she's terrified.

'You think this… Conan something… is your father?'

'I know it sounds mad…'

'It isn't him.'

'You don't know that–'

'Did he tell you he was your father?'

'Well… no. I mean, I didn't really get the chance to ask him… All this, it only happened a few days ago. I wasn't about to go all full-on, *Are you my daddy?* I'm not mental. His Twitter profile said he was involved in politics and so I made it sound like I was doing a project for school about social media and the government and just so happened to find him…'

'Right. And did he seem particularly interested in you personally?'

'Well, only in like a polite way. He asked what kind of things I liked doing… Where we'd been, where I'd like to travel, that sort of thing…'

'We. You told him you lived with your mother.'

'Well, yeah…'

'And did he seem unusually curious about me?'

'Well, I mean… He thought it was cool that my mum worked in a university lab. He said his nephew was looking for a job in that sort of thing and wanted to know how long you'd been working at Flintworth and what year you got your PhD or something like that–'

'And have you spoken to him at all since we've been here?'

'No…'

'But you've logged into your account...'

'Yeah, but only for a—'

'That's enough. Get your things.'

'What?'

'We're going,' Bella gets to her feet so fast Ariana flinches backwards and almost falls over the armchair.

'Why? I don't underst–'

'This person, this *man...* He's *not* your father. He was just trying to get your trust, to get to *me*. Your father... well, he's many things but he wouldn't manipulate you like this... If he knew... If he found out about you... He'd come to me first.'

Bella moves across the room, picks up her handbag, switches Ariana's phone off and throws it in. She then picks up a few more things and places them on top. Finally she realises that Ariana isn't moving and turns to her in frustration.

'You told me my father was a scumbag,' Ariana says, slowly, her eyes narrowed.

'What?'

'You told me my father was some irresponsible lowlife who didn't want to know when you got pregnant and that we should tell everyone he was violent so they'd think he was the one we were hiding from.'

'So? Ri, we can have this debate in the car, now go and *get your things!*'

'But what you just said now... *your father wouldn't manipulate you like this. If he found out about you.* That doesn't sound like a lowlife. That sounds like someone who never knew I existed in the first place...'

'Ri, not now...'

'Conan said–'

'Ariana, I've never met a man called Conan, let alone

borne his secret love-child–'

'So he used a different name, big whoop. Who is my real dad? *Is* he the one we're running from or not?'

Bella glances around in exasperation, but Ariana doesn't budge. She stands solidly, feet still bare and slightly wet on the rug but firmly planted. Bella sighs and puts her bag down on the breakfast bar.

'Fine. You're right. Your father didn't know I was having you. He probably would have wanted to be involved, if he'd known. His sodding family certainly would have. And you'd have been one of *them*.'

'Family? You mean I could have had a family?'

'Ri, you don't understand... You didn't know them... They were–'

'I *don't care!* You should have told me the truth! I had a right to know where I came from!'

'You came from me!'

'I wish I hadn't! I wish he'd kept me instead!'

She storms past Bella towards the front door and begins shoving her feet into her new trainers.

'Ri, wait...'

'Don't talk to me! I don't want to hear it!'

'Ariana, please, you can't leave – I'm sorry, alright? I should have told you the truth about your dad... You're right, he's not the one I'm scared of, he never was... But I was telling you the truth about the person we *are* hiding from... This Conan guy, if he's who I think he is, he's the most dangerous person in the country and there's every chance he knows *exactly* where we are...'

But Ariana isn't listening, she's got her trainers on now and is reaching for the door. In desperation, Bella darts forward and grabs at her daughter's arm, but Ariana snarls and, with a furious strength that surprises even her, pushes back with two hands. Bella flies backwards and hits the ground hard. Ariana doesn't look. She doesn't turn. She doesn't care. She's out of the door and leaving it to bang behind her before Bella can raise a dazed hand to her head.

**October, 2018**

*Sunday*

Felix yawns and stretches as much as she can in the cramped back seat of the Fiesta. She feels horribly grubby in that particular, unique way which comes of wearing the same clothes for too long and not having slept horizontally for over twenty-four hours. She brings a hand up to her head and ruffles her hair, thankful that its shortness means its lack of cleanliness doesn't show too badly. Ralph, with his dark blonde hair just reaching his shoulders in limp, dank noodles, looks far worse and Felix winces a little on his behalf. Having driven for seven hours – they'd stopped for breakfast then promptly hit the morning rush hour traffic around Bristol – on limited sleep reserves, and an ongoing neglect of personal hygiene were not the most ideal circumstances in which to confront an ex-lover. Let alone one who could pass for Angelina Jolie's younger, sexier sister.

'We've got to be nearly there now,' Dominic mutters from the seat next to her. The car has been silent ever since they left the A30 and followed the SatNav onto increasingly narrow roads. Ethan drives with his jaw set as if deeply offended, though Felix knows he's just concentrating. Ethan's never gotten on well with Ralph's battered old

Fiesta, preferring his vehicles heavyweight, with towing capabilities. Next to him Ralph sits motionless. His eyes have been closed for much of the journey, though Felix doubts he's been sleeping. Now his brown gaze is wide and almost unblinking as he stares at the hedgerows, fields and occasional glimpses of the coast. No one bothers to answer Dom and he slides sulkily back into his chair. Felix closes her eyes again.

The car begins to climb and then, abruptly, they're dipping forward. Felix opens her eyes and immediately the world around her is smudged with colour. Dirty yellow gorse rushes from the overgrown hedges, fingering the sides of the Fiesta like eager talons as Ethan eases the car into a second gear crawl down the narrow lane. It's only when he draws to a stop that Felix looks up and sees the tiny cottage perched at the end of the lane like a neglected fairy-tale dwelling. Its white bricks are partially obscured by ivy, though the front garden is neat with only slightly overgrown pampas grass and laurel bushes. Felix remembers a joke she's heard about pampas grass and swingers, but when she sees the whiteness of Ralph's face coupled with the tic in his jaw, she decides to keep it to herself.

'Hey, pampas grass!' Dominic pipes up from her left, 'Fee, didn't you say that was a calling card for sw—'

'Shut up, Dom,' Felix hisses, kicking him hard in the shin.

'Ow! Just trying to lighten the mood,' Dominic grumbles, rubbing his leg as Ralph unclips his seatbelt brusquely and swings his long legs out of the car. Ethan and Felix quickly follow suit.

Felix breathes the salt air deeply, but as she stares around at the surrounding sweep of hills, she can't help but feel boxed in.

'What d'you think?' Ethan nudges her. She has a sudden, fleeting urge to turn into his chest and feel his thick arms burrowing around her. Instead, she shrugs.

'It's remote enough,' she replies, 'But I wouldn't want to stay here... It feels like the bottom of a well...'

'No, I mean *that*,' he takes her by the shoulders and gently turns her round to point at the side of the house. A car has been parked so closely to the wall, so nestled in from the lane that it's stupidly difficult to spot despite its dark blue colour and large, SUV build.

'Oh. Yes, that's definitely hers. Matches the number plate.'

Ralph nods grimly and, before she can add a question about what their plan of action might be, who should go in first, et cetera, he opens the gate and marches up the garden path with quick, nipped strides.

'OK then...' She glances from Ethan, stoic as ever, to Dominic, who is struggling not to look utterly terrified, 'I guess we're going in...'

Twenty minutes later, Ralph sits heavily on one of the covered sofas in the cottage's tiny living room and sighs deeply into his hands. Exchanging a glance with Ethan, Felix crosses the room to sit next to him, placing a hand on his shoulder blade.

'Tell me the truth, Fee,' Ralph murmurs, looking up at her, 'How similar is the way this place has been left to the state of Bella's flat?'

'Nothing like it,' Felix says, straight away. 'The flat was tidy, everything in its place. It was like she knew she'd have to leave at a moment's notice.'

'So how's that different to here? It barely looks like anyone's been here at all!'

Felix smiles at him almost pityingly. 'You're like Ethan. You don't *see* things.' She holds out a hand and begins to tick off her fingers. 'One, there's an open wash bag in the bathroom upstairs, shampoo in the shower and something's been spilled on the bath mat recently and not cleaned up properly. Two, the bed in the small room hasn't been made, there's a dirty pair of socks on the floor in there, a shopping bag of new clothes with the labels still on and a schoolbag containing, among other things, *this*,' she shifts, digs in her pocket and extracts a mobile phone with a pretty, swirling purple cover. Ralph stares at it miserably, but before he can open his mouth, Felix continues, 'I know you're going to say that no teenager who hasn't been taken by force would voluntarily leave their mobile phone behind, but before you do, I also checked the receipt in the shopping bag. It shows they bought two new phones yesterday morning. I'm guessing Bella told Ariana to stop using this one and got her a new one...'

'I thought you said you'd found usage from the original device at two points yesterday. That's how you located them, isn't it?'

'Yeah. I didn't say Ariana did as she was told, did I. She's *your* kid too, remember?'

A shadow of a smile crosses Ralph's face and Felix grins back, adding: 'If all that wasn't enough, there's a bloody nice angora cardigan in the master bedroom that I can't see *anyone* leaving behind, let alone Bella. And there's a washed-up plate and mug on the side over there but a dirty pair still in the sink... What does that tell you?'

'That someone didn't get around to finishing the washing up?'

'Because...?'

'They were interrupted? Shit,' he gets to his feet so quickly Felix sinks several inches into the sofa cushions.

'Not necessarily,' she gets to her feet as well, but Ralph's already striding towards the front door. 'It just means that something broke up the rhythm, that's all... But that could mean anything! A phone call, one of them pointing something out on the TV... Ralph, where're you going?'

Ralph has left the cottage and is already unlatching the gate by the time Felix, Ethan and Dominic have followed him to the front door. He stops in front of the Fiesta and scans the horizon left and right.

'Ralph, look,' Felix jogs up to him and grabs him by the elbow. She feels him twitch under her grip as if his whole body is wired in adrenaline. 'The car's still here... They've probably just gone for a walk or something...'

'Or someone has come and taken them,' he turns to her, wildness in his eyes.

'Think about it. We only found them a few hours ago. Do you *really think* Lychen and his bubble-headed tech guys could have tracked them before then?'

'Think about it, mate, you know they've got no one like Felix,' Ethan says, appearing on Ralph's other side and putting a large, calming hand on his shoulder. 'That's why he was always putting on the sweet talk for her back in the old days...'

'We don't know *who* they've got now,' Ralph replies irritably, though his arm relaxes a little under Felix's grip.

'True. But we do know that they haven't been near Bella. We know it was us who made her run...'

'Well, me,' Felix grins. Ralph shakes them both from him and strides towards the rotting wooden fence of one of the fields.

'There's a path there,' he says, as if to himself. 'And another going that way. They *might* have just gone for a walk I suppose... Forgotten about the washing up...'

He turns back to the others, his face set once again. 'I'm not waiting around for her to come back, see the Fiesta and run off again, though. We'll look. We'll find them ourselves.'

'Alright...'

'There're two main paths here... This one goes up, along that hill there. And this one goes towards the coast. I'm going coastal, you guys take the other one.'

'OK,' Felix says, quickly, because she can see Ethan opening his mouth to disagree. 'But let's be sensible. I'll come with you, Dom and Ethan go together.'

'Fine. Let's go.'

**October, 2018**

*Sunday*

'Are you OK? Really?' Felix has to take two strides for every one of Ralph's and the cottage is still in sight when the stitch begins to burn at her side. Still, she keeps up as best she can with his furious pace.

'I'm *fine*,' Ralph replies, shortly. He holds a large tangle of blackberry thorns out of the way just long enough for Felix to duck under it, though she still has to catch a few errant twigs before they scratch her face.

'Good. You sound it,' she mutters, brushing dirt and debris from her denim jacket.

'Look, I don't want to have some deep and meaningful discussion about my feelings, OK?'

'OK, OK...'

They march on in silence for several more minutes. Felix can't help but notice how frequently they have to duck and dodge the overgrown hedgerows and bushes, not to mention the large tussocks of grass that reach like snakes for her ankles. The ground underfoot looks completely undisturbed. She really can't see how likely it is that anyone else, let alone two someone elses, could have walked this way in the last month or so, let alone hour. If Ralph notices, though, he doesn't say anything. They trudge onwards and, suddenly, they take a corner, climb a stile and there, before them, stretching like a giant, blue-gold blanket, is the sea. They both pause automatically, staring as a boat meanders lazily across the water. Then Ralph snaps back to attention and glances around them. They're standing in another field, but this one seems wilder than the previous one, with large patches of bracken and–

'No path,' Ralph grunts, taking a step into the long grass.

Felix squints ahead. The field slopes gently downwards and then disappears before the sea.

'There must be cliffs over there,' she says. 'Maybe there's a way down to the coast?'

'Let's have a look...' He marches through the grass without waiting for a reply.

It's not easy going, especially for Felix, who finds some of the tangles of grass and bracken reaching well over knee height. Ralph waits for her a few times but she waves him on, sensing his eagerness to keep going. It takes at least ten minutes for them to fight their way across the heavy grasses to the edge of the cliffs, and once there the drop to the water is sheer. Wind buffets and grabs at Felix's coat and she takes several steps away from the edge. Ralph stands as if completely unbothered by the cataclysmic drop just inches from his feet, staring both ways along the cliff.

'We can follow the coast round,' he says, turning back to her with his eyes bright and determined. 'There's more of a path here and it looks like it opens up a bit more around that corner there...'

'Looks like it's covered in rocks to me,' Felix mutters. She's got a scratch going across one cheek where she hadn't been quick enough to swipe away a vicious tangle of twigs, her neck feels hot and sweaty beneath her jacket and, judging by the smell wafting up from her trainers, at some point she's managed to step in some sort of excrement, though there's no sign of any animals anywhere in sight.

'Come on, nothing ventured…'

'You've changed your tune! Was brooding bastard not working for you anymore?'

'Guess I just took pity on your short arse and decided to cheer up. Besides, I've always liked the seaside.'

'We're hardly on a jolly holiday here,' Felix mutters, glancing over the cliff edge which still feels far too close to her right side as she trudges along behind him.

'Better than being stuck in front of a screen in that stuffy hotel room though, isn't it? At least we're out *doing something*.'

'I happen to like stuffy screens and dark rooms, thank you very much. Anyway, the seaside is all well and good when there isn't a bloody great cliff-edge between– what is it, why've you stopped?'

'Here… look, these rocks. You couldn't see it from back there, but there's an opening in between them… And look! A path!'

'Whoop,' Felix mutters, as she puts a hand on the rock and slowly peers around it. Sure enough there's a tiny, wide-enough-for-one-foot-at-a-time spit of a path leading between the rocks downwards. She follows it as far as she can with her eyes, but it winds too much for her to see all the way down. Still, there's no doubt where it goes.

'You think they're down there?'

'It's as good a guess as any,' Ralph says. 'It's where I would go, after all…'

'Ralph, stop a minute,' Felix tears her eyes away from the sickeningly vertical path and battles a sudden wave of nausea. Ralph turns to her, his eyes alight with a mixture of impatience and almost feverish excitement.

'Just suppose they did come this way, on that ridiculously overgrown path through the field, through the wild grass and crazy bracken back there, off any passing resemblance to a *beaten track* to here, where there's a tiny imitation of a path which we only spotted because we literally stumbled across it... Do you really think they looked down there and thought *Hey, that's going in the vague direction of the sea, let's wander off an actual, literal cliff?* Really?'

Ralph frowns and glances from her to the path, which he's already stepped onto. He rests a hand on one of the rocks and opens his mouth, though whether to protest or acquiesce she never knows because he spots something. Something small and gleaming. He lurches forward so quickly Felix has to look away, and re-emerges holding something aloft.

'Look!'

'What?'

'It's an earring! You tell me no one's been down here recently, look at it! It's not been half-buried, it looks pristine!'

Felix reluctantly studies the tiny pearl stud. Not only is he right, she has a sinking suspicion she noticed a matching necklace on Bella's bedside table in the cottage.

'You don't have to come...'

'No, no, it's fine... lead the way.' She sighs, hoping that if she thinks about nothing except where she's putting her feet, she'll be able to keep her breakfast where it is.

To Felix's relief, however, the initial steepness of the cliff path soon eases and after a few minutes they're almost able to walk side by side as the path widens.

'I can smell the sea,' Ralph calls, gently, as he rounds a corner up ahead. Felix catches him up and stops short. The sea is *there.* They are standing at the end of the straggly cliff path where it joins a larger, well-maintained coastal footpath running left and right along the top of a lurch of rocks. The sea laps hungrily at their base, so close that Felix can taste tiny flecks of spray when she licks her lips.

'The tide's in,' Ralph mutters unnecessarily as they both stare, momentarily dazed by the sudden wildness of the waves frothing just feet below them. Felix suppresses the image of a young girl launching herself into the water only to be immediately dashed backwards into the ragged coastline. *Don't be stupid*, she tells herself. *No one in their right mind would go swimming in that*.

'So... they probably just followed the path... Which way, d'you reckon?' Felix glances from left to right, but neither way looks more or less distinctive.

'I... I'm not sure,' Ralph pulls his hands through his hair and Felix senses his previous enthusiasm sinking under a swelling tide of despair.

'Well... what would Bella do?' Felix clenches her teeth a little as she says it. Ralph just shrugs.

'Who the hell knows that? And what if it's Ariana we're trying to follow? What if she was the one deciding where to go...? I didn't even know she existed two days ago, now I've got to try and work out whether she'd choose a right or a left?'

'Well... that way looks like it's going further along the cliff,' Felix turns to the left, and then glances back along to the right. 'This way I think I can just about spot some boats, maybe a harbour... so that way might lead towards a town... Probably that little seaside resort we drove through earlier…'

'Either way, if we pick the wrong turn, we'll probably miss them coming back…'

'Then they spot the car…'

'And we return to another dead end.'

'That's if they're even here at all and we're not just chasing our tails by the bloody seaside while they're being driven miles away by Lychen's henchmen…'

'Come on… You found the earring, right? I'm sure that's hers…'

'It could be anyone's,' he spits, turning around. Felix takes a step back, unnerved by the sudden change in his spirits.

'Let's face it. Lychen could've orchestrated this whole bloody thing. Brought us on some wild goose chase and planted a load of rubbish for us to follow like stupid sniffer dogs… And meanwhile he's made off with the two he's been chasing all along…'

'Or you're a paranoid idiot and they're just along that bend there, admiring the view…'

'Actually, neither of you is entirely right or wrong.'

Felix whips around, her pulse a hum in her ears. There's a small bench set into the cliff behind them, partially hidden by the rocky outcrop next to the path they've just followed. And, sitting upon it, legs crossed, back straight and not a hair out of place, as if she were simply waiting for a bus on an upmarket street in central London–

'Bella!' Ralph gives a strange, involuntary-looking lurch towards her and then seems to catch himself. 'What– Where did you… Where's Ariana?'

If Bella is surprised by his mention of her daughter's name, she doesn't show it. She just stares at him and blinks slowly, languidly, like a cat.

'Did you come through the fields? You look like you've rolled here. There's an easier path if you go up the track past the cottage a little bit and then follow the cliffside...'

'Never mind that, where is she?'

'I don't know.'

'You don't–'

Bella gets to her feet. Though slim and petite as ever, she's on higher ground than both of them and Felix finds herself having to crane her neck to meet her gaze. The effect makes her feel uncomfortably infantile.

'We argued. She stormed off. I thought she'd come here... I told her about the little beach just there – well, there when the tide's out – and she'd seemed keen to visit it. But here she is not. But you are. Which means this place is far easier to find than I'd hoped, which means...'

'Lychen could have picked her up.'

'It's looking more possible every moment. I've been up and down this path all morning. I was just about to set off back to the cottage to see if she'd returned there, but if you've just come from there...'

'We have... no sign of her...'

Felix stares between them. She scowls as the wind whistles and scuffs at her own hair messily, whilst gently lifting the tendrils escaping from Bella's gathered chignon and floating them delicately around her face like the tender caress of a hairstylist. Bella's green eyes bore into Ralph's brown ones and worlds pass between them.

'You look exactly the same,' he says in a soft voice which makes Felix wish she'd taken up his suggestion to stay put on top of the cliff.

'You look... appalling,' Bella replies, and Ralph gives his short bark laugh for the first time in days. Felix clears her throat.

'Right, well loathe as I am to break up this… well, whatever this is… Should we not perhaps try ringing the others to see if they've had any luck? I mean, no offence or anything, Bella, but shouldn't we at least eliminate the possibility that Ariana might simply have wandered off in a different direction rather than immediately assume that you are omniscient and she's definitely been abducted?'

Bella's iridescent green gaze snaps to Felix, and Felix immediately feels as if an icy wash of water has been emptied over her head, but she doesn't flinch or look away.

'By all means,' Bella replies, coolly.

Felix looks away, hiding her relief, and digs her phone from her pocket. She has three missed calls from Ethan and quickly hits the button to call him back before she has time to worry what that could mean.

'Fee?' The line buffets with static as if Ethan's talking from the top of a howling mountain.

'Yeah, any sign of the girl?'

'No, nothing… I've been trying to get hold of you – we got halfway up the hill and the path is totally overgrown so we're heading back to the cottage… Any luck on the coast?'

'Well, we've stumbled across Mama Bear,' Felix turns away from the sight of Ralph helping Bella down from the rocky outcrop of the bench and onto their level. 'But no sign of the kid. Seems they had a little falling out earlier and Ariana took off in a huff.'

'OK…'

'There's a million places she could be… but we think the best thing might be to head back to the cottage and regroup.'

'The best thing would be to track down Lychen and look for her there,' Ralph interrupts, hotly.

'What? Sorry, Ethan, I can't hear you, the wind is bad… Just meet us back at the cottage… Hello?'

The phone goes dead. Bad signal, Felix tells herself as, again, panic tussles with adrenaline and battles to surge into her limbs and power them back up the cliffside path as quickly as she can. She looks up. Ralph, at least, is wearing an expression which mirrors how she's feeling. He's still glancing up and down the coastal pathway as if hoping Ariana will miraculously appear from behind a gorse bush. Bella, on the other hand, looks completely serene.

'Shall we go, then?' She doesn't wait for an answer but sets off up the cliff path, her steps as nimble as a mountain goat. Felix soon finds herself out of breath as she hoists herself up after her. *Maybe not so serene, after all*, she thinks to herself.

**Autumn, 1995**

It was surprisingly easy adjusting to life with the Blakes. Even Ana. She had a strangeness about her, and I soon learned that I wasn't the only one who kept themselves alert whenever they were around her. Overly affectionate one moment, she could switch at the flicker of a heavily-lashed eye and even 'darling Freddie' wasn't immune when one of those moods took her. One morning when Ralph and I were waiting for Dr Blake in the schoolroom – the book-filled room where I'd first met Ralph – he appeared with a long, cat-like scratch smarting across his throat. Another time I arrived downstairs for breakfast only to find Ralph hovering outside the door of the dining room. He put a finger to his lips when I opened my mouth to ask him what was going on and I was answered by the sound of high-pitched shrieks and smashing plates within.

Ana rarely got physical with Ralph, but I sometimes wondered if her occasional choice of abuse for him was worse, for she'd often just go completely cold, call him a disappointment or act as if he weren't there at all. No one ever spoke about Ana's moods. Dr Blake would sometimes say she was 'having a turn' or blame the heavy doses of cancer medication for her less-violent outbursts, but the worst of them were never discussed at all. Often she'd take to her bed for days after the worst incidents and the house seemed to breathe more deeply without her, and yet things were always a little blander, as if some of the colour had seeped from the world. I'd always find myself confusingly glad to see her back at the breakfast table. It seems strange, looking back, that her moods didn't remind me more of my own mother and the way she'd treated me, but she didn't. My mother had been a snake, dealing in hisses and beady, cold glares; Ana was more like a dragon – fiery, passionate, mythic, and infinitely more dangerous. My mother had hissed at me alone, Ana's burns consumed us all.

My days took on a uniformity; in the mornings Ralph and I would study either together or one on one with Blake or Ana at individual, old-fashioned desks in the schoolroom. Ralph was far ahead of me in the sciences, but for literary subjects we were more evenly matched and we would often be assigned the same book to study or composition to write. I soon learned that, despite their love of books, the arts were regarded as more of a pastime than a career path by all three Blakes. That wasn't to say they didn't take them seriously, however. Often I'd find myself reading long past my bedtime to keep up with that week's assignment of literature. Similarly, Ana took on my dance training with a dedication akin at times to obsession. She became a different person in the studio. Her instructions were precise and specific, her criticism overwhelming, but her patience here, at least, seemed endless. She taught me as if she simply did not believe there was a movement I would not be able to do without due practice, and I believed her. It was a style of training I was utterly unused to; my old ballet teacher had fawned and encouraged and gentled. Ana barked, snapped and pushed. I fell far more, but I also turned, leapt and stretched my body further than

I thought I ever could.

And so time passed. I began to wonder whether Dr Blake would ever do the tests he had assured my mother he would perform when she'd brought me here. One day, however, he left Ralph and Ana pouring over a particularly nasty-looking quadratic equation in the schoolroom and told me we were taking a trip to the ARC. I had not been to the large, oily-black building since arriving at the Manor. In my head it had become entwined with the terrifying crushing-embrace Ana had given me when she'd shown it to me that first morning and as Blake and I walked silently along the path on our approach, I found myself having to concentrate on my breaths so they didn't shorten in panic.

'So Bella… Are you happy here, with us?'

I looked up at Blake in some surprise. The weather had chilled over the weeks I had been staying there and though I had found myself needing the warmth of my coat, hat and gloves long before the Blakes had, by now he too was wrapped in a tartan scarf with a padded jacket over the top. I thought about the question, about the way he and Ana didn't watch me with awe and crinkle their eyes in easy affection every time I answered correctly. Sure, Blake was easy enough to manipulate most of the time – I now had a large TV as well as a brand-new stereo in my bedroom – but when it came to teaching, he acquired a focus that made him as relentless as Ana, though perhaps not so aggressive.

I thought about the way Ralph called me *Beast,* how we'd spent hours throwing rotting apples at one another in the garden the other day, how he was showing me the best places to sit quietly and spot wild rabbits and red deer. How his eyes narrowed in easy contempt when I said something he deemed frivolous or girly, but how other times I'd catch him watching me out of the corner of my eye when I said or did something right and know I'd impressed him. I thought about Ramona and how she'd never quite warmed to me, hissing strange Spanish phrases when she knew the Blakes couldn't hear her and, occasionally, making the sign of the cross when I glanced her way. And lastly I thought about Ana. About how just one smile from her in the ballet studio could make me feel like a marathon runner passing through the finish line; about how she sometimes caught me in the hallway and pulled me into a hug for no reason at all. How sometimes that is all it would be, an embrace, warm and gentle, but other times she would hold me too tight or pinch my skin between her bony fingers, as if she had been taken over by some demon partway through, like the cancer in her brain had suddenly whispered to her that I was an enemy and needed punishment.

'Yeah... I think so.'

'I know it's been a bit of an adjustment.' We were heading through the dense copse of trees now, the ARC lurking like a shining shadow just through the thicket. The path was clear, the only sounds coming from the crunch of thin needles and pine cones beneath our shoes.

'But we're pleased with how well you seem to be settling. Your schoolwork is excellent, I have to say. You'll be giving Ralph a run for his money before long if he's not careful. And you and he seem to have built up something of a competitive rapport,' he chuckled to himself, perhaps thinking of the rotten apples and how many of them had ended up smeared across the windows of the Manor's lower floor.

'He's OK,' I shrugged. 'For a boy.'

'And I know Ana adores you...' I looked up at him

again, eyes roving over his roughly stubbled face for hints of sarcasm or irony. He must have sensed my confusion because he glanced back at me only briefly before removing his glasses and rubbing the lenses on the edge of his scarf.

'I know she can be... difficult... at times. It's the illness – she lives with a lot of pain, a lot more than she lets on. You should have known her a few years ago... she was incredible. Like the definition of vitality itself... I used to say she could never simply walk from one place to another, she'd always be leaping or dancing or running or some such. Walking was too dull for an existence like hers...'

'Why can't you fix her?' I blurted, and then blinked. The question had come from me without any warning and I brought a hand up to my mouth, shocked that anything like that could have happened. Before coming here I didn't think I'd ever said anything without considering it carefully first. If he noticed my surprise, however, Dr Blake didn't say anything. He merely replaced his glasses and kept walking up the slope leading out of the trees.

'You mean, why can't we cure her cancer?'

'Yeah... I mean, if you can make babies who are really good at sports or maths and stuff, why can't you make something that will kill cancer?'

'We tried. When Ana was first diagnosed, I almost halted all of our current research entirely to put our scientists onto it... But cancer is a monstrous foe... We had no experience with its particular type of cell multiplication – we were all about creating life, not studying its destruction... We did try, though... But it didn't work. In the end Ana herself told us to stop, to go back to what we knew. She didn't want us to waste years of resources on saving just one person when we could be creating technology to improve the lives of millions… After all, the bigger picture of our work isn't about curing cancer, it's eradicating the need for a cure. You see, by manipulating the genes early enough, we hope to engender a species which wouldn't have the same susceptibility to disease…'

'But what about her? Is she dying? Ralph says she won't get better… but she can still do things on her good days. I've seen her do twenty fouetté turns en pointe without breaking a sweat…'

Dr Blake smiled at me, and this time his eyes crinkled the same way my dad's used to.

'We're all dying, Bella. One way or another. Now here we are – I don't believe you've had the experience of our little laboratory before?'

The blackness of the building shot straight up, punctured only by tall, uniform windows. Dr Blake held a dark, marble-looking door open for me and I stepped into the darkness. *Little laboratory* seemed a particularly inadequate description. The entranceway opened out into a shining reception area. The floor was as polished and dark as the exterior walls, though when I stepped – somewhat gingerly – forward, my feet didn't slip like I thought they would. The walls were also the same oily-black stone, and it would have been terribly gloomy if it weren't for the dazzling crystal chandelier hanging above our heads and the floor-to-ceiling windows slotted into the walls. The room was empty except for a desk at the far end, currently manned by a young black man talking busily into a phone which he held to his ear with one hand while typing on a computer keyboard with the other. He waved at Blake as we walked past, bulging his eyes at me. I didn't see the smooth lift doors until they parted suddenly at our approach and almost jumped backwards in alarm.

'Yes,' Blake chuckled, as he pressed a seemingly invisible button on the lift wall, 'The architecture of the ARC is rather… unique… It does take some getting used to.'

'What exactly are we doing here?' I asked, trying to keep the apprehension out of my voice as the lift lurched unexpectedly sideways and then upwards in a dizzying rush. Blake put a hand on my shoulder to stop me falling, as there were no rails to hold onto. The inside of the lift was as black as everywhere else, the only light coming from a soft orb set into the ceiling. There were no buttons I could see, though the spot where Blake had pressed glowed bright blue.

'It's fingerprint recognition,' he said, softly. 'No one but a small handful of people can access the building.'

'Why?'

He looked at me as if trying to work out whether I was grown up enough to be told. I tried to make myself taller under his steadying hand.

'Some of our research is a little… controversial. Do you know what that means?'

'Like… dodgy?'

He laughed shortly, reminding me sharply of Ralph. 'Well, that's certainly how some people would view it! Which is why it's best to keep them in the dark, as it were.'

The lift stopped less than a second before the invisible doors sprang open in front of us. Blake steered me out into a long, shining corridor with a soft reed mat on the floor.

'This way,' he said, cheerfully. 'We'll pop to my office first before I introduce you to some of the scientists.'

I realised, as we walked past several doors set into the black walls – some bearing name plates, others visible only by the large, metal knobs sticking out of them – that he hadn't answered my question about why we were here.

When I opened my mouth to ask again, however, he answered me unexpectedly.

'You may recall the conditions under which your parents left you with us?'

'Tests?' Again, the word came out before I could catch it and I immediately resented the high, scared edge it held. I scowled.

'Don't worry, it's just a little blood test and a scan. You'll barely feel it, I promise.'

'I'm not scared of needles.'

'Good. We don't need squeamish future scientists... Ah, here we are...' He opened a double set of knobs and a doorway appeared as if it had sliced itself into the wall by his touch. I glanced up just quickly enough to see his name emblazoned on a shiny metal plaque before my gaze was snatched by the room beyond. Like the errant words, my gasp escaped before I could catch it.

**October, 2018**

*Sunday*

*Did you really think she would be on that cliff path?*

Don't be ridiculous. Of course I did. Why else would I go there?

*To draw Ralph and the others. To give him more time. So he could get away.*

Lychen? Why would I want that animal anywhere near Ariana?

*Because you know he won't hurt her if she is bait. And you know she is OK. You feel it here, in this place where I live too. Besides, she's not what he's after. Not yet anyway.*

Shut up. Shut up. How can you think I'd plan something like that?

*Because, Bella, you always plan everything.*

I glance back at the others out of the corner of my eye as we reach the top of the cliff and begin the walk along the track they missed earlier. Felix is breathing heavily but I can tell she has many miles left in her. There's barely a sheen on her forehead and her even strides come easily. Ralph, on the other hand, is puffing like a smoker and when he coughs it's ragged and wheezy.

'Did you bring your inhaler?' Felix asks, just as I open my mouth with the same words.

'I'm fine, let's just go...'

'If you need a break...'

'I've got one in the car, don't *fuss...*'

'Fine.' Felix stamps past us both and leads the way up the track. 'Don't expect the kiss of life from *me* if you keel over.'

I shut my eyes for a moment, remembering the old bickering in the lab. Ralph's face set in rigid lines on one side, Felix's glowing with fury on the other and, often, Dominic or Reuben inbetween, their large eyes flickering from one to the other in worry. Nothing that couldn't be resolved over a drink in the canteen or village pub, of course. Not like the arguments I was involved in.

*They think you don't care, you know. Especially the woman. She thinks you're cold.*

I know.

*She probably has three kids of her own and can't imagine acting so calmly should one of them have fallen into the hands of a psycho...*

Possibly. I don't think so, though.

*How can you possibly tell?*

I know her.

We're in sight of the cottage now. I pull up short as I pass through the gate Felix holds. Everything is focused on Ariana. On finding her in the house, waiting for me, perhaps throwing confused looks at Dominic and Ethan as they perch awkwardly next to her. But still I can't stop my small gasp of surprise as I spot the red vehicle parked in the lane.

'Your car! It's still going?'

'Of course it is,' Ralph wheezes next to me.

'Barely,' Felix snorts.

'It's got to be... what, nearly twenty years old? How on

earth...?'

'I guess it was just built to last,' Ralph says, tightly, as we head around it and he swings open the garden path. I glance at it again, memories jostling with one another. Then I catch Felix's eye.

'Money's not what it was,' she says, shortly. 'We don't all have family trust funds. We can't all swan about in BMWs and angora jumpers.'

I stare her down for a few seconds, just for the fun of it.

'Cashmere, actually,' I remark, as I stride past her and towards the house.

I know as soon as I step through the front door that Ariana isn't here. I let the gazes of Ethan and Dominic settle on me but barely spare them a glance as my eyes sweep over the room. Everything is exactly as I left it earlier, but not. It's all been raked over and put back... like someone reapplying make-up when the first layer hasn't quite rubbed off.

'You searched the house?' I say, crossing to the counter and putting my handbag down. I dig into it for my new phone but there's nothing on the screen. There wouldn't be, of course. I reach for Ariana's phone. Her Twitter page glares at me when I unlock the screen and I quickly swipe it away, placing the phone back into my bag. It's only then I notice the third mobile sitting on the counter, screen down, purple patterned cover striking a brash, gaudy chord in the simply furnished room. I frown as I reach for it.

'Yeah, no one here,' grunts Ethan. I look up at him properly for the first time. Of all of them, he looks the least different. Ralph is greying around his temples and has the beginnings of the stoop he'll share with his father; Felix has wrinkles around her eyes and mouth; Dominic is a beanpole of awkwardness and large, flappy hands. But Ethan is the same thick-set pillar of a man he always was. Perhaps there's an extra tattoo or two on his bare, dark-skinned forearm, but otherwise I could be talking to him thirteen years ago. He's even got the same bristly haircut.

'I mean before, when you first arrived.'

Dominic, who got to his feet from the sofa as we entered the house, flushes violently. Ethan doesn't so much as twitch, however.

'Yeah. No one here then, either,' he grunts with a flicker of a smile.

I look around again. I may be wrong, but the house feels touched by more than just them.

'That's it then,' Ralph says, leaning on the counter next to me and taking a long drag from his inhaler. 'He's got her, hasn't he? Felix?'

'On it,' Felix is already pulling a laptop from a bag resting behind the sofa.

'You've been tracking him?' I ask.

'Where we can... he's picked up a few things in the last few years,' Felix mutters as she sets the computer up on the coffee table and plugs it in. 'Or at least the tech guys he uses have...'

'Don't you want to know how we found *you,* Beast?' Ralph is watching me carefully. He's trying to be gruff but there's a glimmer in the murk of his eye. It's not like his dad's twinkle though, this one is pure Ana. Indulgent, yet carefully cold at the same time.

'I'm assuming you used this,' I hold up Ariana's old phone. 'You found the Twitter account she made from it and, what, tracked it to this location somehow? Even though it was switched off?'

'She turned it on yesterday morning, only for a few minutes... And then again in the afternoon, again just briefly.'

'Ah,' annoyance leaps briefly but the rising worry swats it down irritably. I keep my eyes lowered until it's under control, staring at the blank screen in my hand. Ralph stares at me for a moment. He sees what I don't say. He always had that knack.

*Not the parts you didn't want to tell him, though.*

Of course not.

*That's my girl.*

'I take it you didn't know about the Twitter thing? Is that what your argument was about...?'

'Among other things. What do you think? Should I risk switching it on now?'

'Depends how sure you are that he's got her. If he doesn't, you're risking him finding us.'

'We're not the ones in danger, Ralph,' Felix pipes up from the sofa. Dominic is sitting on the sofa arm next to her, peering from the screen to us and back again. My appearance seems to have had a suppressive influence on his vocal chords.

'I agree,' I say, turning back to Ralph. 'She's been talking to some stranger on Twitter for days, possibly weeks. She's switched the phone on when I told her not to... The damage has been done.'

He nods. I press the power button.

'What if this is all some stupid song and dance over nothing?' Ethan calls through from the kitchen where he's making tea. 'What if Lychen's off building an entirely new empire in New York or Paris like he always said he would and hasn't thought about the ARC or any of us in years... Ariana's just gone off in some strop like any other teenage girl and will be back when she's hungry... We've raced across the country just for the pleasure of your company, Bella... To have a nice cup of tea... And we're all utterly paranoid?'

He plonks a mug in front of me. Black, no sugar. Milk and two for Ralph. Felix glances up and smiles at him as he goes back for hers. The phone lights up and I place it on the counter top between Ralph and I.

'You *could* be right, mate,' Ralph murmurs, not taking his eyes from the screen. A couple of messages pop up:

> Hey, it's Jake frm the beach :) What
> du prefr? Bacardi or vodka? I cn gt
> bth 4 nxt wk.
> U stll cming, rite?

'Who the hell is *that?*' Ralph almost jumps up from his stool. I almost smile. For the short amount of time he's been trying on the cloak of parenthood he's already perfected protective father.

'Some boy she met at the beach yesterday. He's invited her to a party at the weekend. She was *going* to ask me, appar–'

Another message appears. This time we both stare.

> Good afternoon, Bella.

'Shit,' Ralph mutters.

'What? What is it?' Dominic comes over. I can't take my eyes from the screen, but I sense him looming over my shoulder. Ethan, too, places his tea down in the corner of my peripheral vision and comes over.

'Shall I reply?'

'Yes. But let's get the number first. Fee? We've got a mobile number, shall I read it out?'

'Go for it.'

He takes the phone and does so before handing it to

me.

'Go on. It'll have to come from you. You know what he's like, he'll smell me a mile away.'

I nod.

Conan68, I presume?
Forgive me. But you never can trust
teenagers with smart devices these
days, can you? Even when they're
not quite teenagers.

How did you find her?
You have done an excellent job of
erasing your digital footprint, Bella.
I have one photograph of you. One.
My team have been using it for
years to try and trace you on social
media and for years they have been
unsuccessful, until a few weeks ago.
An individual, partially blurred but
clearly discernible in the
background of a 12-year-old girl's
selfie on Instagram. Only a partial
match, but closer than we have
ever come before, particularly
when teamed with a corroborative
metadata tag. At first I thought it
was a ghost, Bella. A ghost of the
perfect child I knew all those years
ago. But then I looked more closely
and realised it wasn't you at all. But
those eyes. Those eyes are
unmistakable.

So you went through Lucy.

Was that the friend's name?
Forgive me. I don't know the
details. Engaging with self-obsessed
pre-teens is a tedium I chose to
delegate, but I'm told it didn't take
long for her to give us what we
needed.

>You had to make Ariana
>believe she found you.

We knew there must be a degree of
carefulness. The photo of Ariana
disappeared almost as quickly as it
had appeared, after all. It was too
late by then, of course. But we
couldn't rush in. So we used the
friend, we used the obsession of
every single-parented child. It was
not my idea, but it did work. I
apologise.

>No you don't.

No, I don't. Isn't this fun? Like old
times. I must say, Bella, I never
pegged you for the maternal type.
Has Felix found me yet?

'He knows,' I say, dropping the phone. Ralph picks it
up and scans the messages, turning pale.

'He knows you're tracking him, Fee...'

>I'll make it easy for you, if you like.
>I'd hate to tempt dear Fee with
>redundancy, but I'm more than
>happy to disclose my whereabouts.
>>Go on then.

You will come yourself, Bella. You
may bring your lap-dog Blake Jnr if
you like, but that's it. Ariana will be
there. We can talk.

Where are you?
First you need to return to the ARC.
There's something I need there.
Blake senior can obtain it for me.
He knows what it is. You will bring
it.

I raise my eyes to Ralph's. He frowns back at me and shakes his head.

What is it?
You know that's not how this
works. Tsk tsk, Bella, I do hope
motherhood hasn't dulled your
keen sense of depravity. That
would be a terrible disappointment.
And you know how I hate to be
disappointed.

'He won't tell us in case we move whatever it is he's after,' Ralph mutters. 'It's got to be something of Dad's. Perhaps one of his instruments... I can't think of anything Lychen wouldn't already have or be able to buy unless it's one of the machines Dad modified himself...' I turn back to the phone, my breathing quick and shallow. I feel the clench of a heavy fist battering against my lungs.

How do I even know you
have her?

The image appears in seconds. Ariana is slumped against the window of a car, her hair – dry now – tumbling in frizzy tufts around her shoulders. Her eyes are closed, her mouth open slightly. Bile rises from my stomach and I'm aware of a strange, growling noise vibrating from my throat. Before I can type, another message appears.

> She is merely sleeping, my colleagues assure me. She may have been given a little assistance in the matter, but no harm will come to her. You have my word.

> You abducted my daughter.

> I acquired insurance. You never can trust a Blake to do a thing properly. And it was they, not I, who chased you down to that hovel in Cornwall, remember, Bella. And let me ask you this – do you know why? Do you really think the life of your insignificant child will be enough for them to let you go again?

> What do you mean?

> I suggest you ask him.

I place the phone on the counter quickly, but still it rattles with the tremor in my hand.

'Beast? What did he say?' Ralph is already reaching for the device, scrolling back through. I don't think he notices me getting up. I run soundlessly up the stairs and into the bathroom, locking the door behind me. The scent of my hair serum tumbles into my nose and churns my stomach. I count in my head; I let the voice screech in protest; I press my fists into my eyes. Then I turn, lift the toilet seat and vomit neatly into the bowl.

**Autumn, 1995**

Blake chuckled at my shocked expression.

'Yes, it is a bit of a sight, isn't it? I call it my office but it's more of a laboratory really... With a few – er – office trimmings...'

I stared. It was all I could do. The room was larger than I'd expected – it must have taken up half the length of the corridor we had been walking down. I'd been expecting something that matched the shiny exterior of the building, the fancy chandelier downstairs, even the crazy lift, but this room was nothing like that. The walls were barely visible and what I could see of them was a neutral greyish colour. One side of the room ached with rows of books much like Dr Blake's office back at the Manor, only these shelves didn't sag but held their loads in rigid rows of metal and strong-looking bolts. The far side of the room was taken up with floor to ceiling windows and for a moment all I could stare at were the tumbling hills, mountains, and far off glittering lakes. I moved a little closer and felt the strange, swooping feeling of being about to walk straight into the landscape in front of me. Snow crested the top of some of the mountains and for the first time I really appreciated how far away from everything the ARC and the Manor were...

'If you wouldn't mind taking a seat over here, Bella,'

Blake said, quietly cutting into the daydream I was having about stepping straight through the glass and flying away. I turned around and took in the rest of the room. A two-person sofa stood between the window and the bookshelves. More books were stacked on the surface of two large desks which took up most of the floor space in the middle of the room. The work spaces also held two tall microscopes, several rows of glass test tubes and a few fragile-looking beakers. In the far corner Blake stood next to what looked like a dentist's chair. It even had a little tray table next to it where the sink would be. I made my way over, skirting carefully past all the glass items, and he lowered the chair with a little pedal so I could climb on.

'Don't worry, you're not the smallest person we've had take a ride,' he smiled at me. I smiled back to show him that I wasn't worried in the least, and really it wasn't the thought of the tests which scared me. It was the lurking memory of the way my mother had spoken about me all those weeks ago when we'd first arrived.

I'd avoided thinking about my family as much as possible after that first night. Thinking about my dad and siblings made me feel horribly squirmy inside, like one part of me wanted to cry and the other wanted to hit and punch and tear the image of them up into tiny pieces until I could think of them no longer. Touching on the idea of my mother just made me burn. It scared me, to be honest. The intensity of my hatred for her was something I'd never experienced before. I'd always tried to think of myself a bit like a robot before – my mother had described me that way enough times, after all – it had become a shield, a comfort almost. I told myself I didn't have feelings. If I didn't have feelings, I couldn't get bored or complacent, after all. If I didn't have feelings, nothing *she* did or said could actually hurt me. If I didn't have feelings, I couldn't be scared, or lost, or alone.

So when Blake took my arm and gently rolled up the sleeve, a tiny needle in his gloved hand, I looked away and tried to tell myself that it didn't matter what the tests showed. A robot wouldn't care if it were defective, after all. The bite of the needle was small but insistent.

'All done,' Blake smiled, whisking the vial of dark red away and placing a tiny plaster over the pinprick in the crook of my arm. 'Now all I need you to do is lie still while I pass this machine over your head for a moment or two. Just lie perfectly still, that's right. Good girl. Nearly done... Perfect. OK, up you get!'

'That's it?'

'That's it. Should have the results in a few days if the workload isn't too bad around here. Come on, let's go and say hello to some of the science folk, shall we?'

'OK.' I slid gracefully down from the chair and tried not to glance at the small vial of blood or the machine he'd passed over my head, currently whirring softly to itself. Blake led me towards a door set into a wall plastered in cabinets. As we passed, I glanced into the nearest one and glimpsed a row of jars holding a variety of fascinating objects, from what looked like a miniature brain to some sort of baby animal all curled up. In truth I'd have liked to have spent at least another twenty minutes in that room just looking around and staring out of the window, but I knew enough by then to realise that Blake was the boss around here. I needed him, so I would do what he said until I was old enough not to.

We passed into a room which was roughly the same size as Blake's office/lab, but with work benches set into rows. A handful of adults, all wearing long white coats and goggles either pulled over their eyes or perched on their heads, were busy peering into microscopes, scribbling notes or, in the case of a tall, fair-haired man with his back to us, washing up in the sinks beneath the windows. It looked a bit like the chemistry classrooms in the secondary schools we'd gone to view for Maya a few years ago. I'd been younger at the time but I'd felt the same intrigue I was feeling now, the need to claw my way up onto one of those high stools, read what they were writing, understand what they could see in the vials of blue liquid and floating gases.

'Morning all, don't mind us – I'm just giving Bella here a mini tour,' Dr Blake announced. The scientists all looked up and most of them muttered greetings back to Dr Blake as they stared at me keenly, except the man at the back of the room who only glanced. It was enough for me to notice something odd about his face, a rippled blur stretching over his left eye, before he squared his back over the sink once again. I turned from him to the others, watching them carefully as Blake waffled about the fundamentals of chemistry never being forgotten here at the ARC no matter how removed they seemed from other, 'flashier' experiments.

'That's why I chose to have my office up here, among the more basic laboratories. It reminds me that one can never truly strive to achieve anything of worth if we forget our origins.'

'Ha! Is that Nietzsche?' One of the male scientists nearest us chuckled as he glanced over the top of his microscope at us. He was slightly older than the others, but he didn't look quite as old as my parents – his hair was thick and brown and his eyes didn't crease when he grinned from Blake to me.

'A Frederick Blake original, I'm afraid,' Blake smiled back at him. 'Though indeed, he who would learn to fly one day must first learn to stand and walk and run and climb and dance; one cannot fly into flying.'

'Don't say that too loudly downstairs, though,' one of the other men said and they all laughed. I took the opportunity to approach the man who'd been looking in the microscope.

'Can I see?' I peered up at him through my lashes and he was mine in an instant.

'Of course!' I let him lift me onto one of the stools and I knelt upon it, peering at the blobs and lines under the long lens as he showed me how to focus the image using the knobs. I half-listened as he explained earnestly about cells and microbes, sensing Dr Blake's scrutiny. I let the man carry on, now off on a tangent about his cat, listening hard as Blake was drawn into conversation with the two female scientists somewhere nearby.

'...one of the Subjects from the C-Project? I don't think I've seen her before...'

'No, no,' Blake's rumbling voice carried so easily to my ears, I wondered if he simply didn't care whether I heard him. 'Bella's actually one of our original genetic selection children from Project A. One of the last, as a matter of fact.'

'Really? Beauty, I presume...'

'Predominantly...'

'So what's the story? Why is she here?'

'She's staying with us... I'm monitoring her genetic properties – her natural parents unearthed a couple of anomalies, it seems...'

'What's Ana got to say about it all? She was at the forefront of the A-Project, wasn't she?'

'Oh, she's having a wonderful time... Did I mention

Bella's a keen ballerina? Ana's got the protégée she's always wanted… And her health has improved, I have to say. Her last scan showed the tumours have stopped growing and one or two seem to have shrunk since Bella's arrival… It's remarkable, actually…'

'Gosh, really?'

'That *is* incredible…'

I smiled at the man showing me his slides and thanked him. As he helped me down from the stool, I glanced over at the women who'd reacted to Blake's news about Ana. Both wore their hair long and feathered around their faces, the larger of the two wore thick, wire-rimmed glasses which made her eyes look bigger and bulgier as she exchanged a glance with the other behind Dr Blake's back as he launched into a discussion about some new equipment with one of the other male scientists. Despite their exclamations, I could tell that neither of them were thrilled about Ana's improvement. In fact, they looked worried.

The bespectacled one spotted me looking and her eyes immediately lost their beady, engorged look as she broke into a grin.

'Hey, Bella, is it?' I smiled back automatically and nodded. 'D'you want to see something really cool?'

'Yeah,' I said, coming over and taking her hand.

'Oh, what a little sweetheart,' the woman said, squeezing my hand. 'I hear you're quite the ballerina. I used to love dancing when I was little, too. Maybe you could show us some moves some time?'

I sensed the test.

'Maybe,' I shrugged. 'But I'd *really* like to see some of your science stuff. Ballet's just a hobby. I want to be a scientist when I'm older.'

They both laughed and, as they steered me over to a large, glass-fronted cabinet with various test tubes of different coloured liquids in it, I could sense Dr Blake's eyes on my back, his knowing nod as he rejoined his own conversation. I made all the right noises as the women introduced themselves and showed me how to pick up the test tubes using tongs, pouring one and then another of the strange mixtures into a beaker.

'Goggles.'

The voice was soft, almost a whisper, but insistent. I turned from the bubbling, shaving-foam-like substance which had just begun pouring out of the beaker. The tall man from the sink was hovering behind the female scientists and me, holding out a pair of goggles. Up close, I could see the strange rippling across his face was a large scar which undulated like flesh-coloured waves. He saw me looking and cringed, bobbing his head as he held out the goggles.

'Thanks, Robbie,' the woman nearest him, the blonder, slimmer of the two, who'd told me her name was Grace, held her hand out for them.

'She should wear them,' the scarred man said, his voice a little stronger, 'If you're showing her experiments. Even from behind a glass.'

He turned around and began to walk away. I stepped out from under the hand Grace had put on my shoulder to follow him.

'Robbie?'

He paused and looked around at me. I took his hand. He stared at it and at my hand within it as if he had never seen such a thing.

'Yes?'

'I'm Bella. Thank you for the goggles,' I smiled. Slowly,

lopsidedly, he smiled back. I opened my mouth to ask him more, but at that moment Blake's voice rang across the laboratory.

'Bella? Come on, kiddo, time to go,' Blake called from nearer than I realised. I gave Robbie's hand a squeeze and dropped it.

'Bye, Robbie! See you soon, I hope. Thank you, Melinda and Grace for showing me your work. And Bert, hope your cat gets better soon!'

They beamed, cuddled and waved me away as Blake lead me back into his adjoining room. Once the door was shut behind us, he stopped next to the dentist's chair and looked at me. I looked right back at him. The vial of my blood and its paperwork stood where he'd left it, between us.

'Did you enjoy meeting those scientists?'

'Yes.'

'Really?'

I frowned. 'I don't understand.'

'OK,' Blake looked away from me, at the blood on the tray. 'Let me try a different question. Do you know what the word classified means?'

I shrugged.

'It means secret. Everything we do here is classified. Those scientists we just met... when they started working here they all signed agreements saying they were not to speak of *anything* they do or see here to anyone. Even the most basic of experiments. If they do, they'll be asked to leave and never return.'

'OK...'

'And yet they showed you. Just like that. I was in the room and not one of them thought to check it was alright. They saw you and they all wanted to give you something.

They *needed* to... Oh, I'm not cross. I just wonder... What you do. Who is it for?'

'What?'

'Do you really want to be a scientist when you grow up?'

'Yes.'

'Are you just saying that because it's what you think I want to hear?'

'I... I don't–'

'Why did you approach Robbie? He was on his way back to the sinks, he'd given you the goggles, there was nothing more he could give you...'

'Because... he was sad. He thought his scars would scare me.'

'Did they?'

'No. Yes. A bit.'

'But you still approached him and took his hand... Why?'

'To make him happy?'

I was stumbling. Something had tripped me and I was trying to catch a foothold. Blake's eyes flashed from me to the books around us, to the scanner he'd used on my head, back to me. His questions came so fast I couldn't think.

'You do it to make others happy? Is that why you work so hard for Ana? Is that why you smiled and let Bert lift you onto a stool we both know you're more than capable of climbing onto yourself? Is that why you told Melinda and Grace you are more interested in science than ballet, so that they are happier? Or is it because you wanted them to like you?'

'Like me?'

'Is *that* what it's about? Like? Love? You charm people to make them love you? Because your mother couldn't?'

'No!'

'Why then? Why bother? Who are they to you? What do you care if they show you their experiments?'

'Because I wanted to see them! I want to know what they know! I want to know all of it.'

'Why?'

'So there isn't anything I don't know. Ever. I want it all in my head. All of it.'

'Knowledge. Knowledge is power. Knowledge *as* power. Is that it?'

'Yes!'

'And what about Robbie, Bella? What knowledge did he have?'

'What happened to his face?'

'Would you have asked him, if we'd stayed in there? Directly, just like that? Don't you think that might have put him off you a bit?'

I thought about it for a second.

'I would have got him to tell me. Somehow. I know how to get what I want.'

'And why did you want to know that?'

'So I can make sure it never happens to me.'

I watched him for the same reflexive spasm of disgust I'd seen cross my mother's face when she'd questioned my motives in the past. It didn't come. Instead he stared at me for a moment or two as if I were the most fascinating science experiment he'd ever come across before reaching into his pocket for a pad and a pencil and scribbling something.

'Interesting,' he said, carefully, looking back at the blood. 'But it's to be expected... Beauty is fleeting... extraordinary beauty demands an extraordinary degree of resilience... And burning, well...' He wasn't really talking to me, I could tell, but then he surprised me by putting his pencil down suddenly and flashing his piercing eyes back to me.

'It's not the first time the subject of burning has piqued your interest recently, is it, Bella?'

I kept my face stony and my shoulders square as a shudder rippled down the inside of my back. He was talking about Katie. I looked down. My hands, I realised, had clenched at my sides. I relaxed them. Robots didn't feel. Robots didn't get confused. They knew exactly who they were. Robots were robots.

'Perhaps that's enough for today,' Blake said, quietly, when he realised I wasn't going to answer.

'So will you fix me or not?' The words escaped before I could stop them. I looked at him and he smiled sadly, the same way he'd smiled earlier when I'd asked about fixing Ana. I wondered if he was going to give me the same spiel about them not being in the business of fixing people or whatever it was he'd said. But then he surprised me.

'You're safe here, you know, Bella. There's nothing you could say or do that would make us give up on you. You don't have to pretend or charm us or impress us... Ana, Ralph and I... We can be your family now. If you let us.'

I blinked, but I didn't move. Finally, he pushed himself away from the chair and picked up the small vial of my blood from the table. I looked up. He crossed the room in long, purposeful strides and threw the vial into a large, metal bin.

'See?'

He raised his empty hands, as if I were pointing a gun at him. I smiled and nodded, but as we left the office together, hand in hand, I noticed he picked up the notepad he'd scribbled in and slid it, swiftly, into his pocket.

**October, 2018**

*Sunday*

Ariana has imagined being kidnapped many times before. When she was younger the shadowed faces and the large, grabbing hands would invade her dreams, reaching for her, winding her in ropes that choked the screams in her throat and held her so tightly she couldn't breathe. She'd wake up sweating, often with the bedsheets wrapped tightly around her and she'd have a few moments of panic as she wrestled herself free. More recently, however, the imaginings had taken on a more whimsical tone. A tall, burly man would burst into her maths lesson with a knife, sling her over his shoulder and then drive off with her in one of those large, tank-like cars people drove in America. Or she'd be whisked off the pavement on the way home from school, plucked from her circle of friends and put into the back of – and again, a Hummer was the only vehicle that would really do here – leaving her friends shrieking and clutching one another in alarm by the side of the road.

In reality, it's nothing like that. She'd huffed away from Mum and stomped along the track leading away from the cottage, realising too late that she had no idea how to get down to the little beach Mum had mentioned. She'd trudged onwards until the road had widened into a junction and there she had looked around, wondering whether she should go back and try to find a way through the fields towards the coast or whether she should push on and try to find a different route. The last thing she wanted to do was come face to face with her mother – who surely would have come after her by now – and see the knowing, pitying look on her face. Hear her stupid, musical voice all slightly amused saying something like, 'Oh Ri, didn't you realise you can't get anywhere around here without me...'

'I *can*,' she'd muttered, taking the right fork and stepping into the long grass of the hedgerow lining the road. She'd only been walking about five minutes when the car pulled up next to her. It was a decidedly ordinary-looking SUV much like the one her mother – and all her friends' mothers for that matter – drove, except this one had tinted windows. The front passenger window glided down and a pretty young woman with blonde hair and bright red lipstick poked her head out.

'Hello! You look a little lost... Are you OK? Do you need a lift somewhere?'

Ariana glanced past the woman to the driver but whoever it was had their face in the shadows.

'I'm alright, thanks...'

'Are you sure?' The woman's voice had a sweet Irish lilt to it and she smiled with all of her face. She reminded Ariana of her old playgroup leader. 'There isn't much for miles around here... Where are you going?'

'Town...'

'Which one, Pethwick or Stokenway?'

'Erm... Pethwick.'

'Hop in,' the woman grinned, 'It'll take you ages to walk and the roads really aren't safe. We'll have you there in a jiffy.'

Ariana had known she shouldn't. She'd practically been able to hear Bella's voice screaming in her head: *This is the very thing I've always warned you about! Don't be so utterly stupid, Ariana!*

Then she'd shrugged. Her mother wasn't right about everything. She didn't *know* Ariana really, did she? She hadn't known about Conan. She hadn't suspected that for one moment Ariana might actually dare to think for herself and take the initiative. She was just bitter than she'd been trying to find a different parent – a *better* one, Ariana had thought sourly to herself, not bothering to really think about whether she actually meant it. Twelve and a half years old and she'd never even been allowed to host a sleepover. Was she meant to just live her life doing everything her mother wanted? Shrugging, she'd reached for the back door handle and, before her mother's voice could reach fever pitch in her ears, opened the door.

I allow myself a few minutes to splash water on my face, breathe deeply and calm the jittery nerves trembling all over my body. It's as if Lychen's words have snaked out of the screen and hissed into my veins, winding upwards and inwards, blackening everything in their path...

*Nothing is hurting you. Calm down. There's nothing there. Now is not the time for hysterics.*

The voice is right. I breathe and slowly the crushing blackness retreats. I resist the urge to strip and scrub my body under scalding water. There's no time.

It takes me less than ten minutes to gather all of my things and Ariana's into my holdall and her schoolbag, then I make my way downstairs. The others are clustered around Felix's computer and I feel a frisson of annoyance that they aren't all busily preparing to leave as well.

'There you are, Beast. Look at this. Felix tried to trace the number he texted from and look...'

The screen shows a map of Britain with red dots glowing all over it. Cardiff is alight, as is London, Nottingham, even the Isle of Skye way up in the corner.

'He's scattered the signal,' Felix says. 'I was right, he's got some real smart-arses working for him. And that photo he sent doesn't give anything away either...'

'OK... Well that's hardly unexpected, is it?' I say, sharply. 'Besides, we know where we need to go...'

'We know where he *wants* us to go. Bella, are you really so keen to just follow what he says, go where he leads you?'

'He has my daughter. What am I supposed to do?'

'Let's just think about it, first.'

*He's right, you know. You weren't so frantic an hour ago when he had her.*

That was before I saw her slumped in that car seat. Before he spoke to me. Before I felt him...

'You think,' I turn away and grab my handbag from the countertop. 'I'm going.'

'Bella...'

'Beast, listen...'

'No, *you* listen! You've had, what, a few days of the fatherhood experience? You haven't even *met* Ariana!'

'And whose fault is that?' He's in front of me now, irises blazing whirls bulging out of the whites. I glare back at him.

'You have *no idea* what he's capable of, Ralph. If you did, you would have been out that door the minute you saw that photo–'

'Look, I'm just as keen to get Ariana back as you are,

but do you really think he'd hurt her?'

'*Yes!* If he chose to! Without giving it a second thought!'

'Can we just wait a moment and see if we can come up with–'

I make to push past him and he grabs onto my arms.

'Let go of me,' I say calmly, even as the recent panic threatens to cloud me into a blind rage. I look him directly in the eyes and say it again and this time, I do it the way I know best.

'Let go. Of me.'

He lets go and steps aside, his eyes glazed.

'Ralph?' Felix gets to her feet as Ethan sidesteps me to block the doorway. I raise my eyes to his and he wavers, off-balance... He's about five times my size but I know I'd be able to floor him with a flicker of my fingernail within the next ten seconds if I wanted. I reach into my handbag and feel the soft, cool leather of the knife's sheath...

'Listen, let's all go,' Felix says quickly from behind me, careful not to look me in the eye as I glance back at her. 'It's far enough to Cumbria, there's plenty of time for us to put our heads together on the way.'

'Fine,' I say, unclenching my fist from around the knife and letting it drop back inside my bag. 'But I'm taking *my* car, and I'm leaving in the next five minutes. So I suggest anyone who wants to come with me gets a move on.'

**October, 2018**

*Sunday*

It is Felix and Dominic who opt to come with me in the end. Dominic claims it's for the leg room, Felix doesn't bother pretending it's for any reason other than keeping an eye on me. She tries her best to keep up her silent, cat's bum face, even when Dominic falls asleep slumped across the X5's spacious back seats with his mouth open and a long line of saliva dangling ever lower over the upholstery. But I break her. It's a long way to Cumbria and I've endured enough moody silences recently. Besides, although it's only been two days since I left Flintworth I can feel the lack of adult conversation like a leech on my brain.

'So how're things at the ARC these days? You mentioned something about money being a little tight?'

Felix sniffs and looks determinedly out of the window. She reminds me so forcibly of a stroppy child just then that I have to bite the inside of my cheeks to stop a wild desire to laugh. Instead, I watch the road and slide the BMW up a gear as we join a dual carriageway. I feel so much lighter now I'm *doing* something – now that I can physically watch the miles ticking down between Ariana and me... The worry is still there, of course – it lurks in the back of my mind like a murmuring shadow, giving voice to all the terrible things

151

that might happen, might *be happening* to her – but the crushing asphyxiation of panic I felt back at the cottage has gone. I can breathe, at least.

'I suppose a lot of the scientists I knew have moved on now... Is Melinda still there? Or Robbie?'

Felix sniffs again, but after a few moments she replies, gruffly, 'No. Both of them left around the same time you did. Lychen took them with him. He took all the good ones after the inquiry. Blake didn't have a leg to stand on after what happened to Rudy...'

'Really? Both of them? Melinda... yeah, I guess I can see that. She always was ruthlessly ambitious.'

Felix snorts derisively and I ignore it. 'But Robbie? I thought he'd be working at the ARC until he was as old as Dr Blake!'

'He didn't want to leave. A lot of them didn't,' Felix's voice has crept into bitterness, though this time it's not all because of me. 'Lychen's terms were along the lines of *Come with me now or go on my hit list*.'

'I'm surprised he didn't try to poach *you*...'

I keep my eyes carefully on the road in front of me as Felix glances my way. I don't need to see her to know she's scanning my words for sarcasm. Her voice when she answers is still brusque, but minutely more friendly than before.

'He did. A few times. It's been about five years since the last time, though. I think he gave up after I told him he and his bloody robots didn't scare me.'

'Robots?'

'Not actual robots. It's what we call his lackeys – he calls them *The Guard*. His own, personal Project D. They're like a mixture of soldiers and bodyguards. I don't know where he recruited them or what he did to them to make them the way they are, but looking at them is like looking at a dead body with its eyes open. It's like he's scooped all the humanity, the spirit, the *everything* out of them and replaced it with muscles and undying obedience. Ethan saw one of them walk clean off a fifty-storey building once, just because Lychen forgot to tell him to stop.'

'Really? Wow...' The image of an expressionless man stepping into certain death mixes with a memory of heady enclosure, clasping hands, a fist clenched in my hair... For a moment I see Lychen's face hovering in front of me, thin lips flecked with wine and a dull gleam in his eyes as he tells me about his plans to take the research further. *Project D takes it all to the next level. It marries genetically-enhanced ability with fundamental reliability... an entire generation of perfect, unblemished soldiers...* I blink several times and shudder until the memory of the conversation and all that came afterwards has gone. Though she isn't looking my way, Felix gives an echoing shiver beside me, as if I've shaken the horror out of my head and onto her.

'It was a lie,' she mutters, quietly. 'Of course I'm scared of him.'

'We all are,' I reply, softly. Then, before she can turn and say something acidic, I quickly steer the conversation back:

'What about old Bert? He was at the older end of the younger scientists back when I was a kid. He must be, what, fifty odd now? He was such a sweetheart when I was little, always showing me what he was working on whether I wanted to know or not! Don't tell me he's gone too?'

'Nah,' Felix is actually smiling now. 'Bertie's still there. And his cats. He's got six of them in his room at the Manor...'

'He lives at the Manor?'

'We all do, now there's so few of us. It's got the space... And it's safer...'

I frown.

'What does Ramona think of that?'

'Who?'

'Ramona? The Blakes' housekeeper?'

'Never heard of her... but I'd be surprised if Blake could afford a gardener these days let alone a housekeeper... What little he does have gets ploughed straight into the ARC. It doesn't run cheap...'

I think about the ARC I grew up visiting, with its shining marble surfaces and glittering chandeliers. I try to picture the Manor full of life, with Bert's cats running underfoot and lively academic discussion ringing across the large dining table and down the flagstoned corridors. I wonder who sleeps in my old room.

'So go on then, ask me. I'm sure you're dying to know, even without Lychen's shit-stirring...' Felix cuts into my daydream with her usual bluntness.

'What's that?'

'Why we were tracking you, of course!'

'Oh... I assumed you'd kept tabs on everyone who knew the truth about the whole Rudy scandal... I knew that if Ralph ever found out about Ariana he'd be after contact... I suppose I thought that if Lychen's people had been able to work out I had a child, you would too...'

I glance at her just long enough to catch her scowl.

'Ah. So when *did* you find out about her?'

'When we went to your flat and saw the photos.'

*I warned you about those photos, Bella. Especially the one on the swing. You should have burned it the minute it dropped through your door.*

It is becoming abundantly clear that there are a million

things I should have done differently.

'Go on then,' I say, quickly, before the voice can pipe up with examples. 'Why were you looking for me, if it wasn't about Ariana?'

'He didn't try for a while, you know. When you left, Dr Blake told us to leave you alone, let you do your thing... It almost destroyed Ralph. Not that he ever talked to me about it... But it all changed a few years ago. That's when Blake came to me and said we had to find you...'

She pauses again and squirms uncomfortably. From the back-seat Dominic gives a loud snort and shuffles jerkily against the seat. I glance at Felix impatiently.

'Why, if he didn't know about Ri? What could he possibly have wanted from me after all those years?'

'Your blood. Well, more specifically, your genes.'

'Project A?' The words sound almost alien. I haven't thought about them in so long.

'Yeah. The other Subjects... well... I don't know how much you've heard through the grapevine or if you've kept up with the journals. A few of them ran the story...'

I realise, like a sudden blow to the head, why she's acting so awkwardly.

'My brother and sister? I know Silas died a few years ago... His heart, wasn't it?'

'Yes, he had a sudden attack in the middle of a race. Dead before he hit the ground. Sorry...'

'I hadn't seen him since I was nine. I barely remember him. What about Maya? We kept in touch sporadically over the years, after I left Cumbria. Never about anything particularly meaningful but I was thinking of taking Ri to go and meet her after Cornwall...'

'She died two weeks ago. She had a brain tumour. She didn't tell you she was ill?'

It hits me with a strange, twisting wrench somewhere in my throat. Far stronger than the dull little ache I'd felt when I'd read about Silas's death some years ago. Felix looks away solicitously and I clear my throat.

'We didn't talk about the heavy things. Except Silas, when he died. Mostly she would tell me little snippets about her life in North Devon. Her partner. Her dogs. I didn't tell her about Ariana. She occasionally mentioned our parents.'

'Well, they're both still alive from what I know...'

'I don't want to hear about them,' I say, more sharply than intended. My voice cuts through the car and even I feel like shivering from its iciness. Dominic's snores stop with a grunt, though I don't bother glancing back to see if he's woken up. Next to me Felix shrugs.

'What about the others from Project A?' I say, bringing my voice back to a slightly more normal tone with effort.

'Dead or dying,' Felix says quietly. 'It seems to happen in the early to mid-thirties... Some without warning, like your brother. Some have slow-growing cancers like Maya... The interesting thing is that their ailments are all linked to their selective abilities... The athletes have heart attacks, the super-intelligent get aneurysms, brain tumours and Alzheimers. Jessie Williers – incredible mathematician, you can look her up on YouTube giving these amazing demonstrations where she performs impossible calculations on the spot – she ended up in a nursing home at the grand old age of thirty-four. Died last month not knowing her own name.'

'I see. So all this cloak and dagger, chasing my daughter and me halfway across the country, tapping my phone and God knows what else... I'm supposed to believe this is all out of *concern* for my health?'

'Blake wants you to come in for testing. You're the last Subject from Project A who seems, to all intents and purposes, to be healthy.'

'Subject. That's what we called the Project C kids...'

'You're not just one of the Subjects now, you're Subject A.'

'Subject A.'

'That's right.'

I try not to think about it, but still the hidden malignancies wind themselves through my imagination, blistering my face, clouding my eyes, choking my voice...

'Tell me about Maya... I assume Blake brought her in when he started to have cause to worry.'

'Yes... He was able to detect her cancer before she was symptomatic... But unfortunately it was too aggressive for chemotherapy and radiation to buy her more than a few extra months.'

'We hadn't been in touch for a while... She... Well, to be honest she began to suspect I had a child. I must have said something incriminating... So I cut her off. She kept trying for a while, but I never replied. Eventually she left me alone a year or so ago.'

'Blake wanted her to contact you when she became ill. Told her time and time again that she should try and reconnect with you while she had the chance. I don't even think he knew that she had been in touch at all since you left the family... But she always refused. I think she thought you deserved your own privacy, after all this time... Even if it meant you didn't know you could be ill... I don't know, I never really got it...'

'I think I do,' I say, softly. My sister, the daughter my parents chose, giving me one last chance to be free for as long as I possibly could be.

'Anyway, it hardly matters now. Blake's got bigger things to worry about if you ask me...'

'Bigger than the whole benchmark of his academic career crumbling around him?'

'Yeah. The benchmarks' families. You remember who signed up for Project A? There were about twenty families, all of them filthy rich. They're not best pleased that their kids, brothers, sisters, et cetera are dropping dead after only thirty-odd years of excellence...'

'They're suing him?'

'Well, they all signed waivers back in the day saying that they agreed that it was all experimental, risks of all sorts, and so forth... But you know lawyers. They're slimy bastards. Only took one of them to find a loophole and it's looking like they've all got a case...'

'Wow...'

'Yeah. So that's another reason Blake needs you. If you can show them all you're healthy and not in danger of dropping down dead anytime soon...'

'They no longer have a case against him?'

'It's impaired somewhat...'

'Right. But we don't know I'm healthy, do we?'

'Well, that's what we were hoping to find out, before Lychen waded in...'

'So what's *he* after...'

'I have no idea. Though from those messages he sent, it sounds very much like he thinks *you* do.'

She stares at me. I keep my eyes on the road. And the silence slowly sifts back into the air around us.

**October, 2018**

*Sunday*

Ariana doesn't like the man with the shadowy face. She can see him more clearly from inside the car, but even though his face dips in and out of the light as the sun streams through the window, the only way to describe it is shadowy. And creepy. He doesn't look at her. He doesn't look at the blonde woman, who keeps her head bent over her phone, her thumbs a flurry of activity. He just looks at the road. His face doesn't change, even when a lorry swerves in front of them and the woman swears loudly, gripping the door handle next to her. Ariana no longer thinks she reminds her of her old playgroup leader.

'We aren't going to Pethwick, are we?' Ariana says, trying not to let the rising fear into her voice. She tries to tell herself that this is what she had always known might happen. That she is having an adventure. That she is sure these people won't hurt her; they're after Mum really, after all. Aren't they?

'I'm sorry, Ariana...' The pretty woman turns around and she really does look sorry. Sorry the same way Mum did when she told Ariana that they *were* going to Pizza Hut for dinner, but that they were also going to the dentist first.

'You know my name. What's yours?' Ariana asks. She

won't show them she is scared. She won't show them anything. She looks out of the darkened window and tries very hard not to think about the shadowy man in the front seat or the dark figure with the spectral fingers from her nightmares. Instead she focuses on her mother. Not the warm, soft figure who curls up with her on the sofa to squirm through celebrities eating cockroaches on ITV, but the hard-faced silhouette in her bedroom doorway, barking at her to tidy up. The cold-voiced replier to her pestering about Instagram and sleepovers and going into town with her friends. The glittery-eyed author of her nightmares. *She* wouldn't show them any fear. She isn't scared of anything. And neither is Ariana.

'Tess,' the woman says, after thinking about it.

'Tess… Where are you taking me?'

'To a small facility just outside York.'

The woman doesn't turn around, but she glances at her in the mirror for a few seconds before turning back to her phone.

'What sort of facility?'

'Classified,' the man snaps in a metallic-sounding monotone, making Ariana jump. She glances at the woman and sees her looking at the man the same way she, herself, is feeling. Ariana settles back into the seat, considering this. *This man is dangerous. But I don't think the woman is. She could be an ally. Engage her. Make her like you.* She shifts in her seat so she faces Tess fully and the man's shape blurs into an indistinct dark blob at the edge of her eyeline.

'I've never been to York. I don't think I've been anywhere north of Norfolk. We went there on holiday once. It was nice.'

Tess glances at the man and then back in the mirror, at Ariana. Her thumbs hesitate above the glowing screen of her phone. Ariana meets her gaze, stretching her eyes as wide as they can go.

'Just you and your mum, was it?'

'Yes. It's always been just us. But I'm guessing you probably knew that, right?'

'No grandparents, aunts or uncles?'

'No...' She thinks about the sister her mother mentioned yesterday. Aunt Maya. She wonders if she will ever meet her. Whether she would prefer being called aunt or auntie. Maybe she has kids. Maybe Ariana has cousins.

'I grew up with just a mum too,' Tess says, softly. 'It wasn't so bad. It was a bit like living with my best friend some of the time... Except when she was nagging me to load the dishwasher...'

'Or tidy your room?'

'Or pick up my books from the living room floor. Is your mum strict?'

'Yes,' Ariana says automatically. 'Sometimes,' she adds, after a moment's thought.

'My mum was *really* strict. Especially when I got to your age. She wouldn't let me go anywhere on my own or even with my friends. Said it wasn't safe. Didn't trust me at all, you know?'

'Mmm...'

'I don't think it's good,' Tess leans back in her chair and looks out of the window. Ariana can see her red-lipped reflection staring without seeing, her eyes half closed. 'Not trusting your child, I mean. Once they're old enough to be trusted at least a little bit... It just means they rebel more, for the sake of it. But you understand that, don't you, *Les Yeux Vertes*?'

Ariana opens her mouth to ask how she knows her Twitter handle. Then she thinks about it. She remembers

161

her mother's rage from earlier. The way she'd gone white and sat down so suddenly on the coffee table. Her own, all-over fury which had felt like a storm raging through her limbs, longing to beat, rip, push... Bella flying backwards from her. She hadn't even watched her hit the ground. Hadn't bothered to hang around long enough to see if she'd really hurt her. *Mum*.

'Were you Conan68, then?'

Tess smiles a little, lazily. She keeps looking out of the window. Ariana reaches under the sudden well of sadness which has reared up inside her and grasps for the remnants of that blinding fury. *Feel that instead.* She lets it swell inside her. Of course Tess doesn't bother answering. She has all the power. *But she won't always. We can break her and we will. We aren't afraid. We aren't.*

**Winter, 1995**

Soon it began to feel as if I had been living in Cumbria with the Blakes my whole life. I teased Ralph as if he were my own brother, kicking him under the dinner table when he stole pork chops from my plate, pulling grotesque faces during morning lessons when Dr Blake's back was turned. It was less easy to think of the grown-ups as parents. To me, Dr Blake would never be anything other than Dr Blake – tall with the glasses that flashed when they caught the light and the clinical, interested way he sometimes looked at me. And those questions, the insistent, yearning way he'd interrogated me back in his office at the ARC, they often lurked beneath the scour of his gaze. Still, most of the time he was just... nice. He praised me when I did well in my lessons, he winked when Ramona or Ana were grumpy, he saved my favourite red sweets for me from the jar in his office. He didn't exactly look at me the same way I sometimes caught him looking at Ralph – proud and always as if astonished by how much so – but he was someone I came to trust.

Ana remained a puzzle, and yet it was with her I became closest. We spent so much time together in the ballet studio, her hands swift to correct me, her voice whippet quick between delight and harsh discipline. And sometimes she'd grab for me as if she could resist no longer. Sometimes she stroked my hair and told me to call her Mamma like Ralph did. Other times I'd be treated to the rib-crushing death-grip. I'd learned it was best not to struggle. The one time I did she slapped me so hard I fell heavily to the floor. Besides, she always let go eventually. My lungs would begin to cry within my chest, my heart would frenzy in my ears and I could feel the darkness seeping into the corners of my mind and then that's when she'd release me.

Sometimes she cried afterwards, long dripping sobs into my hair as she curled around me, all softness, saying she was sorry, she just loved me. And, weird as it might sound, I loved her too. I loved her for the wildness in her eyes when she danced. The fiery depth of her laugh when Ralph said something funny at the dinner table. The glint of adultness when she looked at Blake under her lashes and called him Freddie. The way she couldn't help but flutter a hand along my hair, down my arm, a pat on my shoulder, a finger on my cheek as I passed her by. I loved her because she seemed to exist on a different plane to everyone else, a position where everyone forgave her what she did because she was ill; because she was beautiful; because she was Ana Blake. I never felt the burning urge to punish her for hurting me, like I did with others. Ralph, who'd been pinched until his eyes watered after he'd made me look stupid in front of Blake. Ramona who had found her favourite new frying pan scratched heavily across the base after hissing at me in the corridor.

Blake never mentioned testing me again after that first day at the ARC. I didn't expect to be allowed back there, but to my surprise he began taking me and Ralph across the field to the large, shining building once every two weeks or so. Looking back, I'm sure it was more to do with giving Ana a quiet day to herself in the Manor than anything else, but at the time we couldn't help but feel swollen with our own importance as we followed him past the front desk and into the lifts below the crystal chandelier. Once upstairs we'd usually be given some small jobs to do – cleaning equipment, copying down meaningless-sounding data, listening to one of the PhD students practising a lecture they were to give at some university we'd never heard of. We saw the scientists from time to time and though Ralph often held back shyly, I always took them up on the offer when they asked if I wanted to see what they were working on that day.

'You're such a show off,' Ralph spat at me one day as we made our way back through the trees towards the Manor at dinner time. It was already dark, the year creeping towards its end, and we were both well wrapped up against the freezing air. Blake wasn't with us; he'd been preparing to leave with us when a white-coated man I'd never seen before had burst into his office and said there was an issue with one of the C-Subjects. It was of this I was thinking as I trudged along next to Ralph, so his insult didn't filter through my wool-covered ears immediately.

'What?' I glanced at him. What little of his face I could see over the top of his tartan scarf was pink and his glasses were beginning to steam at the edges. He pulled them down a little.

'You, with those scientists up at Dad's... You're all, Oh yes, Robbie, I'd love to see your mice. And when I grow up, I want to be just like you, Grace. You're such a cool role model. It's gross and embarrassing.'

'*You're* gross and embarrassing,' I muttered, though I couldn't help the ugly rash of shame flaming across my cheeks. His silly, high-pitched impression of me sounded eerily accurate, even to my own ears. I cringed into the powder pink snood Ana had given me only that morning.

'Anyway, at least I'm taking an interest. You're meant to be the next generation of scientific brilliance or whatever around here, aren't you? And yet you can't even mumble two words to that lot...' I muttered, feeling the power in my voice cool the embarrassment on my face. He frowned as my words cut him and I felt a vicious triumph swarm deep in my chest.

'I have nothing to prove to *them*,' he muttered. 'I'd rather be quiet than a silly little nuisance any day. They probably feel sorry for you, you're such an airhead they can't possibly think you've got a hope of growing up to be anything like them.'

'Are you *jealous*? Is that it?'

'*No!*' He stopped walking, and when I turned, I realised he was breathing heavily, as if trying hard to keep control of himself. As if I were mere shades away from being thumped.

'So what is it then? Why've you got such a problem with me talking to them? It doesn't affect you...'

'It's... You're just so... You don't *know*, OK? You let them show you all their little dinky experiments and you don't even know what they're *for...* what they're all actually *doing* back there...'

'Oh, and you do?'

'Yeah, actually.' He looked straight at me and I felt a weird coldness bloom in my chest where the rage had swarmed just moments before.

'What? What are they doing?'

He glanced behind us at the ARC, almost invisible now in the near-total darkness save for the smear of lights blurring down the oily-black walls. He began walking again as if worried the building might be listening, his head down. I jogged to catch up. His stride was almost twice my own; in the short months I'd known him he'd already grown several inches.

'Come on, you can't say all that and then not tell me. Ralphie!'

'Alright, just… Just keep your voice down. And don't call me Ralphie. You know only Mamma calls me that.'

'Not true. I've heard Ramona call you it too. That makes it practically a nickname, right?'

'Listen, do you want to hear this or not?'

'Yes!'

'Shut up then, Beast.'

We were at the edge of the trees by this point, with only the path leading up through the overgrown field and beyond, just an indistinct shape in the darkness, the gate leading into the back garden of the Manor. I could see the great house lurching over the top of the hill, the windows glowing merrily in the darkness. I thought of the warm fire burning in Blake's study, where Ralph and I usually went after dinner to play board games or read. I thought of the large tureen of butternut squash soup Ramona would be getting ready to serve for dinner. Even her sly glances and not-so-accidental jog of my chair as she passed seemed inviting. I didn't know if I was just cold or if I could sense something else about what Ralph was about to tell me, but suddenly I just wanted to walk away. I didn't want to hear what he was going to say, I only wanted to run up to that house where it was warm and safe and familiar. But he was already talking.

'You know the guy who came in when we were leaving and was blurting all that stuff about Project C and one of the Subjects having trouble and stuff?'

'Yeah...'

'And Dad looked really twitchy and uncomfortable when he told us to get going without him?'

I hadn't noticed that, but I nodded anyway.

'Has he told you anything about Project C?'

I thought back to the afternoon he'd first brought me to the ARC. I'd heard something about Project C then, I was sure of it, but I couldn't remember. I frowned.

'I don't think so... I know I'm part of Project A...'

'The genetic selection programme, yeah yeah we *all* know about that. That was shut down years ago, anyway. Everyone knows it was all a load of rubbish in the end, just rich idiots wanting designer babies...'

I scowled at him.

'Anyway, after Project A came Project B. I don't know much about that. No one does. Just that it was short-lived and quickly got shut down in favour of Project C. Which is what they're still working on now... So Project A looked at manipulating the genes of humans before they're born, right? Project C is different in that it deals with the manipulation of human traits in otherwise normal children. Or *Subjects* as they call them...'

'You mean they've got kids in there?' I turned back to the ARC in surprise, remembering, with a crash, the thing that one of the scientists had asked Dr Blake about me on my first day there. *One of the Subjects from the C-Project?*

'Yep, about twenty or so at the moment. They live there, though. That's why there are people there all the time, all night and all day. They have nannies and stuff looking after them. But during the day, the scientists use them in their experiments...'

I had a sudden image of a small girl being tied down in the dentist's chair in Blake's office while Melinda and Bert hovered over her with a needle. *Don't worry, you're not the smallest person we've had take a ride.*

'What sort of experiments?'

'Well I don't know all the details. I just know what I've been able to read and overhear and stuff... But from what I gather, it's about increasing their potential... Taking natural talents and making them extreme... Like there's this one boy who's really good with numbers and codes. They're trying to make him able to control a computer *with his mind.*'

'You're kidding!'

'It's true. I read some of the planning for it. And I saw the boy's head scans.'

'Did Blake show you all this?'

Ralph looked down suddenly and I didn't need him to reply to know the answer to that question.

'No. He has no idea I know so much. If he did, he'd probably stop taking me over there... And I can't stop. Not now. I need to know more...'

There was a weird light in his eyes. It didn't seem to be coming from the yellow glow stretching from the Manor, or the cold lights of the ARC spotting through the trees behind us. It seemed to come from somewhere inside him and it arched through his glasses right at me.

'Why? What's it to you?'

'Well, it's *wrong.* They're using kids like guinea pigs, Beast. You know they're only little? The oldest one is like four or five. They're just babies. It's not right...'

'But they didn't *steal* them or anything?'

'No, they're all orphans, I think. The files I saw said they were anyway. All formally adopted by the ARC or they all had the permission of the parents... Though I don't know why anyone would do that to their kid...'

'Well, maybe they wanted their kid to have a chance to be something amazing. Like a superhero or something...'

Ralph stared at me as if he'd never seen me before.

'I should have known you wouldn't understand...' He said, flatly, before turning around and beginning to walk up the slope towards the house.

'Wait! I don't mean that it's *right*... But I can see why they're doing it... Your dad even said, when he was showing me the ARC, that they were trying to do more than just cure diseases and stuff, they were trying to get rid of them completely. Maybe that's what he meant – by making kids who won't ever get ill!'

'But they don't know what they're doing! They don't know what the long-term effects of what they're doing are! They're not like you lot in Project A – they won't be just good at sports or really clever or stupidly beautiful or anything like that. They're making them freaks. Like the X-Men in my comics. Mutants. And these kids have no idea! They can't exactly consent to it, can they? It's not *right!*'

He stomped on ahead of me, his face lowered so I could no longer see it.

'What are you going to do then, let them all out? Set them free in the mountains and snow?'

'Don't be stupid.'

'Can't help it. I'm *stupidly beautiful* after all.'

'I *will* hit you,' Ralph stopped and raised his fist, but we both knew he'd never land the blow. Still, I could hear his teeth grinding in the darkness and I dropped the annoying grin from my face.

'Well, what *are* you going to do, then?'

'I don't know.' He glared from me to the space behind me where the ARC lurked like a nightmare. Then he turned, angrily, and walked away. I waited a moment, wanting to ask why he'd told me, if he didn't have a plan. I knew he wanted my help. I wasn't stupid. I knew that's why he'd been watching me in the lab with the grown-ups, his expression veering between disgust and intrigue. I knew that was partly why he'd told me. I wondered why else, though. What else was locked in that tall, skinny frame which even now shook with irregular shudders as if it the surge of feelings within it couldn't stay contained?

'I won't tell anyone,' I muttered, my voice low, as he held the gate for me at the bottom of the garden.

'Of course you won't,' he grunted back. 'You want to keep going back there as much as I do.'

It was true, of course. No matter how much it lurked in my dreams and leered blackly as I walked towards it even on the brightest of days, the ARC had become everything Ana had warned me it was back on my first morning with the Blakes. It was the centre of it all. Everything I came from and everything I would become.

**October, 2018**

*Sunday*

As the BMW sails smoothly through Avon and up into the West Midlands, Felix finds herself being lulled in and out of a shallow sleep. Dominic has turned into the window and stopped snoring; Bella is silent as she glances in the mirrors and occasionally changes gears with quick, precise movements; the radio is a dull, soporific buzz. Felix tries not to sleep, tries to gather her exhausted brain into focus, she knows she should be making the most of this time alone with Bella before Lychen interferes again, try and gather evidence that might, in some way, be useful to Dr Blake. But right now she can't think of anything beyond the bland, simple facts.

Bella is still as beautiful, graceful and beguiling as ever, that much has been clear from the moment they'd turned to see her sitting on that bench by the coastal path. That she can still manipulate people into doing what she wants remains a question, though Felix remembers the way she swept Ralph so neatly aside when he stood between her and the front door back at the cottage, the cold focus of her gaze as she'd turned it to Ethan. Yes, Felix is willing to bet that particular *gift* of Bella's is still very much intact as well, if not more powerful than ever… But then, Silas

D'accourt remained an incredible athlete until the moment he dropped dead. Her eyelids slide irresistibly lower. An image swims into her head of Bella bent suddenly double, hands over her face, straightening up to reveal boils, rashes and blemishes. Her hands peel into misshapen claws as she puts them to her head and feels her hair fall away in long, curling tendrils…

Felix turns into the squashier side of the passenger seat and smiles a little as the sleep she's been trying so hard to resist swarms over her all at once. I glance into the rear-view mirror and, to my surprise, meet Dominic's clear, grey gaze.

'When did you wake up?' I murmur softly. He flushes instantly. This is going to be so easy.

'I've been kind of drifting in and out for an hour or so,' he mutters, gazing nervously at the front passenger seat.

'She's out,' I reply. 'Seems like none of you have been getting much sleep recently.'

'No, we haven't,' he replies, glancing out of the window, back at Felix, down into his lap and then, as if he can't help it, back at me.

'Do you remember the first time we met, Dom?' I keep my voice insouciant, my gaze flickering between him and the road. He swallows heavily.

'Not really… I was only a little kid. I sort of remember you and Ralph as kids, though you both seemed so grown up to me… But I don't really remember the first time I met you both…'

'It was only briefly. Back then Ralph and I weren't supposed to know about you Project C kids… We were only kids ourselves, but we didn't think of ourselves that way of course. We were learning under the Blakes themselves, coming to the ARC to *observe* the grown-up scientists... We were extremely carried away by our own cleverness. When Ralph told me about Project C, he couldn't understand why I didn't immediately agree with him that it was an awful thing... I think he had all these grand ideas of rescuing you all and alerting the authorities... Of course it was probably all textbook early teenage rebellion with a smattering of Freudian father-son angst... But at the time... He was pretty passionate about it all.'

Dominic nods, his eyes unfocused as I draw him deeper into the past.

'He used to tell us stories...' he murmurs. 'When he came to visit us... They were always about kids escaping from evil step-parents and gaining freedom and stuff... I didn't really pay a lot of attention, I just wanted to listen to him, do what he did, make him like me...' He blushes. 'I was only little and he was this amazing older boy who seemed to know everything about everything...'

'Of course. He was twelve, thirteen. You were what, four or five?'

'Something like that, yeah.'

We lapse into silence as we both remember the years which followed. Ralph's vicious arguments with his father, the arrival of new, focused scientists and tutors specialising in developing the talents of the Project C Subjects, including Felix and Ethan. And Lychen.

'I was almost scared of you when we first met,' I lie, coyly, teasing the grin across his face. 'You were unlike anything I'd ever known... I was used to my brother running as fast as an Olympic athlete at fifteen and my sister doing A-level papers at twelve, but you... You were this skinny little slip of a kid, with these scraggly little legs poking out of your baggy shorts...'

'I hated those stupid shorts they made us wear. They never fit me.'

'Then you'd open your mouth and start reeling off all these impossible calculations and figures. Then there was the time Blake brought his laptop into the rec room where you were playing and you just stared at it until it started to smoke... I thought he was going to go mad...'

'So did I,' Dom smiles ruefully at his big hands. 'I remember you squealing,' he adds, peering at me with more than a hint of that bashfully quirky little boy in his gaze.

'I did not *squeal,*' I reply, going for mock-indignity. 'I merely alerted my mentor to the smoke coming out of what was a brand new, state-of-the-art piece of equipment...'

'Yeah, by making a noise like some sort of demented gerbil...'

We both chuckle. I blink and remember the room with the looming dark walls juxtaposed with Disney posters and the cheerful polka dot carpet where small piles of toys were scattered. The acrid smell wafting through the air from the desk behind the grown ups' backs, the tiny tendrils of smoke. I had thought about letting it burn. I had looked at little Dominic standing alone, out of their eyesight, staring fixedly at the square, bulky machine. I had wondered how useful his allegiance might be. And that's when I'd decided to point and shriek.

'He didn't even tell me off,' Dominic says, shaking his head at the high-rises and squat factories of Birmingham in the distance. 'He looked his laptop over, and when he couldn't turn it on, he just laughed and ruffled my hair... I didn't think about it at the time, but that laptop must have been expensive… Specially in those days.'

There's a pause, then I bring us gently to the point of all of this.

'When did it leave you?' I ask quietly, holding his gaze in the rear-view mirror so long he gasps as a lorry brakes suddenly in front of us. I look back at the road and slide easily into the right lane.

'How did you–'

'I suspected. The problems with the C-kids were well-established long before I left the ARC. And the ground breaking, glorious headlines Blake and Lychen foresaw never transpired in the years that followed… Putting that with what Felix said about the lack of funding and general decline at the ARC, I figured that the breakthrough he'd been searching for all those years hadn't been discovered…'

'No… It wasn't.'

'But I remember you at the presentation,' I say, softly, one part of my attention on the sleeping woman next to me. 'You were phenomenal. One of the crowning performances. The way you conducted those machines and the lasers. I can still see it when I shut my eyes, even now… And you were what, fourteen?'

'Fifteen…'

'So it wasn't the onset of puberty like it was with so many of them…'

'No… But…' He glances at Felix, clearly troubled.

'Come on, Dom… It's all water under the bridge now. We're on the same side, aren't we? You and I most of all. I'm a Subject too, remember? The others can never quite understand the same way we do… We were at the heart of everything, after all…'

'Well…' I draw his gaze back at me. This would be

much faster if I didn't have to keep breaking eye contact, but fortunately he's not a difficult individual to control. He's mine with the next glance.

'I think that was my peak. Or perhaps a year or two before, I don't know... I remember those rehearsals being the toughest thing I'd ever done, and the performance itself... Well, I wasn't really a natural on stage, which is why they had me mainly facing away from the audience. I knew I wasn't one of the really *amazing* talents – it's not like I was flying or lifting ten times my body weight or vanishing into thin air... There wasn't so much pressure on me, which helped... And my part did go quite well in the end...'

'You were wonderful.'

'Well. I don't know. No one really talked about it afterwards. Not after what happened to Rudy... I think it was that that got to me, in the end. With the aftermath, people leaving... And everything blowing up between Blake and Lychen... I dunno, Felix says it sapped my confidence. I just remember thinking about things differently. I couldn't help but question why things had happened the way they did. And once I did that... I stopped being able to feel the machines the way I had. I stopped understanding so much. It was like I'd been able to speak a language fluently one day and the next, only mostly... And as it went on, more of the nuances and rules of the language would leave me... Until eventually all I could get out were one or two words.'

'And then what happened?'

'Felix persuaded Dr Blake to keep me on as her apprentice. She's been teaching me all she knows... coding, hacking, tracking and so forth. She's pretty amazing, really.'

'What about the other C-kids?'

'A lot of them weren't as lucky as me... Some went into care or stayed on at the ARC in menial jobs until they were old enough to leave. Blake didn't so much turn them away, but it was clear they were no longer *wanted*. And the worst cases... they turned inward. Then there was nothing anyone could do for them.'

'Did *any* of them retain their abilities into adulthood? What about Daniel? Verity? Nova?'

He shrugs, squirming a little now.

'Verity lost hers around the same time as me, though she was twelve or so, so they put it down to puberty onset. She was fostered by a family in Scotland, I believe.'

'And Daniel? Nova?'

'They joined Lychen. He wasn't so interested in us C-kids by then, and after Rudy... it seemed like we were all doomed. But he took Daniel and Nova with him...'

'What about Reuben?'

'No one really knows about Reuben... He was very much part of the gang at one point. He and I were quite close, he was only a year or two older than me and when I began to lose my abilities, he was really there for me... We used to talk about getting a place together in town and working at the ARC together, working our way up and making it great again. Then after the inquiry... he left. We thought at first that he'd gone with Lychen like so many of the others but he never turned up in the searches we did in their personnel files.'

He looks out of the window sadly. I give him a moment or two to contemplate before asking:

'What do *you* think happened to him?'

'I don't know... I'd *like* to think he saw the way things were going and decided to back out. He always hated getting caught in the middle of arguments, it happened all the time with him being one of the eldest C-kids and one of the first to fail. I think he may well have just gone and gotten himself a new identity. We've tried tracing him but we've never had any luck...'

'Clearly he doesn't live with a twelve-year-old,' I say ruefully. Dominic has the grace to blush.

'So you mentioned Nova and Daniel going to work with Lychen... Does that mean they managed to retain their abilities to some extent...?'

'I don't think so. But I don't know for sure. There's rumours, though, that they both turned inward within a year. Nova almost certainly, but Dan – I've heard some *weird* things about him... It's all patchy, though, our intel. Mostly gathered from random snippets Felix or I have hacked. Their system has really stepped up its security over the last few years, but if I'm in the right frame of mind, sometimes I can worm my way in... But yeah, there were some inter-departmental emails that strongly hinted at Nova having gone off the deep end a few months after you left.'

He shudders. I shut my eyes briefly and, for a moment, I have to fight my own reflexes to shudder as well as I think of the small, bright-eyed little girl whose hand had always found mine, even after the other children had been shooed away. She'd have been in her early to mid-twenties by now, I think, as my memory stretches to the rumours surrounding the failed Subjects, the moans you sometimes heard if you walked certain corridors of the ARC at night.

'They never found a cure?'

'Only termination.'

I twitch my head. It happened long ago. There's nothing you can do now. Leave Nova behind.

We lapse into silence. The sun passes behind a cloud and the motorway instantly darkens around us. I glance at the clock on the dashboard. It's after four already. We won't make the Lake District before nightfall. Dominic's stomach rumbles loudly into the silence of the car and he smiles in embarrassment.

'Sorry,' he mutters. 'No lunch...'

'Right,' I reply. 'We should probably stop... Shall we wait for Fee to wake up first? It'll be dinnertime before long...'

'Sure,' he says, making a valiant effort. I smile and reach into the driver's side pocket, drawing out a packet of toffees.

'Here you go,' I hand it back to him. 'Ri has a sweet tooth. You don't want to get stuck in a car with her when she's hungry...'

'Thanks.' He grins and pops a toffee into his mouth. I wait until his jaws are unstuck enough to talk again before I change tack.

'So what's it like to live up there now? It must be kind of fun all being under one roof...'

He shrugs. 'That's one way of looking at it.'

'What's the other way?' I say, quickly, looking at Felix as she stirs and turns her head. Her eyelids flutter but don't open.

'Well, imagine being the youngest of a long line of brothers and sisters, all of whom are bigger and more intelligent that you... Now imagine that that is your life both at work and at home and there's literally no escape...'

'Ah...'

'Yeah. I get the box room, I have to get up at dawn to get any hot water in the shower... there's never quite enough food for us all to have two sausages for breakfast, though somehow Ethan usually ends up with four... He says it's because he's got the most physical job, he mostly works as a painter and decorator now. Earns better money than most of the rest of us. That's the other issue – money. The ARC hasn't been able to develop anything of note for years now – no investors would go near it with a barge pole after what happened. Most of us earn our keep by freelance consulting and contracting for larger facilities and universities. I do most of my work online so I don't leave the Manor most days. It can be pretty lonely.'

'Yes... I imagine it's pretty hard-going on the dating front as well...'

'Well, yeah... I'm the youngest there by a fair bit... And almost everyone else is coupled up anyway... And even if they weren't, most of them still think of me as one of the little kids from Project C...'

'So there's Felix and Ethan...'

'Jemma and Stephen, Dylan and Katya...'

'Ralph?'

'No... he's not with anyone either.'

'So a lot of couples. Any kids running around?'

'No... Fee and Ethan have been together the longest and I know they've been trying for a while, but they haven't had any luck yet.'

'That's a shame...'

'Mmm. People tend to move away once they get to that stage in their lives anyway... I don't really know how it'd work, having little kids at the Manor. It's not exactly the most kid-friendly place. No offence...'

'Well, I was hardly a toddler when I moved in...'

'No, I suppose not.'

'And Blake senior, what about him?'

'What about him?'

'Did he ever remarry? After Ana...?'

'No...' Dominic pops another toffee into his mouth and chews, thoughtfully staring out of the window. 'Everyone thought he went to pieces after she died, you know. I mean, you were there, you probably know as well as anyone... They say that's why he lost his way with the research, why he let Lychen take over so much back then... But I don't know... I don't think it was that...'

'What do you think it was?'

'I think it was a lot of things. You leaving. The C-kids, especially what they had to do with the inward ones once they lost control... And... Well, sometimes I wonder if perhaps Lychen had something on him. Something that made him weak–'

A sudden cough swipes both our attentions to Felix.

'Sorry, don't let me interrupt your little *chat*,' she barks, irritably. 'Go on, Dominic, you've already covered Ralph's relationship status, my barren womb and probably about one hundred more classified details about the Project C research... You carry on and tell her your suspicions about Lychen and Blake...'

Dominic is a nasty shade of purple at this point and doesn't look at Felix as he puts another toffee into his mouth and chews it, caught between contrition and sullenness. I glance at Felix, hiding my flare of irritation with a winning smile.

'We were just thinking about stopping for something to eat,' I say, brightly. 'How about the services just outside Manchester? If we time it well, we can beat the rush hour traffic.'

'Marvellous,' Felix says, watching me through slitted eyes. I smile back at her and turn back to the road, tucking the car neatly in front of a slow-moving Volkswagen.

**October, 2018**

*Monday*

Ariana wakes up with a jolt. She is in complete darkness. There is no car, no seat propping her up, no red-lipped woman peering at her from the front. She is lying on her back, with soft sheets beneath her fingers and a blanket covering her body. She blinks and slowly her eyes seek out the dull shape of a ceiling lampshade, four walls, and a bare wooden cupboard with its doors open, as if someone had emptied it in a hurry. She pushes herself up on what she now knows to be a bed, narrow but comfortable enough, with new white sheets still with the fold lines pressed in. She looks around and spots a door in the corner of the room. There is no window. Apart from the wardrobe and bed, there is nothing else in the room. It's like a cell. Her brain feels fuzzy, as if half of it is still asleep and she wonders what happened to her.

*They drugged you. When that woman gave you the bottle of Coke. I told you not to drink it.* The answer comes cold and certain in her mother's voice, and Ariana focuses on its lack of emotion as a quivering animal of fear rises in her chest. *Don't cry. Crying won't solve anything.* But the tears are already there. *Stop. You need to focus. There's a door over there. Get up and try to open it.* But the animal is

183

in charge, shivering hot tears onto her cheek. She swipes them with the sleeve of her jumper and then holds the soft cashmere against her face. She breathes. There's still an echo of her mother's sandalwood perfume in the creases where she's rolled it up over her wrists. She allows herself a few sniffs, letting the smell sift and gentle over the creature. It's not like a hug; more like the solid warmth of Bella's hand on her shoulder on the first day of school, her smile when it comes unexpectedly but brighter than the sun in July, reaching and warming every part of her – the quick, sharp reminders of care so strong it almost hurts. *Stop now. You're OK. You are.* Ariana wipes her eyes for the last time, looks at the ceiling and sniffs until her nose no longer threatens to drip. Then she rolls her sleeves back up and gets to her feet. Her hair corkscrews in front of her eyes and she combs it back with her fingers, searching her wrists for a band. There isn't one. She took them off before her shower back in the cottage a million years ago. *Never mind your hair. Try the door.*

Ariana crosses the small room in two strides and clicks on the light switch next to the door. She doesn't spare a glance at the cell in her hurry to try the door, fully expecting it to be locked. To her surprise, however, it swings open easily. Ariana blinks. The light is stronger than the dull glow of the cell and it takes her a while to focus, part of her mind still groggy with the remnants of whatever sleeping pill she's now sure the woman in the car gave her. When she does focus it's with surprise. The long, grey corridor stretching out either side of her room is almost eerily similar to the corridors at school. The same condensation-smeared windows line the opposite side to the doors – though the view here is of rain-splattered countryside – dull in the light of either very early morning or late afternoon – rather than the school's quadrangle of picnic benches. The doors, when she peers at them, are a similar cheap-looking wood to the classrooms. There are even coats on coat pegs outside some of them, though they're all white like the doctors wear on *Grey's Anatomy*.

Ariana takes a step onto the grey lino of the corridor. She isn't wearing shoes. They aren't in the room behind her when she glances back over her shoulder. She pulls a face but carries on into the corridor, keeping close to the doors with the vague idea of ducking into one of the rooms should anything unexpected happen. She feels better now she's moving. The trembling creature is still there, shivering somewhere next to her stomach, but she's swallowing it down with her mother's voice, imagining her comments on the drab décor, the marks where the insulation has blown on the windows. It's clean at least. In fact, Ariana can't see even a speck of dirt on the grey sea before her. If anything, its absence is even more unnerving.

About fifty paces from the cell in which she woke up the corridor hairpins sharply to the right and opens up into a larger space. Here the ceilings are higher, there is a large, patterned rug over the floor and comfortable-looking chairs dotted around it. Two desks stand opposite a set of double doors. It's a bit like a reception area in, and again the resemblance is quite eery, a large secondary school. Ariana glances towards the double doors, set with frosted glass that only hints at the grey-green outside world. She thinks about bolting through them. There's no one here, after all… She could flag a car, ask them to take her to the police. *The police will just ask questions,* her mother reminds her. *And how would you even begin to explain what's going on when you don't understand yourself? Besides, you have no shoes on.* Ariana inspects her socks.

They're a new pair bought yesterday but they feel achingly thin between her feet and the cold floor. She wouldn't get more than fifty metres outside before a hole formed.

Looking around, Ariana wonders what to do. A clock on the wall says seven-thirty. Must be morning, she thinks, because if it were evening it would surely be dark outside by now. That would explain why this school-type place is deserted. How long had she been asleep? Had it only been overnight? Her stomach gives a yank of hunger in answer and Ariana tries to ignore it, looking around the rest of the large entrance room. Directly opposite her are two doors which look like they lead into offices, she can just make out a desk through the glass of one of them. Straight ahead of the corridor from which she has emerged lies an identical looking one. She begins to walk towards it and, as she does so, the sound of voices filters through the air. She stops. They're definitely coming from somewhere ahead.

*Go and listen. Maybe they'll say something about where you are. Maybe they'll say what they're going to do with you. Or at least they might mention where they've put your shoes.*

Driven on by the fate of her brand-new trainers as much as anything else, Ariana enters the narrow corridor and, listening hard, approaches one of the wooden doors identical to the ones lining the first corridor. It is the second one along that houses the voices. Pressing her ear against the wood, Ariana listens and instantly recognises the voice of the woman from the car, though she can't catch every word.

'...here, when was the last time?'

'At least a year ago,' a deeper, louder male voice replies. It doesn't sound like the mechanical tones of the robotic man who'd driven yesterday and Ariana feels something loosen a little in her throat.

'...had time to clean up... usual standards... not important I suppose...' says the woman.

'Oh I don't know,' the man rumbles, his brusque, Northern voice filtering easily through the thin wooden door. 'Always been a bit of a stickler for order, hasn't he? I wouldn't worry too much, it's not like this place is running with rats or anything...'

'Yes, but... renovations... meant to be fully converted by now... what he said?'

'Something like that. But these things take time and money – what does he want, a perfectly functional facility which looks a lot like an old school or six months' delay while it's converted into a clone of that shiny, pointed palace he's created for himself down in London?'

*Him,* Ariana thinks. *He's coming.* A spiral of panic shoots so swiftly upwards into her throat that for a moment she's dizzy and senseless, unable to interpret the words she can hear from behind the door, unable to think about anything except the pounding of her heart. *Him.* The figure in her nightmares. The man who inspired that brittle, metallic shine of fear into even her mother's solid green gaze. Ariana shuts her eyes until the panic slides back down. *They won't hurt you. They don't want you.* She opens her eyes because she's worried she might fall over and concentrates on the voices beyond the door, realising, with a start, that their subject matter has turned to herself.

'...girl sleeping in the old sick bay... soon, probably... will need to wash and eat...'

'I still don't understand why we had to bring her in. It's such a messy situation. Why not just intercept D'accourt herself?'

'Dr Lychen felt it would ensure her presence with less

fuss, less need for… well, unnecessary intervention, I suppose. Especially as the Blakes are involved now. D'accourt is confirmed to be travelling with them…'

'Blake's kid, I take it?'

'It's looking more likely than not, yes…'

Ariana frowns. *Blake. Blake.* The name rings a bell somewhere dull and distant in her memory. What did they mean? Who was Blake? Who was Blake's kid? Was *she* Blake's kid? And what was that about her mother travelling with the Blakes? She doesn't think about the woman's words becoming clearer. Doesn't register the sound of footsteps. The door begins to swing towards her and she leaps backwards in alarm, narrowly missing a collision.

'Oh!' The blonde woman, her lips redder than ever and her eyes lined carefully in fresh make-up looks almost as startled as Ariana feels to see her.

'What, did you think you'd given me a stronger dose?' Ariana makes her voice as hard as possible and is pleased when it sounds reasonably like Bella's. The woman flushes deeply and the sound of a deep, rumbling chuckle precedes the appearance of a tall, tubby man who steps out of the room and puts a hand heavily on the woman's shoulder.

'She's got your number, Tess. Hi, Ariana, is it? I'm Alec.'

He holds out a hand and, slowly, Ariana reaches out to shake it. He's oldish, bald and red in the face and reminds Ariana of one of those characters in stories and films who keeps a handkerchief in his breast pocket with which they frequently mop their face.

'Who are you people? Why'm I here?'

'Come on, let's go and get you some breakfast.' Recovering quickly, Tess glances at the man, who is still beaming as if Ariana's said something really funny. She reaches for Ariana's arm, but Ariana lurches away from her. Tess shrugs and gestures along the corridor in the opposite direction to the entrance hall.

'I'll leave you,' Alec says cheerfully. 'Buzz me when he's here, T. I want to show him my new prototype before old Danny-boy whisks him away for an eight-hour tour of his lab.'

Tess nods, not looking at the large man as he plods away towards the entrance hall. Ariana watches him go, noting his white coat.

'Is he a doctor? This doesn't look like a hospital. He said it used to be a school…'

'It did, he is and no, not a hospital. Not that kind of doctor. Come on, I promise I'll tell you more about us and everything once we're sitting down and I've got a coffee in front of me,' Tess takes a step and, reluctantly, Ariana joins her.

**Winter 1995/1996**

Of course it wasn't all simply a case of Ralph and me rushing in to rescue all the poor experimented-upon children hidden away at the ARC. For starters, Blake kept us so busy during the times when we visited the facility, it was months before we even came across one such child. As the season chilled further, the flurry of activity around the ARC stilled as the workers took holidays, and over Christmas the staffing was kept to a minimum. Ralph thought it would be a great idea to *infiltrate* at this time, when security was low, but the festive season brought a flush of good health to Ana and she lost no time in tasking us with several exhausting activities, from decorating the entire Manor with home-made paper chains and garlands to baking Christmas biscuits and cake. Even Ralph, when faced with her bright, shining eyes and beaming grin, couldn't resist pitching in. As if that weren't enough, Ana also decided that my ballet had improved sufficiently for me to give the scientists and other staff from the ARC a brief showcase during the annual Christmas party just before the lab closed for the holiday, so much of my time was soon taken up by rehearsals and planning. I found myself so exhausted by the end of each day that it was sometimes all I could do to change into my pyjamas before collapsing into the large sleigh bed I'd come to call my own.

Most nights I would be fast asleep before Ana or Blake put their heads in to say goodnight.

'You're certainly keeping Bella busy,' I overheard Blake remark one morning as I hovered outside the dining room, about to go in for breakfast. 'Lessons stopped last week, yet I don't think I've seen her actually sitting down let alone watching television or reading a book like Ralph seems to be spending most of his time...'

'Yes, well,' Ana replied. At first I thought, as so often happened, that that would be the only explanation she would offer. At the time I thought it was a sort of adult sullenness, but as I grew older, I realised Ana just had the sort of self-assurance which meant she would often simply not bother entering into discussions she deemed pointless. I put a hand on the door knob, my stomach giving a little nag of hunger, but then I heard Ana again, her voice lower.

'We haven't heard a word from her parents, have we? Nothing. Not even a phone call. I thought if I kept her distracted, particularly in the run up to Christmas, perhaps she'd have less time to dwell on it.'

'Ah, of course... So that's what this little concert is all about, is it? And there I was thinking you were just trying to show off your Project A protégée to the ARC naysayers...'

'Well, the way some of them talk about A... You'd think it was all about flashy recipe babies. That's what they call them, some of them... Let them see my Bella on stage. Let them be ensnared. They won't be able to move.'

'That good, eh?'

'Good? She is magnificent.'

I smiled even as I wondered whether I perhaps should be unnerved by her strange tone. It was almost reverent. Certainly nothing like the way she usually spoke to me when she was correcting my turn out or telling me that I'd landed my grand-jeté like a baby elephant. As for the mention of my parents, of course I hadn't failed to notice that they'd not sent for me or even so much as asked after me. It only bothered me when I thought about them as my parents, though. If I just labelled them Julia and Marc D'accourt, the couple who had brought me up for a few years, it didn't sting so much. It was like Blake had said all those months ago – he, Ralph and Ana, *this* was my family now. Still smiling, I pushed the door open and stepped lightly over the threshold and into Ana's delighted open arms.

Christmas passed in a flurry. Once I'd given my showcase – Ana had been right, as soon as I stepped onto the stage, none of them moved, even *I* was a little spooked by it – I found my days only marginally less busy. By the time Ralph and I finished completing whatever festive preparation Ana set us it was often dark outside. Snow arrived in early December and during long evenings toasting marshmallows or bread on sticks in front of the fire in Blake's office, Ralph and I discovered a mutual, unspoken agreement that plotting a thing was far more fun than actually putting it into action. And so the weeks went by, our schemes to rescue the children at the ARC became ever more far-fetched and I found myself the happiest I had been in a long time. I didn't have to paint my face with delight at every little present the Blakes gave me like I had done with the D'accourts. Over Christmas lunch Ralph bet me I couldn't finish my sprouts faster than him and, somehow, suddenly, my plate was empty before I thought about trying to eat daintily. And through it all Ana smiled as I'd never seen her smile before, a new pair of pearls glowing in her ears, and she and Blake drank glass after glass of red wine until their cheeks matched the liquid.

It didn't last. On Boxing Day Ana snapped at Ralph for playing too loudly on his new handheld games console and took to her bed before it was even dark outside. She didn't emerge the following day and Blake, in hushed tones, told me that she often over-exerted herself over Christmas and that we shouldn't expect much out of her for the next few weeks. Ralph and I continued to talk about the children at the ARC, but now that the festive season was fast disappearing and Blake had already begun to remind us that lessons would be starting up again the following week, the delight of all the possibilities we'd come up with seemed to lose its thrill. We made one half-hearted attempted to trudge through the thick snow to the ARC on the Saturday afternoon before classes resumed, but we barely made it through the garden before the snow began to fall. I stood, shivering even under my thick snood and fur-lined coat as Ralph shoved his shoulder against the back gate, his gloves coated in white flakes and his face shining with exertion as the snow wedged solidly against the other side. He stopped and reached into his pocket for his inhaler.

'It's no good,' he muttered, inhaling deeply, 'we'll have to find another way around.'

We both stared out at the smudge of blackness just barely visible through the furious, white-and-grey landscape. I wrapped my arms around my body as the icy wind snaked through the wool covering my face and bit at my cheeks like a thousand tiny insects. Ralph shoved his inhaler back into his pocket.

'We'll never make it through the field and the trees,' I said, knowing he was thinking it too but, because he was twelve and I was nine, could not say so. He rounded on me angrily.

'Fine! Why don't you go back and warm your poor little toes by the fire then while those poor kids moulder away down there!' He spat, his face still red beneath his snow-coated hood. There were icicles around the edges of his glasses and, to my dismay, his dark eyes shone with wetness behind them. He saw me notice and immediately wrenched his gaze away, back to the ARC.

'I'll go without you,' he muttered, the wind tearing the words from his lips.

'Don't be stupid,' I hissed. 'You can barely breathe as it is. And your dad will go mad. Let's just wait until the snow clears up. There's nothing you could do now, anyway. Those kids are probably having a great time – the scientists are still on leave, it's like being on school holidays. Anyway, we don't even have a proper rescue plan...'

'I don't care!'

'Well if you're not going to be rational,' I preached, changing tack and using the words Blake always threw at us when we got frustrated during lessons. 'I'm not going to entertain you.'

Ralph stared at me. 'You're really annoying, you know that, don't you?'

His eyes were no longer wet and there was a smile tugging determinedly at the corner of his mouth. I grinned.

'I know. Come on, let's go in and play Monopoly. Bet I'll win again.'

'No you won't,' he grunted. I laughed to myself and began to walk away. I kept my eyes ahead and counted to three before I turned around. He was still staring through the storm which had worsened even in the few minutes we'd been talking. The house in front of us was getting hard to see, let alone the haphazard path down to the ARC.

'Ralph,' I said, putting more command into my voice,

'Come on.'

He turned and followed me without a hitch of hesitation.

We didn't know it then, of course, but there was something coming which would blow all thoughts of rescuing the ARC children out of our grasps like a child's glove sent skittering into a monstrous storm.

**October, 2018**

*Monday*

If the corridor and entrance way reminded Ariana of her school, it's nothing compared with the dining hall. She can hear the noise of it long before the unmistakable smell of oil, overcooked beans and boiled pudding reaches her. The cafeteria is large and low-ceilinged, scattered with tables and chairs where people gather in groups, talking, laughing, whispering, peering... The only difference to school kids is their size and the fact that most are wearing suits, dresses or white coats. Several stare interestedly at Ariana as she follows Tess to the serving area.

'Tea? Coffee? Juice?' Tess takes a white mug and presses a button on a machine until steaming brown liquid spurts into it.

'Tea, please,' Ariana replies, wincing at the little-girl wobble in her voice. Tess fills a cup for her wordlessly and gestures to the milk and sugar. Ariana adds what she wants, keeping her hands steady and trying to ignore the rash of gazes she can feel like laser beams on the back of her head. She's suddenly excruciatingly aware of her unbrushed hair and shoeless feet.

'What d'you want to eat?' Tess asks her. 'I'm just having toast, but there's cooked stuff there, eggs, sausages, et cetera. Or cereal…?'

'Toast is fine,' Ariana mumbles and then, unable to stop herself, bursts, 'Why are they all staring at me?'

'We don't usually see a lot of kids here,' Tess mutters back, taking two plates of stacked toast, still steaming, from the server. 'Just ignore them.'

Ariana turns away from the room and looks instead at the people serving the food. She wishes, almost instantly, that she hadn't. They're all dressed in white and black, with aprons and caps and gloves, and though they're all physically different, they all wear the same expression of mechanical blankness she recognises from the driver of the car yesterday. Ariana suppresses a shudder as one of them hands Tess a dish of butter without looking at her or it, moving automatically like a blind person sure of their surroundings. Tess, she notices, isn't looking at them either, keeping her attention on her full tray as she leads Ariana to a small table in the corner of the room, near a window smeared with condensation.

'Here we go, I expect you're hungry,' she says as Ariana sits down and she hands her a plate of toast. Ariana shrugs, but even as she eyes the toast reluctantly, thinking of the gloved, mechanical hands which made it, her stomach gives another great yawn of hunger. Tess takes a bite of her own toast and, with relief, Ariana follows suit. For a few moments they munch in silence as the people around them lose interest and go back to their own conversations.

'So,' Tess clears her throat and looks at Ariana properly. 'I can't promise to tell you everything. It's not my place. And besides, I probably don't know the half of it… But I'll tell you what I can. What do you want to know?'

'Where am I?'

'A research facility just outside York. It's owned by a research company called Beaumont Futura Industries and its official name is the Futura Laboratory, but you'll also hear it called Graysons or Grayson Boys. On account of it being an old boys' school, not because only men work here. As you can see, that's just not true.'

Ariana looks around them. 'All these people work here?'

'Yep.'

'What do they do?'

'I can't really tell you that, mostly because I don't fully know myself. It's not really my area and it's all quite secretive. Just working for BFI means signing all sorts of non-disclosure agreements, they try to keep everything as classified as possible, even within the company itself. All I know is what they're concentrating on here is, among other things, an evolution of something that was once known as Project B.'

'Project B?'

'That's right. Projects A, B and C all came from the ARC, of course. That was started by the Blakes. But I expect you know about that from your mum.'

Ariana stares at her. Too late she remembers something her mother once told her about bluffing information out of people: *Always act like you know more than you do, that way they don't realise how much they're giving away.*

'I guess not,' Tess says, sighing and taking a long gulp of her coffee. 'Urgh. Well. I don't know if it's my place to tell you...'

'Come on, you thought I already knew! It can't be *that* secret...'

'Good point. Well, I don't know all of it. I don't even

work here. I'm London-based,' she says, with a hint of pride that makes Ariana think that the London facility – presumably the *pointed palace* mentioned by Alec earlier – must be far superior to any other.

'I work on the tech side of things. I'm only here because of you. But anyway, enough of that. So, the Blakes. Ana and Frederick. They were the pioneers of eugenic experimentation back in the seventies and eighties. They started a private institution called the Aspira Research Centre – or the ARC for short – up in Cumbria in the middle of the mountains where no one would stumble across them. Using family money; I think she was some sort of heiress or something. Anyway, they launched a private service called Project A whereby rich families could pay to select certain characteristics for their children.'

'Characteristics? Like what?'

'Well... anything, really. Athleticism, tallness, exceptionally big feet...' She grins and Ariana finds herself smiling back.

'Anyway, that's where your mother came from. She was the youngest of three siblings, and actually one of the last kids to be genetically modified under Project A–'

'Wait, what?'

'Your mother, Bella D'accourt. Her parents – your grandparents, I guess – they paid the Blakes to have a designer baby. Three, in fact. Her brother was a sporting star, very well-known in his time, her sister was extremely intelligent and Bella was supposed to be the graceful beauty...'

'Supposed to be?'

'Well, she was – is – by all accounts, exceptionally beautiful. But then her parents began to see traits they weren't so happy about. Manipulation, having a weird hold over other people, getting them to do what she wanted just by looking at them, apparently. I don't know, the rumours are crazy – she's, er, something of a legend in the world of eugenic research, your mum. Some say she could touch a person and they'd instantly become her slave...'

'That's mental.'

'Well... You'd know. You tell me.'

Ariana shuts her mouth and swallows her mouthful of toast too soon. It scratches all the way down her throat but she doesn't wince. She stares Tess down until Tess looks away.

'Or not. OK, so anyway, Bella's mother brought her to the Blakes' place up in Cumbria when she was a child, told them that she wasn't happy and that they had to fix her. Bella ended up staying there for good, being brought up alongside the Blakes' son Ralph... I don't really know much more than that, other than while she was there, the main focus of work at the ARC was Project C.'

'What about Projects A and B?'

'Project A was shut down not long after Bella was born because the government caught wind and put a ban on it – said it was unethical, playing God, et cetera. Project B was developed and abruptly shut down as well, not sure what it was about but apparently ethics came into that one as well. Then Project C came along. That was all about the development of super-humans.'

'Like superheroes?' Ariana stares at her.

'Well... not a million miles off. Let me try and explain... Imagine a new-born baby; a blank slate, no genetic manipulation, no tweaking of DNA, just its mother and father's traits all mixed up and as nature intended, blah blah. Now say that child, once its natural physiology has been studied, is given a dose of manipulated genetic enhancement, similar to that used on the Project A Subjects. But this is only secondary to its utter immersion in a set of beliefs – a law of sorts – that defies what you and I know to be true.'

Ariana frowns and Tess sighs a little, putting her coffee cup down. Her eyes are shining brighter than Ariana's seen them so far and she can tell that the young woman is revealing more of herself – what makes her tick, what excites her – than she realises.

'Look, what would happen if you got up, stood on this table and stepped off of it?'

'I'd fall onto the ground. Obviously.'

'Exactly. Because?'

'Gravity.'

'Exactly. But what if you didn't know about gravity?'

'I'd still fall off.'

'Why?'

'Because not knowing about something doesn't mean it's not there...'

'Ah, but what if you *knew* you *wouldn't* fall off?'

Ariana frowns.

'I don't get it.'

'Let's go back to the child. The blank slate. He is given a genetic cocktail to enhance lightness of limbs, make him as naturally weightless as possible. And he is brought up being told from the very earliest of days that he can float in the air. That if he is not held up by something, he will not fall. That he is made to believe it using mind-manipulating techniques, examples, evidence that you or I would know to be doctored because it is physically impossible, but that he, in his purity, does not...'

'Are you saying that they created a child who could fly?'

'I'm saying they created the *possibility*.'

'Oh...'

'Yeah.'

'So what happened? If this all happened years ago, why isn't the world full of flying superheroes who can walk through walls and stuff?'

'Who says it isn't?'

Ariana stares at her until she looks away again. It's surprisingly easy.

'A lot of stuff happened. A scientist called Dr Josiah Lychen got involved with the Blakes. He helped massively with the development of Project C. He wanted to take it global, get funding to make it a mass-production. By this point the research was still in its infancy, there weren't enough kids to experiment with and they soon realised that not all children were able to be manipulated in the same way. They had to have certain qualities, certain traits, even as small babies, in order to be receptive to the process. Anyway, part of getting more funding meant giving presentations, showing what these kids could do...'

'Like a performance of a kid flying?'

'Sort of...'

'Wow.'

'Yeah. At first it was all on a small scale, but one year they decided to do something really big – the money was running out and they needed something pivotal to bring in the large-scale funding... So they put on this massive production in the grounds of the ARC, invited a select audience of likely benefactors – academic hotshots, rich investors, anyone who'd heard the rumours of the ground-breaking research going on there, providing they had cash to spare and were willing to sign a non-disclosure agreement... Anyway, something went wrong. Massively wrong. Like as wrong as it could go. A kid died *on the literal stage*. Blake and Lychen fell out and Lychen branched away to create his own research...'

'So... what's all that got to do with my mum?'

'Well, she was a young woman at that time – late teens, early twenties. She was working at the ARC along with Ralph – the Blakes' son – and, even by then, she was something of a legend. She and Ralph were unique among the scientists in that they had been brought up practically alongside some of these C-kids... Subjects, they were called. Your mum herself was a bonafide A-Subject. And apparently she had this *way* with the kids. I don't know if it was part of her own charisma or just simply that she understood them better than anyone else, but apparently by the time this big presentation came around she was like a mentor to the best of them, including the boy who ended up dying...'

'What happened to him?'

'I don't know exactly...' but Tess's eyes slide sideways and Ariana can tell she's not being entirely truthful.

'What *do* you know about it?' Ariana channels her mother, putting all the command she can muster into her words. Tess bites her lip, looks around and then leans forward, her voice so low that Ariana has to bend her head low to catch it.

'Look, this is all way before my time, you have to understand that. And when it happened, it was all massively hushed up. Like super-injunctions on *top* of the NDAs, that sort of thing... Even now there are certain... rules... about speaking about all that in a non-academic setting... All I know is that there was a balls-up and it had something to do with the boy's special abilities. I don't know if he lost control of them or lost them completely at just the wrong time... Anyway, he was one of your mother's kids and a lot of the ARC people... they blamed her. Said she hadn't been careful enough with him, that her head hadn't been in the game, that she was too wrapped up in her own part to play in the presentation... Anyway, afterwards she disappeared. Ralph stuck by his father, Frederick. They vowed to rebuild the ARC's reputation and continue the original research. They didn't want to give up on Project C the way they'd been forced to give up on A and B, they thought there might be a way around the problems they'd encountered with it... But Lychen wanted to cut his losses and move onto something different, something more evolved. He saw potential in the Project B research which he thought had been discarded too quickly, but ultimately he wanted to concentrate on plans for a Project D. So Lychen and the Blakes parted ways.'

'And Mum?'

'She disappeared. She was as ambitious as they come, so a lot of people thought she'd go with Lychen. He certainly offered her a position, and a very high up one too, as the rumours go... But she didn't take it. But nor did she stick by the Blakes. She just... left. It's only recently we've been able to discover why, at least partly.'

'Why?'

'Isn't it obvious?'

Ariana thinks. She frowns into the crumbs on her plate, her mind consumed with images of her mother as a young woman, torn between furthering her scientific career or siding with her adoptive family and everything she had known. Then she thinks of the woman she knows, typing away at her laptop at the kitchen table long after she thinks Ariana has gone to bed. Her keen eyes shining at whatever is on the screen with a hard focus Ariana never sees during the day.

'It was because of me, wasn't it?'

She looks up when Tess doesn't answer and sees that the woman is no longer looking at her. Her face is turned and her expression is captured in an eery mixture of rapt focus, admiration and fear. Ariana realises the room has gone completely silent and, as she follows Tess's gaze, she notices that everyone else is looking the same way. It's like there are invisible threads connected to every face in the room and they are all being tugged in the same direction – the door through which she and Tess entered the dining hall. Silhouetted in the fluorescent light is a man. He's average height and build, dressed smartly in a dark suit which Ariana can tell, even from here, has been tailored to fit him precisely. His hair is short and an unusual, amber-like shade but it is his face which steals the breath from Ariana's lungs. The cheekbones are high and delicate. The mouth is curved into a strange, cold sort of leer as if the man has only read about what a smile is and not quite grasped what it is for and what it should mean. His eyes are two dark pinpricks she can't see clearly from where she is, but she can feel them like two punctures of ice as they bore, solidly, straight into hers. The figure is nothing like the shadowy, tall, lurching spectre of her nightmares, but the radiance of freezing malevolence feels exactly the same. *Him*.

**Winter, 1996**

I wish I could say that the first time I met Josiah Lychen, I knew him for what he was. I wish I could say that I, at the very least, did not like or trust him. But I was a nine-year-old child and he was a polite, well-dressed young adult with a haircut like a pop star. I watched him greet Blake and Ana in the hallway of the Manor, peering unseen through the banisters on the first floor, and I knew he was someone important. Someone who demanded attention and respect. Someone who had Blake inclining his bright head in deference and Ana twisting her mouth in grudging respect.

He'd arrived at the ARC among a small group of new scientists a few weeks into January, though it was he alone who was invited for drinks at the Manor on his first day. I didn't think it odd that the Blakes didn't introduce him to Ralph and me on that first evening, though when Ralph joined me at my post, he muttered about being left at the kids' table as we watched the three of them go through to Blake's study. After that the only times we really saw Lychen were the rare times his path would cross ours during one of our visits to the ARC. Even then it was several more weeks until Blake made formal introductions, and when he did so Lychen barely glanced our way. This seemed to particularly rankle with Ralph, who watched him walking busily away amid a small, white-coated crowd, muttering about posh-voices and *all hair and no substance*; though it was long after Lychen had disappeared around a corner that Ralph stopped looking. For my part I soon forgot him in the bustle of my own school lessons and ballet beginning up again, not to mention the several other forms of dance Ana, in a sudden burst of New Year energy following her post-Christmas malaise, had decided I needed to learn. Still, I was aware of him whenever Ralph, Blake and I entered the ARC, even if I couldn't yet articulate how, in the sharpness of the other workers' gazes, the way the surfaces seemed to gleam brighter than ever whilst the shadows loomed longer.

I wasn't the only one hard at work. As the months began to tick down to Ralph's thirteenth birthday, Blake announced he was going to enter him for his Key Stage Three SATs a year early. Our evenings playing Monopoly on the rug in front of the fire soon became a rare occurrence and although we still studied side by side in the school room on a daily basis, the lessons became hushed as Blake clicked a timer and Ralph bent his head over another timed essay or past exam paper. When we visited the ARC the two of them would whisk themselves away into corners of the labs to mutter away together or sometimes Ralph would simply disappear on his own while I milled around the scientists, occasionally amusing myself by picking one and seeing if I could nudge them into telling me more about the Project C kids. I assumed Ralph was off exploring the building and would tell me as soon as he'd managed to locate the place where the children were kept. When the weeks began to pass with no such revelation, however, I was forced to take the matter into my own hands.

'What's happening about those Project kids?' I asked

Ralph one day as we walked a little behind Blake down towards the ARC one crisp morning in February. 'Have you found them? Do you know any more about them? Are you still planning to try and get them out?'

Ralph looked at me as if I were a very young child. It didn't help that he had grown yet further since Christmas and I still fitted the clothes I had arrived in.

'I don't need to,' he said, with the air of talking to someone very stupid. 'I asked Dad about them and he told me.'

'What? I thought it was top secret!'

'I guess he thought I was ready to hear about it... Anyway, he said that if I wanted to meet the children and see that they were well-cared for I can...' He threw the comment at me as if it was nothing he cared very much about, as if he'd spent the last few months doing the very opposite of stressing and planning over those children's predicament. I swallowed my frustration.

'So are you going to go and see them?'

'Oh, probably. At some point. To be honest I'm quite busy these days with all the work I've been doing. Dad's got me on a chemical fusion project, he's given me my own corner of Lab Five for it, actually.'

I stared at him, unable to mask my amazement.

'So *that's* what you've been up to...'

'While you've been faffing about, flirting with the old geeks in Lab Three like a puppy dog, yeah...'

'I've not been *flirting*. I was finding stuff out!'

'Oh yeah, like what?'

I crossed my arms. 'Why should I tell you? You probably don't *need* to know about it all now anyway!'

Ralph sighed and glanced up at the stooped figure of Blake lolloping through the still-bare trees ahead of us. He looked back at me.

'Go on, just tell me… There's no point keeping it to yourself. It's not like you can do much without my help.'

'Says who?'

'Says this,' he dug into his pocket and brought out a shining black key card. I gasped.

'You've got an ARC access pass?'

'Yep. Told you my work was important.'

'So you could just find them and see them for yourself any old time you wanted?'

'Well, not exactly… This is only for Lab Five… And the canteen.' He reddened a little, looking away. I twisted my lip, fighting the sudden urge to mock him. I knew he was right, possibly more than he did. I needed him. At least for now.

'You were right about the basement,' I said, careful to keep my voice low even though Blake was well ahead of us now and humming softly to himself. Ralph turned to me, his eyes as keen as they had been all those nights we'd schemed in front of the fire. He waited for me to continue.

'But it's not just one room, it's like an entire floor – there're bedrooms, a kitchen, dining hall, play room… Even rooms for the staff who look after them. And they go out in the garden as well when it's nice out…'

'I didn't know the ARC had a garden.'

'Neither did I,' I admitted. 'Apparently it's quite small and it's all walled off so no one can see in, but there's a bunch of stuff for them to play with. And you were right about them all being orphans or kids whose parents have, like, *donated* them. Not bought though, not like…'

'Not like the Project A kids…'

'Yeah. Anyway, them being there isn't a huge secret within the ARC. You can't talk about it anywhere else though. And only certain people are allowed to interact with the children. The rest have to just observe... I don't know why, something to do with what they're working on with them...'

'How did you get all of this?'

I shrug impressively. 'I know how to ask questions...'

'Yeah,' Ralph shuddered. 'I've noticed.'

'Anyway, the most important thing I found out is those new guys – you know the one with the suit and the nice hair? And the people who came in with him?'

'Yeah, I know him.'

'Well he's been put in charge of them.'

Ralph stopped short and I sent a small clod of frozen mud skittering onto the path ahead as I pulled to a halt next to him.

'You're kidding! *That's* what he's here for?'

'Yeah... He's leading some crucial aspect of their development or something...'

'Wow... So he's just a glorified babysitter... After all Dad goes on about how brilliant and innovative his ideas are...' Ralph started walking again, faster than before. I had to jog to keep up with him.

'I don't think he's babysitting, he's *studying* them...'

'Yeah, whatever, Beast,' Ralph was chuckling to himself now as he hurried past Dr Blake up towards the boundary of the ARC ahead of us. I scowled as he leapt clear over the wrought-iron gate in one swift show-off movement. I'd been saving that information about the children for almost a week, it had been the result of several days of hard persuasion on my part and it felt like Ralph was trampling all over my efforts with his stupid, adult-sized shoes.

*That's the last time I tell him anything important*, I

thought to myself as Blake held the gate for me and I stepped through. We'll just see how much information he manages to get without me.

**October, 2018**

*Sunday*

Night has fallen as only night can fall in the Lake District – without boundary to its entirety – by the time Bella pulls the BMW up to a crunching halt outside the ARC. Felix blinks at the tall building, relief at being home swimming in conflict with a sense of unease. She doesn't need to see the flash of activity by the front doors to know something is off. She glances at Dominic and sees his eyes widen as two large figures approach the car. Bella, to her credit, does not blink as she opens the car door and slides as smoothly out of it as if the drive had taken only eight minutes rather than hours.

'Bella D'accourt? You will come with us now,' says the hollowed voice of the Guard man. A Guard woman stands by his side. They're both built squarely and wear the plain, grey uniform Felix has seen only a few times before here at the ARC. Neither of their expressions reflect anything and, as she usually does when faced with them, she finds herself imagining Lychen standing over the figures like a puppet-master, unhinging their skulls and scooping out their wills. She shudders and feels Dominic echo the movement behind her.

'What do you think, shall we wait for Ralph and

Ethan?' Bella turns to Felix, her eyes clear and her voice light as if simply enquiring if they should place their drinks order now or give the others a few more minutes to arrive. If she's afraid of the Guard she certainly isn't showing it. Felix can't help but admire her.

'You will come with us, *now,*' the female Guard repeats, stepping forward towards Bella. Bella turns to her sharply, and though she is completely dwarfed height and width wise by the formidable figure in grey, she shoots her the sort of look that would stop anyone else mid-breath. But the Guard aren't anyone. They aren't even people, Felix thinks, and watches in interest as the woman reaches for Bella's arm undeterred.

'You will not touch me,' Bella snaps. The Guard hesitates. Something that isn't as human as confusion but resembles the closest thing a machine can come to it crosses her face.

'Then you will come with us,' the male Guard says, smoothly. Bella sighs and turns back to Felix.

'I suppose the others will have to catch us up. Goodness knows how long it will take them in the old banger anyway,' she shrugs. And Felix sees, just as the smaller woman turns back and begins to walk towards the looming building in step with the two Guard, a flicker of something underneath the careful veneer. Something, if she didn't know Bella, she might have taken for fear. She wonders if this is the first time she's given an order that hasn't instantly been obeyed. But then, she thinks, as she and Dominic follow closely behind the mismatched trio ahead, who ever heard of one of the Guard hesitating before?

As they pass the three Guard men standing motionless, muscle-whittled arms folded, under the crystal chandelier in the large shining entranceway, Felix feels her tired body wiring itself up for a struggle. Her heart rackets in her ears and her limbs tingle with readiness. Beside her, Dominic looks at anything but the Guard, his face a sickly shade of yellow.

'Don't worry,' Felix says, trying to keep her voice a low murmur, though the hallway is so silent her words seem to boom around them like cannon fire. 'If they wanted to pick a fight with us, they'd have done it long ago. They'll just collect up whatever it is they want, take Miss Universe there and go.'

'What about Ralph?' Dominic murmurs as the lift doors spring open in front of Bella and the couple flanking her like bodyguards.

'Ralph can take care of himself,' Felix says, more firmly than she feels, trying very hard not to picture her long, limby friend and compare him to the beefy squareness of the figures surrounding them.

'I'm surprised,' Bella's voice comes as softly as a caress as the five of them step into the lift. 'Lychen never used to be afraid to take on his own battles. He was always so... virile in his work. I would have thought that whatever he wanted from here, he'd pick up for himself.'

Dominic gasps as if he can't help himself, but Felix nudges him into silence, nodding towards the Guard. Bella is watching them as well. The male doesn't give any indication he has heard her and simply jabs at the invisible finger pad on the wall of the lift. The female, however, gives that strange twitch of almost-confusion again and tightens her jaw, though she does not reply to Bella's dig.

'I see security isn't what it once was here at the ARC,' Bella continues cheerfully, smiling directly at the female Guard. Felix watches in awe. *She's testing her*, she thinks to herself. *She's found a chink and is tugging at it.*

'We are security now,' the female replies. 'The ARC is ours. We are jurisdiction here.'

'Ah… is that what Lychen told you?' Bella says, lightly. The female glowers at her and Felix almost gasps to see so much semblance of emotion on her face.

'That is fact,' the woman replies, her voice several degrees less mechanical. 'You just ask your old friend Dr Blake.'

'Blake is no friend of mine,' Bella replies, shortly, with the air of bringing the conversation to a close. The female Guard twitches again and glances at her male counterpart as if for reassurance. The male does not say a word, but when the lift doors spring open on level four, he lets Bella, Felix and Dominic step out first and, when the female goes to follow them, bars her way.

'You, report to headquarters. Now.'

'But–'

'You report to headquarters now.'

The female's face, now fully creased in enquiry, solidifies back into smoothness as the male stares at her.

'Yes,' she replies, simply, her voice a clip of metal once more. Felix catches Bella's smile, small and hidden behind a carefully placed hand as the male Guard turns back to them and leads them along the corridor. She can't help but smile back.

**October, 2018**

*Monday*

'Come on,' Tess mutters, but Ariana is already on her feet and moving quickly through the silent crowd as if the man has her on a fishing line. Tess falls into step beside her, but Ariana barely notices. All she can see is him. His eyes are like two whirling universes, black as mystery, and while they stare into hers looking away is not an option.

'Ariana,' he says, when Tess pulls her to a halt a metre in front of him. His voice is smooth and clips around the shape of her name without wasting a syllable of breath. He holds out a hand and she watches in some bemusement as her own arm mirrors his, her hand slipping coolly into his grasp as if she is no longer in command of it.

'My name is Josiah Lychen. I'm very pleased to meet you. How like your mother you look.'

He drops her hand and motions to Tess before Ariana can open her mouth to mutter so much as an *um* in reply. Lychen turns sharply on the toe of one shiny shoe and marches swiftly out of the cafeteria. Tess gestures for Ariana to follow, but again Ariana finds herself drawn behind him automatically. Like a child caught in the slipstream of the Pied Piper. She can only look around and note, vaguely, the collective exhalation of relief pushing at the back of her neck as the three of them leave the room.

Lychen leads them silently back down the narrow grey corridor and into the entrance hall. Ariana spots the tall blank-eyed driver from yesterday with a small shivery bolt to her stomach. The man is staring straight ahead, seemingly at nothing, but when Lychen approaches he comes to life, stepping backwards towards a door Ariana didn't notice the first time she passed through the hall. He opens the door and bows his head as Lychen leads them through. Ariana looks around and halts with astonishment. If someone had told her the drab entrance hall through which they had just passed was a portal to a different building altogether she would have believed them, for this room is as unlike all the others she's been in so far as a chalkboard from a smooth, shining computer screen. A plush carpet of violet sinks softly under her feet as she steps forward. Her own reflection bug-eyes back at her from several ornate, gold-framed mirrors, and the large oblong table in the middle of the room is so highly polished it looks ready for royalty to dine upon.

'Please,' Lychen draws a beautifully-carved chair out from around the table and motions for her to sit down. She does so, aware more than ever of her unbrushed hair, rumpled, slept-in clothes and shoeless feet.

'Shall I... er...?' Tess mumbles, awkwardly hovering around a chair next to Ariana. Lychen blinks at her once, slowly, and wordlessly she sits down, face glowing.

'Firstly I must apologise.' Lychen stays standing at the head of the table steepling his long fingers on its surface. The reflection in the polished wood mirrors downwards, and for a moment he looks as if he is dipping his fingers into an alternate dimension. It seems to fit with the sense of unreality in the room, and Ariana feels almost giddy as she stares at him avidly. Somewhere, at the very back of her mind, her mother's voice calls a warning, but it is too far away for her to hear properly.

'We aren't usually in the business of plucking young girls from country lanes.' Lychen smiles, smoothly. Ariana finds her own mouth stretching upwards at the corners in response.

'I do hope you weren't too alarmed,' he adds. Ariana shakes her head promptly. He smiles even more widely, his mouth suddenly disproportionate to the rest of his face, like a snake's.

'Good. I must also apologise for the deceit of our online communications. I deplore deceit in all its forms and I can only tell you how pained I have been that we had to stoop to such levels... I'm sure Miss Cochran here felt just as conflicted during your interactions on social media...'

Tess, who has lost a little of the blush she has been wearing since she sat down, colours once again. Ariana frowns a little. *I knew that Conan68 was Tess. I was sad about it. Why?* She feels like she's grappling underwater, trying to hear her own memories and logic through the rush of Lychen's presence.

'I can assure you that I will do my utmost never to lie to you again. And, with that in mind, I can also assure you that while you are under my care, no harm will come to you. Despite what you may have been led to believe, I have only ever been concerned for the safety of your mother and, when I learned of your existence, yours as well. Any deceit we undertook was, however deplorable, in pursuit of this. You have a question?'

He inclines his head politely and Ariana finds her throat unblocked, her voice, momentarily, unleashed.

'What do you want with my mother?'

'Your mother and I were close colleagues once upon a time. But before then she was part of something ground breaking. You have, I presume, heard of Project A?'

'Yes.'

'Your mother is the last of her generation. The others from Project A have all perished, one way or another. I simply want to check that she is healthy, and to offer my help if she is not. That is all. Your mother is an extraordinary woman in almost all senses of the word. I would love to partner with her once again to achieve the levels of greatness I have always foreseen for the pair of us... But any such dalliance would, of course, be up to her.' He holds out his hands, palms lily-white.

'If it's up to her, why not just let her come to you? Why force her to come by taking me?'

'Your mother is a woman of prodigious... skills... as I'm sure you are aware. And she and I did not part on the best of terms. I had to be sure that she would come. Her health is not something with which I am willing to gamble. She herself is undoubtedly unaware of the extent of the danger she is in. Thanks to my colleagues' work in the field of her specific genetics, I know more about it than she does, to put it simply. I care deeply for her. I simply want to make sure she is alright. Is that not what you want as well, as her daughter?'

Ariana frowns again, feeling as if she's missed a step somewhere. Still, she finds herself nodding. Lychen beams but instead of feeling it like the warmth of the sun on her face, Ariana feels it snake into her chest and around her lungs like tendrils of icy malignancy.

'So we are in agreement. Excellent. Now to practical matters – you have eaten, I presume?'

'Yes.'

219

'Well then, Miss Cochran here will take you to a place where you can wash and change your clothes. Then perhaps you can have a little tour of our facility up here. It is not the grandest of our outlets, but it is impressive in what it does. If you need anything at all, just ask.'

Ariana nods again, dumbly, as Tess gets to her feet. Lychen nods curtly and seats himself just as she gets up. He draws a phone from his pocket and begins to tap on its screen. It's as if she and Tess simply no longer exist and she feels almost surprised to see and feel her own body as it moves her to the door.

**October, 2018**

*Sunday*

I let the admiration on their faces sink into me like nectar. They will never know how much I need it right now. We round the corner of the corridors which are as familiar as the creases and curves of my own hands and I feel everything inside me stealing, withdrawing, heaving inwards like a wave about to crescendo on a flat unsuspecting shore. There are no new laboratories. The same doors shine from the same walls. The only difference now is the presence of the strange Guard people, so remote and yet so simple to break into. They are no threat to me. The man we approach, however... I hear him, his low rumble tangling into my ears with a mixture of warm nostalgia and ice-cold dread. We stop in front of Lab Three and the Guard turns the door handle, steps into the doorway – he is so broad that he blocks the rest of us from view – and announces: 'I have brought the D'accourt woman along with two of the errant ARC employees; Dominic Chester and Felix Bryden.'

'Bring them in,' replies a voice that sounds almost identical. The Guard moves, and in we go.

He hasn't changed. That's the first thing I think as I move out of the Guard's broad shadow and lock my gaze onto his as he gets steadily to his feet from one of the lab bench stools. His eyes behind his round glasses are as sharply blue as ever, his hair, though now completely white, is as stand-uppy as it was all those years ago when I first stared up at him and wondered if he'd just put his finger in a plug socket. But as soon as I notice these things, my mind starts crowding with all the other things – all the ways in which he *has,* in fact, decayed and diminished from the man I once knew and loved more than any other. His height no longer stretches so impossibly above my own, his back, always a little stooped, now curves forward like a comma. The wrinkles around his eyes and forehead have become deep grooves and even that shock of white hair is not so thick as before. Still, when he looks back at me and smiles, his eyes crease the way they always did and his voice rumbles around my name as comfortably as a father's caress and I find my own eyes narrowing.

'Bella. You look wonderful. I am so sorry about what's happening with your daughter.'

Somehow he manages to make me feel every bit as wrong-footed as I did when, aged eleven, I'd been handed a maths test with a B across the front and he'd explained that I shouldn't feel bad because I had been studying for a ballet exam at the same time. *But I want to be able to do it all,* I'd thought at the time. *Isn't that the point of being extraordinary?* And now I feel a small part of me emerging with a not-so-small voice to exclaim: *Just because I look one way on the outside, doesn't mean I'm not tearing in half inside because Ariana's missing.*

'Blake,' I reply, nodding, 'You look… the same.'

'My dear, you never were very good at direct lies. Not when your heart wasn't in it,' Blake chuckles as if I've just paid him the highest of compliments. Felix strides over to him, glaring at the Guard people clustering in the room. I look around us and count five of them including our escort: three male and two female. All of them are staring at nothing in particular, like robots on standby, except the one standing nearest to Blake.

'You will begin the procedures now,' he tells him, blandly. Felix frowns at him.

'What procedures? The message said we had to collect something from here and then Bella and Ralph were to travel on to wherever they're holding her kid...'

'They want evidence, my dear,' Blake says, though he is looking at me so neither one of us know whom he is addressing. 'Lychen may have bought the moon and stars in scientific technology, but he lacks the one thing needed to paint the full picture of Bella's genetic make-up.'

'What's that?' I say, sharply, refusing to become a passive subject in this conversation.

'Me,' he replies, almost apologetically.

'We have you,' the Guard man replies, moving forward menacingly. 'We have her. So begin...'

'Ah,' Blake turns to him, his voice still mild but a familiar steeliness creeping into it which I recognise from his old dealings with Lychen and, occasionally, Ralph and me. 'But I have a few conditions of my own.'

'What conditions?'

'That is between me and Josiah. I suggest you facilitate contact between us. Unless you want any further delays.'

He stares at the man over the top of his spectacles and though the Guard man doesn't squirm or wince or anything so closely resembling a normal, human response, he twitches. I see, with a mixture of annoyance and admiration, that like me, Blake has discovered his own way around the Guards' seemingly impenetrable control. The

Guard turns away and reaches into a pocket of his uniform. He glances at us all before communicating something wordlessly to the other Guard and then stepping out into the hall, drawing a phone from his pocket.

'So,' Blake turns to me, his expression softening again. 'Tell me about Ariana. I want to hear all about this granddaughter of mine...'

I blink once and though my recovery is instant I can tell he's seen the flicker of surprise.

'Come now,' he smiles, 'Let's not waste time with petty lies, Bella. After all, our time is no longer our own.'

His gaze is so piercingly stern that I find myself unable to hold it. Instead I let my eyes travel around the lab. The layout is strikingly similar to how it was back when I was a child, being held up to see into the glass beakers set in their clasps above bright, Bunsen flames. Back then everything was clean, shining with novelty, the scientists would handle everything with pride. Now the benches are bare, their surfaces tarnished with burns and deep scores. The glass cabinets lining the walls are warped and thick with dust. Even the sinks at the back of the room look stained and disused. I wonder if they even have a water supply anymore.

'What do you want to know?' I say, slowly, as the whirr of the Guard's voice monotones into the room from the corridor.

'Everything. Whom does she look like? Ralph sent me a picture but it looked a few years old... What does she like to do? Does she play a musical instrument? Does she possess a preference for kittens or unicorns or slow worms?'

I sigh, feeling his attempts to lighten the mood settling bleakly into the mass of spiky worry which has been steadily growing in my throat since the moment I stopped driving.

'Well. Her birthday is April 14th. She's twelve. She has my eyes, but she's fairly tall for her age, like Ralph. It won't be long before she's taller than me. When she stands in the sun, her hair glows like each strand is made of molten gold, but in the shade it could be brown. It's curly like mine, but thicker and coarser. She doesn't need glasses. She hates all insects, grew out of unicorns when she was ten but she's always loved cats. She's been asking for a kitten for every birthday since she was six, but we've never lived anywhere that's allowed pets. She learned the recorder for three weeks when she was eight before we reached a mutual conclusion that her talents lay outside the realm of musicality. She doesn't dance, but she can turn somersaults like an Olympic gymnast and she likes to act. Her favourite pop star is Harry Styles. She is an excellent poker player.'

I am looking at him again now, because I have to. He blinks and nods and I can't tell whether my words are sinking into him with the sentimentality of a proud grandparent, or if he is turning them over in his mind, dissecting them for ulterior motives. Is he seeing the child I see, with her swirling hair and her spring-footed run, turning and laughing with her entire face, her whole body? Is he seeing the lies creeping between the cracks of the picture I'm painting? He says nothing. And then the Guard re-enters the room and the image curls into blackness and smoke.

'Lychen will speak to you in the hallway.' He holds out the phone and, wordlessly, Blake turns and takes it, walking away from all of us.

**Spring, 2001**

'Hullo, Dom. How are you? And Nova? What's that you've got there? Oh wow, did you make that all by yourself?'

I bent forward to study the little girl's drawing; her face flushed with excitement as she slipped a small hand into mine. The other children crowded around us, each one either holding something to me or just reaching, all of them eager to touch, to grasp a tiny nugget of my attention, if only for a few seconds. I'd never really been sure what the thing was with me and children; they'd always been drawn to me like this, even when I was one of them. Like that first day of nursery school as described so scathingly by the woman who gave birth to me. I wondered, as I straightened up and smiled over the small, tousled heads at the schoolroom leader beaming back at me, if Blake remembered that conversation as well as I did. It had taken place over five years ago, after all.

'Hi, Bella,' the teaching assistant – Jacqui – came over to us and reached over the children for my coat, which I handed to her. 'How long are you with us this morning?'

'Just an hour or so,' I replied as my hand was wrenched out of Nova's and taken by someone bigger. I glanced down to see Daniel, his large grey eyes as mournful as ever, holding my hand to his chest like it belonged to him and him alone. I resisted the urge to wrench it back.

With his always-runny nose, awkward features and general dog-like slowness, Daniel wasn't one of my favourites, though I tried my best not to show it. Blake had given me very strict guidelines on how to interact with the Subjects when I'd asked him about volunteering in the school rooms at the start of the academic year. It was only fair, I'd argued, now that Ralph had been given a laboratory of his own. Still, as persuasive as I could be, I wasn't sure he'd have agreed if it weren't for Ana. Still scarf-wearing and erratic, Ana had poured as much of her usual energies into Christmas the year I was fourteen, and when January had come, she had failed to appear in the dining room in the morning to smile at Ralph's latest research paper or nudge me and remind me that my upcoming tap exam was just as important as my GCSE mocks. But now it was March and the doctors had been called, ducking sombre-faced in and out of her rooms. I visited when I could, and tried not to let her see the relief of my body as it unwound, free from the constant scrutiny. *Don't take so much butter on your toast, don't wear that skirt with that top, is that make-up on your face?*

As Jacqui took my coat over to the pegs, I tried to retrieve my hand from Daniel. He held fast. At ten years old, he was one of the oldest of the C-Subjects and big for his age. His doleful eyes, when I met them, were almost level with mine.

'Let go,' I said, straight into his eyes. He, of course, dropped my hand instantly, though not before a flicker of something crossed his brow. Despite his slow movements, he was no fool and I knew that every command I gave him grew closer to the last as he puzzled over how he could overcome it. I moved away from him before I felt his gaze leave my face. Nova followed me, slipping her hand back into my newly vacated one, whispering something so low I had to bend forward and ask her to repeat it.

'I said I did a proper pirouette.'

'You did? That's brilliant! You'll have to show me sometime.'

'Yeah! You can come to my class this afternoon if you like! Madame Glioue won't mind, she always says she wishes you'd come and demonstrate for us. She thinks you're a prodgy.'

'Prodigy. I know she does,' I sighed, thinking of the dance teacher's shining eyes as she gave commands and I followed them, so different to Ana's darting, pincer-sharp gaze, honing in on the mistakes, voice pinched around the improvements still to be made. 'We'll see.'

Jacqui clapped her hands and Nova slipped her hand from mine as she went to join the other six-year-olds at their table. I watched her, her strawberry-blonde hair whisper-straight around her shoulders, her delicate limbs folding neatly beneath her as she took her seat, almost like wings. I imagined her standing on the table in front of her, stretching her arms out and taking flight. I wasn't supposed to know about the children's talents – their *abilities*. I was only supposed to support their *normal* education, help out like a normal teenager might with normal kids. But I knew things. I knew how to ask, to nudge others into delving a little deeper. I knew the little girl with the light limbs could hover in mid-air. I knew that quiet, tall Dominic was the very same little boy Ralph had described to me all those years ago, back in the days when he deigned to give me more than a few minutes of his attention at a time. The boy who could control computers. Next to him sat a girl who could bend metal with a touch of her fingertips, and over there lurked mini-Hulk Rudy who I'd once glimpsed lifting a man-sized log over his head. Then there was Daniel, who with his dishwater eyes and slow fading footsteps, could trick your eyes into not seeing him at all.

I watched them as I moved around the tables, handing out pencils, admiring terrible drawings and laughable attempts at joined-up writing. I listened to painstakingly slow attempts to read. I wiped noses and cuddled sticky, stained bodies and I resisted the urge to throw their pawing mitts off me, just so I could watch and keep watching. I knew Ralph had lost interest mere weeks after Blake had finally shown him the children – from behind a screen, with no interaction – and he had allowed his mind to be flattered into different avenues of study. I knew he was currently running his own research as well as studying for his A-Levels. He was planning to leave for university in the autumn and liked to sneer at me when I passed, still just a silly little girl in his eyes. But I also knew he watched me as I watched the children, a mixture of conflicting feelings swirling in his chest as he saw how I grew, how I learned, how I teased my own fate into the palm of my hands and rolled it sweetly between my fingers. I knew he saw how the others watched me, too. Those with narrowed eyes who let their jealousy shine from them like invisible ropes, urging me to trip and fail. Those with eyed broadened in wonder. And the others, more of them with every week that passed, whose gaze roved over my growing body without restriction, knowing I was young, still, but that I was getting older every day.

Ralph noticed them all and me as I fed them. A smile here, a pitying glance there, a sharp sneer when it was needed to knock back a rising threat. And sweet-faced encouragement, of course, to those who mattered most. To those whose kindling lust needed stoking if I ever stood to benefit from it. I was *so* clever, at fourteen and a half, so acutely aware of myself. I thought I gripped the reigns of my life, my body, and the attention of everyone around me with a certainty that was life-strong. It didn't even occur to me that the horse I rode had other plans.

'Right, blue table! How are those portraits coming along?' Jacqui swooped down on Nova's group to check their work. Nova looked up and caught my eye. I knelt beside her and, so only she could see, tipped a few extra colouring pencils into the space beside her page. She grinned.

'Hey, no fair,' Rudy squawked from the green table. I turned around; my smile ready to meet his frown.

'Oh, I'm sorry Master Rudolphus, would you like some crayons too to go with those sums you're supposed to be working on?'

'No,' Rudy's mouth twisted but I saw his eyes sparkle. He folded his thick arms. He was only eight but his biceps were already double the size of mine and beneath his shirt his torso rippled with muscle. I knew he could lift ten times his body weight; I also knew he was devastatingly ticklish.

'Ow!' He shrieked, giggling as I swooped down behind him.

'Oh, that didn't hurt!'

'How come you never tickle *Nova?*'

'Because Nova doesn't giggle like a baby hyena...'

'No! It's because she's your *favourite! Argh!*'

Jacqui threw us a half-frown and I stopped tickling him. Rudy sank back into his chair and I smoothed out his work sheet.

'Are you jealous, Rudy-licious? Is that it?'

'*No!*'

'I promise, Rudy-poo, if you take up ballet classes like

Nova and don a little pair of tights and a tutu, I will come and watch every single class you do.'

The green table burst into laughter and, as Jacqui came over to settle them down, I slipped back to Nova. She gave me a small, elfin smile.

'I wish you could come here every day,' she murmured.

'I know, me too...'

'Can you ask Dr Blake? He always does what you ask, doesn't he?'

I blinked at her in surprise. 'What makes you say that?'

'*Everyone* says that, Bella. All the grown-ups. They say he's wrapped in your finger or something...'

'Ha! Well, I could ask Dr B... But he isn't really the boss of you guys anymore, is he? Not now Ana's so poorly...'

Nova's small faced clouded over and she bit her lip. 'So you'll have to go to *him* instead...'

'Dr Lychen. Yes. He's the one who can make it happen.'

'I don't like him. No, don't ask him, he's scary.'

'Nah... He's alright... I can handle him,' I whispered back, winking at her until she smiled back, the darkness momentarily broken. I believed every word. Lychen had only really begun to notice me a few months earlier. And though the power which poured from his every movement had most of us scurrying to do anything we could for the smallest of favours, I still believed, at fourteen, I could manipulate him the same way I did everyone else. He may have been in charge of the ARC's biggest project and there were all those rumours about him taking over from Blake someday soon, but at the end of the day, he was just another eye-rover. No big deal.

## 35

**October, 2018**

*Monday*

Ariana brushes her hair quickly, letting the spray trickle down her back. She glances through the half-open door at Tess, who is leaning over her phone in the hallway. The bathroom she's in has three stalls all lined in yellow tiles and though clean, its bland indifference matches the rest of the former school. Except the room with the mahogany table, of course.

Ariana glances in the mirror. Her face is clean, and she narrows her eyes until they become Bella's – cold, unafraid, irresistible. Her hair spirals around her face. She wishes her curls would stay this tight and neat when dry. The clothes they've given her are an adult-sized white top which falls to her thighs, but with the sleeves rolled up several times over it's not too bad. A pair of navy leggings sag around her bony knees and she folds them up around the ankles so she doesn't step on them. She gets a fleeting flash of a memory of her mother tugging up her leggings as a child, but she can't remember which of them was the irritated party. Again she glances at Tess, wondering whether she can slip past her. She still hasn't been given her shoes back and when she steps out of the shower room she realises her old clothes have been taken away as well.

'Hey,' she says when she realises there is no other exit to the dull, yellow room and no hope of skirting past Tess unnoticed.

'Ready?' Tess looks her up and down and nods, briefly. 'That's better. You don't know how fussy they can be about hygiene around here… That's why they kept these old school showers. I'm surprised Dr Lychen saw you before you'd had a chance to wash, to be honest.' She peers at her curiously. 'I guess he was keen to meet you.'

Ariana shrugs.

'Come on then, I suppose I'd better show you around…'

'Where did they put my things? My shoes and clothes and stuff?'

'They'll wash your clothes… Not sure about your shoes – probably in one of the staffroom lockers. It'll be a hygiene thing – look, there are some clogs here you can wear. I think they got your size right. I know they're not exactly the trendiest but we all have to do it,' she offers Ariana a pair of purple rubber clogs and shows her her own pair in silver. Ariana notices a little toadstool badge gleaming from one of the holes.

'Nice…' she says, smirking.

'Yeah, yeah…'

'The jumper's cashmere,' Ariana says as she slips her feet into the rubbery shoes. They sink into the soles comfortably and Ariana feels a small sprig of betrayal towards her mother, whom, she knows, would not be caught dead in a pair of rubber shoes, no matter what the reason for wearing them.

'It's OK, they'll handwash it…'

'Who, exactly?' Ariana thinks of the burly Guard man and the others she's glimpsed like him. The large, impassive workers pushing cleaning trolleys along the grey, narrow corridors. The dead-eyed cafeteria servers. She can't imagine her mother's delicate wool nestled in their thick, nonchalant fingers.

'We have plenty of housekeepers,' Tess shrugs, glancing up the corridor as if keen to get on. 'A lot of employees live on-site both here and at the Beaumont – that's the London facility – it's kind of a BFI thing.'

'The scientists?' Ariana can't imagine the white-coated adults from the cafeteria, so confident with their braying voices and their large coffees in home-brought mugs, bunking down in dormitories, six to a room.

'No, not them. At the Beaumont we do. It's in central London and the accommodation on offer is a lot more reasonable than the alternatives, but here a lot of the scientists are older and have families and stuff so it's more like the lower-level staff... Come on, let's get going, shall we?' She starts walking down the corridor in the opposite direction to the entranceway. 'I'll show you some of the labs – the ones you're allowed to see, anyway, which I'm presuming are the ones *I'm* allowed to know about – then we'll try and think of something else to do...'

'So what's your job, exactly?' Ariana jogs a little to keep pace with Tess, whose strides are betraying a strange mixture of frustration and jumpy nervousness.

'At the moment? Babysitting you.'

'And before then it was talking to me online pretending to be my long-lost dad, right?'

'I never actually *said* I was your dad, you know...'

'No... you just happened to mention you were the right age and had yellowy-brown hair like me...'

'To be fair, I *do* have yellow hair...'

'And that you were a guy and it was funny my

username was French for green eyes because you used to know a girl who had the *most amazing* green eyes... Thirteen years ago... I didn't tell Mum about that bit, you know.'

'Well, anyway... There's no point getting worked up at *me*, most of it was from a script, you know... I was just the messenger, used for my technological prowess... and mainly being one of the few tech employees judged to be savvy enough with social media to adequately communicate with a teenager...'

'So who came up with the script?'

'Who do you think?'

'Lychen said he didn't lie...'

'Right. He doesn't. Except when he does.' Tess glances around, suddenly uncomfortable. 'Look, let's just draw a line under all that, OK. You're here, you're safe. Your mum will be here soon and she'll work whatever it is she needs to work out with Lychen and then you can go on your merry way and I can go back to London. Maybe all this will be a good thing – you won't have to hide anymore after all this... You can have a normal life...'

The thought had occurred to Ariana, but she considered it again. Freedom. Instagram. Selfies. Sleepovers. Trips into town without Bella hanging ten paces behind her and her friends. They round another grey corner and the corridor opens up into a more modern looking part of the building. Ariana can tell it has been added to the warren-like parts of the school as a newer extension because the walls are brighter, taller, and there is light everywhere. Looming windows dapple sunlight across a carpeted floor and, unlike the dingy corridors from which they've come, there are people everywhere. Two of them sit on a sofa, chatting with coffee cups in their hands, their clogged feet crossed and jiggling. Another couple sweep importantly across the middle of the room, talking closely. A few look up and stare as Tess leads Ariana across the carpet, past several drink and snack machines and towards one of several doors set in the far wall. Each bears a name instead of a number and Ariana recognises a few – Pythagoras, Darwin, Hawking.

'I can't promise I'll be able to explain everything they're doing in here,' Tess mumbles as she leads Ariana to the Darwin door. 'Mostly because I don't understand it all myself. I'm an entirely different species of nerd... But I'll do what I can.' She opens the door and Ariana, who had been expecting lab benches, Bunsen burners and petri dishes like the science labs at school, gasps. It's a bit like walking into a spaceship. Everything is gleaming steel, or poised and pointed. In one corner there is something that looks like an actual ray gun. In another a mouse squeaks in a large cage.

'Yeah,' Tess mutters, following her gaze. 'Just wait till you see the Pythag room. They use rabbits in that one...'

'Wow...'

'Hey, Ariana isn't it?' The large, jolly-looking man from earlier – Alec – pops up from behind a large shelving unit full of strange, spindly-looking instruments. 'Want to learn how to shoot a laser?'

**October, 2018**

*Sunday*

'I don't suppose you're going to tell me what all that was about?' I say, as Blake leads me into his old office. A million memories threaten to swarm over me as I glance around at the books, the lab stations, the huge windows and the old dentist's chair, which has been reupholstered in navy blue.

'Oh, you know Lychen… he's never happy unless he's fully convinced that he holds the strings. I merely posited a few conditions of my own. Certainly nothing he wouldn't have already taken into consideration.'

I watch him coldly as he shrugs into an old monogrammed lab coat and switches on a laptop on the desk nearest the dentist's chair.

'You don't trust I can take care of my child?'

'I have every confidence you will take care of *your* child, Bella,' Blake replies, smoothly, though his eyes have hardened behind his spectacles.

'You don't think Ralph can handle himself?'

'It's not about that,' Blake snaps. 'It's *him* I don't trust. Now, if you wouldn't mind taking a seat… Our testing has moved on in insurmountable ways, in some fashions, but in others we are faced with the same methods which have always served us.'

I sink backwards into the dentist's chair, feeling the soft foam nestle gently against my body. I rest my head back against the cushion and sigh, realising just how tired I am. It's late, after all. I wonder whether Ralph and Ethan have arrived yet. I'd left Felix in the room adjacent to us, her thumbs tapping busily on her phone as she frowned at the screen.

*What do you care, anyway?*

I don't. But he's supposed to come with me to the next place, isn't he? No Ralph, no Ariana...

'Bella?' Blake's voice has gentled and I glance over to find him seated on a wheeled office chair next to me. 'If you wouldn't mind rolling up your sleeve, I'll need to take just a little bit of blood...'

'Fine,' I say, pushing back the sleeve on my right arm, irritated with myself. I remember, with a surprisingly big wave of trepidation, why we're here. The diseased, rotting, festering *wrongness* that might at this very moment be creeping unseen along my veins, twisting itself round my organs or waiting, like a grenade with a finger on the pin, in the very clutches of my chest.

'So,' Blake says, tentatively taking my arm and relaxing it, as if unsure whether I might flinch away at any moment. 'She doesn't dance then, your Ana?'

'Ariana. Ri,' I correct, automatically. 'No, she does not. I took her to a few classes when she was younger but she wasn't into it...'

'You didn't teach her yourself?' He taps the crook of my arm with his gloved fingers and I look away as a vein bounces to the surface of my skin.

'No...' I think back to the small flats and apartments we've lived in, over the years. The comfortable but often cramped living rooms, always carpeted, each strand a tiny tug against a ballet-slippered foot.

'It's incredibly tedious, teaching. I have enough trouble keeping my patience with undergraduates at work,' I say, keeping my gaze on the familiar dark mountains which I can just make out – shadowy, indifferent humps of earth and stone and snow – through the windows.

'Oh, I don't know,' Blake mutters softly as he slides the needle into my skin. 'You seemed to display an admirable amount with the Project C Subjects back in the day. They all adored you... At one point I wondered whether you'd take up a teaching post as a career.'

'There's a difference between adoration and respect. They might have loved me, but it wasn't for what I was teaching them.'

'No? Well... It's all moot now, of course. Seems like you've done well enough for yourself despite... Well, no, that's not quite what I mean... that is to say...'

'It's fine,' I say, 'I don't care. You carry on. Despite leaving here, despite not fulfilling all your grand plans for me – being the ambassador for the ARC, the face of the future of science... Leaving it all to live off my family's guilt money, bear an illegitimate child in secret and not even bother to tell its father of its existence...'

'Bella...'

'No, it's fine. You think it'll injure me, somehow, to consider what you really think of me? To realise the extent of your disappointment?'

'I never said I was–'

'There was a time, once,' I say, softly, as I look down and watch the second vial of my blood fill, darkly, between us. 'A long time ago... When your opinion was the most important thing. When Ana died and I realised Lychen wasn't quite the brilliant white knight I'd thought he was... It was all about you... You took on everything that mattered. You were the one I had to prove myself to. And your value of me was *everything.*'

The vial is full but the needle remains in my arm as Blake stares at me, wordlessly. His expression is so exquisitely tortured I almost don't want to deliver the final blow.

'But like I said, that was a long time ago. I stopped caring what you thought of me the moment you showed me that you didn't.'

'Bella... I never stopped caring—'

'Yes you did. The moment you saw him for what he was and still did nothing. That's full, by the way, unless you'd like to drain me until I pass out...'

We both look down at the vial and Blake removes it from the hollow needle, placing it in the tray next to the first one. He places a cotton pad on my arm and slowly extracts the needle. I take my arm from him as soon as I possibly can.

'Bella... With Lychen... You don't understand. Things were complicated back then... It wasn't just a case of asking him to leave... By that point he was so invested – enmeshed – in what was happening here. And we were, too, with him...'

I shrug, lying back in the chair, transferring my gaze to the ceiling.

'It's done, Blake. All of it. Including the conversation about it. Now I presume the next step is a full body scan?'

I shut my eyes and sleep creeps a little closer, its heavy footsteps threatening to trample over the murmurs of worry for Ariana. *She's alright. He won't harm her. Not if he wants me to co-operate.* When Blake doesn't move, I sigh and open my eyes. He's still staring at me, sadness battling with a reluctant comprehension. He doesn't need to ask any more, but I know he will because who wouldn't grasp for a life-ring even if they knew they were destined to drown?

'Bella... When you say I didn't stop him... You– He never–'

'You know Lychen. What was it you said earlier? *He's never happy unless he's fully convinced he holds the strings.* People aren't people to him, they're puppets. All of us. Objects to control.'

'But–'

'That is all I've got to say on the matter. Come on, let's get this done. I would like to try and sleep for at least a few hours before I have to face him again.'

He sighs and though my lids are mostly closed, I watch him beneath the cover of my lashes as he reaches for the scanning machine and sets it into position. His movements are automatic, but his face is broken. I have done it. After all the years of dreaming about it, of picturing him fractured with the beast I've carried within me for so long, finally here he is, crumbling in front of my eyes by my own hand. Yet the triumph feels colder than I expected. Hollow, somehow. As so many anticipated things are.

*He is weak. He always was. There is no glory in destroying a weak thing. I thought I had taught you that, Bella.*

**Spring, 2001**

As it turned out, my chance to talk to Lychen came quicker than I'd anticipated. I arrived home from the ARC to a slightly more chaotic Manor than usual, with Ramona barely pausing in a vigorous rub of the large, ornate mirror in the hallway to glare in my direction as I took my coat off.

'No, in the cupboard,' she barked, as I made to hang the garment over the banister of the stairs like I usually did.

'How come? Who's coming for dinner?' I asked, retrieving the coat and making for the cupboard under the stairs, but she just went back to polishing the mirror as if I hadn't spoken. In five and a half years I was still none the wiser as to why she seemed to prefer to act as if I didn't exist, but I tended not to waste headspace on it. Certainly not when there were more pressing matters at hand, such as our mysterious dinner guest and the fact that, for the first time in several months, I could hear Ana's voice coming from the dining room.

'No, Vinnie, we will be needing the soup spoons *and* the fish knives, Ramona is serving salmon... Yes, the children too...'

'Mamma?' I addressed her the way I knew she liked me to and she was smiling as she turned from Vinnie, the young man the Blakes hired to serve at dinner parties when Ramona was too busy in the kitchen.

'Ah, Bella, there you are. I've been listening for you for an hour already, where were you?'

'I sat in on one of Madame Glioue's primary ballet classes... What's going on? Are you better? Who is coming for dinner?'

She did not look better. Her skin seemed to sag loosely from her bones, which poked almost viciously outwards in sharp angles. Her face had a greyish colour, yet there were two spots of unnatural pink high up on her cheekbones and though her eyes, as always, were beautifully made-up, the lids seemed heavier than usual. Her gaze shone as it always did, yet it was shadowed somewhat, as if she were wearing thick, slightly tarnished contact lenses. Still, she stood tall without leaning on anything and when she held a long, sinewy arm out to me, it was steady. I walked into her embrace easily and wrapped my arms firmly around her chest, afraid to squeeze too tight. She smelled of her usual sandalwood perfume, but there was another smell beneath it. It reminded me of the smell she'd had when I first met her, here in this room, only it was different again. Five years ago, the bread had only been on the cusp of mould, but now it had curled in on itself and powdery green spots were blooming, unbound, across its soft, white flesh.

'We are hosting one of Freddie's rising stars from the ARC. Joseph or Joshua or something. Apparently we've met but,' she gestures dismissively. 'Anyway, Freddie's talked about him non-stop, these last few months. Says this person is keen to be introduced to us all, properly... So I told him to invite him to dinner tonight. Celebrate my recovery. You will wear the white dress I had made for Christmas, yes? It still fits?'

'It fits,' I replied, a little hesitantly. The white dress

was a beautiful creation of delicate lace and ribbon, like a miniature bridal gown… but it made me look about ten. Still, I knew better than to argue with Ana, particularly as one hand had turned claw-like around my shoulder as the other raked my hair back from my face. She bent to look me properly in the eye, moving her hand to my chin to lift it towards the light.

'Is that where it went?' she sighed, her eyes looking duller than ever this close up as they roved over my skin, as if searching for a freckle which she had been sure was there the day before.

'Um,' I replied, my own eyes sliding away uncomfortably. I hadn't got a clue what she was talking about but she was being weirder than ever, which usually either meant she was building up to a fit of temper or she'd taken too many painkillers. Judging from the steadiness of her hand, still gripping my upper arm in a vice I had felt enough times to know I would bear bruises in the morning, and the look of her eyes, I suspected the latter.

'Go on then, go and smarten up, put your dress on. Dinner will be at seven. Perhaps you could do a little dance recital for Signor Science after dinner or something… Like you used to for Freddie's colleagues.'

'Oh, er, if you like… Though my white dress isn't really the best for dancing in… the skirt is kind of heavy.'

I didn't move, kept my eyes on hers. The last thing I wanted to do was perform a cheesy, little-girl dance for Dr Lychen in my stupid, babyish dress, but I mustn't let Ana see. I mustn't give her any reason to narrow her eyes, wonder what this person could be to me. She wasn't holding my chin anymore, but she still had my arm in her pincer grip, and I knew better than to move away before she had decided to release me.

'Fine,' she said, at last, glancing at the tablecloth and sighing. 'Maybe you can play the piano or something. Probably won't be time anyway, you know how long Papa likes to talk when he has one of his *contemporaries* for company.'

She let me go and began rearranging the place settings, her movements thicker than usual, full of fumbling bitterness. I smiled in case she looked up, but when she didn't, I turned on my toe and fled upstairs, my head full of the evening ahead and how I should wear my hair – thank goodness Ana hadn't requested plaits – and whether Ana would notice if I used the smallest amount of the expensive Italian make-up she'd given me for Christmas.

Half an hour later I stared at myself in the mirror. The white dress wasn't as bad as I'd thought – it still hung long enough beneath my knees to be modest, and yet the small buds of my chest, which had emerged in just the last month or so, gave the neckline a new, more grown-up angle that hadn't been there when I'd donned the dress on Christmas Day. My make-up was minimal, just a light brush of shadow to emphasise the green of my eyes and a glimmer of red to my lips. I knew that too much and I risked Ana barking at me to scrub my face, probably in front of Lychen and Ralph, who would smirk and make it all ten times worse. My hair I wore loose because I'd only washed it that morning and it was looking its best – long, curly and, thanks to a new serum I had discovered in Ana's bathroom, sumptuously smooth.

Despite his having worked at the ARC for several years now, I had only seen Lychen a handful of times, and though

I had felt his eyes follow me like a heat spot on the back of my neck the last few times, he and I had never held a proper conversation. *Tonight*, I said to myself as I made my way downstairs, wishing my feet were clad in a pair of killer heels like Ana would be wearing instead of my boring, patent Mary-Janes. *Tonight will be different*.

The sound of laughter filtered up the stairs and I quickened my pace. It was only six-thirty. I thought I had been early, but as I crossed the hallway to Blake's study, I recognised Ralph's voice, twisted into his *yes-aren't-I-clever-I-run-my-own-lab-you-know* tone and a sharp, unfamiliar laugh. I stopped. The sound should have been warm, cheering, inviting… instead it was cold, calculated… Careful. It reminded me of… well, me.

Taking a breath, I pushed the heavy door open and slipped into the room. Lychen, Ralph and Blake were all clustered near the fireplace, which was lit and pressing too much warmth into the room for the mildness of the evening. Ralph, I saw with a frisson of dark glee, was pink under his shirt collar and his too-long hair was beginning to clump with heat at the nape of his neck. Lychen, on the other hand, was as pale as ever under his mop of tawny-coloured hair. He was wearing a neat, plain suit which even I could tell had been tailored beautifully. His face shone whitely over a glass of amber liquid and his eyes darted between the two taller men in front of him, a deep glow of scarlet reflecting from the fire in their black depths. Ana was nowhere to be seen. Ralph, I noticed, also had a glass of the amber spirit in his hand, though his was measurably less full than Lychen's. Though he was still a few weeks from his eighteenth birthday, Ana and Blake had been fairly permissive with allowing him to drink socially over the last year or so. He had a few friends among the younger students who interned in the less secretive departments of the ARC and I'd often watch him from my bedroom window as he got into the brand-new Ford Fiesta his parents had bought him when he'd passed his driving test and roared off into the night to meet them. Sometimes I'd wait to see him return, unease tumbling with jealousy in my chest as I tried to work out if he'd been drinking when he lurched out of the car.

'Ah, Bella! Josiah, have you met our young Bella properly?'

Lychen's eyes fell to me and though his face did not so much as flicker, the glow in his eyes seemed to change, as if the fire within them had been stoked by something altogether more sinister. It reminded me of the way the kitchen cats would stare at something only they could see in the long grass out in the back garden, oblivious to everything else around them as they hunkered their bodies down and readied themselves for the killing pounce.

'I believe we've seen each other around the ARC,' Lychen said, smoothing over the question. I approached the trio almost unconsciously, as if there were some sort of invisible cord between his gaze and my own. I barely even noticed Ralph frowning on the periphery of my vision, barely heard Blake's remark about my volunteering with some of the C-Subjects.

'And how are you enjoying working with those extraordinary youngsters?' Lychen inclined his head towards me as I stood in front of him, wishing I were tall enough to stare him squarely in the eye, prove I was more than just another minion.

'They're fascinating,' I replied, levelly. 'I only wish I could learn more from them. I'm only allowed up to three hours a week, and that's while they're in class learning normal things.'

'But of course, sometimes it is the study of the mundane, these *normal things,* which reveal one's true extraordinariness, don't you think?' Lychen's voice slipped delicately through the air as insidiously as a snake, and before I knew it, I could almost feel it coiled around my neck, testing for weaknesses. I smiled because I knew he was expecting a frown.

'Sometimes, maybe. But I still think it would be cool to see Nova fly. Or Daniel disappear...'

I felt Blake and Ralph's tense intakes of breath beside me, but Lychen didn't flinch at my voicing of those most guarded of ARC secrets.

'Bella! I– I'm sorry...' Blake stammered and this time I did spare him a glance, as I had never heard such a thing before. 'She's not supposed to know about... I don't know *how...*'

'Tsh... It matters not,' Lychen replied, his voice warm but his eyes still roving mine. 'There are all sorts of rumours floating around the ARC. It would be more of a surprise to hear that they *hadn't* reached the ears of your young protégée here. Especially considering she is clearly astute beyond her years. You might want to be careful,' he added in Ralph's direction, making him cough as he gulped the last of his whisky. 'She'll be after your lab once you've left for university in the autumn at this rate!'

Ralph kept coughing, the rest of his face turning as pink as his neck. I smiled and let my eyes flash prettily at Lychen. He smiled back.

'So, you want to spend more time with the C-Subjects?'

'I think I've earned it,' I replied and his eyes immediately narrowed.

'How so?'

'I've invested in them. They trust me. Some of them love me. I'm sure of it. I understand them. Perhaps better than anyone else at the ARC.'

He raised his eyebrows. 'The ARC hosts some of the finest scientific minds in the country. How do you – a child barely grazing her teens – hope to justify such arrogance?'

'Because I'm a Subject too,' I replied, registering Ralph's smirk behind my back but not letting it interfere. 'But you already knew that, didn't you?'

Lychen stared at me for a few seconds, then his thin mouth curved upwards and he began to laugh again, and though the icy fingers of a shudder crept under the shoulders of my dress, I kept myself still, acknowledging his mirth with a twitch of my mouth. Lychen turned to Blake, who was wearing an odd expression caught somewhere between bemusement and something deep and fearful – the same fright, I realised suddenly, that he wore whenever Ana coughed or had to clutch a chair for support.

'I see my long-awaited invitation to dinner is going to be well worth all my not-so-subtle hints, Blake!'

Blake opened his mouth to reply, but at that moment the door to the study swung open and Ana entered, her face drawn but alight with animation above a black, sparkling gown and matching stilettos.

'Dinner is ready,' she announced, inclining her head to Lychen as he swept towards her, her eyes searching for Blake's and finding them. She frowned at his expression and immediately her gaze fell on me. Before she could say a word, however, Lychen was before her, kissing her cheek in greeting and offering his arm to accompany her into the dining room. I hastened quickly ahead of Blake and Ralph, partly to avoid their scrutiny and partly to try and hear what Lychen might be saying.

'...been discussing some of the more privileged snippets of information with your charming daughter. I would be delighted to continue our conversation over dinner, with your permission of course...'

'Oh, ah...' Ana glanced back over her shoulder, from me to Blake.

'Unless, of course, you find my influence... ah... unsuitable...'

'Of course not!'

'Well then, that's settled. Bella, you shall sit next to me at dinner,' he paused and offered me his other arm. I took it, smiling, though part of me ran cold because of that ring of icy command in his voice. I'd never heard it emanate so effectively in anyone else's but my own.

**October, 2018**

*Monday*

'Come on, I'll show you the computer suite. That's where the real magic happens,' Tess nudges Ariana until she reluctantly stops poking shredded lettuce through the rabbit cage. This is nothing like the boring, tame science classes at school where the coolest thing you might come across in the *lab* is a stuffed owl that she can't look at without shuddering. They throw their goodbyes at the two women in white who showed them the animals, though both are bent over microscopes in the corner of the room and just wave vaguely in their direction.

'More magic than lasers and rabbits with pink highlights?' Ariana asks sceptically as they step out of the room on their rubbery shoes.

'I told you, they just put the different colour blotches on so they can tell them apart. If you want to see theatrics, you should see the animal labs in the Beaumont. We've got a chimp who can play Beethoven, honest to God.'

'Really? What can the ones here do, then?'

'They don't have primates here... but I've heard they've got a rat that can read.'

'What?' Ariana pulls up short. They're at the edge of the large open area, about to duck into what looks like another low-ceilinged warren of a corridor. Tess grins at her as she frowns.

'You're messing with me, right?'

'No, seriously. Apparently they've got a maze with signposts and it always follows the right ones...'

'That's... mad...'

'Amazing how often *mad* and *brilliant* can be used in the same sentence. Come on,' Tess motions for her to follow. Reluctant to leave the warm light of the atrium, Ariana glances behind her and, once again, finds herself stopping short. Lychen is standing in the far corner of the large airy room with his back to them. After blinking at the smooth lines of his back for a few moments, Ariana switches her attention to the man with whom he's in deep discussion. He's shorter than Lychen by at least half a head, and his skin is so pale that next to the fair complexion of Lychen he looks waxy and ill. Ariana's close enough to tell he's fairly young – about the same age as her mother if not younger, because his face isn't wrinkled, but his mousy hair is thinning on top and has a strange, wispy texture like a very old man's.

'What?' Tess realises she's not following and comes back, following her gaze. She spots Lychen and her eyes widen.

'Who's that man he's talking to?' Ariana murmurs. At that moment the man himself looks up, as if he's heard her, and their eyes meet. The man's eyes narrow and his entire body seems to give a weird sort of shudder and – it's the strangest thing, but Ariana is sure, just for the tiniest of seconds, that his silouhette seems to blur around the edges. Like he's outlined in pencil and someone has rubbed their finger along his silhouette. A second later, the man turns back to Lychen and as Ariana sees the taller man beginning to turn around in response to something the shadowy man says, Tess takes her arm and begins to pull her away.

'Come on, let's go,' she mutters. This time Ariana follows her happily, glad to put distance between her and the strange, blurry man who gives her far worse creeps than any stuffed owl.

'Who *was* that?'

'His name's Dr Daniel Skaid,' Tess mutters as they round a corner. She's almost jogging and Ariana wants to tell her to slow down, but she's also afraid of what might happen if they do.

'He looked *weird*.'

'Yeah, he is. He's one of the original Project C kids...'

'The kids with the super-human abilities?'

'Yeah... Except once they got older, they either lost them or went mad or died... And then there was Daniel...'

'He's still got his abilities?'

'No one really knows. But for some reason, he's always had this weird thing with Lychen. It's like he's got something on him... After everything went tits up at the ARC, he was brought over here and by the time he was eighteen he was running his own department and had taken over half the laboratories, which pissed off a *lot* of people who were far older and more experienced.'

'What sort of department?'

'No one really knows. Supposedly something to do with the whole reinvention of the original Project B thing I mentioned earlier... That's the rumour, anyway. People tend to keep their distance... there's just something a bit off about him, you know?'

'Yeah, I kind of got that.'

'Well, if I were you, I would try and have as little to do

with him while you're here as possible. Lychen may be scary and cold, but Daniel... he's unpredictable. He was brought over with another one of the former C-kids – Nora, I think her name was. Rumour has it she was his assistant for a year or so until she mysteriously vanished... No one knows what happened to her, but apparently he doesn't have assistants anymore. Not human ones, anyway. No one wants to work with him... Just stay away, OK?'

'OK,' Ariana nodded, feeling as if there wasn't any advice she needed less.

'Ah, here we are,' Tess's voice changes dramatically as she leads Ariana into a small, narrow room full of screens. A few people are working at a couple, sat at individual desks and very much apart from each other. They don't bother looking up as Ariana and Tess enter the room and Tess leads the way to a large computer in a corner.

'This is where the magic happens?' Ariana asks, sarcastically. It looks almost exactly like the computer suite at school. Except the computers don't look as modern as the ones they have at school and the room smells less of unwashed teenagers.

'You'll see...' Tess turns the computer on, sits herself on a wheeled chair and motions for Ariana to do the same. By the time Ariana has wheeled herself forward, Tess's fingers have flown across the keyboard a few times and suddenly there's a map in front of her. Several dots of different colours are clustered in a small nondescript looking area of green with no town name around it. Ariana looks around for some clue as to where they're looking and notices the area's label.

'The Lake District?'

'Yep.'

'What are the dots?'

'*That* solid black shape there, that's the ARC. Unplotted by the original map software, you'll notice. The blue dot there is Dr Blake senior. The grey ones are some of our Guard, those who've been placed there. Looks like one of them has left, there were ten this morning...'

Ariana stares as Tess zooms in and the black shape becomes the outline of a large, square building with smaller areas within it. The blue dot is joined by a green and a purple. In a different corner of the building a pink dot rests stationary with a grey dot on, what Ariana can now see, the other side of a line dividing one room from another.

'Who're these ones?'

'The green is Ralph Blake... He wasn't there last night, must have arrived sometime in the wee hours. He's–'

'The one who was brought up with my mum...'

'Yeah. The purple is a woman called Felix Bryden who is, like, a legend in the cyber world... She's written a ton of programs, practically invented her own coding... We've never met face to face but she's taught me everything I know. The yellow is a guy called Dominic Chester who was also a C-kid but he lost his gifts sometime around adolescence. There should be a navy one somewhere... oh there he is. Looks like he's sleeping or something. That's Ethan Bryden, he's Felix's husband. Don't know much about him except he's built like a tank.'

'Where's my mum?'

Tess points to the pink dot, alone in a room, unmoving.

'Why isn't she moving?'

'She's probably asleep. See, they've put a Guard outside her door? They only arrived late last night and they were up for hours after that... She's probably exhausted.'

'Mmm,' Ariana frowns at the pink dot until it blurs on the screen. Never once in her life has she known her mother go to bed whilst someone else – namely her – in the house was still up. *But then, how well do you really know her?*

'How do you track them? Have you bugged their phones or something?'

'Nah, Felix Bryden is far too clever for that sort of thing, though the software isn't a million miles away. We've specialised it though, so it can be administered on the tiniest device...' her face glowed with pride. 'I helped develop it myself. Even old Felix would be hard-pressed to get round it. We've been using it for years without them knowing.' She stops suddenly and glances at Ariana furtively, as if suddenly realising who she's talking to. Ariana makes her face as bland and impassive as she can, trying to imitate the creepy Guard people. *Don't let her think you understand what she's talking about. Don't let her think you're at all interested.*

It seems to work because Tess looks away and yawns.

'Sorry... Long night. Do you mind if I hop on this machine here and check my messages? Make sure there's nothing I need to be catching up on from work?'

'Sure,' Ariana says, blandly. 'Can I check Instagram?'

Tess is partly caught up in the screen in front of her, but she does frown a little and begins to turn to Ariana.

'I won't post anything, obviously,' Ariana says, quickly. 'I just want to see my friends...'

'Well... OK, I suppose that's alright. I mean, the only people going to be tracking your activity are right there on your screen, after all... It's not like they're not going to know where you are soon enough anyway.'

'Exactly,' Ariana smiles as reassuringly as she can,

most of her attention still on the motionless pink dot in front of her. She pulls up a new tab and begins to search for her friends on Instagram... all the while she's trying to remember something Lucy told her. Something about her dad and her phone and a code to disable a tracking device...

**Spring, 2001**

'So, Miss Bella, what is it about our Project C Subjects which interests you so?' Lychen's eyes blazed into mine with a hard, grown-up sort of intensity. Even close up it was impossible to tell the black irises from the pupils and, set into his pale face, it made him look otherworldly. Ralph, sitting in the blurred recesses of my vision on Lychen's other side, looked flushed and clumsy in comparison as he spooned soup into his mouth and scowled.

'Everything,' I replied, importantly. Lychen smiled widely and took a small sip from his soup spoon. I mirrored him, resolving only to eat when he did.

'So are you hoping to pursue eugenics as a field of study when you're older?' He asked, the test of my understanding shining clearly out of his intense gaze. *Easy,* I thought, dredging up the long hours spent in the classroom with Blake and Ralph, scrawling essays from encyclopaedias and participating in long-winded debates which twisted all of our voices with screeching self-righteousness.

'Yes,' I replied. 'I've covered some of the basics already... History, that sort of thing. It's quite fascinating when you look at how some factors come into play from as far back as the Roman times...'

'Quite,' Lychen inclined his head, clearly impressed. I

felt the glow of it sink into me, far more nourishing than any of the dishes Ramona could place before me.

'Our research would not be where it is without the hypotheses and conclusions drawn from our predecessors,' he added, sipping his water as his eyes flickered from me to Blake, sitting opposite him at the rounded table. Ana, on my other side, said nothing, but I heard her sniff loudly.

'Oh yeah,' Ralph's voice came snide and slurred from Lychen's left elbow, 'The guys who'd leave a baby out on the cliffs because it had a crooked nose... We've sure learned a lot from them, right? And then there were the Goodell types who were all for forcible castration... Marvellous idea.'

'Well, and who is to say that we would be where we are today without those notions?' Lychen turned to him, his voice mild but his scrutiny unyielding. I watched, amused, as Ralph blinked and seemed to shrink a little against the back of his chair. He recovered quickly, shaking his too-long hair and smirking.

'You can't tell me you agree with those barbarians? You'll be saying Hitler had a point with his Arian obsession next...'

'Ralph...' Blake's voice warned across the table like a hand dampening down a rogue flame.

'Forgive me, but I don't see what this has to do with Bella spending more time with the Project C Subjects,' Ana said, her voice quiet and yet every bit as steely as Lychen's. I turned around and noticed that she was gazing at Lychen, her face strangely flushed around the edges of her make-up. Her wine glass, like Ralph's, was almost empty.

'It's all relative, is it not? The history behind how these extraordinary children came into being... How Bella herself came to be...'

'That's right,' I said, keen to show him I could speak for myself. 'I'm like them... More than anyone else at the ARC... I can understand what it's like for them...'

'So wait, hang on a sec, let me get this straight...' Ralph set his wine glass down too abruptly on the table, sending small, purple-red sprays spreading like blood upon the tablecloth. I winced and saw Lychen do the same.

'You think those nutters were right – at least on *some level* – to leave their slightly odd-looking kids out on the cliffs to die... You think forcing a physically or mentally disabled person to be castrated would be the right call? Seriously? And you,' he turned to me, his eyes hot and passionate and everything that Lychen's cool, sober gaze was not, '*you* want to work more closely with this guy?'

Silence fell as Vinnie solicitously removed the soup bowls and replaced them with plates of salmon, vegetables and a large tureen of sauce.

'It isn't,' Lychen eventually said, coldly, 'a case of right or wrong or agreement or condemnation. I would have thought a scientist with your... ah... reputation... would understand that, Ralph.'

'So what *is* it about then?' Ralph demanded, blinking as if trying to rake through Lychen's words to find the insult he could sense.

'Education. We learn from everything – despite our personal feelings about it. Something which I'm sure Bella here would agree with, wouldn't you?'

'Of course,' I said, quickly, not quite understanding why I'd been brought up as an example, but quick to distance myself from the leering idiot across the table.

'Really,' Ralph drawled. 'And you are aware that Beast's parents effectively abandoned her for being, in her mother's words, *defective*, are you?'

'Ralph! That's enough!' Blake snapped, but I didn't turn to look at him. Next to me I felt Ana's hand, cool but pincer-sharp, on my forearm as if she were suddenly afraid she would topple from her chair without me. I glared at Ralph.

'But that is exactly my point,' Lychen said, smoothly. 'Bella can look with detachment at the folly of her biological parents and see that actually, once personal feelings are removed, the situation is fortuitous to her and all of us. If they hadn't done what they had, well there would be no Bella Blake and we would not all be enjoying her charming presence here tonight and for all the days hereafter,' Lychen raised his still-full whisky tumbler to me as if in toast and sipped delicately as, behind him, Ralph scowled deeply, his glasses catching the light and revealing grease smears which hid his eyes.

'D'accourt,' Ana said, sharply. Her fingers cut into my skin but I didn't turn around, so transfixed was I by the man sitting on my right.

'I beg your pardon?' Lychen replaced his tumbler on the table and addressed her politely.

'Bella's name is still D'accourt. We haven't adopted her formally,' Ana replied, her voice slurring almost as much as Ralph's. I noticed Blake watching her worriedly, gesturing to Vinnie not to refill either of their wine glasses as he hovered nearby with the bottle.

'My mistake,' Lychen said, though there was, for the first time that evening, a distinct air of mystification in his voice.

'We have been wanting to do it… For many years now,' Ana said, defensively. 'But we haven't acquired all of the permissions yet from her biological family…'

It wasn't news to me and, by this point in my life, I barely felt the mention of my former family. I certainly no longer let myself dwell on whatever reasons they might have had for not allowing the Blakes to complete the adoption process they had instigated within a year of my coming to live with them. I knew the reluctance came from my father; I knew there was nothing legal that could stop him coming to reclaim me, even after all these years. I also knew that there was no way I would let him. It was only many many years later that it occurred to me that he might also have known this.

Shaking my hair out of my eyes, I watched Lychen carefully. He was regarding Ana with a mixture of respect and something else. Something as close to contempt as I'd ever seen anyone show my fearsome Mamma.

'Extraordinary,' he remarked, cutting his fish into small slivers of pink flesh. 'And this arrangement is satisfactory to you?'

'Sorry?'

'I mean no disrespect... But it sounds to me as if your parental control is somewhat... compromised... by this indecision on the part of her birth parents. That places the young Bella here in something of limbo. Not quite able to settle. Not quite fully... claimed...'

'Bella is ours in every way apart from name,' Ana replied, her voice steady but with a tiny tremble lurking just beneath the surface of the words, like the wobble of a gymnast's supporting elbows as they stood upon their hands. Her nails had become talons upon my skin under the table. I suddenly had a strange, unbidden vision of her dropping down dead then and there and nobody being able to remove her grip from my arm.

'Of course she is,' Lychen smiled, turning to his fish

and placing a small morsel into his mouth. 'Mmm. This salmon is quite excellent.'

'Isn't it?' Blake interjected hurriedly. 'I think our Ramona might just be one of the finest chefs this side of Paris. But you're a travelled man, Josiah – tell us about your recent trip to Berlin…'

Lychen took up Blake's change of subject readily and, as the conversation swerved into boring territory, Ana eventually let go of my arm. The subject of my increasing my time at the ARC did not come up again, but as I bade Lychen farewell after Ana told me it was time to go to bed later on, he shook my hand firmly and murmured that he would be seeing me soon. My hand burning from the smooth touch of his, I did not notice the looks thrown between Ana – who by that point looked almost dead on her feet with exhaustion – and Blake. But it seemed that whatever hold this strange, coldly powerful man had over the ARC and the Blakes within it was stronger than any reservations they might have had about him, for the following Monday saw Jacqui greet me at the classroom door with a distinct air of excitement as she revealed that I had been given clearance to stay for the entire afternoon.

Less than a month later, Ana was dead.

**October, 2018**

*Monday*

Ariana is OK. She is safe. He hasn't hurt her, he won't...

I wake from a dead-like sleep, one so deep that it takes me a full ten seconds to blink myself into the present. The small, cell-like room I'm in is chilly and I don't have to touch the shining black walls surrounding me to know they're icy – it's like they're radiating frost. There's a narrow window slotted in the far wall and as I glance up, I spot a few flakes of snow clinging to the glass. I feel grubby, having slept in the clothes I've worn since yesterday, but when I check myself I'm relieved to see there isn't a spot on me.

*Yes, you always had an uncanny ability to keep yourself clean. Even as a child. Strange, it was. You'd come in from the garden on a warm, summer's day as pristine as if you'd stepped out of a children's wear catalogue. Unnatural, really.*

She's louder here. I don't know if it's because everything feels so close to the surface – my usual veneer of control feels so stretched it's practically see-through. Or maybe I'm just going mad. I straighten up and move towards the window, trying to use it as a mirror as I bring a hand to my head and comb my fingers through my hair. Clean I may look but I hate feeling unkempt. Like the dirt of the last twenty-four hours has turned me inside out. My hair is probably a mess, too. I wonder if there's a shower nearby I can use. I approach the door and, to my surprise, the handle turns easily. There's a Guard man outside the room and as I appear he seems to switch on, turning his head and blinking his eyes back to what little life they have.

'The testing has been completed. You will accompany me to meet Dr Blake now and then—'

'I will accompany you to meet no one until I have washed,' I tell him, firmly, maintaining careful eye contact. He nods, shortly, and although it catches me by surprise, I'm careful not to show it. His orders must include allowances for my personal comfort, I think, which somehow only makes me feel even more grubby. Wordlessly he sets off down the corridor and I follow him. We're on the seventh floor of the ARC and if I've been here before I can't remember it. I had thought most of the upper levels were taken up by private offices, but apparently there were living quarters here as well. Or at least there are now. The Guard unlocks a door bearing an empty name slot and we step into a spacious office with a distinct air of neglect about it, from the thick, dust-covered desk to the dead potted plant in the corner.

'There's a private bathroom through that door,' the Guard gestures towards a wooden door set behind the desk. 'Linens have been provided. I'll wait here.'

I make my way across the room, careful not to look at any of its features. I concentrate on keeping my thoughts at surface level – wondering who would have ordered the bathroom of this clearly long-dormant office restocked, whether it was the same person who ensured that the bed I slept in last night had clean sheets. I try my best not to look at my surroundings as I cross the room, but still tiny details crowd into the edges of my vision, tinged with a dark, fingering shadow of memory. The feel of the chair's leather trim whispers its smooth, cold notes to my hand as I pass. The familiar swirls in the carpet remember the tread of new, high-heeled shoes. The solid, condensation-free panes of glass in the windows gleam with all they've seen. The sleek, cold surface of the desk screams with an unforgotten pain. I haven't been in this office before, of that I'm sure. But I've been in one almost exactly the same. One which bore my own name upon its door, where people knew they had to knock and even then probably wouldn't be admitted. One where I spent years learning, planning, working, glowing with the thrill of discovering new, hidden pathways. The room where everything changed and, all at once, everything broke.

**Spring, 2001**

There was no dramatic grasping of my hand at the breakfast table. No rolling eyes or sudden, hand-to-chest collapse in the ballet studio as I spun around in the foreground, leg stretched in second, toes pointed. There were just days, dull and cold as spring failed to permeate through the large, thick walls of the Manor. Dance and piano practice. Potato-rich dinners. Sore calluses upon the balls of my feet and my toes as I tried, night after night, to raise my number of fouettés. And she was there. Watching, her brow knotted. Quieter than usual, perhaps. And she didn't touch me so much. Once or twice I'd feel a failing flutter at my back or over the surface of my hair, but I didn't stop. I never turned around. I lived for the moments when I could escape into the freshness of the Cumbrian air, let the wind lift the cloak of that house, the sickness and the shadows from my shoulders as I set off for the ARC among the struggling, burgeoning spring buds. And the children. Dominic with his quiet, awkward stoop as his long legs sprouted him almost as tall as I was. Nova with her adoring gaze. Daniel with his slavish dog-eyes. They all reached for me like I was manna, and in turn I listened and held and waited until the day when I might see more than just a glimmer of a glimpse of what they could really do. Now that I was spending whole afternoons with them at a time,

I knew it wouldn't be long; that those in charge were watching me to be sure, to see if I'd pass. And I would. Failure wasn't in my nature.

I barely noticed when Ana didn't come for breakfast a week after the dinner party. When Blake said, with a thickened voice and a heavy gaze, that the doctors had been called, I made the right noises and I promised to go and see her as soon as my lessons were finished for the day. But I didn't feel anything. It was nothing new. The doctors were always coming and going. She would stay in bed for a week, maybe two and then she'd be back, her grip as strong as ever, her eyes narrowing as she demanded I recite the periodic table and then perform one of the solos for my next ballet exam. Her voice sharp if the results were anything less than perfect. Ralph, if anything, reacted even less than I did. I saw him little during those weeks – he would set off for the ARC before I'd come down to breakfast and most of the time he did spend at home was done so in isolation as he studied for his impending A-Levels. If our paths happened to cross, we mostly ignored one another.

It was late when I made my way into her bedroom. I'd stayed behind at the ARC to help Jacqui clear up after the children had gone for their dinner – I had discovered that people were more likely to disclose secrets when their manner was grateful and their hands were busy. I'd been feeling particularly pleased that afternoon after Jacqui had let slip that Reuben – currently our oldest C-Subject – was beginning to show signs of plateau with his ability to perceive hidden desires. He had failed in his last two tests and had only managed to identify *surface wants* when questioned that very afternoon. The news was welcome for two reasons – firstly because I knew the longevity of the

Subjects' abilities was integral to Ralph's line of research and that he had probably not heard the latest about Reuben. The second reason was because I'd always felt a little nervous around the dark, large-eyed young boy; wary that he might suddenly pipe up and tell the rest of them that my primary motivation for spending so much time with them was not, in fact, a fondness for small children.

'You're late,' the voice came, hoarse but threaded with an everlasting note of maternal injustice.

'I'm sorry, Mamma,' I murmured, crossing the room to the large, darkened bed. It was a four-poster canopy but the curtains had been tucked up out of the way of the machines. One fed morphine into her arm, another would be strapped to her face to provide oxygen overnight. Ana was lying slightly propped up by a mound of pillows. Her thin arms were bare and rested on the outside of the duvet, and though her face was completely colourless – not even so much grey as just blank, as if there were nothing under the surface of her skin at all – her eyes followed me as keenly as ever as I approached.

'Liar,' she said, smiling and lifting one arm to pat the duvet next to her. I climbed up next to her as gently as I could, afraid to jostle her in case I disturbed any of the medical leads and wires. Her scarf was slightly askew, revealing a small, snowy white lock of wispy hair. New and soft-looking, like the hair of the smallest children at the ARC. I wanted to touch it, but I also wanted to tuck it away and never have to see it again.

'He keeps you busy,' Ana said, and then coughed harshly into her hand. I reached for a tissue from the box on her bedside table, but she gestured my hand away.

'I like the work,' I said, mostly because it looked like it hurt her to talk. 'I like working with the kids...'

'You ne... never could lie... to me, bambina...' Ana coughed. Her eyes, only slightly watery, stared into mine and saw it all. *Forget Reuben,* I thought, *here's the person who sees everything.*

'OK, I want to see what they can do,' I admitted, twisting my mouth ruefully.

'Why?'

'I don't know... I just want to see it...'

'You want to see... if they're better... than you...'

'No. They're different. Their gifts have been introduced differently. There's no point of comparison,' I said, though we both knew I was reciting what I'd been told. She waited.

'OK, fine. I want to find out if there *is* any comparison...'

'You feel... threatened by them...?'

'I don't know,' I shrugged, looking at the tank of oxygen standing next to her bed. Her sudden grip on my arm was cold but surprisingly strong. I looked down at her hand before I looked up at her. Her eyes were still on mine, but there was also something strange about them. Something filmy and uncertain, as if she was unsure if I were really there or not.

'You must be careful, Bella. With Lychen. He is *not* just interested in your intelligence...'

'He said I was the brightest young person he'd ever met!'

'Whether that's true or not... that's not why he's interested. You're not stupid... You can see it.'

'You don't know him,' I said, sulkily.

'I know men... like him... they're all about possession. He will try to possess you... if you let him.'

'What if I want to let him?' I whispered, putting my

hand over hers and slowly prising her fingers away from my skin. Her eyes bulged in surprise and possibly pain. For that moment, I didn't care. For that moment, I just wanted to stop her for all the times I hadn't tried before. But then she shrugged and before I had finished removing her hand, her grip disappeared and she settled back into her pillows, her eyelids fluttering.

'You don't...' She said, her voice stronger though her gaze flickered with looming unconsciousness. 'The possessor has the power. You will not give that up so easily. Not after all I have taught you.'

'What have you taught me? How to twirl and pout and point my toes? A few quadratic equations? I could have learnt all that from anyone,' I snapped, harshly. I didn't know why I was angry; I just knew that something about her giving up so easily made it easier to be angry than anything else. She smiled, her thin mouth a weak ghost of the beaming elegance in the portrait hanging downstairs.

'You couldn't. Not the same way. You're my spirit child, Bella. Ralph, he came from my flesh. But you were born of my spirit... The binds are inside. They won't be silenced... Not if you speak back.'

I frowned. The door opened behind me and made me jump a little, which made me scowl as I always did when caught unaware. Blake dipped into the room, his eyes searching between Ana and I.

'She's really tired,' I whispered. 'Been rambling all sorts of nonsense...'

He nodded. I slipped gratefully off the bed and made my way across the room. She didn't call out to me again. She didn't tell me goodbye or repeat her strange warning about Lychen. Blake didn't say anything either, and as I turned I saw he had taken my spot on the bed, his hands gentle and soft as they took the one I'd prised roughly from my arm a few minutes before. They were utterly each other's, I thought, as I left the room. I could have swelled to the size of a giant and broken through the ceiling, and they wouldn't have looked up as the plaster rained upon them. My anger shrivelled like plastic in a fire as I padded down the corridor towards the stairs and my own bedroom, where I could rake and dwell over her words with the self-obsessed toothpick of the chronically-misunderstood teenager.

**October, 2018**

*Monday*

I've known for quite some time – since I was a child, in fact – that being me takes a great deal of resilience. I wouldn't say I'm a mother who doesn't worry unduly about her child. Some might call me cold, being concerned for my appearance and wanting to shower whilst my daughter is in the custody of someone I know to be one of the most evil men in the country. When I allow myself to think about it, just the thought of Lychen being anywhere near Ariana catches in my throat and makes it impossible to breathe. During my shower my mind, already fragile, wanders there and I almost collapse, my heart pounding, my lungs feeling as if they are wringing themselves inside out like a sponge. But then I stop. I tell myself that this *will not do*. I feel the flutter of her shadow heart beneath mine, I recall the echo of her voice in my head. I remind the emotional, clutching beast inside that I am doing everything I can to get her back. He won't hurt her. He doesn't want her. He doesn't know. He only wants me, and that I can handle because I know – even the raging, weeping mess inside knows – that he won't risk hurting her when she is the strongest piece to play on this chessboard between us.

It *is* a coldness, I suppose. This resilience. The part of

me which takes over and steps, calmly, from the shower and reaches for a towel, all traces of panic washing down the plughole with the water. It's what my mother called *coldness,* anyway. Cold, creepy, defective Bella. It doesn't mean that I don't ache for my child. It doesn't mean that the small girl I once was didn't blink as hidden parts of her crumpled and died under her mother's open contempt. It just means that I put it away, I actively don't think about it because what good would dwelling on it do anyone? Maybe that's part of my *ability*. It certainly seemed to be part of why my mother could no longer bear the sight of me by the age of nine.

I follow the Guard man after I've dressed and styled myself as best I can with the small make-up supplies and comb I have in my handbag. It's mid-morning so I'm not surprised when we exit the lift on the third floor and he leads me to the staff canteen. As we walk, I take in my surroundings – the broken ornaments cluttering the hallways, the cobwebs in the high reaches, the general air of decay. Even the black walls seem less shiny than they were thirteen years ago. The sound of voices reaches us as we approach the canteen and the Guard swings one door open to admit me. Blake, Ralph, Dominic, Ethan and Felix are all there, clustered around a table which I recognise, with an odd pang, as the one we often used to share in the old days because it stood adjacent to a window overlooking the mountains. They look up as we enter, their expressions ranging from relief to surprise to impassivity. Apart from Dr Blake, who just looks terrible.

'You have thirty minutes to refresh yourself, then we will be leaving,' the Guard man barks, loud enough for everyone to hear. He goes to join the other three Guard people positioned around the room. I glance over at the food service area, which I remember being full to the brim with everything from doughnuts to fresh lasagne. Today there's a small box of stale-looking pastries, a meagre selection of small cereal boxes and a choice of tea bags or instant coffee next to the boiling water tap. I heap a teaspoonful of dry coffee into a mug, pour on water and grab what might be a Danish. I feel them all watching me. I let them.

'So, what's the word on the tests?' I address Blake, as I sit myself in the chair one of them has drawn up for me at the table. A small part of me is surprised they didn't leave it for me to drag over myself.

'Can't tell you,' Blake says, glancing from me to the Guard and back again. His whole face seems to have greyed and sagged since yesterday, like he's suddenly put on a mask of elephant skin. The beast in my chest shivers worriedly and I swallow hard, wrapping an icy hand around it to keep it still.

'They won't let you?'

'No, I mean I don't know... The results take a few hours to process and I was hoping to review them, but it's like those... those *things*... knew exactly how long it would take. No sooner did numbers appear on the screen than I had one of them hovering over me, barking at me to print everything and place it in a sealed envelope... I barely got a glimpse of anything. Though what I did see looked perfectly fine.'

I swallow a large, hot mouthful of bad coffee and keep my eyes on him.

What, then? If I'm not dying... Why do you look like you've had a stroke overnight, Blake?

Maybe it's not the test results. Maybe something else has happened.

'Figures,' snorts Ralph, hoarsely. I turn to him. His hair is sticking up in peaks and troughs all over his head as if he's been running his hands through it all night long, and there are deep grooves under his eyes. He almost looks as terrible as his dad. 'I mean it's only *your* health... Can't expect Lychen to just let you find out if there's anything wrong before he does, can you?'

I take a bite of pastry, staring at him until he looks away uncomfortably.

'So what's the plan?' I ask, staring from Ralph to Felix, Ethan, Dominic and back to Blake. None of them look like they've had more than a few hours of sleep between them. Dominic can't stop the yawns from shuddering through his body and flushes deeply red with every one he tries to suppress. Felix frowns irritably as if she has a bad headache and, next to her, Ethan looks blank as he rubs a spot between Felix's shoulder blades seemingly unconsciously. I watch the way she leans back into his broad hand even whilst scowling in my direction, as if he is simply an extension of her own body, his permanence unquestionable.

'Well... You and I have been summoned, of course,' Ralph mutters, keeping his eyes on the nearest Guard.

'And...?'

'And that's all you need to know, if you ask me,' Felix hisses.

'Why? I assume there is some underlying plan in place that doesn't just involve following Lychen's trail... Surely I of all people–'

'You of all people *do not* need to know,' Felix's hisses turn guttural and Ethan moves his hand from her back to her shoulder. She glances at him and frowns as he raises his eyebrows.

'Stay out of it,' she mumbles, though he hasn't spoken. I battle a sudden, visceral urge to leap up and push her over, chair and all. I breathe in slowly, and out again.

'Look... It's just...' Ralph starts, haltingly, but Felix cuts across him.

'We can't trust you, Bella. Not with Lychen. Not with everything...'

'I see,' I say, slowly, placing my empty coffee cup next to my full plate. The pastry has turned into sawdust in my throat but I won't let them see that. I just swallow, hard, until it's gone, and push the plate away. 'So we're about to go on a rescue mission for *my* daughter, who is currently being held by the man who has been trying to find me for God knows how long. And has requested the results of specific genetic tests performed on *me*... As the last surviving Project A Subject. And you don't think I deserve to know the full story as to how you all presumably plan to thwart him?'

'No,' Felix snaps. 'You might tell him.'

'Might I?' I'm not looking at her, though. It's Blake whose watery blue eyes are staring at anything but my own clear gaze. I turn from him to Ralph, who meets my eyes at least, though with rather a lot of blinking.

'You really think I'd risk further danger to Ariana?'

'No, of course not,' Ralph says, too fast. 'But he's... powerful... Beast, you don't know him anymore. What he's become... it's almost monstrous. They say he's almost impossible to overcome, even without all the resources at his disposal,' he gestures at the Guard, who have begun to cluster together, their voices a low, monotonous murmur. I check my watch and see that my allocated thirty minutes are nearly up.

'People have said similar things about me in the past,'

I remind him, mildly, though it's a battle now, keeping the inner rage from bursting out of me and leaping at his throat.

'It's just... It's safer if you don't know,' he says, firmly. 'For everyone. Ariana included. You're going to have to trust us.'

'Trust you?' I get to my feet before I can stop myself, and this time my fists are balled as I turn to Blake. 'Trust *you?*'

'Trust Ralph,' Blake says, his voice barely more than a whisper. 'He'll do what he can for Ariana and you both. You know that, Bella. No matter what else there is... here... you know *that,* don't you?'

They're all staring at me now. I can feel their gazes as I could when I first entered the room. Confusion, hurt, blandness from the Guards, that keen, jealous hatred from Felix which I have yet to fully unravel, and from Ralph a deep-seated mystification. He opens his mouth, his eyes flittering between his father and me, framing the question that could undo everything if I dared to answer it... A Guard man arrives at my elbow.

'Come. It's time to go.'

I turn and join him without another word.

**Summer, 2005**

Ralph slammed his fist down on the desk between us, making the glass instruments shiver angrily.

'It's not that simple! It *can't* be that simple!'

'Maybe it is…'

'No. I refuse to accept that. The problem is biological. It has to be. We isolated that specific gene pattern in Reuben and it's why Verity is rapidly declining as well… Rudy has it too, so it's only a matter of time before it catches up with him as well. It's linked with what makes them receptive to genetic manipulation…'

'Blah, blah, blah, Ralphie. It's adolescent self-awareness and outsider influence.'

'It's *not!* Reub, did anyone come up to you when you were thirteen and tell you that all the stuff you could do with your mind was put there by careful suggestion, manipulation and isolation?'

'Leave me out of it,' Reuben blushed from his perch on the stool next to Ralph, folding his arms and fluttering his long-lashed eyes downwards.

'We can't, mate,' Ralph switched into his grin as quick as he had been to flare up in anger. It was an impetuous mood change that reminded me painfully of Ana. 'You're kind of the basis of the whole argument.'

'What are you two snarling at each other about now?

And why have you dragged poor old Reub into it?'

Felix entered the room, frowning at us but unable to hide the frisson of amusement creeping into her voice. Her hair was purple and in need of a trim; curls were beginning to infiltrate her usual cropped style. She shrugged a white coat over the top of her rolled-up sleeves. I pretended to regard her punky fashion sense with scorn, but deep down I admired the way she always seemed to dress and act as if she knew exactly who she was. Having turned nineteen just a few weeks previously, I still hadn't quite figured it out for myself.

'Reuben's fine,' I said, perhaps a little too sharply.

'Yeah, he looks it,' she scoffed, coming over and bending down to murmur in Reuben's ear. He flushed again but began to unscrunch on his stool, a smirk pushing at the corner of his lips.

'What did you say?' Ralph asked, suspiciously.

'Not much,' Felix shrugged, innocently, reaching into her bag for her laptop. 'I just pointed out that whatever you guys were saying had less to do with him and more to do with your own semi-incestuous lust for one another...'

'*What*!' I'd begun to turn away but at her words I swung back around, my long hair splattering my back as if as appalled as the rest of me at the suggestion.

'That's complete... You're off your head!' Ralph spluttered, turning a violent shade of purple.

'You're *disgusting*. He's like my brother,' I added, venomously. Felix's smile faltered a little as she took in my fury, but then she caught Reuben's eye and grinned wider.

'Methinks they doth protest too much, too, Reub...' She said, though Reuben hadn't spoken.

'Because what you're saying is ludicrous... Not to mention disrespectful and downright insulting!' Ralph spat.

'Insulting? Yeah, to me!' I glared. 'Like I'd ever go for someone who used to be able to peel grease strands out of his own hair with his fingernails...'

'Yeah, well, at least I never threw up into my own school desk...'

'I had the flu!'

'There they go again,' Felix muttered to Reuben as he shrugged, gathering up his belongings.

'Well, I'd better get going,' he said, his voice soft as ever but several degrees more cheerful than it had been when Ralph had dragged him into the lab from the corridor and thrust him onto a stool as he'd tried to make his point. 'Got to get these test results to Dr Bletchley before lunchtime...'

'Sorry you got pulled into it, Reuben,' I said, watching the hunch of his shoulders as he bent over a large sheaf of papers and hauled them into his thin arms. He raised his large eyes to mine and, though it had been years since he was able to tell so much as what number between one and ten someone might be thinking of, I still had to resist the urge to look hastily away.

'That's OK, Bella,' he replied, a hint of surprise in his voice.

'Drop by my office later, Reub,' Felix added, 'I'll show you some new software I've been developing.'

Grinning at her gratefully, Reuben bent forwards over his heavy load and backed hurriedly out of the room.

'Poor kid,' Felix murmured, watching him go. 'Why'd you have to drag him into it, eh? Don't you think it's hard enough he has to work alongside his former classmates without having it shoved in his face that he isn't one of them anymore? That he's a failure?'

'Yeah, alright,' Ralph looked down guiltily. I frowned, not so much because I disagreed with Felix but because I hated the way she was looking at us, like we were stupid school kids. Plus I couldn't let her implication about me and Ralph slide so quickly.

'It wasn't like that,' I said, acidly, 'and anyway, it's not like Dr Bletchley works with any of the C-Subjects these days. And Reuben chose to stay. He didn't have to.'

'Oh right, and what's the alternative for a kid his age? He's never known anything different to here, of course he was going to stay!'

'Well then, he should accept the consequences and let us learn from him. As it is, he's no use to either of us really, when it comes to the argument of what makes the C-kids fail...'

'I *just said* he possessed the gene–' Ralph rounded on me as Felix rolled her eyes and turned back to her computer screen.

'Yeah, and I maintain that it's got less to do with that and far more to do with the psychological develop–'

'You and your head games! Don't think I don't know where this is all really coming from, Beast. If the problem is biological, it means more experiments, more research, more resources. If it's all in their heads, well...' he looked me up and down scathingly, 'Forgive me for not jumping to the *cheap* conclusion.'

I felt Felix's sharp intake of breath beside me but I didn't spare her a glance, I just glared at Ralph and channelled every ounce of hatred I could summon until he flushed to the very roots of his short gelled-up hair and looked away.

'Look. I've been doing this a lot longer than you,' he said. 'I've been studying this angle for *years*... If I could just hire more assistance... Proper, specifically-skilled researchers who can help me isolate whatever biological characteristic–'

'But it's *not* biological! Can't you see that after all this time – surely even *you* could have proven it by now if it was! If you just *look* at the studies on self-actualisation. Hell, if you just *think about it*, can't you see that it's all connected to the progression of puberty, the loss of childhood grace and innocence...'

'I hate to interrupt,' Felix cleared her throat, glancing between us with a mixture of exasperation and awkwardness. 'But what about Dominic? He's what, fifteen? Older than Rudy, at any rate... And still doing great by all accounts...'

'Exactly! *Exactly!*' Ralph slammed a fist onto the workbench again, making Felix jump. 'Dominic's a scrawny little bean-stalk but he's well into puberty... You should see the way he looks at *you,* for God's sake, Beast... And he's doing just fine, right Fee?'

'Yep,' Felix replied, but her eyes slid away from mine as I turned to her and I could tell she already regretted her interjection.

'Is he?' I asked, quietly. Felix glanced up, bit her lip, swallowed angrily and nodded. Ralph ran his fingers through his already-spiky hair in frustration.

'Course he is,' he barked. 'He's in your bloody pantomime, isn't he? One of the star performers, right Fee?'

'He's *not* one of the stars,' I said, quickly, knowing I sounded petty but too wound up to stop myself. 'Nova and Rudy have the finale slot... And Dan, of course.'

'Yeah, well, he might not be the *flashiest* talent... And let's not forget who comes up with the final running order.

Oh *wait*,' Ralph tapped his forehead in mock confusion, making me want to punch him. '*That's* right, it's the same person who allocates funding. Your boyfriend *Josiah*...'

'He is *not* my boyfriend,' I hissed. Felix was no longer pretending to look at her computer anymore; Ralph glared at me and I glared back at him just as hard. Something pounded furiously between us like a living, breathing pulse of energy. He batted it to me, I thrust it straight back at him. I didn't know *why* Felix had been spouting off about us liking each other earlier, all I could feel was rage from the tips of my fingers to the balls of my feet. All I wanted to do was tear him down, wipe the self-righteous blindness out of his stupid eyes; make him see me for more than the silly pretty little girl who'd pointed her toes, batted her eyelashes and flirted her way into the spacious office and private laboratory that was twice the size of his.

'So he doesn't know you're in here peddling all this psycho-babble rubbish at me? It's not his way of sugar-coating his rejection of my latest funding application?' Ralph snarled, his eyes so narrow beneath his glasses that they were just brown slithers.

'Actually, didn't you say the other day, Ralph, that you thought there could be an aspect of mental blocking going on when you were working with Verity?' Felix said, mildly, though she's quick to duck her head back to her computer as we both turned to stare at her. I recovered first.

'Oh, *really*?' I said, sweetly, turning back to Ralph. 'Well, isn't that interesting?'

'That's... This is *not* the same thing, Fee. Beast's going on about psychological damage and outsider influence — for which she has *no* basis of fact...'

'Look, all I'm doing is making a simple suggestion for an avenue of thought...' I replied, letting the anger dissipate now I could feel the moral high-ground solidly under my feet. 'I would have thought that, with *resources* being so pressured and all, you would at least be open-minded enough to give it some consideration before rejecting it completely. Even if it did come from me.'

We stared at one another. The pulse of energy quivered between us, ears fronted for danger, fully alert for any sudden movements from either side.

'Fine. Whatever. I'll look into it. At some point,' Ralph muttered, furiously, turning back to the two heavy textbooks he'd been studying before I'd entered the room.

'That's all I ask,' I replied, keeping my voice sweet but unable to resist putting a little wire of triumph into my words. 'Now I'd better go, I've got a rehearsal to oversee.'

'Fine. Wouldn't want to hold up preparations for your latest show-boating opportunity,' Ralph muttered bitterly.

'Oh come on,' I replied as I removed my lab coat and hung it on the peg near the door, not because I needed to but because I was wearing one of the outfits Lychen had sent me as a possible choice for the presentation. The dress – green as my eyes – clung to every inch of my body and shimmered with pinpricks of emerald crystals. I felt rather than heard Felix's low whistle of admiration; I was looking at Ralph. I watched him glance up and his eyes freeze upon my body even as his chin began to dip back into his book.

'We all know you're just jealous *you* weren't asked to be the ambassador of the ARC presentation...'

'Oh right, yeah... I'm *so* jealous no one asked me to be the pretty face of Lychen's latest display of money-grabbing frivolity. The eye-candy pimped out onto the stage for everyone to stare at... Cos you couldn't find another one of them anywhere else in the world, could you, Beast?'

I smiled, though it cost me far more than I would ever let him see.

*Should have left when you had the upper hand*, the voice hissed. *Now you look foolish.*

Not in this dress. Not while he's looking at me like that.

'Keep telling yourself that, Ralphie...' I said, sweeping my way out of the door, making sure he got a good view of the dress' plunging dip towards the small of my back as I went. As the door swung shut behind me, I could just make out Felix's words:

'When you guys finally throw caution to the wind and end up getting down and dirty on one of these benches, at least have the decency to hang a pair of goggles or something on the door so none of us have to walk in on you, OK?'

**October, 2018**

*Monday*

It is surprisingly easy, once Ariana has her fingers on the familiar keys and begins to remember what Lucy told her. Even the coding bit... all she had to remember was the name of it, and that was easy enough because she and Yas had giggled that it sounded like a fancy STD. Then, after a quick Google – no restrictive controls exist in *this* computer suite – she has all she needs. Next to her, Tess has begun to hum as she clicks from one window of code through to a long list of unread emails. She doesn't spare a glance for Ariana, and none of the other workers in the room are anywhere near her screen. Ariana quickly types in a few strings of code – copying and pasting when she needs to – until the map spasms angrily into an error message. Then she clicks off of it, deletes her history and brings up Lucy's Instagram.

Ariana spends the next half hour clicking through pictures from the weekend. Lucy and Yasmin in town, holding up Halloween costumes they've just bought. Ariana had forgotten about their plans to go *ironic* trick-or-treating. She remembers last year, with a strange, hunger-like pang, when Mum had agreed to accompany them only at a respectable distance so that no one would think she was with them. How she had waited in the shadows even as her careful eyes glittered in the glowing lights of pumpkins, always watching. Ariana remembers the weird feeling it gave her, the mixture of embarrassment and security all tangled up with a worry that her costume wasn't as good as Lucy's. *What a stupid little kid,* she thinks now, though she can't help the jealous acid burning at her throat as she spots Michelle Crossley, who has been trying to get in with Lucy since the first term of year seven, in the background of one of the selfies, mouth hanging open as she laughs too widely at whatever they're saying.

'Ariana? Ari?'

'Yeah,' Ariana peels her eyes from her friends' laughing faces and turns around in her seat. Tess's screen is now blank and she's standing up, phone in hand.

'Come on, we'd better get to the lunch room before the hoards descend. It's fish and chips today but if it's anything like Beaumont they'll run out of the good fillets before twelve thirty and the stragglers will be left with fish fingers...'

'Just like school,' Ariana mutters as she closes the window of her grinning friends and gets to her feet.

The journey is silent, but totally unlike the silences which had fallen during the previous day's long drive. The vehicle is large and heavy and makes me think of the corny crime dramas I've watched with Ariana when the baddies drive Hummers. With the windows blacked out and the only view of the mist-smeared, rolling grey hills and churning lakes available through the boxy front windows, it certainly feels more like we're rolling into a war zone rather than just meandering slowly – for the wide vehicle's handling is clumsy and the Guard driver moves methodically – through the winding lanes of the Lake District.

'What was all that about between you and Dad, Beast?'

I turn to Ralph in some surprise. He's been white-faced and tight-lipped since he clambered into the seat next to mine in the middle row of the vehicle, and with two Guards up in front and two in the rear seats behind us, I haven't been expecting him to strike up conversation.

'What do you mean?' I ask, playing for time. Neither of the two Guards in front nor the ones behind give any indication of listening. In fact, their expressions appear to have all slumped into the same impassivity; I'm coming to think of it as *standby mode*.

'Don't be stupid,' Ralph scoffs and, for a moment, we could be kids again, sitting around the breakfast table as I deny, blank-faced, flicking the cornflake which has just landed in his glass of juice.

'Ethan and I rocked up in the wee hours and found him all white and twitchy, saying you'd gone to rest and he was busy processing your blood work...'

'And?'

'Come on, it hasn't been that long. You know Dad. He doesn't get all white and twitchy over nothing... What did you do to him?'

'How do you know it was anything *I* did?' I glance from him to the Guard and back again. 'He might have been mad with worry for Ariana – she is his granddaughter after all. Or it could just have been *them* crawling all over his facility.'

'No... We've dealt with the Guard at the ARC before...' Ralph says, thoughtfully, his eyes sliding away as he frowns. 'They used to come and *check in* and make searches...'

289

'And Blake couldn't stop them?'

Ralph frowns and I can tell I've touched a nerve.

'He tried… Or he said he did… At first. But they aren't like normal people. If that's what their orders are, they just do it… There's no getting round it…'

'Isn't there?'

'Well… I mean, usually there isn't. I don't know what you did to that Guard woman but Felix said you found a way around her. Got her confused or something. Probably why we've got an all-male contingent with us today. Anyway, Dad's not… he's not really been the same since everything began to fall apart with the funding and everything… He doesn't really work on anything much. I tried to get him engaged in some of the work I've been doing… Nothing flashy, just exploring ordinary genetic mutations and how they can be adapted, but it didn't really engage him. Even the cancer stuff. He said he'd tried it years ago, that it's not what Mamma wanted, but when I ask him what she *would* want, he can't answer… It's like… what happened with the A-Subjects just made him lose faith in anything he ever achieved… And meanwhile, Lychen has got all the investments and the control of the original research for Project D and has built an empire…'

'Right…' The car turns onto the wider A66 and begins to pick up speed. I can feel Ariana coming closer like an elastic band slackening a little around my chest. But then there's Lychen, too… He looms like a spectre and for a moment everything is dark, there is a smooth, cold surface pressing hard into my cheek, hands around my throat…

'Beast? You alright?'

'I'm fine,' I say, quickly, though my breath is coming faster than normal.

'You looked weird for a minute… All whitish. Do you

want some water? Oi, Gregory! Some water for the lady please?'

'He has a name?' I murmur as the Guard in the passenger seat turns and hands a bottle of water to Ralph.

'Probably not, but I'm hopeless at telling them apart if I don't call them something,' Ralph says, almost cheerfully, handing me the water. I take a sip and my heart calms. *You're going to get Ariana. That's all. Nothing else. He is nothing else.*

'So you're not going to tell me what it is with you and Dad, then?' Ralph says, after watching me for a bit. 'Cos just now, that's who you reminded me of.'

'It's nothing. Really.'

'It's to do with why you left, isn't it? I thought it was because of me... Because of how I acted that day...' He turns to me and I see pain flicker over his face and suddenly we are standing on the path between the ARC and the Manor and even the thick blackness of the summer night cannot hide the crumple of his eyes.

'It wasn't you... Well, not *just* you, anyway.'

'So it was Dad? What did he say? He's never told me...'

'It wasn't really him, either,' I lie, carefully. 'It was everything. I was just... done. After everything happened with Rudy...'

'It wasn't your fault.'

'That's not what you said at the time,' I say, quickly, unable to stop the thirteen-year-old bitterness creeping into my words.

'Yeah, well... I was angry. I hated the whole presentation thing.'

'You called it frivolous show-boating, if I recall correctly...'

'Yeah... It wasn't just that though. You know.'

'It was because it was Lychen's project.'

'Yeah. His and yours... I just couldn't trust him, ever. The amount of times I told Dad, I tried to warn him about Lychen. Tried to get him to talk to you, try and make you see that you needed to keep your distance. Mamma would have...'

'She tried. She told me, after that dinner party, that she didn't trust him, especially with me. But she also told me that Ramona was trying to poison us all and that I was her spirit child and that if I practised my grand jetés enough I would truly learn how to fly... Which, when you consider that we had an actual flying child living less than a mile away from us, is even weirder than it sounds...'

'It was the disease... The medicine...'

'Yeah. I know. But still, she was right about Lychen.'

We lapse into silence as the car rumbles onward. I take another sip of water.

'I would have done it all, you know. The nappies and the night-feeding and the tooth fairy and Christmases...' Ralph says, staring out of the window.

'I know,' I reply, softly.

'I suppose you were punishing us. Me and Dad. For the way we left things...'

'No,' I turn to him in surprise. 'It wasn't that. I know you'd have done everything you could. You'd have been a great dad. It wasn't your fault I didn't give you the chance... I knew that Lychen was taking over the ARC. I knew it wouldn't be long before everyone there was dancing to his tune... I couldn't bring Ri into that. I didn't want her growing up with him lurking over her, watching her the way he watched me... I knew that if I turned up at the Manor with her that he'd be all over us like a rash...'

'We could have found a way around it... We could

have met in secret. Like we used to.'

'Could we? Would you really have taken that chance, if you were me?'

'Well, we'll never know now,' Ralph says, bitterly, to his knees.

'No,' I agree, softly. 'And there's not much point debating it now, is there?'

'I suppose not.'

And we lapse back into silence as the car rumbles south onto the A1. When I'm sure none of the Guard are looking and Ralph is gazing out of the window, I reach into my handbag until my fingers close around the sheath of my knife. I slide it into the front pocket of my jeans in one quick, fluid movement. Its unfamiliar bulk presses into my thigh and I try to focus on it and the loosening band in my chest. But still, as the miles vanish beneath our tyres the shadow grows with every extra ounce of oxygen I inhale and by the time signs for York appear I can feel my face growing colder. Ralph doesn't say anything, but I know he notices. And, as the miles tick into single digits, he reaches over and takes one of my hands in his. Dry, warm and still.

**Summer, 2005**

'Humanity. It is the great binder; the thing that unites us all... Or so we thought. It was Nietzsche who questioned the confines of humanity; who pondered what cords could *almost* not be torn. And tonight, ladies and gentlemen, we will answer him. We will show you the next generation, the latest in eugenic evolution–'

'No.' Lychen stepped into the space between the lights and the stage, holding up his hand. 'Don't use eugenic as an adjective next to evolution, the gravitas of both words are lost. They need to each be the subject of their own sentences.'

I stepped forward so I could see him better. Even though I was the one on stage, he still wielded command throughout the grounds of the ARC, where a semi-circular amphitheatre had been constructed over the last few weeks. We'd done presentations before, but they had been far smaller, involving up to five selected children with demonstrations scaled down into whatever space we had been given in university lecture halls, business offices, even the corner of a staff canteen once. This was to be something else altogether. There was a twenty-foot stage, laser effects, smoke machines, flame stretchers... It wasn't so much a presentation as an extravaganza.

'What about the latest in eugenics. The cutting edge

of human evolution?'

'Better... The Nietzsche stuff, though. Do you think it's strictly necessary...? Just seems a little... old school and uptight...'

'I think it lends an authoritative overture, balances out the glitz and glam a bit...' I said, staring him down. We both knew the real reason he didn't want a Nietzsche mention in the opening speech was because it was the sort of thing Blake would include. Lychen shrugged and motioned for me to continue. I resumed my place in the centre of the stage and picked up where I left off. The glaring spotlights didn't bother me; Ana had had me dancing on stage from the first winter I had lived with the Blakes. The feel of the eyes upon me – from the admiring to the envious, the lustful to the bored Subjects waiting in the wings – that didn't bother me either. The only thing that ticked irritably in the back of my head as I gestured where I needed to, paused for emphasis, moved to catch every beam of the spotlight and smiled gracefully, was the memory of my argument with Ralph.

It had been four years since Ana's death; four years during which I had finished my studies with marks equally as high as Ralph's, watched as Dr Blake had sunk into an echo of the vibrant, passionate man I had once known him to be, and Lychen had swollen like a God over everything the ARC did. Sometimes at night I dreamed that the ARC itself had transformed into one of his black, fathomless eyes – shining and soulless as it gazed unblinkingly upon all of us. Over the last year, since I joined the ARC staff full-time after choosing to defer my place to study genetics at the University of London, my salary had doubled and I'd been given a large office and lab of my own. I still hadn't decided when, if ever, I would be taking up my university place; Ralph had completed his degree in Durham some years previously and, though it had made him generally more superior and arrogant than ever, he'd returned to the same laboratory and office he had occupied at eighteen. He maintained it was his choice, that he wanted to *work* for his gains and that was also the reason why he'd chosen to move out of the Manor and into a tiny basement flat in Kendal rather than continue living rent-free with his father and me. I didn't know whether he actually believed that or if the chance to prove himself somehow more moral than me was such an ingrained habit by then it had become a rule to live by.

The last four years had also seen the progression and demise of Project C as the Subjects grew up and, more often than not, saw their extraordinary abilities begin to diminish. Already the eldest of the Subjects I had known as a child had either been redistributed as apprentices to the senior ARC staff, Reuben among them, or had been removed altogether. The official line was most had either gone to family members or been fostered... But there were other rumours, too. Rumours of sickness and madness. Rumours that the disappearance of the former C-Subjects tied in with new sounds that could be heard, at certain times of the night, from the subterranean levels beneath the ARC.

I mentored a choice few of the remaining C-Subjects, having known them longer and worked more closely with them than anyone else at the ARC. These Subjects of mine were, naturally, the stars of the presentation – Nova was to round off the finale with a spectacular balletic aerial display as Rudy lifted objects of increasing size, culminating in a Morris Mini-Minor, and hurled them at Daniel, who would dodge into thin air at the last minute.

'Good,' Lychen cut into my brief reverie in his cool clipped way, as I stepped out of the spotlight and moved to the wings. I watched him watching me. That was another thing which had changed over the last few years; the twitch of his hands as I passed him, the prowl of his eyes unbound over my body, the burn of his gaze. I knew by now that Ana had been right, that his interest in me was rooted in his need to possess that which he desired; I just didn't know how far I could stretch the tension.

Lychen met me by the curtain, holding out a hand as I stepped lightly down the steel steps, Rudy darting past me to rehearse his show opener. The ordering ranged from the high end to middling, to the groups of little ones who were more there for cuteness than anything else, and then straight into the spectacular. Lychen's eyes never left my face even as Rudy heaved a ten tonne log over his head and the children's minders filling in for the audience whooped and cheered.

'I hardly need say it, I think, but that dress is even more spectacular on you than I imagined it would be when I saw it in the dressmaker's studio,' Lychen breathed, his gaze leaving a hot trail over my body.

'Thank you,' I said. 'The red needed adjustment around the waist, but the black was also a contender.'

'No, this is the dress for you. I knew the emeralds would match your eyes perfectly.' He still had my hand in his. I raised my eyebrows inquisitively, knowing there was something more he wanted to say.

'Will you join me in my office later? I want to go over your speech again. I've an excellent Bordeaux I've been saving… We will toast the sell-out event.'

It wasn't a question. We both knew that.

'Of course,' I smiled, stepping lightly onto the mat

covering the ground so that my heels didn't come into contact with any mud.

'Great. Let's say nine,' Lychen replied, moving closer towards me as a small group of Subjects approached the stage, staring at us both in terror. Lychen's hand was light, like the flickering tongue of a snake, on my back and, because I felt my shudder building like a tidal wave, I twisted away in pretence of needing to call after the children.

'Remember your spacing, girls,' I called, 'especially when you turn into the final movement, Emma!' They all nodded with wide eyes, dipping their heads in respect.

'It's all in the choreography,' I said, smilingly, into Lychen's brows, which had twitched together the moment I'd moved out of reach.

'Later, then,' he said, placing his hands behind his back as I hurried away. I felt his eyes upon me like the flickering of a snake tongue the whole way back to my office. It was as unlike the look Ralph had given me as ice from fire.

**October, 2018**

*Monday*

Ralph's hand stays warm on mine as I feel the coldness beginning to spread outwards and onto the surface of my skin. The frosty air as the car door opens barely registers. Ralph leads me out and squeezes my hand as if he knows. As if he knows everything. But he doesn't. He can't. I smile and squeeze his hand back as we stand in front of the squat, ugly old building in front of us. On the front it says *Futura Laboratory* in fresh-looking lettering, but when I squint and move in the bleak sunlight, I can make out the engraving *Grayson Boys' Academy* underneath. The Guard move to surround us and I breathe in the ice-tinged air and let it sharpen everything. Bury the darkness. Bring the image of Ariana into focus; dancing on the sand with her hair twirling around her; her hand reaching for mine on the first day of school, the slightest tremble hidden deep in our clasp; her large eyes bright and innocent in a way mine never had been as she sees her presents on Christmas morning. My girl. My heart. She is close and I can't be anything less than this bastion of icy resolve I have created of myself when I face her. I let go of Ralph's hand, square my shoulders and march briskly forward. I won't think of anyone else.

It's almost a little anti-climactic when we enter the drab grey building in front of us. There are no gathered forces of Guard men and women waiting for us, just our meagre little escort. There aren't even any employees goggling eagerly. There's no one... I feel Ralph practically twitching as he strides beside me, can almost taste the spark of the adrenaline flooding from him. The Guard surrounding us lead us briskly across a carpeted entranceway and towards one of several doors. There they pause and one holds out a hand to me. At first, I think he must have seen the outline of the sheathed knife in my pocket, but then he gestures at my handbag. I hand it over without a flinch. They frisk Ralph, who mutters and turns red when they pull out two phones and an old penknife I remember him receiving for Christmas in 1995. There's no room for reminiscing now, though. I am a robot. I *have* to be a robot. I cannot feel because if I do, I know I will feel *him* like an icy rush against my face as I head towards the door in front of me. And I know that if I let it, that icy breath will turn to the memory of a hard surface and then I will be lost completely. No. I will be a robot. I am ready. I wait for the door to be opened and I stride through it before anyone can lead me, and I seek those coal-black eyes of emptiness with emerald shards of purpose. *I feel nothing, I feel nothing*, I tell him. *Robots don't feel.* And the steel of my resolve shimmers in slices around the dark threat of memory, muffled and bound deep inside. Lychen stands up from where he has been sitting at the head of a large, mahogany table.

'Bella. Ralph.'

'Josiah,' Ralph snarls, his hands balling into fists at his side. There are two more Guard in this room and with the four who entered with us, we are hopelessly outnumbered. Lychen keeps his eyes on mine as he reaches out a hand and one of the Guard from the ARC strides forward to hand him a file. My test results, I realise, with a cold little shock. I'd forgotten that I might drop dead at any moment; the realisation is so utterly ridiculous I almost laugh. Lychen slides the papers from the envelope and, as he does so, he turns slightly away from us until I catch a glimpse of the stubby black handgun at his waist. I know from the sharp little intake of breath next to me that Ralph has seen it too. I'd spotted the larger, plastic-looking guns worn by the Guard who had escorted us from the ARC, but their whole presence was so bizarre, so surreal in a toy-like way, that they didn't seem half as threatening as Lychen with his pistol, its silencer gleaming with intention.

'Bring them in,' Lychen barks, suddenly, without looking up. One of the Guard positioned near a door at the back of the room springs to life and opens it. A young woman, all red lips and nervous, quick eyes, steps in, but before I can spare her more than a cursory glance my attention is wrenched by the smaller figure behind her.

'Mum!' Ariana launches herself across the room, skirting a wide berth around Lychen. I take two paces and she is there, warm, soft, and real in my arms. My heart swells, and emotion like I've never known before spills out, trembling my hands, bursting tears from my eyes... It's all so messy and undignified but for once I couldn't give a damn because she's *here*, at last. I clasp her so tightly I feel the breath whistle from her lungs but still it takes a conscious effort to loosen my arms. She smells unfamiliar and her too-big clothes are strange – not to mention the bizarre rubber footwear – but her hair reaches into my nostrils in the same way it always has when I press my face to her head, and her fingers clasp into my shirt as if searching for the grooves they've worn into my back. It's a while before I look up and I feel her begin to fidget long before I can persuade my arms to let her go. I meet Lychen's eyes first – creased a little in something between fascination and disdain. I look away and glance at Ralph beside me, whom Ariana is already regarding with a keen interest. Ralph glances from me to her and back again awkwardly, one hand running through his hair absently and then pushing up his glasses.

'Ariana… This is Ralph Blake… He's–'

'My dad.'

I turn and stare at her.

'How did you know–'

She shrugs my question away and I experience one of those strange, shadowy swoops of discomposure you get when your child does something that mirrors you almost exactly.

'Doesn't matter. It's who he is, right?'

'Well… yeah… Ralph, this is Ariana. Ri.'

He bobs his head but when she holds out her hand, his face splits into a more familiar grin and he shakes it.

'Nice to meet you…'

'You too…'

'I'm sorry,' I say, though neither of them look my way. I can see them measuring one another's physicality, spotting the similarities and pondering on the differences. 'I should have let you two meet a long time ago… I hope you'll both understand one day why I didn't feel like I could…'

Ralph wrenches his eyes from the girl in front of him and opens his mouth to say something, but at that very moment the door through which Ariana and the woman entered bangs open with a sound so like a gunshot I grab

Ariana in surprise, ducking my head. A Guard man rushes towards Lychen, already murmuring in the low version of their metallic voices. Lychen listens and frowns and mutters a few things back to him. I glance at Ralph, who is frowning, but doesn't look half as confused as I feel, particularly when I look back at Ariana and see the same expression she wore just last week when I discovered half the wrappers for the sweets I'd bought for Halloween under her bed.

'What's–' I begin, but before I can finish there's another loud bang and I clutch Ariana reflexively as the very walls seem to shudder around us.

'*Go*,' Lychen barks at the Guard, who is staring at the door to the entranceway through which Ralph and I arrived with an expression as close to befuddlement as I imagine he could get. He immediately gathers himself and rushes at the door along with two of our escort. The remaining two stay where they are, eyes on Lychen. I'm holding Ariana around her shoulders and Ralph has a hand on my arm too, as if scared I might leap into action and join the Guard. Two more bangs shock around the room and Lychen turns quickly to the woman who came in with Ariana. Her eyes are almost bulging out of her face, which has drained of all colour.

'Apparently there's been a breach in our tracking system, Miss Cochran,' he says lightly, as if remarking on the weather.

'I... I don't know how–' she stumbles. Another explosion, closer this time, throws all our attention at the door. I'm half expecting it to be blown from its hinges at any moment.

'Delta, take the girl back to the living quarters. Beta, restrain these two and take them–'

Another thunderous sound makes the whole floor wobble and we all stumble. The air shimmers with sudden dust and one of the Guard begins to cough in loud, echoing booms. I feel the other approaching, one hand reaching for Ariana.

'You *will not* touch her,' I hiss right into his face. He falters and it's all I need, I thrust Ariana towards Ralph and he meets my eye for a nano second. I barely have time to think what I need him to know before he is striding towards the back door, pulling Ariana along with him. More bangs, and there is smoke everywhere and a smell of searing stone and rubble in my nose and suddenly I'm not holding onto anything but there's an iron-tight fist closing around my arm. I look around and meet the terrified gaze of the young woman as she ducks and shrieks as another boom shudders the room, and suddenly she's running away and I try to follow but something has me. Something icy like a snake, cold-skinned and intent only on squeezing tighter.

**Summer, 2005**

'Have you given any more thought to my proposal?'
Lychen's tone was clipped, his gaze burning as he raised
the wine glass to his lips. I sipped from my own, letting the
dark rich liquid slide easily over my tongue. The window
was open and the heavy air swirled around us, bringing a
distant scent of woodsmoke and the buzz of crickets.
Summer was easily my favourite season in Cumbria,
perhaps because it always seemed so brief between the
long exaggerations of winter. The fleeting flavours given to
my everyday routine – the sweetness of the few fruit trees
overhanging the walk from the Manor to the ARC, the
novel tease of night air on my bare limbs as I returned late
– it all seemed to give the days an extra dose of possibility.
That summer in particular, there were times when I felt my
own invincibility like the blaze of a second sun on my skin.

'Leaving the ARC for London, you mean?' I slid
backwards onto the desk behind me, tipping my head back
a little, knowing the dimmed lights would catch the shine
of my hair as it tumbled down my back. I had changed back
into my usual work clothes – tailored trousers and a short-
sleeved blouse in sapphire silk. The fabric clung to my
warm skin despite the air conditioning wafting lazily from
the unit behind Lychen's desk. Everything about his office
was luxurious, from the crystal chandelier in the ceiling to

305

the designer sofa and chairs rarely used in one corner, but it was built for a winter climate and without the breeze from the window and the tickle of the recirculating air behind me it would have been uncomfortably warm.

'Yes,' Lychen said, closer than I had realised. I dipped my head forward and instantly realised my mistake. I had sat down. He was standing between me and the door, dominantly upright before my relaxed recline. I smiled to hide the sweep my eyes had made between him and the exit, but I knew he had seen it. Still, he returned the smile with his own tight, wolf-like gleam, one hand clasped around his wine glass. With the other, he reached lazily forward, as if he had all the time in the world, and traced the silk of my left sleeve with one finger.

'I know you cannot be blind to what has been happening here, Bella,' his eyes were lasers. It hurt to hold their gaze, but I couldn't look away.

'The failing C-Subjects, you mean?'

'The failing everything,' he replied, shortly, his finger reaching my skin with a sharp iciness. His nail was long but didn't leave a mark as it trailed downwards over my pale forearm. We both watched as the tiny hairs raised in his wake.

'The ARC is finished, you know that,' he said. 'Dr Blake is an old man. He wants to retire. He doesn't care about the failure of Project C... Ever since your dear Mamma... Well, you know as well as I that he hasn't been the same,' Lychen tried for sorrow, his eyes pinching in sympathy, but his voice remained steely, his finger cold, his eyes... blank.

'He's just a bit down... maybe he has a touch of depression... Perhaps if the funding team managed to procure–'

'The funding team have halted their efforts on behalf

of Blake,' Lychen snapped, business-like once again. He moved a little closer, his finger now trailing back up my arm. I could feel the danger of him now, a subtle emanation like the faintly metallic scent of scalding water. I wanted to shuffle forward on the desk, place my feet more firmly on the ground, but it was as if that one finger was a clamp holding me firmly in place.

'I didn't know that...' I said, slowly.

'Of course you did,' he replied, equally slowly. 'You know everything that happens here, Bella. Don't think I haven't seen your potential. Don't think that just because some might say I parade you out for your exceptional beauty and charisma that I don't appreciate your brilliance.'

His finger had reached my cheek now and hovered for a moment over my skin. I couldn't help but shut my eyes as the cool tip traced gently over it, part of me envisaging the sharp nail turning talon-like, gouging away the very beauty he described. The other part just hoped he took the shudder that flamed from my face through my shoulders and downwards for nerves.

'I'm sure you give me too much credit,' I said, looking down.

'No. I do not. In fact I possibly do not give you enough. You are, after all, a very young woman still. Not quite twenty, if I'm correct. Why waste all that vibrancy on a dying institution tucked away in the depths of forgotten mountains? Why deny the world yourself? Why deny your*self* the world? This is no place for you anymore. Your place is with me, out there...'

'In London?'

'London, Paris, New York... Everywhere, anywhere. You could take up your university place if you wanted – live in the finest apartment and work part-time at my Beaumont facility at the same time. Or forget about it completely, it's not like you *need* it. I could put you anywhere in the world, Bella. The plans are in place. The funding is secure. Project D has been underway since the week after I arrived here... That's what the presentation is for, that's what the investors will be putting their money into. The C-kids, they're just a flashy demonstration... I mean, don't get me wrong, there are still those who will be blown away by the sight of a flying child,' he snorted contemptuously. 'Of course, if they knew what we know... Well, that's my point. There's no certainty. All it takes is one whisper, one slip of the truth and young Nora might wake up tomorrow no more able to step across thin air than you or I.'

'Nova.'

'Whatever. My point is, these children... they're all so... flimsy. Project D takes it all to the next level. It marries genetically-enhanced ability with fundamental reliability, eliminating the aspects which make the C-Subjects so weak... The mess, the emotion. No. This will be an entire generation of perfect, unblemished soldiers.

'And do you know what inspired it all, Bella? You. Your control, your resilience, your cold, unyielding perfection... So you see, it only makes sense. You're already a part of it. I need you by my side. I want you there...'

His finger had traced back down my arm and he had taken my hand in his. I don't know if it was the gesture – his grip tight but less threateningly suggestive than the trace of a nail upon my skin – or the stirring of how Ana would react, indignant and burning on my behalf – but my eyes snapped open fully and my body rocked forwards, into my shoes.

'By your side,' I turned to him, bolstered by the extra height my four-inch heels gave me. I saw the annoyance of my move register with a dull smouldering anger that flamed briefly behind the coal blackness of his eyes.

'As *what*, exactly? A one-up on Ralph and Blake? A pretty face and an eloquent voice to chime in when necessary in front of press and investors?'

'No, Bella,' he placed his wine glass behind him and reached for my other hand so he was holding both. To an outsider we might look like hand-clasped lovers, but for the blaze in his eyes, the steely warning of his grip and the sudden bite of pain as his nails found the soft parts of my palms.

'You'd be my partner. Working alongside me on all *my* projects. D and beyond. Travelling the world, reaching further into the realms of eugenics than anyone has plunged before... Taking the experiments to the very edges of possibility and beyond. My equal; my counterpart. In every sense, if you would accept me.'

We stared at one another and I didn't look away. I saw it all. The facade of earnest sincerity, so *almost* convincing. The burning wolfish lust in his eyes, twitching like fingers around the trigger of a gun concealed in a pocket of fabric. The path he was offering, narrow and scrutinised and entirely under his control, no matter what he said about equality.

'I... I need to think about it...' I said, making my voice a little breathy.

'This isn't the first time you've asked me to wait, Bella,' he replied, his voice hard once again and his grip tighter than ever.

'I know. It's just... the presentation and everything... it's all so mad at the moment. I just... I want to... I need to see it through, there're only a few weeks to go...' I stared at him, willing him not to make me fight my way out.

Don't ruin it now. We're so close. The balance is so frail. Not long now. Just a few more weeks. Let me go. Let me go.

He released me with a sigh. I smiled and kissed him sweetly on his cold cheek. It was like brushing my lips against a dead radiator.

'I won't wait forever, Bella,' Lychen murmured, and as I began to move away he struck, clenching a fistful of my hair and jerking my entire upper body backwards. It lasted less than a second. Less than a second and less than a twinge of pain and imbalance, but the warning rang clear between us; with one flex of his arm he could throw me backwards onto the soft carpet and wrench away everything I held so precariously from him. As I jolted upright, Lychen turned back to the desk and casually picked up his wine glass. I took three steps across the carpet.

'Sooner or later you're going to have to choose a side, Bella.'

I kept walking.

'Before the choice is taken from you.'

I didn't reply. I didn't trust my voice. Instead, when I reached the door, I turned and looked at him. He lowered his glass and licked the wine from his lips, his eyes blazing into me as hard as they had when he'd gripped my hands. I turned and ran.

I didn't feel my heels. I didn't register the frenzy of my heart juddering my entire ribcage under the flimsy silk of my shirt. I didn't think about where I was going. I didn't even notice the tears, cold against the warmth of my face, until Ralph looked up, his eyes widening in surprise.

'What the—? Beast? Are you OK? Are you *crying?*'

'No,' I said reflexively as I shut the door behind me and waited, my hand upon it, until I was sure. Until *he* definitely hadn't followed me. He wouldn't. Not here.

'You *are*,' Ralph was behind me, too close, and when he put his hand on my shoulder to peer more closely at my face I flinched violently.

'Woah, sorry,' he held up his hands. I stood alone, chest heaving, heart hurting, trying with everything I had to control it all, to cool it all down but it was all wrong. My face was red, the worst colour for a face to be. My armpits were damp and the silk shirt was clinging to my body. My hair felt scattered and wrong where Lychen had grasped it. I stared around at the laboratory to try and calm myself down. It was dark, the only light coming from the lamp hovering over the same work area Ralph had been using that morning, the two textbooks still open but at a further point now, I could see. No one else was here. Outside, darkness had finally overtaken the heavy twilight and the cool air from the open window lapped at the heat tumbling from me like chaos.

'What's happened to you?' Ralph's hair was still sticking up, he'd lost his lab coat and rolled the sleeves of his checked shirt up, but he still bore sweat patches beneath his raised arms. He looked as discombobulated as if one of the red deer we sometimes spotted from the ARC's western windows had just leapt through the door.

*And do you blame him? You never lose control like this. Calm down. Nothing happened.*

'Nothing happened,' I echoed in a mutter, bringing a shaking hand up to try and smooth my hair back into place. As I did so I realised my palms were stinging. I brought them down and saw tiny crescents of blood embedded across the soft pads beneath my thumbs. I closed my fists but Ralph was too quick. He took my hands in his large ones and gently prised them open.

'Who did that?'

'Nobody. I must have done it myself... I was watching the kids rehearse earlier... I got nervous; you've seen Nova do that big swoop through the fire...'

'Bella. I've heard you coach the kids – you told Nova last week that you'd ordered extra-flammable feathers for her costume to make sure she flew straight through the fire hoops and didn't keep arching her back in mid-air. Besides, we both know you'd sooner trek through the moor out there in your designer heels than do something to disfigure yourself in some way... It was Lychen wasn't it?'

'It– he... it was *nothing*...' I said, all in a whoosh, and suddenly Ralph's arms were around me and the smell of him, sweaty but safe, was in my nose and to my horror I could feel the tears coming properly this time, like a surging hurricane devouring everything in its path. *Robots don't*– but it was too late. My self-control crumpled like a house made of sticks.

I don't know how long we stood there; him just wrapped around me, cocooning my shudders and sobs until they slowly began to subside. I didn't care that he was supposed to be like a brother to me, or that only that morning I had wanted to hurt and humiliate him as much as I ever had. He didn't say anything, even when I stopped sobbing and pointed out, in a muffled, shaky voice most unlike my own, that really, nothing *had* happened. I'd been offered a new job. That was it. Really.

'Not *really* really, though, is it?' He said, gruffly. I looked up. His eyes were there – brown, solid, waiting. 'I *warned* you about him. Mamma tried to warn you... He won't stop, he won't ever let you go until he—'

312

I kissed him. I don't know what made me do it, but I know it *was* me – even if it was just a small, impetuous part of me that I'd kept buried for years – that decided. That reached my body upwards and found his lips with my own. Maybe I was grateful to him for providing me with what I'd needed to claw my way back into myself. Maybe it was the only way I could think of to answer him, to *choose my side*, as Lychen had put it. Or perhaps I simply wanted him to shut up.

There was no time, in the end, to hang anything on the door.

**October, 2018**

*Monday*

'Run, Ariana! Ralph, *go!*' My words struggle from my throat as another explosion shatters the air with dust. Shapes move uncertainly across the room as I'm pulled backwards. Another icy limb wraps around my chest and suddenly I know who has me and I can't breathe, let alone reach for the blade in my pocket. The blackness of memory swells within me until it reaches my throat and my eyes, blotting out everything but the cold hardness choking me from all angles. I try to inhale and my lungs flounder weakly, there is a hard surface pressing into my face and pain clenches like a knife, reaching for my softest parts and wrenching them inside out.

I don't know if I pass out. I don't know if hours go by or mere seconds, but eventually the snake around my ribcage eases and a tiny parcel of oxygen filters through my lips. Then a tiny bit more. And then I blink and can see the dark shadow of the table, the empty spaces where Ariana, Ralph and the woman have fled. Nothing is pressing into my face. Nothing is knifing me. And, slowly, Lychen's arm loosens until it's merely a chain around me.

'Be still,' he croons, too close, and when I flinch, he tightens his hold again until I obey. 'Good… Just relax.

You're fine...'

We're alone in the room. The dust has begun to clear, only shimmering a little with the bangs that have become distant. He is behind me, holding me with one arm while the other slowly twists my wrist up in between my shoulder blades. As I realise it, my shoulder gives a sudden yawn of pain and I gasp.

'It hurts, doesn't it?' He remarks placidly, and I shudder again as *that* memory, so spectrally close, threatens to take over once again.

'Yes,' I breathe. He sighs slowly and I can feel how much he's enjoying himself. I can't see his lips but I know they are moist with the pleasure of dominance, his tongue flickering over them like a serpent's. He shifts a little so I can feel the cold knuckle of the handgun at his hip.

'I'll let you go if you promise not to run.'

'Fine.'

'Good girl,' he sighs into my neck, and I feel his lips graze me there for a second just before his grip loosens and the pain in my shoulder retreats. I stumble forward, coughing as my desperate lungs suck in the debris-laden air around us. More distant bangs drift into the room as I grasp the back of an ornately carved chair for support.

'Well, well,' Lychen mutters, striding around to the head of the table. I cough into my hand and look up at him. His face is more animated than it used to be; or perhaps I've simply forgotten how he looks when something surprises him.

'It seems, once again, that I have underestimated you. Or at least one of you...'

'I don't...' I cough and he passes me a bottle of water from a side table. I take it because there's no sense in not being able to speak. The water is like cool nectar on my scorched throat. I remember, suddenly, that there is a knife in my pocket.

'I don't understand,' I say, evenly.

'Let's just say these little explosions we're hearing aren't fireworks I put on for your benefit. Not that I'm not pleased to see you, of course.'

'What is it, then? What's going on?'

Keep him talking. Give them a chance to get away. Ralph can handle the Guard. Maybe. This is Ariana's biggest threat, right here.

'My best guess is that a small band of vigilantes from the ARC followed you here and are attempting to... ah... rescue you. They're no match for my Guard, of course... But I would have given them a slightly less *bangy* greeting had I known they were to join us... Which begs the question of how they managed to thwart our tracking software...'

'I've no idea,' I say drily, my eyes skirting from him to the door behind him and back around to the one through which we entered.

'No... It's more Bryden's style, isn't it...? But *how* could she have accessed our system remotely... Unless...'

More bangs sound and this time they're closer again. Heavy footsteps pause only briefly outside the door before pounding on. Shouts rip through the air. I think I recognise Felix's voice, twisted in anger and pain.

'Well. I shall be able to ask Ms Bryden soon enough, by the sound of things,' Lychen smiles coldly. 'So let us proceed while we have some semblance of privacy.'

'Proceed?' I tear my eyes away from the door, swallowing hard against the flutter of panic in my stomach. Lychen is holding Blake's report, which now wears a fine layer of dust.

'Don't you want to know why I went to so much

trouble to track you down through your hapless child?'

He brushes the papers clean and taps them gently against one of his white, glistening teeth.

'I presume it's to do with the demise of the other A-Subjects,' I say as more blasts echo into the room. I'm still holding the chair, my body carefully angled so he doesn't see me reach into my pocket for the knife. Keeping my eyes locked on his, I ease it slowly out of its sheath and slide it up my sleeve.

'Partly, yes.'

'Go on, then. Am I dying? Am I *defective* like my mother said all along? Don't keep me in suspense.' I screw the sarcasm into my words even as I realise, to my own surprise, that at this particular moment I really don't give a damn what those pages say.

'You're fine,' Lychen says softly, looking at the papers and then up at me. The old, wolfish flames stir into his dead eyes. 'You're perfect, in fact.' He moves closer. 'As ever you were...'

'But it could change any moment,' I say, quickly. 'Look at what happened to my brother. He was fine too, then boom.'

As if in support of my point, the room gives another shake. Someone shouts thickly nearby. I shut my eyes for a second and hope with every particle of my being that Ralph has Ariana somewhere safe. When I open my eyes again Lychen is closer still and his hand is reaching and once again I get a flash of that hardness, that terrible, unyielding pain just as he brushes his fingers into the hair by my right ear.

'Bella... You know why I brought you here. You *must* know. It's not because of this,' he throws the report onto the table. 'That was just... a means to an end. A justification. To myself as much as anyone. I know you

317

think me cold. Monstrous even, perhaps. And I've undoubtedly given you reason in the past.' His fingers find my neck like they never left. I shut my eyes again as nausea shudders through me. I can't move.

'But the truth is... Ever since I first met you when you were little more than a child, wearing a clean, white dress and gazing at me with such pure, unblemished beauty... I haven't been able to look at anything the same way. Bella... You make me weak in a way I never thought a human being could. I need you. I love you.'

My eyes snap open and I raise the blade to his neck in one swift movement. He blinks as he feels the cool metal press into his skin.

'You don't love or need anyone, Lychen,' I hiss, mustering everything to keep my voice level. 'You *want* me, perhaps...'

He frowns. 'What's the difference?' His hand falls from my throat, eyes flickering between me and the knife under his chin.

'Everything,' I whisper.

*Now,* the voice murmurs. *Do it now, before he remembers he has a gun.*

He's furrowed in confusion and my mind shudders as the memory crowds in again. *Use it.* His hand slamming against my head, knocking me half senseless. *Make him pay.* My own desk a cold slab against my cheek like a butcher's counter. *Make him bleed.* His fingers at my throat, squeezing the scream from my body. His other hand busy wrenching my clothes aside. And pain. Deep and knifing and crushing in every possible way. *Do it now.*

I push the knife upwards and Lychen gasps as a ruby gleam shivers onto the blade... There's a crash, the floor shivers beneath us and the door bursts open. It's a second of distraction but it's all Lychen needs to knock the knife out of my hand. It skitters across the table in front of us and I look up to see smoke, and Ethan, half his face swelling and bloody but wearing the beginnings of a grin as he takes a step towards us and turns to shout behind him. And Lychen glances over, raises his gun and shoots him in the chest.

**Summer, 2005**

It lasted for ten days. Ten long heady days of whispered glances, hidden touches and clutched moments where we could melt into one another and forget the empire around us. We thought we were careful in every sense of the word. We agreed that no one should know, pretending it was because Felix's smugness would be unbearable, glossing over the real dangers the way we glossed over everything. So we continued to spar with one another in front of our friends in the lab and at our usual table in the canteen. Ralph rolled his eyes and mocked me when I brought my speech notes with me to lunch, imitating my voice when I read parts out to Felix, Ethan and Reuben. I kicked him with the sharpest part of my heel under the table. Felix rolled her eyes, Ethan chuckled and Reuben watched with his dark dark eyes and said nothing.

Of course it was obvious. I know now. I know that though it was an affair confined to locked doors, the backseat of his Fiesta and several uncomfortable sofas (I drew the line at doing anything on a work bench after that first time) where we lived from one breathless kiss to the next, it was painted upon our bodies, it radiated from our voices. The tired shadows under Ralph's eyes lifted and he laughed more. My skin glowed in the mirror; my very hair seemed alight. And through it all, Lychen watched me and his eyes gleamed like cold onyx stones set into his face. He invited me for drinks again and I made my excuses, pleading the necessity of spending every free moment possible in preparation for the show. His hands reached for me, fingers already clenching, but I turned, slipping away before he could grip, and all the while Ana's warning trembled a constant buzz in my head. *You're walking a dangerous line, Bella. You must act. You can't have them both.*

I could have told Ralph I was afraid, but then I would have had to have admitted what I was doing, why I was leading, nudging, nettling Lychen. And I was. I knew it. I didn't want him to stop watching me, I didn't want him to stop wanting me. While he wanted me so desperately, I had all the game pieces in my hands and he knew it too. I could have told him to leave me alone, that I was a Blake, last name or no. That's what Ralph would have told me to do and sometimes, when he held me and loved me and I could see nothing but him, that's what I wanted, too. But then I would button my shirt and leave the room and Lychen's eyes would find me and the glint of his gaze would whisper of all the things I could have with him; the newness, the glamour, the endless world right there, waiting for me to take the first step. *Choose a side, Bella.* In the end, of course, I waited too long.

He had followed me. I hadn't heard him. I had only gone to my office to retrieve my notes for my speech so I could go over the Nietzsche references with Blake. With less than two weeks to go before the presentation, its imminence was beginning to overtake my distractedness over Ralph. I picked up my latest draft, frowning as I tried to decipher something Ralph had scribbled in the margin. I'd let him read it the night before and he'd marked it all in red and told me to check my references before admitting, finally, that it was *quite good,* he supposed. I didn't realise anyone was in the room with me until I heard the click of the office door closing. Even then, my eyes were still on the scrawled words in front of them as I began to turn, thinking it was Ralph. I only caught a flash of his eyes – blazing, deathly – before his hand came between us and cracked against the base of my skull so hard I was thrown, like a doll, forward onto my desk. I began to fight, once the shock gave way... I think I began to fight.

I didn't hear him leave afterwards. I think I was so shut off at that point, so closed up that I didn't perceive anything outside the strangely calm, blurry blankness in my head. I blinked and realised I was cold. I breathed and realised I was still alive. I stared at my own arm for thirty seconds as the unfamiliar red marks hazed in and out of focus. On unfolding myself, I realised I had been huddled in a ball of a person under my desk. The cup I had drunk my coffee from that morning was lying a few inches in front of me, the handle sheared clean away like a neatly severed limb. I placed my hands on the swirly-patterned rug and pushed myself upwards.

The door was closed in front of me. The room was dark. It was late, after all. I fastened my clothes with cold, unfeeling hands, hiding the ripped parts. I shook back my hair and used my fingers to comb it into a ponytail so nobody would be able to see where it had been grasped and pulled with the weight of my body behind it. I folded the collar of my blouse upwards so no one would see the marks around my throat, and used a spare scarf from my coat rack to hide the rest. I smoothed myself down and waited for my heart to stop trying to flee from my broken, used cusp of a body. Then I crossed briskly across the office to my bathroom and vomited neatly into the toilet.

Of course I didn't tell anyone. Who could I tell? Who could change anything? Ralph would be furious, but he'd also look at me the same way I met my own eyes in the mirror. Like I was something less than I had been. Used. Tainted. Blake would be broken. No one else mattered.

I couldn't clean away the feeling of it, of *him*. I showered under water so hot it turned my skin red and I hid the bruises with make-up and clothes. I even found a matching wrap for my green presentation dress to hide the scratches his nails had made on my neck, the bruises on the palest parts of my skin. But I could still feel his breath, wet in my hair. I still ached with the shame of the desk pressing into my cheek as the night air flared upon my naked skin. I still burned with the sharp, shocking pain as he'd forced his way in. It would catch me unawares at random times; during dinner, clattering my fork onto my plate and making Blake jump in surprise; coaching Nova on stage during last minute rehearsals so I'd need to step backwards into a stalls seat, my heart clutching in my chest. I began to avoid Ralph, pretending I was busy with preparations for the presentation. I stopped eating in the canteen and avoided his rooms at the ARC. Lychen tried, just once, on the eve of the presentation, to invite me to a private dinner in his office by way of an inter-department memo. I burned it. I wore a mask of icy dedication and kept them all at arm's distance. No one asked if I was OK. No one noticed I was anything different to normal. I'd finally turned myself into a robot; the congratulations of both my mothers echoed sourly in my head.

The night of the presentation drew in with a deep velvet sky bringing ideal conditions with just the meanest hint of approaching autumn. Nova found me as I waited in the wings, her feathery costume quivering as she hopped on one foot, simply unable to stay still.

'It's clear! You said if I wished and wished it would be and it is! They'll all see me fly really well, won't they?'

I stared at her small face and suddenly all I wanted to do was wrap her into my arms and cling onto her until she couldn't see the world and the world couldn't see her or what we had made her into. Instead I smiled and bent down to detangle a few strands of her wispy strawberry-blonde hair from her feathery shoulder.

'That's right, little darling,' I murmured as the orchestra began to tune up and a hush, heavy with anticipation, fell over the audience. 'So you'd better point your toes and fly extra well, hadn't you?'

I remembered Ana saying similar things to me when I was Nova's age and about to take to the stage for a ballet show. I remembered the seriousness with which I made her words sink into me, permeating every muscle from fingers to toes, making sure every part of me *knew* that anything less than perfection was unacceptable. But Nova was a different child to me; she grinned and threw her arms around me, kissing me on the cheek. I gasped at the physical contact – the closest I'd been to anyone since it happened – and she'd let me go, running daintily on bare feet through a curtain and into the backstage area long before my heart had stopped thundering enough for me to recover. A few minutes later the music swelled, the cue was given and I strode out onto the wide, gleaming stage; my face composed, my hands steady, my shawl in place and the thousand tiny emeralds ready to shine in the spotlight.

**October, 2018**

*Monday*

'This way, *quick!*' Tess hisses, as Ariana throws her hands over her head and another distant bang chases them down the dingy corridor. Her father is running beside her, his great big feet flapping noisily and one of his hands warm around her arm. She looks up at him, his unfamiliar face taut with worry as he glances behind them, glasses flashing in the light.

'In here,' Tess murmurs, throwing open a door Ariana wouldn't have noticed otherwise, for it is the exact same shade of grey as the walls and floors. Ariana follows her into a dark room without hesitation and Ralph clambers in beside them, his breath heavy as he pants. He reaches into his pocket and draws out an inhaler, which he puffs on slowly. Ariana recovers before the adults, looking around her as her heart slows and her face slowly begins to return to its normal temperature. As her eyes adjust to the darkness, she can make out a long bench with similar instruments to those she's already seen, and a wall lined with empty cages. The room is smaller than the other laboratories and there's another door set in the opposite wall. She frowns, thinking for a second that she can hear murmurs beyond it, but then the walls shudder with another explosive echo and she shakes her head, sure the noise came from outside. The reality of the situation dawns on her and she turns sharply to Tess.

'Was that... Were they *shooting?* With *guns?*'

'I don't know,' Tess says, still breathless, her hands on her knees.

'Home-made bombs,' says the man who is her father, straightening up and putting a hand on the door behind them as if wondering whether to go back. 'Ethan's work. He's always had a bit of a flair for explosives.'

'Mum!' Ariana lurches guiltily towards the door. Ralph immediately puts a hand out to stop her.

'She'll be OK... Lychen won't hurt her.'

'How do you know? He's... He gives me the creeps.'

'I just know,' Ralph says, quietly, not quite looking at her. 'Your mother can handle herself, trust me...'

'But there's *bombs*. And those Guard things–'

'Won't do anything without Lychen's say so. Trust me, your mother is probably the safest person in this building besides Lychen himself... You,' he turns to Tess, who seems to shrink a little under his sudden glare. 'Just before it all kicked off back there, your boss man said there'd been a breach in tracking or something... Seemed pretty pissed off about it if you ask me. Is that why you legged it with us?'

'I...' Tess turns red until her cheeks match her vivid lipstick. 'I don't–'

'That was me,' Ariana says, guilt swarming into her chest and making her speak against her better judgment.

'What?' Ralph turns to her in amazement. 'What did you do?'

'Tess was showing me the computers... She showed me where the ARC was and the dots that were all the people they're tracking here... You, Mum, your mates, your dad... And I remembered something my friend Lucy told me about how when she found out her parents were tracking her phone, she used this coding hack to scramble the signal... So when Tess wasn't looking, I looked up the code and put it into the back-end of the website... So they couldn't track you anymore...'

Tess stares at her in horror. Ralph's face, on the other hand, breaks into a huge grin which seeps into Ariana and lifts the dull, clanging dread that's been lurking within her ever since she woke up.

'That's brilliant,' he says. She smiles back at him. She can't help it.

'It wasn't much... Only a simple bit of coding. I had to Google most of it. I'm sure their tech guys have already overcome it...'

'They will have,' says Tess, through clenched teeth. She's glancing around her as if trying to decide whether she should bolt again, only this time alone.

'Still, it couldn't have come at a better time. The others... We had a plan for them to follow at a distance in one of the vehicles Lychen and his lot don't know about... But we knew they'd probably still be tracking us individually. I'm not sure how they do it, exactly. Anyway, Felix was planning to mess with their software once they got closer – she has a programme but it only works close range, so although they'd know they were being followed, they wouldn't be able to literally see our lot coming... But I guess thanks to you, they were able to catch at least some of the Guard completely unawares...'

'All this just to break me out?'

'Ha! Don't flatter yourself,' Tess spits, though she still looks more terrified than bitter as she carries on glancing around the room. Ariana frowns again as a strange, puppy-like wail murmurs from the door opposite them. *Probably just more test animals. God, though, I hope it* isn't *a puppy.*

'What d'you mean?' She wrenches her gaze back to Tess, who is also looking nervously at the other door.

'They've been trying to break into this place for years... Isn't that right, Ralph?'

'Well, yes, but that wasn't the main objective. We wanted to get you and your mother out safely,' Ralph said quickly, frowning, though he had gone back to not quite meeting Ariana's eye.

'And get a good look at whatever Daniel's been up to on the Project B continuation...'

'If you're asking whether or not we'd take the opportunity, if presented, to monitor what that little slimeball has been doing for the last few years, of course we would,' Ralph says, defiantly, though his cheeks are reddening. He takes his glasses off and wipes them.

'I knew Daniel at the ARC. He was creepy as hell even as a kid... And I heard the rumours of the sort of experiments he tried to do when Lychen gave him that department to run...'

Another wail, louder this time and accompanied by a shrill, birdlike shriek, draws all their attention to the other door again.

'Where are we, exactly?' Ralph mutters, moving across the room.

'One of the old labs. I didn't think it was still in use, so I thought it would be a good place to hide,' Tess says, a distinct tremble in her voice as Ralph reaches for the door handle.

'Don't!' she says, quickly, but it's too late. Ralph throws the door open and all three of them blink confusedly before they recoil, as one, in horror.

**Summer, 2005**

The first few performances went without a hitch. Rudy's log lifting received gasps of incredulity and a standing ovation. One of the little ones burst into tears during their slot when the spoon she was trying to bend telepathically fell to the stage with a heavy clatter, but – whether by surprise at the sound or by happy coincidence – the small boy next to her levitated a metre into the air a moment later and the audience was distracted enough for one of the helpers to run on and grab the crying child. I waited in the wings, reading the faces as they waited to go on and delivering firm, Ana-style encouragement, gentle hugs or simple, sparsely-worded assurances depending on what was needed. I almost forgot the shaky, dark feeling which had lurked so close to the surface over the last few days. I almost forgot the aches within my body and mind.

During the interval I joined Felix and Ethan for a glass of wine and let their congratulations lift my spirits further. I started to believe that it would all be fine, that once this was over, perhaps I could even go to Dr Blake and tell him what had happened in my office. The wine bolstered my nerve – surely something like this would be the tipping point he needed to rally those still loyal to him and overthrow Lychen? *He'll do it for me. I know he will.*

Do you?

The bell rang for the end of intermission just as Ralph approached our small group. I met his eye and he smiled.

'I suppose you'd better get back,' he said, though as the crowd pushed our bodies closer together, he traced a warm, dry finger along my forearm. The soft skin tingled into life in response.

'Yes... I'm due back on shortly to give the spiel about investment... and then later on I introduce the finale performers.'

'Ah, of course.'

Still, neither of us moved.

'I'm surprised you made it out for tonight,' I remarked. 'I thought you said all this was a *money-grabbing display of frivolity* and could ruin us all...'

'I wanted to see Dom... Anyway, since when do you actually *listen* to what I say?'

He grinned and, just like that, it was as if everything dark and dank and ruined inside me was swept aside. Not gone, just not so important anymore. I wondered if it showed in my eyes because he lifted a hand to my cheek and his expression turned concerned.

'Are you OK? You seem a bit... troubled...'

'I'm fine. Just... tired. You know?'

'Sure. Well hopefully after tonight you can relax a bit...'

'Yes. Hopefully,' I glanced behind him and spotted a sleek, tawny head bobbing as its owner talked ingratiatingly to Rex Silverton, head of a large research facility in Scotland and one of the wealthiest audience members in attendance. The bell rang again, giving us our two-minute warning. I clenched my jaw and moved my face away from Ralph's hand, suddenly claustrophobic even though the room was emptying by the minute. I caught Felix's eye as she and Ethan moved away from the bar and back towards the stalls and I looked away, unable to face her knowing grin.

'I'd better go,' I said, clutching my wrap around my shoulders and placing my wine glass down on the nearest surface.

'Beast? All this... It may be frivolous and everything but it's still pretty impressive,' Ralph said, talking quickly as if pained by what he was saying.

'Thanks,' I muttered, unable to stop the echo of the smug little sister escape into my words. 'I appreciate that...'

'Yeah, I mean I'm not saying it isn't playing with fire... All those kids – especially the older ones – around all the outsiders... Anything could happen...'

'We *do* take every precaution to keep the children away from outsider influences,' I pointed out, a little insulted.

'Yeah,' Ralph looked over my shoulder and I watched his eyes narrowed as he took in the sight of Lychen with Silverton. 'Maybe it isn't the outsiders you should be worried about. I don't like the way I've seen Lychen with some of the kids lately... Especially Rudy and Dan. The way he whispers in their ears... It's creepy.'

I opened my mouth to reply, not really knowing what I would say, when the bell rang once again and his attention switched.

'Better go,' I said, shaking my head and running through the beginnings of my second half speech, though I had been word perfect for weeks. 'Oh,' I paused and looked up at him, 'Dom's second up. Definitely worth getting a good seat, he conducts a laser show using twenty-eight laptops... The dress rehearsal was stunning...'

'Right,' he replied, still looking over my shoulder and

frowning. I turned around and left. When I glanced back over my shoulder at the passage leading towards backstage, he was still staring at Lychen, his face as dark as a cloud full of an electric storm, ready to burst at any moment.

'...and so, without further ado, I present to you our final act. These Subjects have been with us for almost their entire lives – lives of extraordinary development which has led them all to this moment. For your delight and amazement, ladies and gentlemen, I present the rising stars of the Aspira Research Centre...'

The audience erupted in applause as I lifted my arms and gazed upwards into the spotlight, waiting until it switched to abrupt darkness before I began to move backwards into the wings. Their eyes flicked excitedly from my retreating form to the sides of the stage, eagerly searching for more. A burst of flames ignited, right on cue, from a large hoop set high above the stage and by its light a shimmering, feathery figure could be seen swooping through the air. The audience exclaimed, gasped – one woman even screeched in alarm – as Nova looped around the air above the stage three times and then dove, her lithe body elongated like a human arrowhead, through the flaming hoop. I smiled and stepped further back into the wings so that no hint of my dress would catch the light tumbling from the shimmering flames. Nova paused mid-air and began to spin, her arms in arabesque and her toes pointed prettily. Her face, from what I could see of it, was a mask of concentration and I made an automatic mental note to tell her to relax it next time.

*What next time? If you leave... you'll never see Nova*

*again...*

I could take her with me.

*No you couldn't. Not her. They'd chase you down. She's too important and you have no claim upon her or any of them.*

I can't leave her. Not with him.

Even as the thought gripped me, tightening itself around all the pain and uncertainty and resolving it into white, cold anger, I spotted him. He stood next to Rudy, who was waiting, shirtless, to go on. One of his hands rested on the boy's shoulder like a brace of long, white snakes curling around Rudy's honey-kissed skin. He met my eyes and bent forward, unblinkingly, to murmur something in Rudy's ear. Ralph's voice echoed back to me under the shouts of amazement from the audience. *The way he whispers in their ears. It's creepy...* Beside me I sensed someone's presence and turned to meet the watery-grey eyes of Daniel. Taller now than I was, he still retained something of the snotty little boy who would grip my hand clammily, staring doggedly through my flinches. He looked at me then with a mixture of unashamed adolescent lust and something else... Something strangely triumphant, as if... The crass thought came unbidden and impulsive, but it fit the way he was watching me so well I couldn't quite dismiss it: *As if Lychen's told him what he did to me and promised him he can have the same...*

'Alright, Dan?' I made myself say, keeping my voice low as Nova swept straight over the heads of the audience and earned herself a few more shrieks. Daniel kept staring at me, his eyes hard and unwavering and far, far too old for a fifteen-year-old. He didn't reply, even as I glanced back on stage to make sure the Morris Mini-Minor was in the correct position and back again. In my peripheral view,

Nova touched lightly down on the X in centre-stage, bent her knees and prepared to spring into the air once again, Daniel's cue.

'Good luck,' I murmured. He smirked and kept his eyes on mine until the very last moment, before rushing out onto the stage with his arms held high. From the opposite wing, Rudy stepped out as well in mirror to him. Rudy's jaw was set, his hands had balled into fists and his expression bore none of his usual, easy-going manner. When he'd taken to the stage just a few hours earlier he'd practically skipped over to his props, beaming as the audience had cheered for him. Now his movements were jerky as he and Daniel performed their faux-chase around the Mini. Something was wrong. I looked past him, but there was no sign of Lychen.

As Nova soared higher, Daniel crept around the front of the car and promptly, just as Rudy went to follow him, vanished completely. The audience gasped, lapping it up. Rudy, who was supposed to stare all around him in amazement, simply jerked his head back and forth. He barely flinched when Daniel reappeared on his left side, smirking silently as the audience cheered. I watched helplessly as Rudy gritted his teeth and marched towards the Mini. I couldn't do a thing. There was no reason to do a thing. Rudy might just be nervous, after all... Except he never got nervous. I knew him better than anyone. I'd sat with him, coached him, sternly steered him into line when his attention waned, encouraged him with soft words and motherly sweetness when he'd needed it... No one else knew Rudy like I did. No one else felt the same dread I did when he braced himself and placed his hands firmly on the vehicle's undercarriage. No one knew that he shouldn't even be breaking a sweat as he began to lift it, let alone grunting the way he was...

Then it was done. The Morris Mini-Minor was lifted high above Rudy's head. Daniel vanished and reappeared at different points all over the stage just as he was supposed to. High above us, Nova twirled and twisted and prepared to dive. For a second, everything was perfect. Silence bloomed over the audience as if some creature had swept among them and stolen every morsel of breath from their lungs... Then, quietly at first but like the growing rumble of a tsunami, they began to cheer. Rudy heard them and for a moment he seemed to relax. The Mini inched higher into the air, he broke into a smile; far stage right, just a few yards from where I stood, Daniel reappeared, his face sour as the audience failed to react to him, all eyes on the figure in the centre. Above, Nova began to dive, her outline a shimmering dart of feathers as she aimed for the Mini. She would land upon it and perform a series of complicated ballet turns it had taken the two of us years for her to get just right... The audience were on their feet, some of them already pointing upwards at the girl in the air, most of them cheering for Rudy...

A hiss. Cold and soft as the rustling of autumn leaves, inaudible to all except the figures on stage, it reached me only as the shadow of words. I glanced towards Daniel, but he wasn't there... And Rudy's expression faltered, his arms wobbled and he stepped backwards and Nova was only a few feet from him now, though her dive had slowed with the movement of her landing target and Rudy turned to me, his eyes searching, pleading... Trembling limbs... A roar of sudden, broken anguish... And the Mini swayed and tumbled as an ear-wrenching sound ripped the very fabric of the night apart.

**October, 2018**

*Monday*

'Ethan!'

   'Ethan!'

   Bodies swarm into the room amidst the smoke. I cough and gasp and realise I'm being held again, dragged backwards. Felix, her face blackened either by a bruise or dirt, I can't tell, has thrown herself on the bleeding figure on the floor. She makes a noise like a wounded beast and doesn't seem to notice when a Guard bursts into the room behind her, followed by a young woman I don't recognise. The woman glances around at us, sees my knife still spinning slightly on the large table and, in one movement, grabs it, raises it and leaps onto the back of the Guard man before he can reach Felix. In a heartbeat the Guard man grunts, reaches around behind him and removes the knife in one fist, the woman's throat in his other. Felix looks up and meets my gaze as the Guard twists and slams the young woman against the wall. I watch her and notice the length of her limbs, the honeyish hints in her short hair and I think of Ariana and I stop fighting.

   'Stop! Stop hurting them! Josiah, call your Guard off!' I put everything into it. All the command I've ever used, but though I twist until my body screams in pain, I can't see his eyes and I know I don't hold the power. He doesn't loosen his grip, even as my limbs fall still.

'I did not start this,' he reminds me lightly.

'I know, I know… Just… Let them go. Please. Tell me what it will take to let them go.'

'I only ever wanted you, Bella. None of this had to happen… All this… *mess*. It's all your own doing. You know that, don't you? If you hadn't defied me. If you hadn't run…'

'Bella. Bella, he's still breathing. We need to get him to a hospital…' Felix stares at me, her voice nothing more than a guttural plea. I look at her and blink and there's Rudy, staring at me because he doesn't understand what's about to happen, why I'm not rushing forward to save him, why I have brought him into so much pain… Beside Felix, the woman's breath gasps from her, her lips turning blue as the Guard man continues to hold her, impassively, by the throat. Where is Ariana?

'We have the means to save him, Bella,' Lychen hisses. 'We have excellent doctors, the instruments, even an operating theatre right here in this building… Just give the word and dear Ethan here will be fighting fit in no time…'

'Bella! *Please!*' I can't look at Felix anymore. I can't look at anything anymore.

'Alright,' I murmur. 'Help him.'

'I'm afraid I'm going to need a little more–'

'It was my fault, OK? All of it. What you did to me. What happened at the presentation… Rudy's death. And all of this. It's all my fault. I'm sorry. I'll do what you want… I'll go with you now, if you still want me. I'll work for you. I'll be your spokesperson. I'll be your partner. Whatever you want. I'll do it. Just let them all go.'

I don't see him. I can't see if he thinks about it, or if his shark eyes simply blink in acknowledgement, but there must be some signal for the next thing I know, the Guard has dropped the girl and she's on her knees, gasping and retching. Three more Guard men appear, one of them bloody but the rest as pristine as if they had simply been patrolling the halls.

'Find Ralph Blake and the child,' Lychen tells two of them. 'Bring them to the entrance hall.'

They nod and disappear. I feel his body turn as he addresses the other two. 'Remove this man to the hall. Administer first aid and inform Doctors Skaid and Crane that the operating theatre will be required.'

'You really have an operating theatre?' Felix spits as she reluctantly allows Ethan to be scooped up by the larger of the men. The tattooed, bleeding man is almost as large as his bearer, and yet the Guard man doesn't so much as stumble as he carries him out of the room.

'It was a necessary requirement for Daniel's work,' Lychen tells her.

She scowls, starting forwards, 'That... That *animal* is not going anywhere near my husband! If he needs an operation, I want him to have it at a *hospital*...'

'You are hardly in a position to make demands, Ms Bryden,' Lychen loosens his grip around me and though I still can't see his face, something about it halts Felix in her tracks. She throws me a look caught somewhere between concern and contempt as she shudders, turns on her heel and runs from the room. The other woman hurries after her, still coughing, her eyes streaming. Lychen releases me and I fall forward, catching the back of a chair for support once again. He moves around the table until he is facing me and slowly, I look up.

'I wouldn't have accepted another outcome,' he says,

simply. 'Your co-operation was always the price for Ariana's freedom. I control the ARC. I have done for some time, despite what Blake might have told you about his father's lingering resistance. That… *rabble*… have only been tolerated for so long because of you.'

'Looks like they managed to do some damage here today, though,' I reply, my voice made low by the smoke. Lychen shrugs and glances at the dust on the floor, the dirty smears of Ethan's blood.

'More to themselves than us, I think,' he remarks. Raised voices can be heard from the entrance hall as if summoned just to corroborate his point. 'Was it worth it, I wonder?'

'To save Ri? Of course. Ralph would risk anything for his family.'

'But Ariana was never in any danger,' Lychen frowns. 'Why do all this – why risk so much to achieve something that was already agreed upon in the first place?'

I must look blank, for his expression changes suddenly. 'Ah… I see I am questioning the wrong person. He did not involve you in his plans for Ariana's rescue, I take it?'

'No.'

'How… interesting.'

'Hardly.'

He opens his mouth, but at that point we both pause as the sound of pounding feet and raised voices carry from the front entranceway. We listen as Felix answers and says something urgent but inaudible and wheels squeak, presumably beneath the weight of Ethan's body. A few words leap into the space between us. *BP. Pulse. Blood loss.* Mere minutes pass before footsteps, now accompanied by the squealing wheels, rumble away again and silence resumes. I frown.

'What sort of work can Daniel be doing that requires a working operating theatre?'

'We are a unique facility here,' Lychen says, quietly, looking towards the door. 'Pushing the realms of possibility far more than Blake originally dreamed up for Project B...'

'What *is* Project B, exactly? What's Daniel working on?'

'All in good time,' Lychen snaps with sudden impatience. 'All you need to know is that Ethan is in skilled hands. And that he will be fine. The others are free to go. Isn't that what you asked for?'

I glare at him and he frowns back.

'Come now, Bella. Do not sully those good looks of yours with such petulance. After all, none of us know how long they are ours to enjoy...'

'I want to see my daughter,' I say, coldly.

'By all means,' he straightens up and inclines his head towards the doorway to the entrance hall. I look down as I round the table. My clothes are covered in dust. His suit, however, is as unblemished as it had been when I'd first walked in. As if all the restraining – that iron-grip around my lungs, the choking of air as I'd gasped through the laden atmosphere – all of it had merely been a means to use me as a human shield against the mess.

The entrance hall is oddly unblemished as I follow Lychen into it. Judging from the explosive noises we'd heard, I'm half expecting collapsed ceilings, bloody bodies, piles of debris. But the only damage I can see is a gash in one of the archways leading into a corridor, spilling a few bricks and plaster. Dust has settled on much of the carpeted floor and blood surrounds a desk where Ethan was presumably placed temporarily.

'Beast?'

'Mum!'

I turn and Ariana is there, whole and only a little dusty, though her face is pale and her eyes blink too much as she stares between me and Lychen. Ralph has a hand on her shoulder, his other is held in a wrist lock behind his back by a Guard soldier. Behind them slinks the young woman who accompanied Ariana into the room before. I feast on the image of Ariana, whole, Ariana unblemished, and then I wrench my eyes back to Lychen.

'Where are the others? Felix and the young woman who was nearly choked to death? Dominic – I don't even know if he was here or not...'

Lychen gestures to one of the Guard soldiers accompanying the trio. He murmurs in his ear and Lychen nods, curtly, before turning to me.

'Bryden is waiting outside the theatre where Ethan is undergoing treatment. The others have been disarmed and are being contained in one of the laboratories. There have been no serious injuries sustained among them.' He frowns slightly and brings a hand up to his neck to touch the small nick made by my knife as if he's only just remembered it's there.

'No *serious* injuries?'

Lychen takes his time reaching into his pocket for a clean handkerchief which he brings up to his neck and dabs against the tiny pearl of blood nestled there. Then he sighs.

'Bella, I have more than sixty employees working in this facility today. They have all been affected, one way or another, by your friends' little rebellion stunt. Now that the most serious injury has been taken care of, my priority is them.' He turns to the Guard. 'I will be delivering an address in a few minutes. Monitor the staff and see that any unduly distressed are taken care of.'

'Sounds like you're going soft in your old age, Josiah,' Ralph remarks, lightly, though I can see the cold hatred twisting behind his gaze.

'Distressed workers are not productive,' Lychen replies, softly, putting the handkerchief back in his pocket. 'Though,' he gazes from him to me and back again. 'I don't think I should expect you to understand that.'

'Oh and I suppose you're the expert on preventing undue distress,' Ralph spits. Lychen just sighs at him as if all this is beyond tedious. He turns to me with the air of a parent reaching the end of their tether with a disobedient child.

'We have work to conduct,' he says, simply. He glances at his watch. 'I will leave you under the care of my Guard for ten minutes. My offer extends to your child, if you so wish. From what I gather, she has caused a significant amount of damage today, but I admire her enterprise. She may prove a valuable asset in a few years. And she has your eyes.'

He looks at Ariana and I resist the urge to lunge at his face with my nails. Instead, I force myself to nod. He turns and marches swiftly away, beckoning to two of the Guard and leaving just the one holding Ralph. The Guard drops his arm and stands at ease with a vacant expression. Ariana bolts towards me and I catch her. For a moment I just hold her and breathe. The dust lifts in tiny puffs as my breath ruffles her hair and I feel her heart thundering alongside my own and I wonder when it was I last felt mine beat without the echo of hers beneath it.

'What did he mean, Beast? What offer?' Ralph approaches us, stepping a little awkwardly around the worst of the dirt and patches of blood. I can tell he would

'I don't *care!* I don't want to stay with *her.* What kind of a mother do you think you are, anyway? I've seen you – the way you cloud over when I come into a room and interrupt whatever precious work you're doing... Why would anyone want *that?* I'll stick with *Dad.'*

She crosses her arms and turns away from me. I watch her, my face is still. My breathing is normal and my heart flips in echo of her furious beats, even as it rips with her words. The pain radiates upwards into my head and I grip onto it because it's real and it's her.

*She's just venting. She's angry because she's hurt...*

And she's hurt because she thinks I don't care about her as much as I care about myself and my own ambitions. Of course she's bloody angry.

*You've had nine minutes. They should go before he's back. He can change his mind. You know that as well as anyone, Bella. What did I always tell you?*

Don't trust him. Don't push him. He's all about possession.

*Let them go. Even like this.*

I reach into my handbag and draw out the small phone with the purple swirling case.

'Here, Ariana. Take your phone. You call me... I will always answer, understand?'

Ariana pauses for a moment, then, without looking at me, she turns and rips the phone from my hand in one swift, furious movement.

'You have to go,' I say it to Ralph, and he glances at the clock on the wall behind me. He nods once and takes Ariana by the arm.

'And Ralph? I mean *go.* Don't hang about waiting for the others, don't wait for any orders to be given or received or whatever. You take Ariana and you *go.'*

Ralph nods again, and I recognise the swift glaze of obedience with relief. Ariana still refuses to look at me as they begin to walk away, but I see a tear tracking slowly down one cheek. The woman with the red lipstick follows, silently. Ralph pauses suddenly.

'Daniel's working here, Bella. Did you know?'

'Yes, he's Dr Skaid – the one with the operating theatre where they took Ethan,' I frown irritably, the news barely sinking into the writhing, wrenching swirl of what I'm feeling. I can barely keep my body upright. Why is he telling me this now?

'That's not all he has... There's a whole load of labs... We stumbled into one of them just now. They've got... monsters. I don't know how else to put it... They're animals but also... people... Or used to be. I don't... I don't even know. You have to go and see for yourself.'

'OK...'

'It might make you feel differently about staying on, that's all.'

I shrug and he turns away, arm tightening around my daughter as the sunlight blots onto their heads.

'I love you, Ariana,' I call to her, softly. She doesn't say anything, but her narrow shoulders stiffen beneath Ralph's grip. They step out of the door and into the weak light of the afternoon. The woman follows behind them, and the look she throws me is a strange one. Worried and afraid and respectful all at the same time, but I can't tell if it's me she's scared of or for.

'Good luck Bella,' she says, quietly. And she steps out and away, taking my heart with her.

**Summer, 2005**

'Beast! *Bella!* What are– Where are you going?'

I shut my eyes for a moment, but I didn't stop. I'd made it this far, I was so close now. I'd been dreading a confrontation with Lychen – I knew I'd be pushed beyond any lie I'd ever told if I came face to face with him. I couldn't risk it. Luckily he'd been ensconced in meetings with lawyers and police as well as the ARC's other directors and stakeholders in the few days it had been since the presentation. Still, the inevitable confrontation was bound to happen if I didn't make a move soon. I was done taking chances, I would never wait too long to act again. I had been called to participate in the meeting scheduled for the following day, presumably to go over my version of events. I couldn't wait any longer.

No one had spotted me using my all-access pass to enter my office and grab the bag I'd hidden there the morning after Lychen's assault. No one had seen me slip away from the building like a shadow and begin walking along the path I knew so well I could have identified the month of the year just by glancing at a square inch of it. That's what I'd thought, anyway.

'Beast! Stop!' Ralph was closer than I realised and I jumped when I felt his hand on my arm.

'What?' I turned around and stared him down. He

looked from my set expression to the plain jeans and light jacket I was wearing, my heeled boots, the large holdall in my hand.

'Where are you going?'

'What do you want, Ralph?'

The night was dark. I could just about make out the gleaming shadow of the ARC behind him and, hulking like a shameful creature on its coattails, the amphitheatre. Ralph's face softened as he watched me.

'I... I heard you were going to give evidence tomorrow. I thought you might... need a bit of support...'

'I'm not *giving evidence.* It's not a court, the police have my statement. They don't *need* me–'

'And what about Rudy, Beast? You know he hasn't shown any brain activity. You know they're talking about switching off life support tomorrow?'

'I know.'

'So why aren't you with him? Why does it look like you're about to do a bunk to God-knows-where in the middle of the night instead of rushing to his bedside? I thought you *cared* about these kids, Bella!'

'Of course I care,' I hissed.

'Really?'

'I... there's nothing I can do for him. There's nothing I can do for any of them anymore...'

'What the hell does that mean, Bella? What's going on? Where are you going?'

'I just... I can't be here anymore, OK? It's not working for me. I don't want this... *any* of this anymore.'

He dropped my arm as if it were burning him. I couldn't bear to see the disgust on his face, but I made myself feel it, I opened myself up to it and let it in, because it was no less than I deserved.

'So you're throwing in your lot with Lychen? After all these years... After my parents bloody *raised* you? This is the thanks you're giving them? Swanning off to be the pretty face at the end of Lychen's leash?'

'No,' I said, coldly. 'I'm just done. I'm not going with *him*. I'm not staying with *you*. I'm just done with all of it.'

He stared at me, chest heaving though I didn't know if it was from running to catch up with me or from what I'd just said. Then, abruptly, all the fight left him and his face seemed to collapse.

'Bella... Look. All that happened with the presentation... You can get past it. *We* can. I'll stand by you... I'll help you get out of it... Just don't go, OK? I can't lose you as well...' He reached for me but I stepped backwards.

'I'm sorry, you'll *help me get out of it*?'

'Yeah. What happened to Rudy. You can't let it ruin everything for you...'

'You think it was my fault.' I said it slowly, looking at him and seeing, suddenly, the young, serious boy who stood in this very spot in another season of a different year and told me about the extraordinary children who lived at the ARC. The children we had to save.

'Not entirely... Not all of it.' He had begun to recover his composure now he could see I wasn't about to fall into his arms. 'Lychen played a part, I'm sure...'

'Lychen played *all* the parts,' I hissed, 'Him and his little minion Daniel. You weren't *there*. He spoke to him, just before he went on stage. And just before it happened, I heard Daniel hissing something at Rudy... Whatever it was, it was *that* that made him drop the car...'

Ralph stared at me in horror. Then, slowly, his face began to flood with colour.

349

'I *told* you. I *warned* you about that creep–'

'So what was I supposed to do, run across the stage and tackle him to the ground? For daring to speak to one of the kids he has part guardianship over?'

'Even *Mamma* tried to tell you about Lychen, all those years ago… But you wouldn't listen. You were so caught up in your own importance. It's been the same since you were a kid – you're so bloody in love with yourself, Bella. No one else stands a chance!'

'Oh what, like you?' I sneered. He blinked at me. Then his face twisted in bitterness and, abruptly, he turned away.

'Go on then. Run away. Run away with your dirty little conscience and see how far you get without my parents' money and influence. I'm sure you're bound to be the *only* pretty girl with green eyes out there in the real world.'

And he was gone.

I didn't want to be there. I didn't want to be in that room, where I'd slept for more nights than I hadn't. But, of course, nothing was as simple as packing a bag for a possible exodus and actually having remembered everything I needed. There was my hair-dryer, for example, still plugged in from that morning. And the stuffed dog. I couldn't quite bring myself to leave that behind, especially now. Especially since that skinny but insistent line had appeared in its little window and changed everything. I looked around the bedroom, at the large sleigh bed with its velvet covers, the heavy curtains at the windows and the gentle, striped rag rug on the floor, worn to softness with a thousand touches of my feet, ten thousand stretches and poses, handstands, turns and balances.

Memories of my first bedroom blurred into pink obscurity next to the hours spent sleeping, studying, practising in here.

'You're leaving,' Dr Blake said, making me jump and frown. He'd been involved in the meetings at the ARC, which often ran long into the evening. I'd thought he would still be there. I turned around and there he was, stooping, in the doorway. I remembered the way he'd bade me an awkward goodnight on my very first night here. The warmth which had grown as we'd settled with one another. The hugs and pats which never had anything sinister behind them, the eyes which crinkled with nothing but pride and love. I stared at him and, suddenly, I *hated* him.

'I have to.'

'No, you don't *have to*,' he said, annoyed. Despite the sudden, tumultuous anger that had sprung into my chest, I still registered surprise. I couldn't remember ever having irritated him before.

'I can't stay here with *him.* Not anymore. Not unless I'm willing to go with him to one of his new facilities and be... his glorified arm-candy. Or whatever it is you all call me.'

'I've never called you anything like that, Bella. You know that. And you know your only option isn't to submit, should you stay...'

'Really. Don't you know you're finished? Don't you realise everyone thinks you're a washed-up old man? Ever since Mamma died you've crumbled away... I might be *the pretty one* but at least people know I have some influence... They probably only have you in all those damage-control meetings with the lawyers to try and make Lychen look slightly more human. You're nothing but a husk. Just some old guy who once owned an empire and is now nothing but a failure–'

'Why are you so angry?' He stepped into the room, frowning curiously at me as if my words meant absolutely nothing. As if they were the petty tantrum of an overtired child. I swallowed, my anger tumbling under a wave of fright. I couldn't always command my will, I knew that now, but never before had my words been so easily dismissed. Especially by Blake.

'Why are you really leaving now? What's happened to you?'

'Nothing!'

'Is it Ralph? Has something happened between the two of you?'

'No,' I looked away and threw the hair-dryer into my case. I zipped it up furiously, hoping he hadn't seen the dog.

'Are you worried about speaking up tomorrow? Bella, what happened to Rudy wasn't your fault...'

'Ralph doesn't agree.' I wrenched the case from the bed and took a step towards him. He didn't move, still peering at me curiously.

'Ralph has his mother's passion and impulsiveness. He doesn't always express himself... appropriately... But he loves you. And *not* as a sister. You must know that.'

'Then he loves wrong.'

'Bella...'

I skirted round him, lifting the heavy bag over my shoulder and making for the doorway. He followed me, his heavy strides creaking into the floorboards.

'Bella... Please. *Is* this about Ralph? Did you... Are you pregnant?'

I stopped. I knew I shouldn't stop. Everything

screamed at me to keep going. We were on the stairs, him above me, and I could see the front doors up ahead. My car was beyond them. The car he'd bought me when I turned seventeen and passed my test on the first attempt. I couldn't leave but I shouldn't have stopped.

'We can sort it out,' he said. 'We can work it out. Whatever you choose to do. Bella... It's not the end of the world.'

'I'm not pregnant,' I spat. I knew I couldn't leave with him thinking that. Knowing that. I turned and looked straight at him, putting everything I could muster into the lie on my lips, but I didn't know if it was enough.

'I'm not pregnant. I'm just... moving on. I don't want to be here anymore. I don't want to sit around and watch everything I loved being torn away by some maniacal dictator.'

'So stay and fight back.'

'Why. You've already lost. You've already rolled over and let him take it all.'

'We haven't. Not all of us. Bella, trust me... We're working on taking it all back. Ralph, Felix, Ethan, and several others. More every day. If we have your help, I know we can do it – people look to you for guidance... We didn't involve you before because we weren't sure of where your loyalties lay... Forgive me, I should have known better.'

'Yes, you should,' I spat, my fury rising again as, deep inside, something gave a sharp yank of pain. All those times Ralph and I had been alone, all the burning looks and blazing touches and still he hadn't fully trusted me.

*Well, can you blame him?*

'But it's not too late, you can join us now. We'll protect you. You can even go to university if you like, we'll work it out – we can protect you from Lychen.'

I turned away, sighing, and stepped down the last two stairs. When I turned back, he hadn't followed me. He stood there on the stairs, not quite at the top or bottom, hovering as he always had done. Waiting to decide what to do, whilst all around him the world fell.

'Don't you understand?' I murmured, the pain catching in my throat no matter how hard I tried to swallow it back down. 'You've already failed. He's already taken it all. Everything. Everything you were worried about… Everything Mamma warned us about… He's taken it all.'

I didn't wait to see if he understood. I didn't wait to watch it sink into his old, sad features. I couldn't. So I turned away and walked, smartly, across the hallway. My heels tapped sharply against the cold flat stones of the floor and the sound jolted me back to my childhood, my mother's quick steps on this very ground.

*She was never your mother. Not really. Not like I was.*

It doesn't matter. I'm not like her.

*No. You're not. She left her child behind. You're taking yours with you.*

Yes.

*And you're sure? Completely? That it isn't ours, after all?*

I am sure. Besides, I can't take that risk. I can't let Lychen see and wonder. I have to get away.

*To save it?*

To save us both.

*How long for?*

For as long as I'm still breathing.

**October, 2018**

*Monday*

I wait there, long after the murmur of their voices fade and the sound of the ancient Fiesta splutters into the distance. I wait until I feel Lychen approach my side like the cold counterpart to my shadow.

'Blake left with Ariana?'

'Yes.'

'I don't understand…'

'I wouldn't expect you to.'

'Well. I'm not a parent, after all,' he says it coldly, matter-of-factly, but I sense the challenge lurking beneath. And, once again, I put everything into the lie on my face as I slowly turn to face him.

'No. You're not.'

**EPILOGUE**

Felix waits. Her face aches and her hands are dirty but she doesn't want to find somewhere to wash them. She doesn't even want to blink in this place in case something happens. She perches half on and half off the unyielding plastic seat, staring at the blown condensation of the window in the corridor, her nerves still jingling with the echoes of the bombs. They had been more powerful than she'd been expecting, but then she hadn't been on one of these missions for a long time. She's tech support. She doesn't usually see all this. She shuts her eyes and there's Lychen dragging Bella backwards, her eyes screaming in pure terror. She shakes her head and there's Ethan, drowning in blood on the dirty floor...

'Felix?'

Felix looks up and meets the gleaming-grey gaze of the wispy man in the white coat. Daniel Skaid has aged badly since he left the ARC. He can only be in his late-twenties but he could pass for forty.

'How is my husband?' She gets to her feet. She is the same height as him and more powerfully built but he doesn't flinch as she approaches. He stares too long and blinks too slowly. She never liked Daniel Skaid. No one did.

'He's fine,' he said, smiling. 'You can go and see him. He should be waking up any minute...'

Felix pushes past him before he's even finished speaking, her shoulder twitching where it touches him. He's oddly non-solid, like a ghost, but she doesn't pause to think about it as she pulls open the door in front of her. She doesn't register the surgical room, the lights, the instruments, the sinks and the cabinets all full of glimmering equipment. She doesn't look at the strange X-rays still pinned to the light-boxes on the walls. She only has eyes for the figure lying prone on the bed in the centre of the room.

Ethan is fine. He lies as solidly as ever, bandages swathing his right shoulder. Relief almost hamstrings Felix as she reaches for his thick, tattooed arm.

'You're OK,' she murmurs, as she reaches down and kisses him hard on the mouth. He stirs under her touch and his eyelids flutter. 'It's OK, I'm here,' she says, 'We're all OK, too. Ralph and the others – no one got hurt. No one except you, you big idiot. We got the kid out... she's fine. You can just rest if you want to... You can sleep...'

But his eyes continue to rove under the lids as if he's determined to wake. Behind her, Felix doesn't notice Daniel slip back into the room with two of the blank-faced Guard. She only has eyes for Ethan as slowly, his eyelids flutter and open. And she sees it, in an instant. He's not fine. Because he's not Ethan.

'Ethan! *Ethan!* What have you done to him? Let me *go*!'

The men behind her have grabbed her by the forearms and they're dragging her backwards, and she kicks and connects with the steel of the bed, but the figure upon it doesn't so much as flinch in response.

'Ethan!'

He sits up smoothly and turns his head, but there's

nothing in his gaze, it's like he can't see her at all.

'No! Ethan!'

The last glimpse Felix has of her husband before she's thrown from the room are his eyes. Blank, empty, impassive. As if everything he has ever been and all she's ever known of him has been scooped away and replaced with nothing at all.

## END OF BOOK ONE

J M (Jenny) Briscoe is a sci-fi author, journalist and stay-at-home-mum of three based in Berkshire, UK. She writes a strong female lead, bakes a mean birthday cake and has been known to do both simultaneously. This, her publishing debut, was long-listed for The Bridport Prize 2020. It is part one of a soft sci-fi trilogy called *Take Her Back*.

Jenny penned her first 'novel' at the age of 12. Several melodramatic tales (often involving twins, one of whom would invariably end up dying extravagantly) later, she honed her craft enough to earn a place on an English and Creative Writing BA at Royal Holloway, University of London. After graduating, she began her journalism career as a reporter with the local newspaper in her home town of Dartmouth, Devon, before completing a PGDip in Broadcast Journalism at Cardiff University. She has worked as a journalist for radio, TV, news websites and b2b trades magazines, but her true passion has always been writing fiction.

After becoming a mum in 2013, Jenny took the opportunity to write, launching a light-hearted parenting blog called Insert Future Here and penning a Young Adult novel (featuring twins) called *The Thing About Amelia*, long-listed for the 2016 Mslexia Children's Novel Competition.

Jenny wrote *The Girl with the Green Eyes* in 2018/19 while pregnant with her third child. In 2020 it reached the top 20 of over 1,600 entrants to The Bridport Prize: Peggy Chapman-Andrews First Novel Award. Jenny is currently working on its two sequels. No twins have been hurt in the making. Yet.

Follow J M Briscoe on Twitter @jm_briscoe or subscribe to her website www.jmbriscoe.co.uk for updates and exclusive *Take Her Back* content.

Just when you thought it was safe
to go back in the bookstore...
www.badpress.ink

BAD PRESS iNK,
publishers of niche, alternative and cult fiction

Visit

www.BADPRESS.iNK

for details of all our books, and sign up to
be notified of future releases and offers

WHILE NOBODY IS WATCHING

MICHELLE DUNNE

They called it peacekeeping.
For Corporal Lindsey Ryan it was anything but.

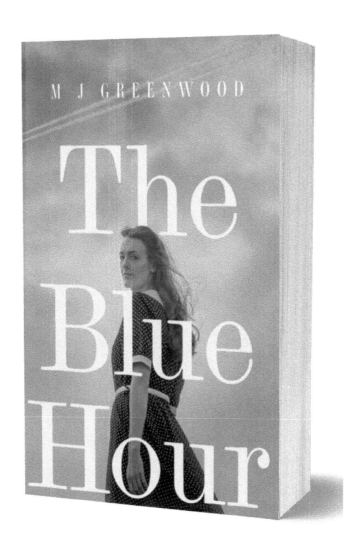

M J GREENWOOD

# The Blue Hour

Caring for the elderly was
never meant to be like this.

Lightning Source UK Ltd.
Milton Keynes UK
UKHW021013111021
392014UK00009B/159

9 781838 457723